S0-BXB-976

VOICES AND INSTRUMENTS OF THE MIDDLE AGES

Frontispiece *A fiddler, probably a minstrel, accompanying himself as he sings. A twelfth-century sculpture from Cluny. Musée Ochier, Cluny.*

VOICES AND INSTRUMENTS OF THE MIDDLE AGES

Instrumental practice and songs in France 1100–1300

Christopher Page

J. M. Dent & Sons Ltd
London Melbourne

First published 1987
© Christopher Page 1987

All rights reserved. No part of this publication may be
reproduced, stored in a retrieval system, or transmitted,
in any form or by any means, electronic, mechanical,
photocopying, recording or otherwise, without the prior
permission of J.M. Dent & Sons Ltd

This book is set in 10½pt Baskerville
by Tradespools Ltd, Frome, Somerset

Printed and bound in Great Britain
by Mackays of Chatham Ltd for
J.M. Dent & Sons Ltd
Aldine House, 33 Welbeck Street, London W1M 8LX

British Library Cataloguing in Publication Data

Page, Christopher
   Voices and instruments of the middle ages:
   instrumental practice and songs in France
1100–1300.
   1. Musical instruments—France—History
   I. Title
   781.91'0944   ML497

ISBN 0-460-04607-1

ML
182
.P24
1987 / 54,787
C.1

CONTENTS

CAMROSE LUTHERAN COLLEGE
LIBRARY

For my parents and for Régine

Bele amie, si est de nus,
ne vus sans mei, ne mei sans vus.

Preface

We must all find our own doorway into the past. For some it is the study of what can be seen in paintings or read in poems. For me the best entry has always been through what is heard in music. The performance of old music is perhaps our strangest way of confronting the past, for in order to do it we must collaborate with the dead; when we hear a performance of a medieval song we are hearing an echo of voices which, as if by some miracle, have not been silenced despite the passage of seven or eight hundred years.

This book is an attempt to move a little closer to the source of that echo. Of all medieval music, the monophonic songs of the troubadours and trouvères seem to have a special fascination for modern listeners—the twelfth-century troubadour lyrics, for example, constitute the earliest repertory of Western vernacular song in existence and lie at the centre of the Occidental tradition of love-lyric. Yet for all their musical and poetic interest, these songs sound very faintly now under the wind of seven or eight centuries and little can be said with certainty about how they were performed. Despite an enormous amount of scholarly effort, the question of their rhythm will remain a matter of controversy until the great day when musicologists will have the opportunity to consult the troubadours in person.[1] Nothing will ever be known for sure about the way in which medieval singers paced and phrased them, about the vocal timbres which they cultivated or their use of dynamic shading.

The past is nothing without its mystery, and these enigmas will probably ensure that troubadour and trouvère songs will retain their fascination for ever. Yet there is one area of performance practice where I believe the mist needs to be cleared a little: the question of instrumental participation in the delivery of these songs. In recent years performers and instrument-makers have done a great deal to lift medieval instruments from the frozen silence of church sculptures and from manuscript borders; many reproductions have been made and some skilled performers have emerged. Now that the initial burst of activity in this area has passed, along with the 1960s and 1970s when it reached a peak, the time has come for a dispassionate assessment of where musical instruments belong in the surviving repertories of music.

This book is an attempt to take a step in that direction. In writing it I have been helped by many friends and colleagues, amongst whom it is a pleasure to mention David Fallows and Stephen Haynes (both of whom read parts of the book in draft and made many valuable suggestions), Ann

Lewis (who spotted many errors and helped me to clarify numerous arguments), Mark Everist, Lewis Jones, Edward Wilson (the best critic any author could wish), Daniel Leech-Wilkinson, John Caldwell, Jeremy Montagu, Eph and Djilda Segerman, and Ronald Woodley.

It is impossible to express what my wife, Régine, has contributed to this book. May it help towards a better understanding of the medieval music of her country.

Introduction

More often resting at some gentle place
Within the groves of Chivalry, I pipe
Among the Shepherds, with reposing Knights
Sit by a Fountain-side, and hear their tales.

Wordsworth *The Prelude* (Text of 1805)

Wordsworth's image of the Middle Ages, when shepherds played their pipes amidst 'the groves of Chivalry', evokes a world of pastoral innocence and simple dignity where there is always music of instruments in the air. With the rise of interest in the troubadours during the second half of the eighteenth century, those were often the terms in which men of letters imagined the medieval past. The poems and biographies of those Provençal songwriters—virtually forgotten, at least in France, since the sixteenth century—were a revelation to the literary public of Europe when Lacurne de Sainte-Palaye published his *Histoire Littéraire des Troubadours* in 1774;[1] at a time when any traveller in southern France could still hear the language of the troubadours spoken even in high society,[2] this pioneering book showed that Occitan had once been a great literary language cultivated by flamboyant poets whose lyrics stood at the fountainhead of European love-song.

This interest in the troubadours was accompanied by a developing appreciation of the role which minstrels and professional entertainers had played in medieval life. Between 1759 and 1798 a hoard of references to *histriones* and *joculatores* was made available to readers in Mansi's volumes of ecclesiastical *Concilia*, and these documents left no doubt that the medieval monk in his cloister, like the chivalrous lord in his keep, had drawn upon a host of itinerant singers and instrumentalists for his entertainment.[3] At the same time the revival of interest in medieval literature—especially in England, where Chaucer had been continuously read since the fourteenth century—prompted antiquarians such as Thomas Percy, Joseph Ritson and Walter Scott to study the part played by minstrels in composing or performing the romances and ballads which survived in manuscripts and in oral tradition.[4] Their disagreements were sometimes public and acrimonious, but they were agreed that 'the groves of Chivalry' had been thronged with minstrels, especially singers and instrumentalists.

It was perhaps inevitable that these interests in troubadour lyric and minstrelsy should coalesce, bringing eighteenth-century antiquaries to the view that troubadour songs had been originally performed by minstrels as combined vocal and instrumental music. Fresh discoveries only seemed to confirm it. By 1774 substantial extracts from the *Vidas* ('Lives') of the troubadours were available in paraphrase in Lacurne de Sainte-Palaye's volumes mentioned above, and one of these relates how Guiraut de Bornelh went from court to court leading two singers (*cantadors*) with him, while another records that the troubadour Perdigo 'knew very well how to play the fiddle'.[5] Such evidence seemed definitive, and by the time of Charles Burney's *A General History of Music* (1776–89) it was in order for the songs of the troubadours to be presented as the first concerted art-music for voices and instruments in Western history:[6]

> It was about this time [*c*1119] that Provençal Poetry arrived at its
> greatest point of perfection; and that it began to be sung to the sound
> of instruments: for at this period *Violars*, or performers on the Vielle
> and Viol; *Juglars*, or Flute-players; *Musars*, or players on other
> instruments; and *Comics*, or Comedians, abounded all over Europe.

By the nineteenth century the troubadour has become the story-book figure of a romantic wanderer, an instrument slung over his back as he makes his way from castle to castle.

It is easy to smile at this romantic image of the Provençal poet. Yet it is by no means an obsolete picture like some Victorian print of the Last Supper relegated to the dust of the vestry. It is with us still, for it is generally assumed that the songs of the troubadours and trouvères were first heard above the clamour of inventive instrumental playing:[7]

> The following transcription of Bernart de Ventadorn's *Ab joi mou lo
> vers e.l comens* . . . may serve as an illustration of the kind of approach
> to the performance of monophonic songs that I have tried to
> outline . . . A suitable instrumentation would be harp for the drone
> and fiddle for the heterophonic line but portative organ, hurdy
> gurdy, rebec and recorder would make suitable alternatives.

This view has recently been questioned by Hendrik van der Werf in his book on the songs of the troubadours and trouvères. In a few paragraphs he clarifies the accompaniment question in a most useful way. The central issue, he argues,[8]

> . . . is not whether medieval singers ever sang to instrumental
> accompaniment. In some of the narrative literature of the Middle
> Ages we find clear indications that this was done, but that does not
> prove that the chansons of the troubadours and trouvères were

accompanied too . . . we have to reckon with the possibility that
medieval Western Europe . . . knew many kinds of songs, popular as
well as esoteric ones; some of these may habitually have been
accompanied, but not necessarily all of them.

I take my point of departure from these lines. The task is not to establish
'whether medieval singers ever sang to instrumental accompaniment', for
there is a good deal of literary evidence that they sometimes did (see
Appendix 3, *passim*). My purpose is to distinguish the kinds of songs which
were considered more appropriate for instrumental accompaniment from
those considered less suitable for performance in that way.

When the issue is expressed in these terms, much of the literary evidence
for accompaniment is disqualified for being too vague; it does not reveal
what kind of song it is that lies behind such terms as *chanson, son, lai, vers,* and
so on.[9] I have therefore based the argument of this book upon the few
sources which refer to different kinds of songs in contexts where it is clear
what kinds of songs are meant, and where instrumental accompaniment is
mentioned in explicit terms. The pattern that emerges from these sources is
probably only a fragment of the whole truth, and nothing more can be based
upon it than the most tentative conclusions. In a situation such as this the
danger of exhausting the reader with qualifications and multiple hypotheses
is clearly very great; I have attempted to be brisk and plain as an invitation
to the reader to consider the issues afresh.

The book is in two parts. The first is an attempt to determine which kinds
of songs may have been associated with accompaniment, and which not.
The second gathers evidence relating to the kinds of accompaniment which
stringed instruments may have supplied in performances of monophonic
songs. This restriction of the field of view to stringed instruments seems
justified by the lack of any definite indications that wind instruments
participated in the performance of courtly monody during the Middle Ages.

In the Appendices I have gathered source material relating to various
matters which, though important, do not belong within the substance of my
argument. The first deals with the terminology of medieval instruments,
since no attempt to use literary evidence as I wish to use it can be justified
without some clarification of the nomenclature employed by medieval
writers. The second offers a selective typology of musical references in Old
French literature such as is necessary, I believe, to interpret what comes
next in Appendix 3, a collection of literary references to musical
performance. Finally, Appendix 4 confronts an issue which bears directly
upon the sound of courtly monody: the string-materials used on medieval
instruments. Here I have attempted to establish a tentative chronology for
gut, metal, silk and horsehair strings as a guide to instrument-makers and
performers who wish to do in a much more effective way what this book
attempts to do: to capture sounds after a lapse of many centuries.

PART 1
SONGS AND INSTRUMENTS

chascuns doit s'amie
requerre d'amours...
pour ce sont fait tuit istrument melodious...
mais j'ai trouvé
et esprouvé
que sour toute melodie
bele vois a la seignourie
par biau chanter.

Anonymous 13c (Bamberg codex)

1

Epic and Romance

Rollant est proz e Oliver est sage.

Song of Roland

I

During the period 1050–1200 the arts of lyric poetry and string-playing were transformed. The troubadours emerged with their range of lyric genres in the vernacular and their highly self-conscious approach to the art of song-writing. At the same time, bowed instruments proliferated in many shapes and sizes throughout Europe and the fiddle became the chosen instrument of the Provençal courtier. These are just some of the most obvious manifestations of a transformation in the art of being a poet or an instrumentalist. Yet the most vivid testimony to these changes is to be found outside the realm of songs and instruments. It can be sought in the narrative poetry of the period where the change from Epic to Romance embodies so much of what is significant in the making of the Middle Ages.[1]

The early French epics, of which the *Song of Roland* is probably the earliest and certainly the best-known, are often approached as if they were windows onto the eleventh century. They reveal a generally harsh and 'uncourtly' feudal aristocracy, constantly engaged in tragic conflicts over rights and inheritances. In this respect these Epics have often been contrasted with the new genre of French vernacular romance (new, that is, around 1150), for the tales of Arthur, Tristan and other heroes, so much admired in the later twelfth century, mirror a new and 'courteous' life-style. We hear less of draughty, torch-lit castles, and more of window-seats and private chimney-corners in well-appointed chambers.

This is a simplified view, of course, for in many ways the genre of Epic becomes increasingly hard to disentangle from Romance as the twelfth century progresses. It may also be an unguarded view, for we have become reluctant to look in the 'mirror' of literature for a reflection of life as it was lived in the past. Yet as far as the history of music is concerned this interpretation of the contrast between 'feudal' Epic and 'courtly' Romance has much to offer. Anyone who brings an interest in music to the *Song of Roland* (c1080) and then, let us say, to Thomas's *Roman de Horn* (c1170), is

3

bound to notice a significant difference. The *Song of Roland* has no music—
none, that is, apart from the alarums of trumpets and the cry of Roland's
horn. Roland inhabits a world where there is neither time nor place for
anything else; he passes (and ends) his life as a great soldier in Charlemagne's warrior-band, pursuing the communal and aggressively Christian purpose of a crusade against the Saracens in Spain. The scenes of his
story take place in public or crowded places where only men are present: the
great war-councils before Charlemagne; the column of *chevaliers* riding to
combat; the press of the battlefield.

Almost a century later, the hero of the *Roman de Horn* belongs to a different
realm.[2] He is a great fighter—good enough to have fought with Roland—
but he is not a soldier. In his world there is a measure of freedom from
urgent military obligation and the range of human experience deemed to be
consequential has widened as a result. It is not just Horn's warriorhood that
matters—although that was all that mattered for Roland; Horn can
converse with ladies and deport himself in a way that inspires emulation in
his peers and delight in his superiors.

Above all, he can both sing and play the harp. The passage where
Thomas celebrates Horn's musical skills is possibly the finest account of
accompanied vocal performance anywhere in medieval literature. Here we
leave the stern keeps of Epic behind and walk along the galleries of
Romance; private chambers, their floors 'strewn with flowers, yellow, indigo
and vermillion', lead off on every side, and the air is full of music:[3]

> Lors prent la harpe a sei,   qu'il la veut atemprer.
> Deus! ki dunc l'esgardast   cum la sout manïer,
> Cum ces cordes tuchout,   cum les feseit trembler,
> Asquantes feiz chanter   asquantes organer,
> De l'armonie del ciel   li poüst remembrer!
> Sur tuz homes k'i sunt   fet cist a merveiller.
> Quant ses notes ot fait   si la prent a munter
> E tut par autres tuns   les cordes fait soner:
> Mut se merveillent tuit   qu'il la sout si bailler.
> E quant il out (is)si fait,   si cummence a noter
> Le lai dunt or ains dis,   de Baltof, haut e cler,
> Si cum sunt cil bretun   d'itiel fait costumier.
> Apres en l'estrument   fet les cordes suner,
> Tut issi cum en voiz   l'aveit dit tut premier:
> Tut le lai lur ad fait,   n'i vout rien retailler.

> Then he took the harp to tune it. God! whoever
> saw how well he handled it, touching the strings
> and making them vibrate, sometimes causing them to
> sing and at other times join in harmonies,
> he would have been reminded of the heavenly harmony.
> This man, of all those that are there, causes most

wonder. When he has played his notes he makes the
harp go up so that the strings give out completely
different notes. All those present marvel that
he could play thus. And when he has done all this
he begins to play the aforesaid *lai* of Baltof, in
a loud and clear voice, just as the Bretons are versed
in such performances. Afterwards he makes the strings
of the instrument play exactly the same melody as he
had just sung; he performed the whole *lai* for he
wished to omit nothing.

We need not concern ourselves yet with the meaning of the word *lai*; it
suffices here to note that the *lai* is clearly a song which Horn both sings and
plays. Other passages reveal that the *lai* was composed by Baltof, a young
aristocrat and son of the king of Brittany, to celebrate his beautiful sister
Rigmel who is Horn's beloved. The episode implies an audience closely
interested in songs and instrumental playing.[4]

There is nothing new about the figure of the amateur string-player in
royal society; we find him in *Beowulf*, for example, and much earlier still if
we cast our net wide enough.[5] What is new, however, is the tacit but
unmistakable admission in the *Roman de Horn* that refined love is the passion
which music most readily stimulates and feeds. There are no love-songs in
Beowulf, only lays of the ancient epic heroes of the North; yet in the *Roman de
Horn* there is a keen sense that Horn's musicality is part of a disposition to be
elegant and amorous which is the heart of courtliness as interpreted by
secular individuals.[6]

This is not simply a change in the ethos of songs and instruments; it is
something new in the ethos of masculinity and in the awareness of male
beauty.[7] The Epic knights of the *Song of Roland* may have magnificent
physiques, but they are generally shown to us as seen through the eyes of
their admiring male peers in the banqueting hall, in the council chamber or
on the battlefield. Women barely figure in these places and therefore the
Epic hero's magnificence is generally without any sexual nuances. Here is
Ganelon before the war-council of Charlemagne in the *Song of Roland*:[8]

> De sun col getet ses grandes pels de martre
> E est remés en sun blialt de palie;
> Vairs out [les oilz] e mult fier lu visage.
> Gent out le cors e les costez out larges.
> Tant par fut bels tuit si per l'en esguardent.

> He has thrown down his great marten-fur from his neck
> and is left standing in his under-tunic of silk;
> his eyes are flashing and his face is haughty.
> His body is fair and his chest is broad.
> He was so fine that all his peers watch him.

'He was so fine that all his peers watch him': this is a man seen by men. What a difference, then, if we move forward a century and encounter Thomas's description of Horn. Here is a man whose beauty is seen through the eyes of a woman who desires him to distraction:[9]

> [Rigmel] pense de Horn,   ki ele tient trop fier,
> ....
> 'Cheveus ad lungs e blois,   que nul n'en est sun per;
> Oilz veirs, gros, duz, rianz,   pur dames esgarder;
> Nies e buche bien faite   pur duz beisiers prester . . .'

> Lady Rigmel thinks of Horn, whom she thinks too proud,
> ....
> 'He has long blonde hair so that none can equal him;
> he has blue eyes, large, sweet and laughing to look upon
> ladies; he has a fine nose and mouth to give kisses . . .'

The image of the courtier-amateur skilled in singing and playing upon instruments was a potent one in both North and South. Here it is, for example, in the twelfth-century Provençal tale of *Daurel et Beton*:[10]

> Qua[n]t ac .vii. ans Beto sap gen violar
> E tocar citola e ricamen arpar
> E cansos dire, de se mezis trobar. . . .
> Qua[n]t ac Beto .ix. ans foc del rei escudiers,
> Foc bels e gens e covinen parliers,
> Joga a taulas, et ad excas, a diniers,
> E va cassar ab cas et ab lebriers,
> Ab los austors et ab los esparviers;
> Baissa las astas, abriva.n los destriers.
> Ama.l lo rei, la regina a sobriers,
> Sa genta filha que lo te motz en chiers;
> Ama lo domnas, donzels et cavaliers.
> Et a las taulas servia als mangiers,
> Denan lo rei estava prezentiers,
> Servi li fort do so que.l fa mestiers;
> Peussas los viola e canta volontiers.
> Vi o Daurel; ac ne grans alegriers.

> When Beto was seven years old he knew how to
> fiddle well, and to play the citole and harp
> in a noble fashion, and how to sing *cansos*,
> and how to compose by himself. . . .
> When Beto was nine years old he was a squire of
> the king, he was personable and courteous and

an eloquent speaker. He plays drafts and chess
where money is bet, and goes hunting with dogs
and greyhounds, with hawks and with sparrowhawks;
he lowers his spurs and drives warhorses on.
The king loves him, and the queen adores him greatly,
and her courteous daughter who holds him very dear;
ladies love him, young men and knights. He served
at table during meals and stood graciously in the
presence of the king, serving him diligently with
everything pertaining to that craft; then he fiddles
to them and sings willingly. Daurel watches him and
takes great delight in what he sees.

No doubt there is a good deal of elaboration and idealisation in this passage, yet it is impossible to dismiss it as pure fiction. It is unlikely to be a coincidence that the *Vida* of the troubadour Pons de Capdoill records that Pons was a gifted composer, singer and fiddle-player; nor that it sets his musical talents like stars within a brilliant constellation of chivalrous values: 'Pons was a fine knight in arms, a gracious speaker and a gracious wooer of ladies, large and fine to look upon...' (Appendix 3:10). In case we are tempted to dismiss this encomium as yet another literary fabrication we have the seal of Bertran II, Count of Forcalquier from the year 1168 (Figure 1): on one side the count rides in characteristically chivalrous pose, armed with lance and shield; on the other he plays a fiddle.

Figure 1 *The seal of Bertran II, count of Forcalquier, 1168. Paris, Arch. nat., collection de sceaux Supplément 4512 et bis. Reproduced by permission.*

A document of great interest in this context is Gervase of Tilbury's *Otia Imperialia* (Appendix 3:13). Here Gervase describes how the Catalan magnate and troubadour, Guiraut de Cabreira, used to play the fiddle in the palace at Arles. The passage is a remarkable one in which almost every chivalrous theme which we have touched upon is displayed: the emphasis on youth, *jeunesse*; the value placed upon courteous behaviour; the association between musical skills and male sexual allure:

> ... There was in our own time a knight in Catalonia
> of very high birth, dashing in warfare and gracious
> in manners, whose name was Giraldus de Cabreriis ...
> This knight was in the flush of youth, charming,
> lively, highly skilled on musical instruments, and
> madly desired by the ladies....

Guiraut de Cabreira, like Pons de Capdoill, was both troubadour and string-player, and his story reminds us that it was not only performing skills which might be expected of the accomplished courtier but also poetic ones. Here again we meet a new conception of masculinity and the skills which it may entail. If we retrace our steps back to the *Song of Roland*, and specifically to the line quoted at the head of this chapter, we find that Roland is *proz*, headstrong and brave, whilst his companion Oliver is *sage*, wise and circumspect. Now it is almost exactly at this time—the decades before 1100—that the adjective *prudens* ('wise') becomes by far the most popular epithet to join to the word *miles* ('soldier') in Latin narrative texts.[11] In other words the ideal knight of c1100 was closer in some ways to Oliver the *sage* than to Roland the *proz*.

How did the knight develop and display his *sagesse*? Above all, perhaps, in his eloquence, as revealed in the counsel which he gave his feudal lord. We cannot miss the importance of this kind of warrior *sagesse* in the *Song of Roland*; even the best Saracens have it. Thus the pagan king Marsilie calls upon his dukes and counts for counsel:[12]

> Cunseilez mei ... mi savie hume

and the poet dwells upon the *sagesse* of the pagan warrior Blancandrin: 'He was one of the wisest pagans; he was a knight well-endowed with the qualities of a vassal; he was a man of valour to serve his lord.'[13]

In some measure the lyric art of the troubadours and trouvères probably arose as a transference of the eloquence which a knight was expected to display before his male peers into the realm of leisure passed in mixed company. In some chivalric narratives both kinds of eloquence are associated. In *Folque de Candie*, for example, Thibaut is said to be *amez de dames et sages de plaidier*: 'loved by ladies and wise in pleading a case',[14] and this because of his *beles paroles*, his attractive eloquence.[15] The fictional figure of Thibaut finds its historical counterpart in Conon de Béthune, the knightly trouvère who was active in the late twelfth and early thirteenth centuries. In 1203 we find him conducting delicate negotiations at Constantinople on behalf of the Crusaders; he was chosen, it seems, because he was *sages et bien emparlez*; 'wise and most eloquent'.[16]

II

We have seen that the arts of string-playing and song-writing were endowed with a new ethos in the twelfth century. These were clearly important arts in secular society and it matters that we should have some understanding of how they were combined.

In some respects the issues before us may seem simple enough and even half-decided. Surely the existence of troubadour fiddlers like Guiraut de Cabreira and Pons de Capdoill shows that the marriage of courtly song to instruments was a natural and easy one. Perhaps it was, but there are signs that performers were not always faithful to it. Here, for example, is a young member of a courtly household, a *vallet*, performing a song by a noted trouvère, the Vidame de Chartres (Music example 1). A king, a single knight and a minstrel named Jouglet are listening:[17]

> [li bons rois] onques n'ot conpegnon ne per
> q'un sol chevalier et Juglet,
> s'oïrent chanter un vallet
> La bone chançon le Vidame
> de Chartres. . . .
>
> *Quant la sesons del douz tens s'asseüre*
> (remainder of stanza, and one other stanza,
> both without music, follow)
>
> [The good king] never had any friend or companion
> with him other than a lone knight and Jouglet; and they
> heard a *vallet* singing this fine song by the
> Vidame de Chartres. . . .

This passage from Jean Renart's romance of *Guillaume de Dole* (c1220) is one of the most convincing descriptions of performance practice in Old French literature. The quietness of the scene, the domestic character of the performer (a young household servant), the citation of a specific song by a named trouvère—all of these details suggest that the passage may be rooted in contemporary practice. As far as we can discern, the *vallet* is not accompanied as he sings; indeed the minstrel Jouglet, who elsewhere in Jean Renart's romance shows no reluctance to accompany singers on his fiddle, may not be involved as the *vallet* performs.

This brief reference is already enough to suggest that there can be no simple answer to the question of instrumental practice in troubadour and trouvère lyric. Despite the evidence that string-playing was endowed with a powerful courtly ethos, here is a performance at court where instrumental accompaniment is available, but is not used. No doubt the simplest way to resolve this opposition is to assume that a trouvère song might be sometimes accompanied and sometimes not, and that Jean Renart is describing a performance in which one is not. Yet however sensible this may seem as a solution to the conflict which I have (perhaps artificially) created, in the long term it is an admission of defeat, for it is likely *a priori* that some performances involved instruments and some did not. It seems more interesting to ask whether the use of accompaniment was entirely dependent upon whim and the chance availability of appropriate resources, or whether it was subordinated to certain artistic principles and traditions. For example, is it because *Quant la sesons del douz tens s'asseüre* is a trouvère song in the High Style manner that the *vallet* sings it without accompaniment in Jean Renart's romance?

As this example shows, questions of instrumental usage in troubadour and trouvère song are essentially questions about *genre*—about the differences between different kinds of song. This is to carry our subject onto ground that medieval performers and listeners would have recognised, for it mattered to them to know the genre of a song. That is why there is humour in these mischievous lines by Raimbaut d'Aurenga (d.1173):[18]

> Escotatz, mas no say que s'es,
> Senhor, so que vuelh comensar.
> Vers, estribot, ni sirventes
> Non es, ni nom no.l sai trobar....

> Listen, lords! although I do not know what it
> is, this song that I want to begin. It is not
> a *vers*, *estribot* nor *sirventes*, nor can I find
> any name for it....

Where did instrumental sounds and techniques fit into the genre system of Old French and Old Provençal lyric? Practices that were appropriate in a performance of a High Style song like *Quant la sesons del douz tens s'asseüre* may not have been suitable for an anonymous (but no less courtly) refrain-song intended for dancing. We cannot hope to rebuild these, or any other, medieval traditions of performance practice. Yet I believe that we can sometimes glimpse, as if in an aerial photograph, faint traces of the lines which their foundations followed.

Example 1

Quant la se - sons del douz tens s'as - se - ü - re,

que biaus es - tez se ra - ferme et es - clai - re,

et to - te riens a sa droi - te na - tu - re

vient et ret - ret, se n'est trop de mal ai - re,

chan - ter m'es - tuet, car plus ne m'en puis tai - re,

por con - for - ter ma cru - el a - ven - tu - re

qui m'est tor - ne - e a grant mes - a - ven - tu - re.

2

The twelfth century in the South

e auziratz, si com yeu fi,
als trobadors dir e comtar
si com vivion per anar
e per sercar terras e locx.

Raimon Vidal, *Abril issia*

I

Any attempt to place instrumental accompaniment within the genre system of troubadour and trouvère poetry must take its bearings from the genre which dominates the surviving corpus of lyrics: the elaborate love-song which Dragonetti has termed the *grand chant courtois*. I shall also refer to it as the High Style song. Throughout the later twelfth and thirteenth centuries this kind of song, which the trouvères inherited from their predecessors in Occitania, was the 'classic' form of the courtly songwriter's art. As an example of the prevailing poetic and musical manner of the High Style, here is the first stanza of a song by Arnaut de Maroill:[1]

Las grans beutatz e.ls fis ensenhamens
e.ls verais pretz e las bonas lauzors
e.ls autres ditz e la fresca colors
que vos avetz, bona dona valen,
me donan genh de chantar e sciensa,
mas gran paor m'o tol e gran temensa,
qu'ieu non aus dir, dona, qu'ieu chant de vos,
e re no sai si m'es o dans o pros.

The great beauty, the fine discrimination, the true
worth, the fine praise, and other things and
the fresh colour that is yours, good and perfect
lady, give me skill and ability to sing – but my

great fear and fright take them away from me for
I do not dare mention, my lady, that I sing of you
and I do not know whether I will come to harm or good.

Example 2

1. Las grans beu - tatz e.ls fis en - se - nha - mens
2. e.ls ve - rais pretz e las bo - nas lau - zors
3. e.ls au - tres ditz e la fres - ca co - lors
4. que vos a - vetz, bo - na do - na va - len,
5. me do - nan genh de chan - tar e sci - en - sa,
6. mas gran pa - or m'o tol e gran te - men - sa
7. qu'ieu non aus dir, do - na, qu'ieu chant de vos
8. e re no sai si m'es o dans o pros.

Like many other melodies for High Style songs this one is essentially
rhapsodic in character. Lines 1 and 2 are set to the 'same' music as lines 3
and 4, but this is a conventional patterning in this repertory and in this
instance (as often) it is far from strict; line 2 has a 'closed' ending but 4 has
an 'open' one. There are other relationships, but the essence of the
rhapsodic musical style of the *grand chant courtois* is that they are disguised.
Thus there are significant resemblances between the settings of lines 1/3, 2
and 6:

13

Example 3

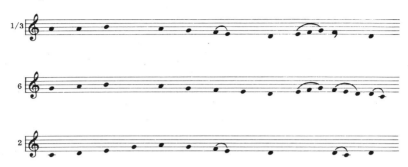

while the music for lines 2 and 4 is closely related to the melody for line 7:

Example 4

These relationships do not necessarily strike us when we hear the first stanza; they gradually materialise as we hear the full song. As the performance proceeds, our sense of coherence and focus in the rhapsodic flow of the music becomes more pronounced. This is part of what is *grand* about the *grand chant courtois*: these songs reject the conspicuous and short-range patterns that give an easy and instant tunefulness to dance-songs such as the *rondet de carole* (see Music example 5).[2]

In contrast to dance-songs such as this, the essence of a High Style song like Arnaut's *canso* is that it makes us aware of the voice which is singing to us. In a performance of a dance-song like *C'est la gieus en mi les préz* the voice of the singer dissolves into the voices of the dancers (who sing the refrains) and thence into the dance; but the high seriousness of Arnaut's song forbids us to sing or to do anything which will remove the song and the singer from the centre of our attention.

14

Example 5

C'est la gieus en mi les préz,

J'ai a - mors a ma vo - len - té!

da - mes i ont baus le - véz.

Ga - ri m'ont mi oel.

J'ai a - mors a ma vo - len - té,

te - les com ge voel!

Whence the characteristic manner of the High Style song: neither gregarious in impulse nor indulgent towards its listeners, it usually lacks any choric refrains which might invite us across the space that separates us from the singer and draw us into the song. Arnaut de Maroill maintains the distance between singer and hearer by a great show of decorum achieved by an accumulation of potent courtly words (*verais, valen*) and by strewing his poem with connectives that give it the appearance of discursiveness and debate (*quand...car...perque...*). Presented in this way the *grand chant courtois* becomes a form of oration and the antithesis of a 'performerless' dancing song. Indeed the idea of the song as the composition of a self-conscious artist is constantly kept in the listener's mind and is a crucial element of the *grand chant* manner:[3]

> The expressive technique of the Provençal love-song...the
> exploration in the first person of an emotional state which the poet
> alleges to be his own, evidently supposes that, by convention if not in
> literal fact, the poet is presenting himself. To this extent, then, the
> poet is self-conscious. But, in Provençal practice, he is not self-
> conscious merely as (according to the convention) a happy or
> dejected lover, but as a poet. The *canso* does not only present an
> emotional state: it often presents the poet in the act of presenting

15

that emotional state or in the act of reflecting upon the artistic means of presenting it. The troubadour is not only self-consciously a practitioner of the art of poetic composition, he says, even boasts, that he is so, sometimes at considerable length.

The contrasts which we have drawn between Arnaut de Maroill's *canso* in Old Provençal and an Old French *rondet* can be gathered into a rudimentary typology of twelfth- and thirteenth-century songs:

HIGH STYLE	LOWER STYLES
	POETRY
Tendency towards stanzas of isometric lines	Tendency towards stanzas of polymetric lines, especially brief lines multiplying short-range and conspicuous effects of rhyme and metre
No refrain or refrain rare	Refrains common
Exclusively lyric	Lyrico-choreographic Lyrico-narrative
Beloved not named (except in enigmatic terms)	Beloved may be named, or protagonist(s) named
	MUSIC
Rhapsodic	Conspicuous short-range repetitions and effects to create an instant 'tunefulness'
No strict metre (Figure 2)	Strict metre in many forms (especially those connected in some way with dance) (Figure 2)

16

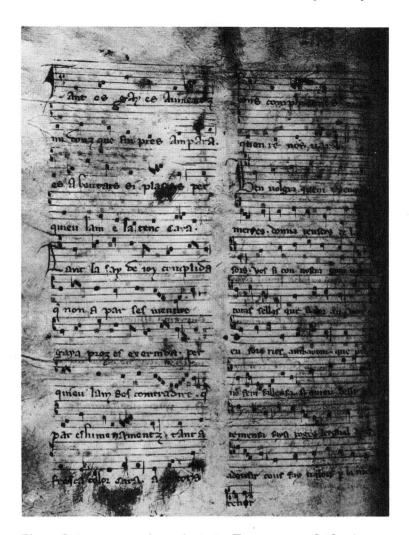

Figure 2 *An anonymous* dansa *beginning* Tant es gay es [sic] avinentz *and a High Style* canso *by the troubadour Blacasset, beginning* Ben volgra que.m vengues mer[c]es *(commencing on the third stave on the right hand side). The* dansa, *whose form reduces to ABBa[A], is in mensural notation, whereas Blacasset's through-composed* canso *is in unmeasured notation. Both songs are additions of the early fourteenth century to the Manuscrit du Roi. Paris, Bibliothèque Nationale, MS fr. 844, f.78v. Photographed under ultra-violet light. Reproduced by permission. See further Chapter 4.*

II

Where did instrumental accompaniment belong in this system of contrasts? The search for an answer begins with an aristocratic musician whom we encountered in Chapter 1. He is the Catalan nobleman, Guiraut de Cabreira, 'dashing in warfare … gracious in manners … [and] highly skilled on musical instruments'.

It may have been as early as 1150 that Guiraut addressed a mocking *sirventes* to a certain minstrel named Cabra (?Guiraut himself), playfully rebuking him for the accomplishments he had not mastered. Guiraut's own mastery of the fiddle—remembered long after his death by those who had heard him play—sharpens the edge of what is already a pointed *sirventes*.[4] 'Whoever taught you to bow and finger the fiddle made a bad job of it', he proclaims to the unfortunate minstrel in the hearing of all; 'you fiddle badly and sing worse, from start to finish':[5]

> Mal saps viular e pietz chantar
> del cap tro en la fenizon.
> . . . . . .
> Mal t'ensegnet cel qe.t mostret
> los detz a menar ni l'arson.

At one point Guiraut rebukes Cabra for not being familiar with a variety of lyric genres, including the *sirventesc, estribotz, retroencha, contenson* and *balaresc*—a useful but rather featureless list which does not mention particular works or name individual troubadours. Yet, in the lines which follow, Guiraut finds a more specific charge to level against Cabra: he cannot sing songs by the famous troubadours of the last and the present generation: Jaufre Rudel, Marcabrun, Ebles II de Ventadorn, a certain Anfos, and 'en Egun' (perhaps a mocking pun on *negun*, 'nobody'):[6]

> Ja vers novel   bon d'en Rudel
> non cug que.t pas sotz lo guingnon;
> De Markabrun   ni d'en Egun
> ni d'en Anfos ni d'en Eblon.

This suggests that some minstrels who fiddled and sang for a living included songs by celebrated troubadours in their repertory. As we might expect from one who was probably a younger contemporary of both Marcabrun and Jaufre Rudel, Guiraut de Cabreira refers to their songs in the correct way; by referring to their *vers novel* he is following the usage of both Marcabrun:[7]

> dist Macabruns lou vers del son

and Jaufre Rudel:[8]

No sap cantar qui.l so no.m ditz
ni.l vers trobar qui.ls motz no fay

So there is no doubt about Guiraut's meaning; but what do his words imply about performance practice? Here I have to confess that I have been as mischievous in beginning with Guiraut's *sirventes* as Guiraut was mischievous in writing it. For while the poem deserves pride of place in this chapter on chronological grounds, it also illustrates the principal difficulty that besets any attempt to answer questions about medieval performance practice with the aid of literary texts. This is that many literary sources are suggestive in a way that supports conventional wisdom (which is how that wisdom arose), yet prove, in the final analysis, to be vague and inexact. Guiraut de Cabreira's *sirventes* is a particularly vexing example. There is no doubt that Cabra's talents (if that is the right word to use in his case) include singing and playing the fiddle (*viular e chantar*), and it is implied that *vers novel* by Marcabrun and Jaufre Rudel are songs which a minstrel of Cabra's stamp would normally be expected to know. So it seems that some *joglars* in twelfth-century Occitania played the fiddle and had songs by noted troubadours in their repertory. What we cannot so readily conclude is that these minstrels used their instruments to accompany the *vers novel* which they performed.

At first sight this may seem a precious or perverse objection. Medieval courtly monody has been regarded as an art of instrumentally accompanied song for many years; an effort is needed to recognise that there is no *prima facie* case in favour of that view. Much of the literary evidence bearing upon the question of accompaniment suffers from what might be called the 'discontinuity problem': it mentions *this* (singing, perhaps), then mentions *that* (string-playing, let us imagine) but rarely allows us to establish whether this and that happen at the same time, whether they happen in the same place, or even whether they are associated with one another.

Then there is the problem of unwritten and lost repertory. Guiraut's *sirventes* offers an excellent illustration. In his determination to embarrass Cabra, Guiraut spends six lines on troubadour lyric, but he lavishes one hundred and fifteen lines (almost twenty times as many) on the epic stories which Cabra does not know. As Guiraut gets into his stride, names (some famous and some obscure) come tumbling out pell-mell: Charlemagne, Ganelon, Aiol, Erec, Amic, Berart, Aimar, Merlin, Alexander, and so on until Cabra must have despaired of ever finding employment again. This litany of heroes from Antiquity, the Bible and medieval epic tradition leaves us in no doubt that southern minstrels, like their northern counterparts, passed a great deal of their professional lives telling stories, and if a wealth of northern evidence may be believed, these narratives were often sung to instrumental accompaniment.[9] None of these songs has survived with music, yet this kind of material may lie behind many of the literary references to vocal and instrumental music which scholars have associated with the surviving troubadour and trouvère repertories.

III

After Guiraut de Cabreira's harangue against the unfortunate minstrel Cabra (whose bad luck must have begun when he took on the professional name 'Goat'), it is a relief to turn to the roughly contemporary epic of *Daurel et Beton* and two passages which may bring us a little closer to the kind of information which we seek.[10]

The story of this epic tells how Daurel, a minstrel, sacrifices his own son to save his boy-lord, Beton, from being massacred by a French duke named Guy. To guarantee Beton's safety Daurel sets off with the boy in a boat, and this stage of the narrative brings the first musical reference. When the child cries during their hazardous and uncertain voyage, Daurel takes his fiddle (*viola*) and[11]

> . . . fai .i. lais d'amor.

A second reference to vocal and instrumental music involves Beton, now matured into an expert instrumentalist and so courteous that nobody at the court of the Emir of Babylon can believe that he is the son of a minstrel. To test the point they arrange for Beton to play in the chamber of the princess while other courtiers hide; the trick being that if Beton refuses to accept the money offered to him after the performance then he cannot be a minstrel's son. Needless to say, Beton does refuse it; but what interests us most is not the outcome of the story but its incidentals. At first, Beton is requested to play some *laices* upon his fiddle for the princess, but Beton's name for what he has to offer is *bels verses*, and the poet follows Beton's usage: 'he sang his *verses* and was courteously attended to':[12]

> 'De bels verses sai, dona, vueilh que n'aujatz.'
> E dit sos verses e fon ben escoltatz;
> Lo rei l'auzi que s'era amagatz
> Entorn la cambra e.il reïna delatz,
> Et ab lor so .c. cavaliers prezatz.
> Que tuh escolto cossi s'es deportatz.
> Una gran pessa s'es laïns deportatz,
> Canta e vihola, es se fort alegratz.

> 'I know beautiful *verses*, lady, I wish you to hear
> some of them.' He sang his *verses* and was courteously
> attended to; the king, who had hidden himself within
> the chamber, heard him, and the beautiful queen, and
> with them are one hundred excellent knights who all
> listened to how [Beton] rejoiced in himself. [Beton]
> lingered within [the chamber] a good while.
> He sings and fiddles, and enjoys himself
> a great deal.

In the first extract the term *lais* is a suggestive one whose meanings in Old Provençal are many and various, often amounting to little more than 'a song', 'a tune (whether vocal or instrumental)'.[13] The context shows that Daurel's *lais* is played upon the fiddle, and that it is a love-song, *.i. lais d'amor*, which he is presumably either singing to his own accompaniment or

Example 6

S'al cor pla - gues be fora huei may sa - zos

de far chan - so per jo - ia man - te - ner,

mas trop me fay m'a - ven - tu - ra do - ler

cant ieu es - gart los bes e.ls mals qu'ieu ay;

que ricx dis hom que soy e que be.m vay

mas sel c'o ditz no sap ges ben lo ver,

car be - na - nan - sa non pot hom a - ver

de nul - ha re mais d'ai - so que.l cor play

per que n'a may us pau - pre s'es jo - yos

c'un ric ses joy qu'es tot l'an cor - ro - sos.

playing as instrumental music to soothe the troubled child. The likelihood that Daurel's *lais* is a lyric lai—a polymorphous lyric where each sub-division of the text has its own metrical form and musical setting—seems remote at this date (possibly as early as c1150). However, *lais* could also be applied to lyrics in the High Style, including the *canso*. Folquet de Marseilla (d.1231) calls his song *S'al cor plagues be fora huei may sazos* a *lais*, even though its subject matter and musico-poetic form mark it as a *canso* in the High Style tradition (see Music example 6).[14]

The *lais d'amor* played by Daurel to comfort the young Beton may be a High Style troubadour *canso* sung to the fiddle, although it seems to have been an unusual practice for a troubadour to refer to his words, his music, or both together as a *lais*.

In the second extract Beton's pieces are called *vers*, the prevailing term for a troubadour lyric until the later twelfth century when *canso* began to make an appearance.[15] Unfortunately it is not clear whether Beton is fiddling and singing at the same time, or whether the *verses* in his repertory are to be identified with troubadour songs such as those by Jaufre Rudel, since *vers* seems to have been used by the early troubadours for any kind of poem.[16] On balance *Daurel et Beton* only seems to offer hints in whispers.

A brief passage from *Jaufre* (c1170) speaks in bolder tones. In this romance, the only Arthurian verse narrative in Old Provençal, there is a description of a court celebration where[17]

> ...joglars que sun el palais
> Víulon descortz et suns et lais
> E dansas e cansonz de gesta.
> Jamais nun veira hom tal festa.

> ...minstrels who are in the palace play
> *descortz* and *suns* and *lais* and *dansas* and
> *cansonz de gesta* on the *viula*. No-one will
> ever see such a celebration again.

The *suns* are probably instrumental melodies, for *so* (<Latin *sonus*) in the sense 'a tune, a melody' is attested in numerous troubadour lyrics (where the *so*, or melody, of a lyric composition may be contrasted with the words, the *vers* or *motz*).[18] Perhaps the same meaning may be assigned to *lais*, given the frequency with which this word carries the sense 'melody, whether vocal or instrumental' in Old Provençal.

As for *descortz* and *dansas*, there is another twelfth-century source which joins these two terms to the minstrel's fiddle: a *partimen* with stanzas by the troubadours Raimbaut de Vaqueiras, Perdigo, and the nobleman Adémar II of Poitiers, Count of Valentinois and Diois, 1188–1230. The first *tornada* of this poem opens:[19]

Senher n'Aymar, vos etz vencuts primiers;
e.n Perdigos viule descortz o dansa. . . .

Lord Adémar, you are the first to lose; and let
sir Perdigo play a *descort* or *dansa* on his fiddle. . . .

This double confirmation of a link between the fiddle and the genres of *descort* and *dansa* is striking and surely significant. Both of these lyric forms may be said to occupy a very minor position in the corpus of troubadour lyrics with music. Only a handful of *descort* settings have come down to us with music[20] and only a few *dansas*, all of which are written in various forms of Franco-Occitan and preserved as additions of the early fourteenth century to the Manuscrit du Roi (Figure 2). In terms of survival, therefore, this association between the fiddle and the genres of *descort* and *dansa* carries instruments to the very periphery of the troubadour corpus.

Patterns of survival can be the result of accident or caprice, but there is another sense in which both the *descort* and the *dansa* lie on the edge of the troubadour art. Each one, in its own way, subverts the High Style manner as represented above all by the *canso*. The *descort* was a polymorphous lyric in which each subdivision of the text had its own metrical form and musical setting. Its form therefore subverted the dignity of the *canso* in which each stanza has the same form and the same melodic setting. As Baum has argued, the *descort* is not simply unlike the *canso*; it is the anti-*canso*:[21]

> The study of different writings concerning the
> *descort* and a preliminary examination of the Old
> Provençal *descorts* suggests the following hypothesis:
> for the troubadours of the classic period, the *descort*
> was the anti-chanson. Beside the regular *canso* which
> followed the principle of regularity, they conceived
> the irregular *canso* which followed the principle of
> irregularity . . . the opposition of the categories regular/
> irregular is the generating principle of the *descort*.
> This opposition may manifest itself on one level or
> on several levels at once; on that of form, on that
> of music, or on that of content.

This interpretation sets us wondering about the relationship which seems to have existed between the *descort* and the fiddle; was this relationship also designed to counter the High Style manner, this time in the realm of performance? Was instrumental accompaniment therefore inimical to the High Style manner in music and poetry?

This brings us to the *dansa*, associated with the fiddle in both the romance of *Jaufre* and the *partimen* between Raimbaut, Perdigo and Adémar. The *dansas* of the twelfth century have passed into eternal silence, for not one survives—neither words nor music—but their poetic form is probably preserved in the *dansas* which began to be written down in the next century (none of which are much older than c1250). Here is the outline of that form:

A   called the *respos*

b   the stanza, using different rhymes and a
     different metrical form to the *respos*

a   the closing section of the stanza, using the same
     rhymes and the same metrical form as the *respos* (but not
     necessarily reproducing its whole form).

If the *respos* were repeated at the end, then the result could be identical to the French virelai:[22]

A bb a A

A glance at the list of High Style and Lower Style characteristics on p.16 is enough to show that the *dansa* belongs in the region of the Lower Styles. The *dansa*, as its name implies, was a lyrico-choreographic form which must often have been performed for dancing; on those occasions, at least, it will have been performed in some kind of strict metre. When the *respos* was repeated at the end of the stanza the *dansa* had a refrain (in the strict sense: a combined musical and textual reprise); at all times the *dansa* had a conspicuous musical reprise (A b a). In all these respects it is a Lower Style form.

But what of the texts? Here we may be able to pursue the link between instruments and unwritten repertory a little further. For the most part the surviving *dansa* poems are courtly in the sense that they are love lyrics which exploit the conventions of literary love whose natural home is the *canso*. Yet no twelfth-century *dansas* seem to have survived, and there are no *dansas* surviving among the works of the major thirteenth-century troubadours.[23]

One explanation for this state of affairs is that the *dansa* began life as a trivial, ephemeral and perhaps even popular form: one which lay too low for the troubadours to cultivate. This would not stop *dansas* from being played and enjoyed at court, but it would prevent them from becoming the vehicle of a High Style lyric genre.

There are traces here and there of what these unrecorded *dansas* may have been like. A song by the Catalan troubadour Guillem de Berguedà (d.1192/6) claims to take its melody from a song sung 'by the young men of Pau', and the verses end with a (slightly variable) refrain which may well incorporate material from a dance-song:[24]

Puis van xantan liridunvau,
balan, notan gent e suau.

. . . . . .
Puys van xantan liridunvar,
balan, notan autet e clar.

Then they go singing (?playing) 'liridunvau', dancing, singing
sweetly and pleasingly.

At once they go singing 'liridunvar', dancing, singing
loudly and clearly.

The nonsense words 'liridunvau' and 'liridunvar' carry us some considerable distance from the High Style manner, as do these closing lines
from a disembodied verse:[25]

Varalalito
varalalito
deu!
varalatitondeÿna.

If this is an accurate picture of the prehistory of the *dansa* then we can
shed some fresh light on the association between the fiddle and the *dansa*
which we have met in two sources of the period 1170–1200. We have
already seen that the musical style of the thirteenth-century *dansas* lies in the
region of the Lower Styles; it now appears that the texts and general ethos of
dansas in the twelfth century may have been foreign to the High Style.

Our most explicit twelfth-century sources therefore suggest that fiddle-
accompaniment was associated with one form which subverts the musico-
poetic decorum of the High Style (the *descort*), and another which, at the
time we hear of it in relation to the fiddle, may well have been an ephemeral
genre which the troubadours ignored, the *dansa*. Thus we have a provisional
answer to the question of where instrumental accompaniment belonged in
the system of contrasts presented on p.16. As far as the twelfth century in
the South is concerned, the evidence—admittedly very meagre—suggests
that instrumental accompaniment did not have a High Style ethos.

It may be that these two references to accompanied *descorts* and *dansas* are
misleading, but I believe the next chapter will show that we have reason to
trust them. Let us leave the twelfth century with a text of c1210 which offers
a remarkable portrait of a minstrel with High Style troubadour songs in his
repertory: *Abril issia* by the Catalan poet and poetic theorist of the early
thirteenth century, Raimon Vidal.

IV

In this poem the narrator tells how he walked out one morning when 'April
was leaving and May entering'. Low in spirits, he enters the town square of

Besalú (in Catalonia) and is pleased to see a minstrel approaching him, 'dressed and shod after the fashion of the time in which valour and worth were both found in the barons'.[26] The two characters fall into conversation and it becomes clear that in some measure the minstrel is an archetypal figure found throughout medieval literature: the professional entertainer nostalgic for a vanished age of generous and discriminating patrons when inferior entertainers, 'bad men who have come to work their vile and ill desires', did not displace men of true talent.[27] Raimon Vidal's poem therefore gives an idealised and archaising picture of minstrelsy, but this increases its value as a testament to the high seriousness and sense of professional pride which the minstrel craft could encompass in the twelfth and thirteenth centuries.

The minstrel introduces himself by listing his skills:[28]

> Senher, yeu soy us hom aclis
> a joglaria de cantar,
> e say romans dir e contar,
> e novas motas e salutz,
> e autres comtes espandutz
> vas totas partz azautz e bos,
> e d'en Guiraut vers e chansos
> e d'en Arnaut de Maruelh mays,
> e d'autres vers e d'autres lays ...

> Sir, I am a man inclined to the profession of minstrelsy of
> singing, and I know how to tell and narrate romances and
> many tales and love-greetings, and other charming and
> good stories known everywhere, and *vers* and *chansos* of
> sir Guiraut [de Bornelh] and more by sir Arnaut de Maroill,
> and other *vers* and other *lays* ...

Although he specialises in *joglaria de cantar*, 'the profession of minstrelsy of singing', this minstrel seems to have no wish to advertise any instrumental skills that he may possess.

As the story unfolds it emerges that this *joglar* has a high opinion of his own craft. In his view minstrels have a responsibility to promote the highest values of courtly society by conversation, songs and tales. The minstrel craft therefore deserves to be regarded as a kind of learning (*saber*) which can only be acquired by men of great personal gifts; they must be both charming (*avinens*) and wise (*savis*).[29] Accordingly, the best minstrel travels to courts where he may seek out 'select' people (*chauzitz*) and 'increase wisdom and excellence amongst them' (*a lur pujar sens e valors*), for his professional satisfaction comes from inspiring noble people to magnanimous actions and virtuous thoughts—to courtesy in the fullest sense of the term.[30]

As for troubadour songs, Raimon Vidal presents them as an effective means of moral instruction through pleasure, *solatz*. His taste in troubadour lyric is an elevated one, for it centres upon Guiraut de Bornelh (*honratz per los valenz homes*, according to the Vidas),[31] and Arnaut de Maroill (*onratz hom de cort*).[32] Since a minstrel lives entirely by his voice, and since his art, in all its manifestations, is an art of eloquence—of 'how one should speak' (*si co hom ditz*)—the narrator takes a lofty view of lyric genres, disdaining performers whose only concern is to learn love-debates in verse, or *jocx partitz*, together with 'every wisecrack that one says to fools'.[33] In contrast, he regards the *canso* as an art of eloquence in the service of moral instruction. Thus a poem of Arnaut de Maroill 'instructs undiscriminating people', while Guiraut de Bornelh is pictured as a teacher of 'refined people in order to strengthen their good behaviour'; viewed in this light the troubadour's chief gift is his wisdom, or *sen*, and his task is to instil it into others, whence, to *ensenhar*, or to 'teach' those who hear his works.[34]

To anyone familiar with the idiosyncratic works of the first troubadours, whose sexual morality is sometimes less than exemplary, this earnest view of a lyric repertory which is often concerned with erotic love may seem somewhat ingenuous,[35] and it is certainly difficult to believe that a theorist of poetic art like Raimon Vidal, who acknowledges the primacy of didactic aims in poetry with such candour, can capture more than a fraction of what was truly enjoyed by those who cared for troubadour poetry. Yet it is doubtful whether Raimon Vidal's contemporaries would have considered his faith in the moral seriousness of troubadour song to be misplaced, nor need we assume that the troubadours and their listeners would have turned to some other defence of their art than the moralistic one which Vidal offers. The articulate mind of the Middle Ages was never dissatisfied with the view of good poetry as something *utilis* as well as *dulcis*.

In accordance with his elevated view of the High Style song the minstrel in Raimon Vidal's *Abril issia* is accustomed to be listened to. When he asks the narrator to listen to his account of himself 'as attentively (*puramen*) as if it were a message of love', he may be alluding to High Style love-songs of the troubadour tradition, and the adverb *puramen*, whose meaning in this context may amount to something like '[listen] in a pure fashion, unsullied by any base thought or distraction', suggests that a minstrel with High Style songs in his repertory held high expectations of his listeners.[36]

Needless to say, these songs could not be sung to any audience at any time; they needed to be prepared for, and one of the most fascinating sections in Raimon Vidal's poem is the passage where the narrator explains how a minstrel should bring his audience to the point where they are ready for them.[37] It seems that a skilled minstrel began by working his way into the flow of conversation; then, *petit à petit*, he manoeuvred himself into a dominant position within the party by exploiting his learning, his *saber*. On the simplest level this *saber* consisted of traveller's gossip, for in any courtly circle a minstrel enjoyed a conversational advantage by virtue of his travels that enabled him to report items of news he had learned as he moved from place to place. In the opinion of Raimon Vidal this was one way that an entertainer could help to maintain and stimulate aristocratic courtesy, for courtesy was the common culture of a network of *cortz* and it was the privilege of minstrels, who travelled regularly between these courts, to report which lords of the region were the most courteous, and which ladies the most virtuous, as an example to all. Conversation such as this was the minstrel's first deployment of his *saber*. Next, if he saw that the company was with him and eager for more, he turned to *novas*, or stories in verse which retained the themes of courtesy and noble deeds but which represented a move away from conversation as the company (which the minstrel had by now turned into an audience) fell silent to listen to his material in rhyme.

Once the *novas* were over, the minstrel reached the most sensitive point in the management of his audience. His next and final stage was to offer to sing, but it was only worth proceeding to *chantars* if the audience had shown itself *adreitz, prims* and *entendens*—to be clever, of fine sensibility and discriminating. This, it seems, was the kind of audience, moulded and tested at each stage by a skilful performer, which proud *joglars* sought for the performance of songs by troubadours such as Guiraut de Bornelh and Arnaut de Maroill. Raimon Vidal seems to regard all his skills as facets of the same gift—the gift of eloquence. Whether it be the improvised eloquence of conversation, or the prepared eloquence of tales and troubadour songs, a good minstrel sees himself as one who, in all the manifestations of his art, shows how one should speak to the pleasure and moral profit of others. He does not emerge as a manually skilled or dexterous individual, whether the skills be those of the knife-thrower, the juggler or the instrumentalist.

The evidence assembled in this chapter might suggest that the High Style troubadour *canso* was not generally accompanied in the twelfth century. However, we have found no positive evidence for that view, for none of the texts that we have so far encountered mentions the High Style *canso* in clear and unmistakable terms (although a passage from Daurel et Beton may do so; see above). All that can be said is that as early as the second half of the twelfth century there are signs of an association between instruments and certain song-forms (the *descort* and the *dansa*) which, in their own way, stand well apart from the High Style *canso*.

3

The thirteenth century in the North

[Telamon] fu mout de grant valor.
Mout ot en lui bon chanteor,
Mout aveit la voiz haute et clere
Et de sonez ert bons trovere.

Benoit de Sainte Maure, *Roman de Troie*

These lines from the *Roman de Troie* show that the courtly singer-trouvère was a recognisable figure in northern France by c1165. In some ways this is a remarkably early date; we will not hear of any named trouvère for several decades yet; there will be no written source of the trouvère art for almost a hundred years. Yet Benoit de Sainte Maure shows that a male courtier who was a good *chanteor* and *trovere* could expect to be admired in French society less than a generation after the earliest known troubadours such as Marcabrun and Jaufre Rudel.

In terms of lyric production, the half century from 1170 to 1220 was a brilliant one in northern France. Yet in terms of information about the way in which those lyrics were performed, it is a dark period; not until the very end of it does the obscurity surrounding instrumental practice in trouvère song begin to recede. Yet although the way is dark during those years, it is not impossible to follow, for the main path must lead from south to north, from the *cortz* of Occitania to the lands of magnates in France. The central genre of the northern trouvères, the *chanson*, was directly based upon the *canso* of the southern troubadours,[1] passing easily from Occitan to French in the repertory of travelling performers who found a willing audience for these and many other songs from Occitania which the northern barons lumped together as 'songs from the Poitou', *chansons poitevines*. We can even see the process at work in some of the twelfth-century epics; in *Garin le Loheren*, amidst an evocation of a fierce warrior society, we suddenly encounter minstrels who[2]

Vïelent, notent maint bel son poitevin.

Whether such musicians as these respected the performing traditions which began to emerge in the previous chapter will never be known for certain because of the insuperable problem of song-terminology. The *son poitevin* which is performed here before a set of warrior barons at their banqueting table might be anything from the most weighty of troubadour *cansos* to the lightest and most trivial of *dansas*.

Two striking references to accompanied singing will serve to illustrate this problem of terminology further. Here is a knight named Gerars, riding to a tournament in the thirteenth-century romance of *Gille de Chyn* by Gautier de Tournai (Appendix 3:27):

> Gerars Malfillastres li frans,
> Li prex, li gentix, li soufrans,
> A cel tornoi tout ensement
> Ala mout acesmeement.
> Vi. compaignons o lui mena
> Ou il durement se fïa;
> Et s'ot o lui .ii. vïeleurs,
> .I. son d'amors cantent entreurs,
> .I. dïemence par matin.
> Cevauçoient tout lor cemin
> Tout droit le premier jor de may,
> Qu'erbe est vers et florissent glay,
> Que tote riens trait en verdour.
> Li vïeleur .i. son d'amour
> A haute vois mout cler cantoient,
> O les vïelez s'acordoient. (lines 447–62)

> Gerars Malfillastres, noble, valiant, courteous
> and forbearing, went in this magnificent way to
> the tournament. He took six companions with him
> in whom he put the deepest trust; and he had two
> fiddlers with him who sang a *son d'amors* between
> themselves, one Sunday morning. They rode straight
> along on the first day of May, when the grass is
> green, the gladioli are in flower, and everything
> takes on a verdant hue. The fiddlers, with loud and
> clear voices, sang a *son d'amour*, according themselves
> with their fiddles.

These lines offer an uncommonly detailed reference to accompanied performance. The outdoor setting is made from layers of rhetoric common to both lyric and narrative tradition (*Que tote riens trait en verdour...*), but the company of characters in the foreground is independently imagined, as shown by the concentration of incidental and unconventional detail (the six companions; the two fiddlers). The fiddlers are clearly singing to their own accompaniment as they ride, and the piece which they perform is twice described as a *son d'amour*.

Gautier de Tournai's passage, arresting though it may be, is not the only description of its kind to survive. Here is another, this time from the thirteenth-century epic of *Hervis de Metz* (Appendix 3:29):

> Dist Hervis: 'Frans jongleres, bien soiiés vous trouvés!'
> A mengier li a fait maintenant aporter,
> Après souper commence moult tost a vïeler
> Et cante sons d'amours, belement et souef,
> Et Hervis l'escouta li gentis et li bers. (lines 2469–73)

> Hervis says: 'Noble minstrel, you are welcome!
> He had him brought to the banquet, and after the meal he
> began to play the fiddle at once and to sing *sons d'amours*
> in a beautiful and sweet way; Hervis, courteous and
> noble, listened to him.

The accompanied *sons d'amours* mentioned in these passages might conceivably be High Style troubadour songs. In Old French literature the term *son* is often associated with melodies from Occitania or the border between north and south; there are *sons poitevins, sons gascoins, sons auvergnaus*, and even a *son* with Gascon words and a Limousin tune (Appendix 2, 4:9, last example). In the epic *La Prise de Cordres et de Sebille* a *son d'amors* is particularly associated with minstrels from the Auvergne:[3]

> Tubent ces guaites, chantent cil jugleor,
> Lai[s] de Bretaigne chantent cil vielor,
> Et d'Ingleterre i out des har[p]eors,
> Li Auvreignas dient .j. son d'amors.

> Watchmen play their horns, minstrels sing,
> fiddlers sing *lais* of Bretaigne and there were
> harpers from England; the men from Auvergne sing
> a *son d'amors*.

Jean Renart's romance of *Guillaume de Dole* (c1220), where over forty lyric songs are quoted or cited, also suggests that the term *son* had meridional associations for French speakers. Renart reserves it for High Style songs by the troubadours Bernart de Ventadorn and Jaufre Rudel. His only departure from this usage takes us back to the Auvergne, for he calls the following High Style *canso*, attributed to the troubadour Daude de Pradas in one of its three sources, a *chançon auvrignace*. Here it is with the heavily Gallicised text that Renart gives (Music example 7).[4]

Example 7

It is therefore tempting to see a reflection of contemporary practice in the extracts from *Gille de Chyn* and *Hervis de Metz* quoted above. They suggest a world in which High Style troubadour songs are performed for northern audiences, their texts heavily Gallicised but still emitting the heady perfume of the South with such non-French forms as *altane*. Perhaps it was performances like this which helped to spread the troubadour *canso* into the north. Instrumental accompaniment may have been a necessary prop to performances of songs whose words cannot always have been wholly intelligible to northern listeners. No doubt most French speakers could recognise many individual words, but not when the Occitan was seriously garbled. How many northern listeners would have been able to twist a meaning from this troubadour line as it appears in Jean Renart's romance:

no coir dont desier non fon.

This has come a long way from Bernart de Ventadorn's

lo cor de dezirier no.m fon.

Modern performers of medieval music have repeatedly found that instrumental accompaniment is a great aid in building attractive performances of troubadour songs whose texts are not fully intelligible (if intelligible at all) to their audiences; perhaps the minstrels of twelfth- and thirteenth-century France, keen to exploit the vogue for *sons poitevins*, made the same discovery.

This is only supposition, of course; what is certain is that the term *son d'amors* is not a precise one and could be used to denote songs very far removed from the High Style, as here:[5]

> Au tens nouvel   que cil oisel
> sont hetie et gai,
> en un boschel   sanz pastourel
> pastore trouvai,
> ou fesoit chapiau de flors
> et chantoit un *son d'amors*
> qui mult ert jolis:
>   '*li pensers trop mi guerroie*
>   *de vous, douz amis.*'

> In the spring season when birds are excited and
> joyous, in a small wood I came across a shepherdess
> without a shepherd; she was weaving a head-garland
> of flowers and she sang a *son d'amors* which was
> very pretty indeed: *Li pensers trop mi guerroie/de*
> *vous, douz amis.*

In this *pastourelle*, by the thirteenth-century trouvère Perrin d'Agincourt, talk of *son d'amors* seems to be pointing us in exactly the opposite direction to the one we have been taking up to now. In Perrin's poem a *son d'amors* is identified with the world of Lower Style song associated with shepherdesses in the rich lyric repertory of the *pastourelle*. Taken in isolation, the lines *li pensers trop mi guerroie/de vous, douz amis* are obviously too short to give an impression of the song which the shepherdess is singing, but shepherdesses in Old French *pastourelles* do not sing High Style lyrics by troubadours; their songs belong with the huge repertory of floating refrains (many of them probably from dance-songs) and rondeaux scattered throughout Old French manuscripts.[6] On balance it may be safer to rest with the conclusion that *son d'amors* was flexible in meaning during the thirteenth century (as we would expect it to be, since it is not a precise term), and that the lyrics which are sung and accompanied in *Gille de Chyn* and *Hervis de Metz* may be High Style songs by troubadours, but might equally well be lyrics of a very different cast: simple refrain forms such as the *rondet de carole*.

To escape from this tangle of terms and hypotheses we need evidence in which specific kinds of songs are associated with accompaniment. Fortunately, there is one such source compiled by an author who had heard *chansons poitevines* and who was a connoisseur of the whole range of monophonic lyrics known in France, from little dancing songs up to *chansons* by trouvères such as the Chastelain de Couci and the Vidame de Chartres. His decision to insert lyrics into a romance narrative of c1220 provides an outstanding source of information about instrumental practice in northern courtly monody, and one which suggests that performing traditions did indeed pass northwards along the roads which linked Occitania to *Fransa*. This is the romance of *Guillaume de Dole* compiled by Jean Renart in the first decades of the thirteenth century. Jean Renart seems to have initiated the fashion of inserting lyric poems into romance narrative; his poem contains more than forty lyrics which, taken together, provide a conspectus of the song-forms known in his day.[7] They include sixteen High Style songs, six *chansons de toile* (see below), two *pastourelles* and twenty refrain-songs comparable to *C'est la jus en la praele* (see below). Since they are presented as arising from the story—being sung by characters in the tale— Jean Renart is committed to some narrative involvement with the way in which they are performed.

In three cases Jean Renart refers to the presence of instrumental accompaniment (which, in every case, is provided by a minstrel upon his fiddle), and if we put the accompanied songs together then we begin to discern various patterns.

The first accompanied song is a *rondet* beginning *C'est la jus en la praele*. The context of the performance is informal and festive, for the piece is sung at the hostel near the palace of Conrad, Emperor of Germany, where Guillaume de Dole is staying. Guillaume and his party return from a night of entertainment at the palace taking with them Jouglet, a minstrel. Jouglet is commanded to carry his *viele* back to the hostel in response to a request made earlier that same evening by the daughter of the hostel-keeper who had playfully upbraided the minstrel: 'you have sung nothing, Jouglet, since you came through our door', offering to pardon the omission if he would return with his fiddle that night. 'I shall do so willingly', replies Jouglet, 'if we are to have *caroles*' (1566–7; 1799–1801). When the party arrives at the hostel (which is clearly no country inn but a well-appointed lodging which the Emperor judges to be appropriate for his guests) they seek out the owner's daughter. Once they have ascended to the upper floor where the valets have laid out fruit and wine, the girl sings the *rondet* to the accompaniment of Jouglet's fiddle:[8]

...car el a chantee	...for she sang
ovoec Jouglet en la vïele	to Jouglet's fiddling
ceste chançonete novele:	this new *chançonete*:
C'est la jus en la praele,	It's down there in the meadow,
or ai bone amor novele!	now I have a new true love!
Dras i gaoit Perronele.	There Perronele rinsed her clothes.

Bien doi joie avoir:
Or ai bon'amor novele
a mon voloir.

I have good reason to rejoice:
Now I have a new true love
to my desire.

A glance is enough to show that this *chançonete* (whose music does not survive) is an example of what we have called a Lower Style; indeed it is exactly the kind of lyric which was used to illustrate Lower Style characteristics in the previous chapter: a light, informal song whose brisk and essentially trivial character is caught, in this instance, by the diminutive suffix in *chançonete*. There are many features which set this poem apart from the High Style: the refrain; the pastoral setting signalled by a formulaic, half-narrative *C'est la jus en la praele*; the mention of the beloved's name (a gesture which is foreign to the decorum of the High Style, unless the lady be referred to by some enigmatic name which the poet has given her); the use of the conventionalised rustic name Perronele; the implication that the speaker himself is of Perronele's social class; and the evocation of an insouciant rustic life (Perronele rinsing her clothes).

The second of the songs performed to instrumental accompaniment in Jean Renart's romance is *Bele Aiglentine*, a *chanson de toile* sung by a young Norman squire as he rides into the fields before a great tourney. Once again the accompaniment is provided by the minstrel Jouglet on his fiddle. He is commanded to play by the squire (*si la fist Jouglet vïeler*).[9] *Bele Aiglentine* presents many of the characteristic features of the *chanson de toile* (literally 'a song to sing while sewing cloth'). It is narrative, opening as the heroine, Aiglentine, converses with her mother whilst sewing. She is busied with other thoughts and proves so inattentive to her work that she pricks her finger with the needle. Her mother notices this and suspects that Aiglentine may be troubled in love—indeed that she may be pregnant:[10]

'Bele Aiglentine, deffublez vo sorcot,
....
Je voil veoir desoz vostre gent cors.'
'Non ferai, dame, la froidure est la morz.'
   Or orrez ja
[conment la bele Aiglentine esploita].

'Fair Aiglentine, undo your dress for I wish to look
at your fair body underneath.' 'I shall not do it,
mother, for the cold can be fatal.' Now hear how the
fair Aiglentine won through!

Aiglentine admits that she has fallen in love with Count Henri. 'Will he not have you?' asks Aiglentine's mother; 'I do not know,' replies Aiglentine disarmingly, 'for I have never asked him'. On her mother's prompting, Aiglentine goes to visit Henri in his *ostel* where she finds him in bed and asks him if he will marry her. Henri gladly accepts, and the final verse of the poem runs:[11]

> Oit le Henris, mout joianz en devint.
> Il fet monter chevalier trusq'a .xx.,
> si enporta la bele en son païs
> et espousa, riche contesse en fist.
>   Grant joie en a
> li quens Henris quant bele Aiglentine a.

> Henri hears her and became very joyful. He commands
> twenty knights to mount and carried that fair one
> to his own country and married her, making her a
> rich countess. Count Henri is overjoyed now that he has
> fair Aiglentine.

Here we have a fully narrative poem whose stanzas (except the last) end with a refrain which calls us into the tale with an almost minstrelish insistence:

> *Or orrez ja*
> *conment la bele Aiglentine esploita.*

Bele Aiglentine is characterised not only by its narrative framework but also by its para-folkloric tone. The tone is established by the archetypal nature of the characters (a sorrowing pregnant maid, an anxious mother, a lover), and by the incremental repetition of the narrative technique—as when Aiglentine's mother calls to her at the beginning of one strophe:

> Bele Aiglentine, or vos tornez de ci . . . (2271)

and then the narrator begins the next strophe:

> Bele Aiglentine s'est tornee de ci (2277)

This device of completing an action with the words in which the action was commanded or predicted figures in many traditional forms of narrative (English balladry provides a parallel); it contributes to an impression of the world as a place where events have a momentum of their own, largely independent of human will and choice. Yet it does so without establishing any mature sense of tragedy or even of fate. Motivation and causality become cryptic and the narrative can be pared down to its essentials, leaving the reader with a stirring sense of mystery. Who is Aiglentine? When and where does her story take place? Why does she wait for her mother to discover her pregnancy before speaking to Count Henri since he seems quite happy to marry her? Why is Count Henri abed when Aiglentine visits him?

At the same time the direct speech assumes a para-folkloric tone with a stylised and sometimes proverbial manner—as in the stanza quoted above when Aiglentine's mother asks to see beneath her dress:

Je voil veoir desoz vostre gent cors.

and Aiglentine replies:

Non ferai, dame, la froidure est la morz.

Or when Aiglentine enters the hostel of her lover and cries:

Sire Henri, veilliez ou dormez? (2283)

The last of the accompanied lyrics in Jean Renart's *Guillaume de Dole* is performed at the command of the king and accompanied on the fiddle (*li fet chanter en la vïele*):[12]

Cele d'Oisseri
ne met en oubli
que n'aille au cembel.
Tant a bien en li
que mout embeli
le gieu soz l'ormel.
En son chief ot chapel
de roses fres novel.
Face ot fresche, colorie,
vairs oils, cler vis simple et bel.
Por les autres fere envie
i porta maint bel joël.

She of Oisseri does not forget to go to the combat;
she is so fine that she graced the game under the elm.
On her head she had a garland of new,
fresh roses. She had a fresh, high-coloured visage,
shining eyes with a clear, sweet and beautiful face.
She wore many beautiful jewels there to make others
covetous.

This is an enigmatic little song to say the least. Jean Renart describes it as *une dance* composed by maidens of France to commemorate the toils of a certain *bele Marguerite*. This is quite plausible since there are references to commemorative dance-songs of this kind scattered here and there in medieval writings from at least the ninth century on.

These are the songs which Jean Renart associates with instrumental accompaniment in *Guillaume de Dole*. Several points can now be firmly

37

stated. Firstly, only three of the forty-six songs quoted or excerpted in the romance are associated with accompaniment, a proportion of one in fifteen. Secondly, the accompaniment is provided in every case by a solo fiddle, a circumstance which suggests a degree of standardisation of performance practice (since the same, solo instrument is used each time) and also betrays a certain sobriety of taste; *Guillaume de Dole* provides no evidence for the mixed bands of wind, stringed and percussion instruments which have figured so prominently in modern recordings of this repertory.

But the most important conclusion to emerge from this survey is that in poetic terms, at least, every accompanied song in *Guillaume de Dole* shows pronounced Lower Style characteristics (the music of these songs does not survive). There is a strong link with dance, with narrative and with refrain-form. There is no instance in the romance where accompaniment is associated with a High Style poetic manner.[13]

This picture, if an accurate one, seems to accord with the evidence of the Old Provençal sources examined in the last chapter. There we found that instrumental accompaniment seems to have been particularly associated with the *descort* and the *dansa*, both of them genres which, in their own way, subverted the High Style manner. With Jean Renart's *Guillaume de Dole*, instruments seem to lie on the periphery of the surviving corpus of trouvère monody.

The distinction between High and Lower Styles in lyric, together with the patterns of instrumental usage appropriate to them, is not a distinction between what is courtly on one hand and what is uncourtly on the other. A Lower Style song with a simple, refrain-based melody, sung to the fiddle for dancing at court, would not be an 'uncourtly' song; indeed the fresh and primaveral ethos of most aristocratic dancing lay very close to the essence of court-culture in the twelfth and thirteenth centuries and characterises the scene where the Catalan troubadour Guiraut de Cabreira plays the fiddle for dancing in the palace at Arles.[14]

Courtliness is not the main issue here, but art. While any simple *dansa* could be as courtly as a High Style troubadour song, its appeal was not to good taste or judgement, but to the feet. In the same way narrative songs, whether in the form of epic or lyric like the *chanson de toile*, catered for a basic human desire—the desire for stories—in a way that the High Style songs of the troubadours and trouvères resolutely refused to do. If we have uncovered a general principle here it is a very general one and seems to be this: a song was less appropriate for instrumental accompaniment the more it lay claim to self-conscious artistry.

We may be confronting a fundamental characteristic of twelfth- and thirteenth-century string-playing here: instrumental music does not seem to have been associated with the kind of profound creative endeavour which demanded serious and considered attention from the listener. Time and time again, medieval literary sources convey the impression that string-playing was spontaneous, ephemeral and associated with very few emotional feelings beyond those which are inspired by gregarious dining and dancing. The minds of the twelfth and thirteenth centuries, both northern and southern, could find a wide range of significance in poetry, as they could in poetry with music; but music by itself—*so desturmens ses verba*—does not seem to have existed for them on the same plane.

4

Late traditions in the South

Dansa...deu [haver] so plazent; e la
ditz hom ab esturmens...

Doctrina de Compondre Dictats

I

The value of Jean Renart's romance of *Guillaume de Dole*, explored in the previous chapter, is that Renart's narrative allows us to establish whether instrumental accompaniment is meant and precisely what kind of song is being accompanied. In the final analysis this is the only kind of evidence upon which we can hope to build an understanding of instrumental participation in courtly monody, and since so little of it survives, every scrap counts, no matter how late or peripheral it may seem. The purpose of this chapter is to examine two southern sources which offer explicit information about the place of instruments in a system of lyric genres, but which are very late for our purposes, perhaps even too late. Both are treatises on the writing of lyric poetry in Occitan: the Catalan tract entitled *Doctrina de Compondre Dictats*, probably of c1300, and the annotations to the A text of the celebrated *Leys d'Amors*, compiled in Toulouse during the first half of the fourteenth century. As far as instrumental accompaniment is concerned, we shall find some grounds for believing that these treatises endorse the picture traced in Chapters 2 and 3.

The *Doctrina de Compondre Dictats* was probably composed by Jofre de Foixà as a supplement to his *Regles de Trobar*, commissioned by Jacme II when king of Sicily (Jofre is known to have had connections with the Catalan court in Sicily after 1289).[1] The methods and treatment of material employed in the *Regles de Trobar*[2]

> ... presuppose the existence of a circle of amateurs
> anxious to write Provençal verse in the manner of the
> troubadours without making linguistic and metrical

errors . . . for Jofre, and presumably for his intended
readers, Provençal verse was an object of living
practical interest, not merely of antiquarian
curiosity; their interest was in continuing, to
the best of their ability, a tradition still felt
to be alive.

In Jofre's eyes, therefore, the writings of the troubadours formed a
classical tradition: a canon of literary models from the past setting standards
of excellence in diction and expression for later lyricists to follow. It is
perhaps from just such a man as this that we might expect to derive a
conservative, retrospective view of troubadour practice with regard to
accompaniment.

The *Doctrina de Compondre Dictats* defines numerous poetic genres according to their characteristic stanza-forms, subject matter and length, offering a
few brief remarks on the type of musical setting with which they should be
provided: the *plant* may have 'any type of melody you like', the *vers* 'a new
tune', the *dança* 'a pleasing melody', and so on. In this manner Jofre works
his way through the *canço, vers, lays, sirventez, retronxa, pastora, dança, plant,
alba, tenso, discort*, and a few minor forms. Suddenly, towards the end of the
treatise, we hear of instruments in Jofre's account of the *dansa*:[3]

> Si vols far dança, deus parlar d'amor be e
> plasentment, en qualque estament ne sies. E deus
> li fer dedents .iij. cobles e no pus, e respost,
> una o dues tornades, qual te vulles; totes vegades
> so novell . . . Dansa es dita per ço com naturalment
> la ditz hom dança[n] o bayllan, cor deu [haver]
> so plazent; e la ditz hom ab esturmens, e plau a
> cascus que la diga e la escout.

> If you wish to compose a *dança*, you should speak
> well and pleasingly of love in whatever state
> of mind that you may be in. And you should
> compose it with three stanzas, and no more, with
> a *respost*, with one or two *tornadas*, as you may think
> fit; it should always have a new tune . . . A *dansa* is
> so called because it is normally sung whilst dancing,
> hence it should have a pleasing tune; and it is sung
> with instruments, and pleases everyone who sings and
> hears it.

Jofre's passing comment that the *dansa* 'is sung with instruments' carries
some weight in the full context of his treatise, for no other lyric form in the
Doctrina is associated with instruments in this way. Here we seem to have a
point of contact with performing traditions reaching as far back as the last

decades of the twelfth century, for the *dansa* is associated with the fiddle in two Old Provençal texts produced in that period, as we saw in Chapter 2. In that chapter it was suggested that the *dansa* (and the *descort*) may have been distinctive among the lyric genres known to the twelfth-century troubadours for their association with instrumental accompaniment (or instrumental performance); I went on to propose that this was one aspect of a distinctiveness of form and poetic content which set both *descort* and *dansa* apart from other lyric genres. As far as the *descort* is concerned, Jofre at least knows that it stands on a limb for its melody, 'the contrary of all other types of song', as he puts it,[4] while the distinctiveness of the *dansa* seems apparent in his treatise for exactly the reason which twelfth-century sources have led us to expect: it is linked to instruments.

Fortunately it is possible to form a relatively clear impression of what the *dansas* known to Jofre were like, for it is in early fourteenth-century additions to an important French chansonnier, the Manuscrit du Roi, that we encounter *dansas* with their music for the first (and last) time (see Music example 8).[5]

II

By way of Jofre de Foixà's treatise we come to the most exhaustive and systematic of all treatises on troubadour poetry, the *Leys d'Amors* ('laws of love'), compiled, for the most part, during the second quarter of the fourteenth century by Guillem Molinier.[6] This treatise, which exists in several versions, was produced for the Academy of the Gai Saber at Toulouse, an association which sought to encourage the composition of lyric poetry in Occitan by organising poetic competitions, probably on the model of the northern French *puis*, and the purpose of the *Leys d'Amors* is to reduce the art of writing lyric poetry to rule so that it may be taught, propagated and judged.

Like Jofre de Foixà, Molinier and his collaborators in the Toulouse Academy can have had no direct knowledge of earlier traditions of performance-practice, but this does not affect the issue of whether the practices of their own day—*aquesta prezen art*—enshrined long-established conventions—*long uzatge acostumat*. Our judgement of that issue (insofar as we can hope to judge it) must rest upon a comparison of the *Leys d'Amors* with the two independent sources which we have already examined: Jofre's *Doctrina* and Jean Renart's *Guillaume de Dole*.

In an important section of the *Leys* Molinier describes the characteristic subject matter and metrical forms associated with each genre of poem, usually adding a brief note on the kind of melody associated with them. In this way he works through the principal genres, or *dictatz principals*, a category which embraces the traditionally significant troubadour genres. There is no reference anywhere to instrumental accompaniment or to purely instrumental forms, and an anonymous member of the Toulouse Academy,

Example 8

with access to the manuscript, seems to have been struck by the omission. To remedy it he added an extensive marginal note (Figure 3) which mentions the purely instrumental *garips* and also the *estampida* (which, he explains, may be either a purely instrumental melody or an instrumental tune to which words have been added).[7] He also mentions the *bal*, a form which, he relates, is usually composed as an instrumental tune and then supplied with words, resulting in a song which is 'more apt for singing to instrumental accompaniment than the *dansa*' (*mays apte per cantar amb esturmens que dansa*).[8]

Figure 3 *An extensive marginal annotation to the A text of the* Leys d'Amors. *There are several references to the use of* esturmens. *Toulouse, Académie des Jeux Floraux, MS 500.007, f.41v. Reproduced by permission.*

We glimpse the outlines of a familiar picture here. As in Jean Renart's romance of *Guillaume de Dole* and Jofre's tract, instruments in the *Leys d'Amors* seem to occupy a minor position within the system of lyric genres, being closely associated with minor forms that are linked in some way to dancing. With the exception of the *garips*, all of the forms which the annotator of the *Leys* links with instruments have some direct or historical connection with dance: the *bals*, the *estampida*, and the *dansa*.

Yet the *Leys d'Amors* has more to reveal, for a close reading of the text shows that instrumental accompaniment had a distinctive ethos for the members of the Toulouse Consistori. It is possible to sense this ethos, for the members of the Consistori seem to have ranged their lyric genres across an aesthetic spectrum which corresponds closely to what we have called the High Style and Lower Styles. At one end of the spectrum lay the principal High Style forms, the *chansos* and its didactic equivalent the *vers*,[9] together with the *sirventes*, the *tenso*, the *partimen* and the *plang*. By piecing together various remarks scattered through the treatise we learn that all these genres were associated with the same kind of tune, fully described in the section on the *vers*:[10]

> . . . lonc so . e pauzat . e noel . am belas e melodiozas
> montadas e deshendudas . et am belas passadas e plazens
> pauzas.

> . . . a slow and sedate tune newly composed, with
> beautiful and melodious ascents and descents and
> with pleasing [?] phrases and with pleasant pauses.

This was the kind of melody required for a *vers*, but also for a *chansos*, a *partimen*, a *sirventes*, a *tenso* (if it is to have music at all), a *retroncha* and a *plang* (although Molinier does not entirely approve of the *plang* having a tune of this kind).[11] So it seems that the passage quoted above describes the musical style and ethos of High Style poetry as the members of the Consistori knew it.

'Ethos' seems the appropriate word in this context since Molinier is attempting to define this musical style in terms of both its aesthetic effect (*belas passadas e plazens pauzas*) and its objective properties (*so noel*). As every music critic knows to his cost, the character of musical sound cannot satisfactorily be captured in language; whence it is no discredit to Molinier if some of his references to melody seem impressionistic, or if some of his meaning must remain in doubt (is a *lonc so* a 'long' tune, a 'sedate' one, or something else again?). Yet we can salvage this much: Molinier viewed the performance of these major genres as a heightened form of declamation in which singers, like trained readers, pointed the sense of their texts with *pauzas*, matching the High Style of the words with a restrained and imposing style of delivery.

So much for the *vers*, *chanso*, *sirventes*, *tenso*, *partimen* and *plang*. With the *pastorela* this musical register changes: the melody of this genre should be 'not so slow as that of a *vers* or *chansos*, but it should have a tune which is a little more fast and lively'.[12] This fits well with the light tone, outdoor setting and semi-narrative content of the *pastorela* and its northern equivalent, the *pastourelle*.[13]

At the other end of the spectrum in the *Leys* we find the dance-related genres, most of which seem to be associated with instruments. In a particularly revealing passage the anonymous annotator records that the tune of a *bal* should have more short notes and be more likely than that of a *dansa (so mays minimat e viacier)*, whence the *bal* is 'more apt for singing to instrumental accompaniment than the *dansa*'.[14] This suggests that the quality which made a song more apt for accompaniment in the view of the Toulouse Consistori was a pronounced gaiety and dance-like character, quite in order in certain *dictatz no-principals* but foreign to the decorum of the High Style and principal genres.

Turning back to the *Doctrina de Compondre Dictats* we can now see that Jofre de Foixà reveals something similar. Writing of the *plant*, which must treat *d'amor o de tristor*, Jofre says that such a poem may be set to 'any kind of melody you like, save that of the *dança*'.[15] This surely implies that the music of the *dança*—the only genre with which Jofre associates instrumental accompaniment—was somehow distinctive and unlike that of any other lyric genre.

Here, then, is the aesthetic spectrum of the *Leys d'Amors* (including the annotations) showing the position where instrumental accompaniment and performance seem to be located:

Instruments and the *Leys d'Amors*

Toulouse, Académie des Jeux Floraux, MS 500.007

f.40r MAIN TEXT
lonc so . . . pauzat   Vers
                                            Chanso
                                            Sirventes
                                            Tenso
                                            Partimen
                                            Plang
                                            Retroncha

f.41r MAIN TEXT
no pero ta lonc cum
vers o chansos . . .
.i. petit cursori
e viacier   Pastorela

f.40v MAIN TEXT
ioyos et alegre per
dansar . no pero ta
lonc coma vers ni
chansos mas .i.
petit plus viacier
per dansar   Dansa

f.41v ANNOTATOR   INSTRUMENTS
mays minimat e   HERE
viacier [que dansa]
e mays apte per   Bal
cantar amb esturmens
que dansa

III

A pattern has emerged from *Guillaume de Dole*, the *Doctrina de Compondre Dictats* and the A text of the *Leys d'Amors*, the most explicit vernacular sources that bear upon the problem of instrumental accompaniment. With the *Leys d'Amors* this pattern has formed itself into a musico-aesthetic spectrum in which instruments are associated with songs (or instrumental pieces) whose music is of a predominantly joyful character, and which have a refrain (or a musical reprise of some kind) often linked to dance.

These conclusions help us to refine some ideas about the aesthetic status of instrumental sound which were floated at the end of the last chapter. It seems that during the twelfth and thirteenth centuries instrumental sound had its own aesthetic colouring—at least when considered as a potential accompaniment to songs. It was not a colouring which could be painted onto any kind of lyric. This sense of propriety—of performing decorum—is not difficult to account for. At this time the apprehension of instrumental sonorities was in a 'pre-composer' phase, for instrumental colours did not lie on the composer's palette waiting to be combined for whatever expressive ends he desired; nobody composed in that way during the Middle Ages (or so I assume). Instrumental sound therefore had its own, closely-defined, expressive range according to the kinds of music which, by convention, it was directed to perform, and according to the kinds of occasion which, again by convention, it was called upon to adorn.

During the period that we have been examining, this expressive range seems to have been strongly influenced by the ethos of vivacious dance-music. According to the annotator of the *Leys d'Amors* it was because the *bal* had a rather more vivacious tune with more short notes than the *dansa* that it was 'more appropriate' for instrumental accompaniment. Since a high proportion of medieval instrumentalists were professionals whose livelihood depended upon their ability to rouse a courtly company to festiveness, and especially to dance, it is apparent that much instrumental-playing of the time must have been gay, tuneful, and closely linked to dance. Virtually all of the medieval dance-music which survives, whether in the form of textless (and therefore presumably instrumental) pieces, or of songs which could be sung for dancing and accompanied, is characterised by an instant tunefulness achieved by conspicuous, short-range melodic patternings (see Music example 9).[16]

Only one piece of instrumental music survives from before the thirteenth century and it bears out these observations. According to a famous account in the *Razos* (explanations of how certain troubadour songs came to be composed), Raimbaut de Vaqueiras composed his lyric *Kalenda maya* to the tune of an *estampida* played at the court of the marquis of Montferrat by two fiddlers (Appendix 3:11). Fortunately, Raimbaut decided to write a High Style *canso* to fit the fiddlers' melody. The combination of a High Style text and a Lower Style melody is part of the wit of the piece—for it is a

Example 9

Example 10

flamboyantly Lower Style tune, packed with conspicuous and short-range patternings (see Music example 10).[17]

So far we have considered north and south from 1150 to 1220, and have made a momentary foray into the fourteenth century with the *Leys d'Amors*. This leap seemed desirable in order to bring out the patterns which unite our earliest and latest sources, for those patterns amount to an artistic tradition for the role of instruments in courtly monody.

An artistic tradition may be a fragile thing. The one which we have been describing must have been vulnerable in all kinds of ways; we have already found some suggestive evidence that northern minstrels may have accompanied southern trouvère songs in order to make their performances more accessible to northern audiences who could not fully understand the Occitan words (or to cover their own incompetence if they could not understand them themselves!). Up to now we have only glimpsed part of the story; it remains to be seen how things were in the region where most of our later-thirteenth century evidence from the North congregates: Paris.

5

Paris

Bonus autem artifex in viella omnem
cantum et cantilenam et omnem formam
musicalem generaliter introducit.

Johannes de Grocheio, *De Musica*

I

It is time to introduce two Parisian authors of the thirteenth century with much to offer: the music theorists Johannes de Grocheio and Jerome of Moravia. I have kept these two celebrities backstage until now for they are exceptional writers who are reporting the musical customs of an exceptional city.

Viewed in the context of this book, Paris is exceptional for many reasons. It is a city, not a court; a hive of ambitious *clercs* packed into tenements and hostels, not an assembly of courtiers and knights in a chamber or hall, 'around the bright fire . . . amiable and agreeable'.[1] Above all, Paris is full of men who can *lire et chanter*—read from script and sing from musical notation—the two basic skills of every *clerc* and the foundation for all of his ambitions for lucrative office. In later life these skills, acquired in childhood, perhaps on a bench in a parish school, could help to nurture a taste for the savant forms of music which reigned in Parisian musical circles, the motet and the Latin conductus, both monophonic and polyphonic. As Johannes de Grocheio says, these were forms for *litterati* and *divites*—for men made learned by study or made rich by worldly success; trouvère song, in contrast, was for magnates whom it would be inapt to call *litterati* and vulgar to call *divites*; in Grocheio's scheme of things they are *reges*, *nobiles* and *principes terre* (Figure 4).

It is this contrast between courtliness and the world of clerical literacy, both verbal and musical, which provides the theme for our prolegomenon to Johannes de Grocheio and Jerome of Moravia. In Chapters 1–4 of this book I have suggested that in the predominantly notationless world of the troubadours and trouvères before c1250 there existed a courtly tradition of instrumental usage. It was courtly because it rested upon a collective moral and aesthetic apprehension within aristocratic society that it was *courtois* to

Figure 4 *The opening page of the Chansonnier de l'Arsenal. The compilers of this manuscript were clearly anxious to present a traditionalist and (by the later thirteenth century) somewhat archaic image of trouvère monody as an essentially aristocratic art. Thus a composition by the royal trouvère Thibaut king of Navarre is placed here on the opening leaf, complete with a picture showing a fiddler before a seated king and queen as courtiers stand nearby. This recalls another late view of the trouvère art, that of the music theorist Johannes de Grocheio; in his judgement trouvère songs were to be performed for 'kings, nobles and princes of the earth', and indeed to be composed by them. Like the painting which opens the Chansonnier de l'Arsenal, Grocheio's words suggest that by the later thirteenth century the trouvère art was involved with a nostalgic mythology of kings, queens and courts. Paris, Bibliothèque de l'Arsenal, MS 5198, f.1. Reproduced by permission.*

mix instrumental sound with some kinds of songs but *vilain* to mix it with others.

This austere ethic of instrumental usage—for an ethic it deserves to be called—was vulnerable to abuse by the ignorant who had not the taste to appreciate it, but it was also under threat from the learned and literate who had the manoeuvrability of mind to bypass the tradition and come up with something else. This manoeuvrability was already there in the act of recording courtly songs with neumes and staves, for once a lyric has been written down (as happened to many troubadour and trouvère songs after c1250) it ceases to be an event. It becomes an object and can therefore be objectively perceived. Any moorings which may have tied it to a kind of occasion, or a kind of performance, become loosened.

The emergence of a literate tradition of troubadour and trouvère song in the second half of the thirteenth century may therefore have exerted a profound effect upon performance practice in that repertory, for musical notation enabled songs to be lifted out of the behavioural conventions in which they had become embedded. So it is important to look at some of the ways in which string playing interacted with literacy, both verbal and musical, in the Parisian milieu which nourished Jerome of Moravia and Johannes de Grocheio.

II

'Music', writes Jehan des Murs, who attained the academic title of *magister* at Paris in the 1320s,[2]

> is immensely refined through the efforts of the moderns,
> and not only as a result of the service and artistry of
> cultured and studious men in this region; the general
> populace, especially young men and girls, are also
> motivated to it.

These lines point us towards a fundamental change in the musical experience of literate men which took place in the twelfth and thirteenth centuries: a change from rural silence in the monastery, broken only by the sound of liturgy, to the clamour of dancing songs, work-songs and love-songs in the streets and tenements of cities. Jehan des Murs's view of music is that of a city-man whose experience of a wide range of music, both sacred and secular, has brought him to the generous belief that the *subtilitas* of music is maintained by human effort on many fronts: by the 'general populace, especially young men and girls', as well as by monks entrenched in their monasteries to resist the siege of Satan. What is more, Jehan senses that this is all new; it is the *moderni* who, together with the people, are helping to refine music.

In this Jehan is expressing the conviction, shared by many musicians of his generation, that musical composition and notation had been transformed to the point where a new art, an *ars nova*, had arisen. Yet his words cut deeper than that, for the 'newness' he senses involves a recognition that a new kind of urban community has developed, one which forces the literate man to widen the range of human activity which he judges to be consequential.

This sense of the city as a place where a wealth of music comes together animates Johannes de Grocheio's *De Musica*, probably written in Paris around 1300. It is strongest in what might be called Grocheio's 'urban morality', for in his view music contributes to the stability of the city and anything which serves the *civitas* cannot be bad in itself, although it may have evil applications.[3] Sometimes this philosophy leads Grocheio into opinions that are surprisingly liberal for the thirteenth century and wildly at variance with contemporary teaching from the pulpit and confessional. Consider, for example, Grocheio's view of the public ring-dances, or *coreae*, which were so popular amongst the young men and girls whose musical initiatives are praised by Jehan des Murs. In the eyes of most contemporary moralists these *coreae* were services in Satan's church, but Grocheio, in defiance of some of the most respected churchmen of his day, takes the opposite view: 'these dances keep young men and girls from vanity and are said to have force against the passion of erotic desire.'[4] Even the simplest and most popular music, it seems, had a role to play in maintaining civilisation on the banks of the Seine.

As we shall see later in this book, Grocheio has much to tell us about instrumental practice, and it is probably because many *clercs* shared his background of urban experience that we begin to find an increased awareness of musical instruments in many Latin works of the thirteenth century: sermons, tracts on the Vices and Virtues, Bible commentaries and manuals of confession, to name only a few. This new awareness of instruments is apparent in this kind of vocabulary which these *clercs* employ. For many centuries monastic writers had been content with a repertoire of instrument-names derived from the Bible or from classical literature (*cithara* and *psalterium*, for example), and these words were luminous with the splendour of Christian history and prophecy. *Psalterium* evoked Mankind's long journey towards the Incarnation, foretold by David as he sang *in psalterio*, while *cithara* spanned the history of Man from Tubal in the first generation after the Flood to the Revelation of St John where the sound of *citharae* is heard amidst the marvels that signal the end of all earthly music.

From the thirteenth century on, however, Latin writings begin to fill up with a new generation of words which could not be found in the Bible, in Ovid, in Isidore of Seville or in any other standard and revered source. Indeed it was precisely this lack of literary charisma which recommended these new words; they were useful because they were current in vernacular speech and were directly tied to instruments in daily use. Grocheio gives us *viella*, and the highly exotic *quitarra sarracenica*. Jerome of Moravia has *viella* and *rubeba*, while other theorists have *liuto* and *cistolla*. It is hard to imagine an eleventh- (or even twelfth-) century Latinist comparing the seven words of Christ on the cross to the 'seven notes of a *viella* tuned up to breaking point': *.vij. note vielle que usque ad rupturam cordarum fuit tensa*, but it does not

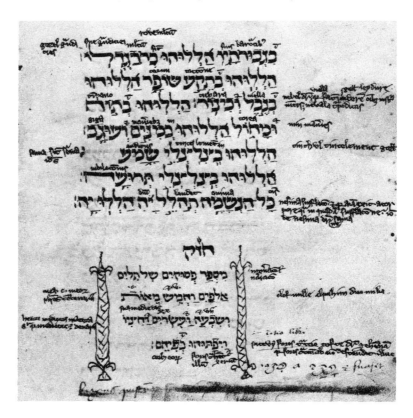

Figure 5 *An interlinear commentary and gloss, in Latin and French, upon a Hebrew text of Psalm 150. The vernacular-derived terms* viella *and* giga *appear in lines 3 and 4. Instrument-names like these, based upon words in current vernacular speech, hardly ever appear in Bible commentaries before the thirteenth century. In the right-hand column the annotator has written:* nebel dicitur viella quia facit pudorum Gallice 'leydure' omnibus instrumentis musicis ... ('*The nebel is interpreted as* viella *because it puts to shame (in French 'leydure') all other musical instruments'). This is based upon the commentary of Rabbi H̱iyya ben Abba in the Jerusalem Talmud, Sukkah V:6 (55c), where the* nebel *is said to put all other instruments to shame. The term* viella *therefore seems to have been chosen as a gloss for the Hebrew* nebel *by a commentator who had observed, in the words of Johannes de Grocheio, that 'the* viella *takes pride of place over all stringed instruments'. Lambeth Palace, MS 435, f.131v. Thirteenth century. Reproduced by permission.*

surprise us in a thirteenth-century collection of sermons.[5]

A more dramatic demonstration of the way in which instruments had become more vivid in the mind of the *clerc* is provided by developments in Bible commentary. For many centuries monastic readers of the Bible had been content to know that the *psalterium* of King David was to be interpreted as an emblem of praise, the *cithara* the admission of lowliness, and so on through countless similar explanations.[6] In most of this enormous literature of commentary the literal sense of words like *cithara* and *psalterium* was allowed to shrivel and die; it did not matter to the commentator to have a clear impression of the instruments behind the names in terms of wood and strings; the names were left hollow, like vacated shells upon a beach, their meanings having withered and gone to be replaced by an echo of eternal truth.

By the later thirteenth century there were many scholars whose curiosity about the instruments of the Bible went far beyond what a millennium of Bible commentary had stored up for them. The renewed study of Hebrew, for example, set many scholars thinking again about the meanings of the instrument-names used in the psalms, and terms such as *viella* and *giga*, drawn from contemporary life, begin to appear in commentaries, sometimes with reflections on the status or properties of instruments in current use (Figure 5).[7] In some commentaries, curiosity about the meaning of terms such as *psalterium* and *cithara* led to the production of small treatises, complete with illustrations (Figure 6). The friars were particularly active in this field; here, for example, is Jerome of Moravia's contemporary and fellow-Dominican, Petrus de Palude, weighing the proposition that the *viella* (Figure 7) may have been the very instrument upon which David composed the psalms:[8]

> Isidore says in Book III of his Etymologies that the *psalterium* has a soundbox in its upper part, and also that its form was like that of the Greek letter which is called Delta, so it is clear that the *psalterium* of the Ancients was not the same in form as the one now in use. Whence it should also be noted that, in the realm of modern instruments, all kinds of *vielle* (some of which have more strings than others) have a soundbox above which is rested against the left shoulder. While these strings are sounded by means of a haired stick, the sound is modulated below by touching the strings with the fingers of the left hand so that they sound now higher, now lower. The *psalterium* [of the Ancients] is comparable to the *viella* in two respects: firstly, that it has its soundbox in the upper part, and secondly, that its sounds are modulated by the touch of fingers below. Yet these two instruments are also to be distinguished in three aspects: firstly, in the shape and form [of the *psalterium* of the Ancients] which, according to Isidore, was like the Greek letter Delta which looks like this Δ, yet I do not remember ever having seen [a *viella*] of this form amongst those in modern use; secondly,

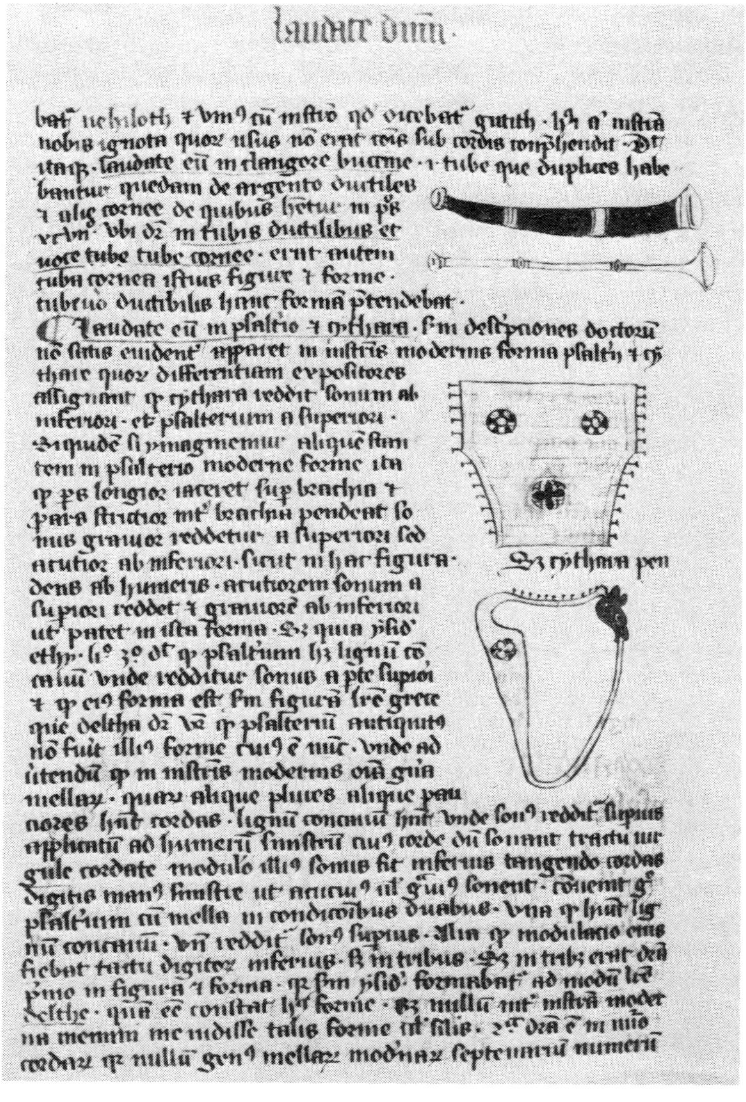

Figure 6 *An illustrated treatise on the musical instruments mentioned in Psalm 150, part of the psalm commentary of the Dominican friar Petrus de Palude. This kind of 'archaeological' interest in the literal sense of scripture is a characteristic of the Franciscan and Dominican commentators active in the later thirteenth and fourteenth centuries. Douai, Bibliothèque Municipale, MS 45, volume 9, f.262v. Reproduced by permission.*

there is the number of strings, for no type of modern *viella* is
equipped with more than seven, yet the *psalterium* [of the Ancients]
was equipped with ten or eight; a third difference, perhaps, may be
that the *psalterium* was not played with a bow like the modern *viella*,
but was plucked with the fingers.

Without taking account of writing like this it is almost impossible to
establish an intellectual tradition in which to place lines like these by
another Dominican, Jerome of Moravia:

Another [tuning] is necessary for secular songs and
for all others—especially irregular ones ... Then it
is necessary that all the five strings of this *viella*
be fixed to the body of the instrument, and not to
the side.

III

Jerome of Moravia's treatise points us to the most obvious way in which
musical instruments came increasingly to impinge upon the lives of *clercs:*
they were increasingly played by *clercs.* Jerome's chapter on the tuning of the
rubeba and *viella* is embedded in a compilation which, according to his own
testimony, is for the 'friars of our order or of another'. We can only conclude
that there existed—at least in Paris—a population of well-educated and
musically literate friars who wished to learn the rudiments of the fiddle from
Jerome's last chapter just as they wished to learn the rules of Franconian
notation from the *Ars cantus mensurabilis* which is one of the treatises included
in Jerome's compilation. Some of them may even have done so because of an
interest in Bible commentary such as we found in Petrus de Palude's
treatise on the instruments of the psalms; at least one thirteenth-century
friar was of the opinion that the ideal commentator would be one who not
only knew the properties of the instruments mentioned in scripture but who
could also *play* them.[9] Others may have been attracted by the savant ethos
which had begun to gather around string-playing in the wake of Aristotelian
studies. According to this, the first genuine alternative to the courtly ethos of
string-playing which medieval culture evolved, the skill of playing upon
instruments was regarded as a rational and teachable technology: a *scientia.*
The Dominican Albertus Magnus, the leading scientific personality of
thirteenth-century Paris and the Germanies, deals with this point in several
places while commenting upon Aristotle's *Ethics*:[10]

Haec solutio confirmatur per hoc quod dicit
Aristoteles in II *Topicorum*, quod una scientia
est plurium velut amborum finium: unius tamquam
finis, alterius tamquam ejus quod est ad finem.

Hujus exemplum est quod Avicenna ponit, quod duae
scientiae exiguntur ad viellare. Una quidem quae
est chordarum compositionis, et altera quae est
de motu vel tactu chordarum. Scientia enim
compositionis chordarum docet componere et
dividere chordam ad sonum gravis vel acuti vel
medii, et hoc per causas et rationes hujus
compositionis. Alia autem scientia utens quae
ex frequenti motu digitorum et chordarum tactus est acquisita.

Aristotle relates in the second book of his *Topics*
that in any science there are many facets of two
ends: one is the aim, the other is what is directed
to that aim. Avicenna gives this example of this
principle: there are two sciences in fiddling; one
which is the arranging of the strings and another
which is the stirring or touching of the strings.
The science of arranging strings teaches how to
adjust and stop the string into low, middle and high
according to the rudiments and principles of the
process. The other science uses those things which
are acquired by frequent exercises of the fingers
and touching of the strings.

Here the intricate art of fiddling is well on the way to being unravelled by
rational thought. Albertus, following Avicenna, and sharing with him a
rigorous, Aristotelian terminology, classifies *viella*-playing as a *scientia*: a skill
which rests upon a knowledge of principles, and since principles, by
definition, are 'intelligible things' (*intelligibilia*), fiddling can be taught.
Hence Albertus's careful choice of words: 'the science of arranging strings
teaches how to adjust...'. Yet a *scientia* is more than a set of teachable
principles; it is also something to practise and master: a *usus*. Hence, once
more, Albertus's careful use of terms: 'the other science *uses*...'. Here, once
again, is writing without which Jerome's treatise on fiddles seems unimagin-
able; Jerome imparts what Albertus calls the *scientia compositionis chordarum*,
the skill of measuring (i.e. tuning and stopping) strings into high, middle
and low notes. It was because the *viella* had been drawn into this special
constellation of ideas that Jerome thought it worthy of treatment, specifying
three tunings, itemising the stopped notes, mentioning an advanced
technique, and even giving a moment's attention to repertory.

The most likely place for this constellation to have been formed is among
the students, friars and priests of later thirteenth-century Paris. The
attraction of string-playing for young university students seems to be
everlasting, and it is no surprise to find Gilles li Muisis (1272–1352)
reporting that he had seen the students of Paris returning from the schools

and playing *chistolles* as they went.[11] Yet there could be more to this musicianship than the natural ebullience of the young. Konrad of Megenberg, a *magister* at Paris in the fourteenth century, rules that stringed instruments 'are sensibly classed amongst modest activities and philosophical pastimes when intervals from study are given',[12] which suggests that a more serious notion of string-playing was sometimes involved. Konrad's description of string-music as worthy to be classed among the 'philosophical pastimes' (*philosophicis solatiis*) shows how far instrumental skills had become immersed in a savant ethos owing much to the recovery of Aristotle's philosophy in the thirteenth century.

What fragments these may seem, however, beside the reminiscences of Henri Bate, a student at Paris around 1266–70 and later a distinguished theologian. In the *Nativitas magistri Henrici Mechliniensis* Henri gives this lavish and detailed account of his musical interests while a young student:[13]

Hic enim servus Dei a pueritia calamis cantus et
fistulis omneque genus instrumentorum musicorum
libenter audivit et interdum delectatus est in
eis ut quasi de qualibet artium huiusmodi partem
sit adeptus; etenim flatum in tibiis et calamis
diversoque fistularum genere artificio se modulari
novit, organis quoque et choris clavos pellendo
melos elicere. Sed postquam philosophie limites
ingressus est et effectus alumpnus eius animique
magis colens intellectus factus obedentior actum
fistularum amplius exercere non curavit iuxta
illud Philosophi in 8° Politicorum: aiunt enim
palladem cum invenisset fistulas abiecisse . . . . Novit
equidem natus iste viellam baiulare melodiosam
tactum cordarum eius et tractum arcus
proportionaliter conducendo . . . . Amplius omne genus
musici cantus sibi notum est . . . et diverse species
cantionum vulgarium in diversis linguis ipseque
cantans libentius, rithmorum quoque inventor et
cantionum, hylaris, iocundus, amativus corearum
ductor et dux tripudiorum in virgultis ludos
convivia et iocos parari affectans, ludum quoque
saltatonis aliis interponens. Hec autem et
huiusmodi non sunt operationibus studiosis
inimica maxime in iuvenibus.

This servant of God gladly heard music performed
upon reed-instruments, pipes, and every kind of
musical instrument, and meanwhile he delighted
in them as keenly as if he wished to become
skilled in every aspect of those arts; for truly,
he knew how to rule himself when blowing wind into

59

CAMROSE LUTHERAN COLLEGE
LIBRARY

flutes and reed-pipes and instruments of
that kind with varied artistry; he also knew how to
elicit melody from organs and *choros*[?] by striking
the keys. Afterwards he entered the regions
of philosophy and became a pupil, cultivating his
mind and disciplining his understanding; thus he
did not wish to pursue wind instruments further,
in line with what Aristotle reports in the *Politics*:
Athene, having invented wind instruments, is said
to have cast them away. This boy knew how to
play a fiddle, bringing together, in harmonious
fashion, a melodious touching of strings and drawing
of the bow . . . . Further, he was familiar with (and
willingly sang) all kinds of monophonic songs in
diverse languages; he was a trouvère (*inventor*) of
poems and melodies, and a merry and amorous leader
of *coreae* and master of dances in wooded places,
arranging parties and games, and interspersing
the sport of dancing with others. These and such things
are not inimical to the student life, especially amongst
the young.

Clearly it would be anachronistic to describe this as autobiography; quite apart from the exaggerations (Henri wants us to believe that he played everything as a boy), the passage is shaped to project an image of youthful and almost pastoral insouciance, adorned with the pipings of semi-rustic wind instruments, followed by an image of the courtly cleric who proceeds from boyish amusements to the very embodiment of courtly *jeunesse*: composing, singing and dancing. Yet for all this rhetoric and literary burnishing it is a revealing passage. Above all, it highlights what might be called the 'Latin quarter' of medieval courtliness. Henri makes no mention of courts; he is referring to a period of his life passed in the provincial town of Malines (now in Belgium) and in the urban environment of Paris, and his reminiscences therefore show how effectively the aristocratic notions of courtliness discussed in Chapter 1 found their way into the culture of town-bred clerics; there is the same cult of youth, the same vocal and instrumental skills that we found in Occitanian courtliness of the twelfth century, and the same emphasis on dancing (which here, as so often in the Middle Ages, has a bucolic timbre, as witness Henri's image of himself dancing 'in wooded places').

Henri is a trouvère—an *inventor cantionum*, to use his own words—but the confines of the trouvère art are here expanded to embrace the 'songs in diverse languages' (presumably Flemish, French and Latin) which Henri so willingly sang. He plays the fiddle, but he surrounds that art in exactly the bookish and savant ethos which this chapter has led us to expect; on one hand he places fiddling in the context of Aristotle's teaching that stringed instruments are the most appropriate ones for young boys to learn, on the other he aligns himself with the doctrine (so important in thirteenth-century theology) that it is legitimate to relieve the tedium of earthly activities and duties with some kind of play—in this case, play of instruments, 'not inimical to the student life, especially amongst the young'. We also notice how, as in Johannes de Grocheio's *De Musica*, ideas which originated independently of Christian belief as strictly formulated by theologians could succeed in stifling any cleric's doubts about the moral legitimacy of secular music and its pleasures; for Grocheio, it is a view of the city as an organism, derived from Greek philosophy; for Henri de Malines, it is the imagery of courtliness as projected in a thousand romances. With these thoughts in mind, neither shows any reluctance to speak highly of dancing, for example, despite the passionate opposition of countless sermonisers and preachers, among whom were some of the most distinguished literary men of the age.[14]

IV

Henri de Malines allows us to draw the Parisian evidence for instrumental practice in monophonic song together. As a literate fiddle player active in Paris during the later thirteenth century, he is probably just the kind of musician who might have encountered Jerome of Moravia's treatise on the fiddle, and whose views about performance practice may be embodied in Johannes de Grocheio's *De Musica*. We are unlikely to find a better candidate for the kind of man whom Grocheio means when he speaks admiringly of what a 'good fiddler'—a *bonus artifex in viella*—can do.

One thing is certain: Henri, and many *clerc* fiddlers like him, would have been musically literate to the point of being able to read plainchant notation. The Paris schools stood on the highway to success in ecclesiastical or secular office but they were staging posts along a road that began in the parish schools of the towns and villages where young *clerçons* learned their alphabet, the psalms and some antiphons, together with staff-notation when their teachers had some proficiency *in cantu*. Gautier de Coinci portrays such an education in his *Miracles de Nostre Dame*; a poor woman's son is put to school at a tender age, 'to the honour of God and our lady', and 'soon he knows how to sing and soon how to read' (*Tost seit chanter et tost seit lire*).[15] The ability to draw words from script and to elicit song from musical notation was regarded as the characteristic talent of the cleric and the pair of verbs *lire et chanter* is found throughout medieval French literature in this context.

The task of learning to sing from plainchant notation would have involved *clerçons* like the young hero of Gautier's story in study of solmisation and the gamut, for solmisation was the scaffolding for most musical literacy in the later Middle Ages and was 'very familiar even to boys only just setting out on the study of music', in the words of the theorist Engelbert of Admont;[16] it was the way that a novice learned to draw sound from musical notation. So it is revealing that the technique of solmisation seems to have made inroads into instrumental playing during the later thirteenth century. The English theorist Amerus, author of the *Practica Artis Musice* (1271), mentions a device of solmisation which operates 'as much with [human] voices as with the strings of musical instruments' (*tam in vocibus quam in cordis instrumentorum musicorum*),[17] while a passage in Engelbert of Admont's treatise suggests that literate players ascribed gamut letters to the appropriate places on their instruments:[18]

> Advertendum ergo est non sine diligentia, quod .vi.
> sunt notae omnium vocum, videlicet *la. sol. fa.*
> *mi. re. ut.* secundum modernos, quae singulis
> litteris in manu musicali et in instrumentis
> musicis loco propriorum nominum ipsarum
> vocum adscribuntur.

> It is to be diligently noted that there are six
> marks of all pitches, that is to say *la sol fa*
> *mi re ut* according to the usage of today's
> musicians, which are ascribed to the [Guidonian]
> musical hand and to musical instruments with
> single letters [A B C D E F G] in place of the full
> names of these pitches.

Jerome of Moravia's chapter on the tuning and fingering of the *rubeba* and *viella* leaves us in no doubt that solmisation had found a secure place in the primary stages of learning the fiddle. He describes the intervals set between the strings of these instruments and then inventories the notes produced by stopping each string within the resources of the first position. In every case he employs the alphabetic letters of the *musica recta* gamut to do so, and with the *rubeba* (the first instrument to be described) he uses the hexachord denomination as well: the first string makes *C fa ut*, with the application of the first finger *D sol re*, and so on.[19]

The scales of the *rubeba* and *viella* as Jerome presents them are a perfect marriage of manual technique and literate theory. He stresses that each finger of the left hand must be put down 'in a natural fashion' (*naturaliter*) and his implied teaching is therefore that the physical structure of the hand welcomes the *musica recta* gamut, for that is what his stoppings produce. He does not discuss *ficte musice*, but it is obvious that they will be produced by deploying the fingers in a fashion which is not 'natural': by 'twisting' them, 'bending' them, or drawing them up towards the pegbox:[20]

musica recta	*musica ficta*
digitus naturaliter cadit	digitus non naturaliter cadit
	girando
	girati
	supra ad caput rubebe tracti
	retorti

In this way Jerome's conception of manual technique is shaped by music theory: just as medieval musicians thought of *ficte musice* as separate notes inserted into the *musica recta* gamut (rather than as modifications of adjacent notes as in the modern concept of sharps and flats), so Jerome regards the production of *recta* notes as requiring one kind of finger technique while the formation of *ficta* notes can be seen (by implication) to require another.

With these instructions Jerome provides the means for reading notation onto an instrument. This is not to say that any medieval fiddlers 'played from music' in the manner of a modern violinist; medieval pictures hardly ever show instrumentalists using notation in this way. The literate *viellator* probably used notation as a source of repertory to learn by heart. The mechanics of the process are straightforward. Notation told the fiddler exactly what it told the singer: where the semitone-steps lay in an otherwise even series of tones. A c-clef placed upon a line, for example, revealed that beneath that line was a semitone-step, beneath that a tone, then a tone again, and so on, according to the *musica recta* gamut. In terms of solmisation the crucial syllables in the hexachord were *mi* and *fa*

	T	T	S	T	T
ut	re	mi	fa	sol	la

for *mi* had a semitone-step above and *fa* a semitone-step below. In a notation like this, therefore,

Example 11

the c-clef establishes the second line as *fa* and the f-clef does the same for the fourth line. To play from this notation a fiddler needed to know where to find a *fa* on his instrument; this is what Jerome tells him. In the first *viella* tuning, for example, there are three stopping points that may be solmised as *fa* and the player can build upon that knowledge to assign the correct pattern of tone and semitone steps to the notation:

(The lateral bourdon string has been omitted since it is not stopped by the fingers.)

		ut Γ		sol re ut G		la sol re dd
first finger	A	re	a	la mi re	e	la mi
second finger			b	fa	f	fa ut
second finger	B	mi	♮	mi		
third finger	C	fa ut	c	sol fa ut	g	sol re ut
fourth finger					aa	la mi re

Literate string-players equipped in this way would have been able to play from any of the surviving trouvère chansonniers.

Our best understanding of the repertory of Parisian fiddlers comes from the music treatises of Johannes de Grocheio and Jerome of Moravia, so often mentioned in what has gone before. In his account of tunings used on the *viella*, or five-stringed fiddle (Figure 7), Jerome makes several direct and indirect references to repertory in his descriptions of tunings 1 and 2:[21]

Tuning 1

d G g d' d'

> Et talis viella, ut prius patuit, vim modorum omnium comprehendit.

> And such a *viella* as just described encompasses the material of all the modes.

Tuning 2

d G g d' g'

> ... necessarius est propter laycos et omnes alios cantus, maxime irregulares, qui frequenter per totam manum discurrere volunt.

... is necessary for secular and all other kinds of songs,
especially irregular ones, which frequently wish to run
through the whole [Guidonian] hand.

The second of these statements is designed to balance the first, for
whereas tuning 1 'encompasses the material of all the modes', tuning 2 is
useful for music which is *irregularis*, and the meaning of that adjective here is
probably 'heedless of modal constraints'.[22] There is no difficulty in deducing

Figure 7 *The* viella. *New York, Pierpont Morgan Library, MS 638, f.17r.*
French (Paris?), thirteenth century. Reproduced by permission.

what Jerome means when he records that tuning 1 'encompasses the material of all the modes', since the compass of every mode is essentially an octave, and tuning 1 seems designed to produce a ninth (the *d* string is not stopped, and the *Gg* strings are surely an octave course).[23] It is also clear why tuning 2 should be useful for music which may 'wish to run through the whole hand' (that is, the complete gamut of two octaves and a sixth); from *G* at the bottom to *d''*, stopped by the little finger on the top course, is two octaves and a fifth.

This contrast between a tuning which suffices for modal music, and another designed for music that flouts the modes, gestures towards a contrast between 'sacred' and 'secular' repertory, or at least a distinction between the repertory of lay-people (*laycos . . . cantus*) and another kind of repertory imagined here as the special province of the *clericus*. What is this clerical repertory? The question is a difficult one to answer satisfactorily since the music concerned might be 'clerical' by virtue of its function (liturgical, perhaps, or para-liturgical), by virtue of the social station of those who normally performed and enjoyed it, or perhaps, if it were song, by virtue of its language (Latin), poetic style and subject matter. One possibility is that this 'clerical' repertory includes the Latin hymn, a genre whose formal similarity to the trouvère chanson (where every verse is usually metrically identical and shares the same musical setting) is noted by Johannes de Grocheio.[24] It is possible that some of the fiddlers amongst the orders of friars for whom Jerome's *Tractatus de Musica* was compiled would have thought it appropriate to plunder the rich repertory of Latin hymns for hall or refectory music; some hymn settings are certainly as lush and melismatic as any secular melody by a troubadour or trouvère:[25]

Example 12

cho - rus no - vae Je - ru - sa - lem

no - vam me - li dul - ce - di - nem

pro - mat co - lens cum so - bri - is

pas - cha - le fes - tum gau - di - is.

With Jerome's 'secular and all other kinds of songs . . . which frequently wish to run through the whole hand' we are on less solid ground, for no secular music has survived from Jerome's day which exploits the full gamut of two octaves and a sixth (an exceptional compass for any medieval piece, whether monophonic or polyphonic, until the second half of the fifteenth century). Troubadour and trouvère songs, for example, rarely exceed a twelfth, and the same may be said of Ars Antiqua motets (most of which appear to have been written for three voices of approximately the same kind; a singer who wished to sing tenor parts one moment and triplum parts the next would find himself required to cover no more compass than he might expect to exploit in performing a monophonic song). Jerome's secular music which wishes to run through the whole gamut of two octaves and a sixth therefore seems impossible to identify in terms of contemporary compositions and the answer presumably lies with performance practice; perhaps the fiddle-postludes, or *modi*, described by Johannes de Grocheio were virtuosic improvisations that exploited the whole compass of the *viella*.[26]

We shall return to Jerome of Moravia; for the moment his source has run dry and it is Johannes de Grocheio who now offers the fullest information about fiddle repertory in late thirteenth-century Paris. Grocheio's *De Musica* refers several times to the central genre of the trouvère art, the High Style *chanson*, using the terms *cantus coronatus* (for the most sublime examples of the genre) and *cantus versualis* (for those specimens which fall short of the very highest standards of literary and musical excellence).[27] These passages leave us in no doubt that the *cantus coronatus* was customarily performed by the best fiddlers, and Grocheio even describes a performing technique which these *viellatores* used when playing trouvère songs:[28]

> Est autem neupma quasi cauda vel exitus sequens
> antiphonam, quemadmodum in viella post cantum
> coronatam vel stantipedem exitus, quem *modum* viellatores
> appellant.

> A *neupma* is like a coda or ending following on the
> antiphon, just as an ending may be played on the
> *viella* after the *cantus coronatus*, or the stantipes,
> which fiddlers call 'modes'.

In some ways this is a confusing passage since it is not clear whether Grocheio is saying that fiddlers accompanied High Style songs when they were sung, or whether they performed the melodies of such songs as purely instrumental music. Be that as it may, the interest of Grocheio's treatise seems to reach beyond the realm of the High Style song to embrace virtually every secular genre, both vocal and instrumental, for in a revealing passage he assures us that 'a good fiddler generally plays every kind of *cantus* and *cantilena*, and every musical form' (Appendix 3:42).

In some important respects Grocheio's distinction between *cantus* and *cantilena* corresponds to our distinction between the High Style and the Lower Styles. *Cantus* is a generic term in Grocheio's usage, and it embraces:

cantus gestualis	sung epic poetry; the chanson de geste
cantus coronatus	the High Style trouvère song
cantus versualis	similar to the above, but lacking its excellence and containing some Lower Style elements

The *cantilena* register embraces Lower Style songs, all of which have a reprise or refrain of some kind:[29]

rotunda vel rotundellus	the rondeau
stantipes	the estampie
ductia	as a vocal form, apparently a virelai as a purely instrumental form, closely akin to the estampie, but having three or four *puncta* (thus: A open/A closed; B open/B closed; C open/C closed).
cantilena entrata	uncertain

This is a long list of forms and we may begin to wonder whether the best fiddlers of thirteenth-century Paris set any limit to their repertory. At first sight Grocheio's words suggest that they did not: 'a good fiddler generally plays every kind of *cantus* and *cantilena*, and every musical form.' Yet it would be hasty to proceed from here to the view that the expert *viellator* played every kind of music. It is striking, for example, that Grocheio discusses musical instruments in the section of his work devoted to 'monophonic, popular or un-learned music' (*musica simplex vel civilis vel vulgaris*); this might be taken to imply, as Gushee has pointed out, that instruments did not perform in polyphonic forms such as the motet and polyphonic conductus—forms which Grocheio treats under the separate heading of 'composed, regulated, rule-bound or measured music' (*musica composita vel regularis vel canonica vel mensurata*).[30] Since there is a third category of music in Grocheio's treatise ('Church music', or *musica ecclesiastica*) in which instruments were probably not used (at least as a general rule), then Grocheio's statement that good fiddlers played 'every musical form' may actually embrace less than a third of the musical forms discussed in his treatise.

Be that as it may, the key to forming a proper understanding of Grocheio's evidence surely lies with the question of literacy versus illiteracy, and the kinds of performing mentality bred by these two conditions. At the beginning of this chapter we suggested that when trouvère and troubadour songs began to be written down, as they were in great numbers from the mid-thirteenth century on, then they became objects which could be objectively perceived in isolation from any performing conventions that may have clung to them when transmission was largely or exclusively oral. As this written tradition of courtly monody grew, I suggest, then literate instrumentalists whose minds were shaped by literacy began to approach their string-playing as if it were the art of reading: something to be applied wherever there was scope for pleasing or interesting results. The courtly decorum which we have glimpsed in Chapters 1–4 was bred in a predominantly notationless and aristocratic environment; it rested upon a consensus about performance decorum which could not survive transplantation into the intellectual and urban environment of Paris where there had been so much experiment with musical forms and practices. By the time of Johannes de Grocheio's *De Musica*, composed when the trouvère movement was all but dead, this courtly decorum of performance seems to have collapsed altogether, and a good *viellator* could perform a High Style trouvère song one moment and a light, tripping *rondeau* the next.

V

If this is an accurate picture of performing traditions in Paris, how did these literate *viellatores* accompany High Style trouvère songs? The question is out of place here since it belongs with later chapters on performance practice, yet we have spent so long in the Parisian milieu of Jerome of Moravia and Grocheio that it becomes irresistible. Surely Paris, with its vigorous polyphonic traditions, supported by an ancillary literature of music-treatises, is exactly the place where we might expect to pick up an echo of the way a *bonus artifex in viella* performed a trouvère song.

I believe that there is such an echo in Jerome of Moravia's chapter on the *rubeba* and *viella*, although it is one that has often been distorted. At the close of the chapter Jerome describes what seems to be an advanced playing technique in these terms:[31]

Finaliter tamen est notandum hoc quod in hac
facultate est difficilius et solempnius meliusque,
ut scilicet sciatur cum unicuique sono ex quibus
unaqueque melodia contexitur cum bordunis primis
consonanciis respondere, quod prorsus facile est
scita manu secundaria, que scilicet solum provectis
adhibetur, et eius equante que in fine huius operis
habetur.

One thing must be finally noted, namely that which is
most difficult, serious and excellent in this art: to
know how to reply with the *borduni* in the first
harmonies to any note from which any melody is woven,
which is certainly easy with the fitting second hand
(which is only used by advanced players) and its equivalent
which is to be found at the end of this work.

The exact meaning of this passage will probably never be clear, for Jerome is saying too much in too few words. What is meant by *replying* in the first harmonies to any note from which any melody is woven?

At some time before 1306 the owner of the only complete surviving copy of Jerome's treatise, Pierre de Limoges, decided that these lines about an advanced *viella* technique were too cryptic to be of use. Like many medieval bibliophiles, Pierre was happy to scribble over his books and he felt that Jerome's explanation of the advanced fiddle-technique required an extensive annotation. This is what he made of it:[32]

> Quod D bordunus non debet tangi pollice vel arcu
> nisi cum cetere corde arcu tactu faciunt sonos cum
> quibus bordunus facit aliquam predictarum consonaciarum
> scilicet diapente, diapason, diatessaron etc. Prima enim
> corda, scilicet superior exterior, que dicitur bordunus,
> secundam primam temperacionem facit D in gravibus, secundum
> terciam facit Γ, id est gamma. Per manum autem sequentem
> scitur cum quibus litteris hae due faciunt consonanciam.

> The *d bordunus* must not be touched with the thumb
> or the bow save when the other strings, touched by the bow,
> produce notes with which the *bordunus* will make any of the
> aforesaid consonances, that is to say: fifth, fourth,
> octave, and so on. The first string, that is the upper,
> outer one, makes *d* according to the first tuning and Γ,
> which is gamma, according to the third. It may be known
> from the following hand with which letters these two make
> consonances.

In this annotation Pierre understands Jerome to mean that the lateral bourdon string (which runs to the side of the fingerboard; see Figure 7) should not be sounded constantly, nor may it be sounded in an arbitrary way; for Pierre the *ars* of Jerome's advanced technique lies in the fact that the *bordunus* is only to be touched with the thumb or the bow when the melody lights upon a note which forms a fifth, a fourth, an octave 'and so on' with the note to which the *bordunus* is tuned. Here, then, is one explanation of what Jerome means by 'replying in the first harmonies to any note from which any melody is woven'; the fiddler plays the melody and sounds the bourdon when the tune steers into a perfect consonance with it.

Closer inspection suggests that this explanation of Jerome's meaning presents certain problems of its own. If we take Jerome's first *viella* tuning, for example, it is a simple matter to map the notes which would sound with the *d* bourdon in one of the 'first consonances' (Music example 13).

According to Pierre's account the advanced technique would have involved the player in learning these points of contact and then performing

Example 13

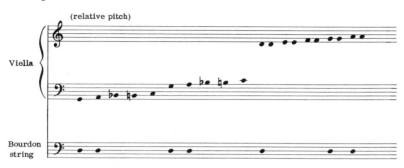

melodies in which the drone (if that is now the right word to use) was
sounded here and there as the tune threaded its way in and out of the
required relationships with the bourdon. Yet, as example 13 shows, there
are several notes in the fiddle's compass which cannot be sounded with the
bourdon 'in the first harmonies' (unless we expand what is meant by 'first
harmonies' to the point where it embraces thirds and sixths; in that case the
rules of the technique would permit an almost constant drone—presumably
the device which the 'advanced' way of playing is intended to supplant).
The difficulty here is that some of the stopped notes on the fingerboard
cannot be sounded in the first harmonies with the bourdon, yet Jerome
requires the skilled player to reply to *any* note from which *any* melody is
woven with the bourdon 'in the first harmonies'.

One way out of this impasse is to assume that Jerome is describing a
playing-style analogous to the contemporary vocal practice of 'fifthing'.
Sarah Fuller has shown that four music treatises from the thirteenth and
fourteenth centuries contain the same core of basic rules for creating a
second voice, largely in parallel fifths over a given melody, and these rules
describe a note-against-note technique in which the singer who is fifthing
must know the octave or fifth of any note in the melody he is accompanying
so that he may sing in parallel fifths above it (and supply occasional passing
notes).[33] With this basic knowledge he should then proceed to follow a few
simple directives to negotiate his way into fifths at the start of phrases:[34]

Example 14

Jerome of Moravia may be describing a similar practice. Viewed in this
light the key words in Jerome's account are that the expert fiddler should be
able to 'reply to *any note* from which any melody is woven' with the bourdons

in the first harmonies. This means, I suggest, that the fiddler should know
how to 'fifth' a given melody, played or sung by another musician, upon his
instrument.[35] Jerome's advanced fiddle-technique would therefore have
evolved as a form of improvised note-against-note counterpoint over
another melody. This interpretation helps to explain Jerome's insistence
that this is a 'serious' and 'advanced' way of playing (these are not epithets
one might readily apply to the selective use of the bourdon envisaged by
Pierre de Limoges); it is difficult and specialised because it involves literacy-
based musical devices (albeit simple ones) taken from the realm of the
discantor.

At a time when a great deal of instrumental playing must have been based
upon drones (as Jerome's fiddle-tunings suggest), this 'advanced' technique
required the *viellator* to study the learning of the *discantor*. He needed to know
contrapuntal formulae like the ones listed above and to consult the
Guidonian hand in order to locate the octave and fifth of every note in the
melody. This technique must also have involved the use of musical notation,
for Jerome records that it is more easily accomplished by those who know
the 'second hand' (presumably the Guidonian hand transposed up a fifth)
or the normal hand, which implies that players consulted notated melodies
and then built up their fifthing-style accompaniment using the hand as a
mnemonic to tell them where the semitones should lie.

If this interpretation is correct then we can reconstruct a literate style of
accompaniment which may have been used in Parisian circles (and surely
elsewhere?) around 1300 to accompany High Style songs of the trouvère
tradition:[36]

Example 15

Dex est aus - si com—me li pel - li - cans Qui fait son ni ou

plus haut ar - bre sus;

There are two striking things about this style of accompaniment. The first is that it looks like a tidied version of an illiterate, heterophonic technique of doubling a melody in parallel fifths. No doubt this is exactly what it is, just as the vocal technique of fifthing was a slightly savant version of the kind of parallel singing in fifths, octaves and twelfths described in the 1270s by Elias of Salomon.[37] In other words there must have been illiterate fiddlers who could produce something quite like Jerome's advanced technique, and this is indeed what several sources suggest. 'Many succeed in the art of fiddling', says Albertus Magnus, 'who cannot explain the rational basis of harmonious accord,'[38] and Engelbert of Admont makes the same observation, hemming it with a citation from Aristotle: 'there are many who, without scientific mastery, accomplish the things which such mastery accomplishes.'[39] However, only the advanced and literate fiddlers, playing *ex arte* as well as *ex usu*, would have been able to produce contrary motion such as we see in example 15 on a rational basis, enjoying the satisfaction of being able to explain their procedures with technical terms and concepts.

The second striking feature about the style of accompaniment shown in example 15 is that Jerome describes it as an advanced form of playing; yet, in vocal terms, it is quite rudimentary. Amongst the *discantores* who had proceeded to the performance of motets and polyphonic conducti the technique of fifthing was regarded as material for the novice. This discrepancy between vocal and instrumental practice suggests that the artistic horizons of voices and instruments were differently placed in the thirteenth century, even amongst literate players.

It is in this last respect, perhaps, that Jerome's advanced technique is of most historical interest. The purpose of the technique is clearly to create a style of fiddling regulated by literacy-based concepts about consonance, dissonance and contrary motion. This can only have happened because written vocal polyphony was fast becoming the respected form of musical endeavour and fiddling was trying to catch up and imitate some of the savant techniques of conductus and motet. Indeed the aim of the technique seems to be to turn a monophonic song into a kind of rudimentary two-part conductus. With Jerome, in other words, we see an art-instrument coming under the sway of vocal polyphony for the first time in the West; this was the force that was eventually to produce the art of string-instrument intabulation in the late fourteenth and fifteenth centuries and to shape the whole course of instrumental music in the Renaissance.

Example 15 may therefore represent a late thirteenth-century—and particularly Parisian—style of performance for three reasons. Firstly, in the fact that accompaniment is used at all in a High Style song of the trouvère tradition. Secondly, in the use of a mildly savant and literacy-based technique of counterpoint as a basis for accompaniment. Thirdly, in the question of rhythm. Example 15 uses a non-mensural notation in accordance with the way in which the song has been preserved. Yet it is well known that there are some trouvère sources in which High Style songs are recorded in mensural notation. Jerome's advanced technique of fiddle-accompaniment uses note-against-note counterpoint, and this is surely a device that requires standardisation of rhythm between singer and instrumentalist. The free and declamatory rhythm which probably represents the traditional mode of delivery of both troubadour and trouvère songs of the High Style kind is not possible in this context. It has often been suggested that the mensurally notated trouvère monodies are an adaptation of an originally free-rhythm genre to the fixed rhythms which 'Parisian' listeners associated with polyphony (the musical example below is a case in point: a *chanson* by the trouvère Gace Brulé); Jerome's advanced fiddle technique seems just such an adaptation, this time in the area of harmony. Perhaps the sound which the fiddlers of Grocheio's Paris produced when they performed a trouvère song was something like this:

Example 16

De bone a - mour et de le - aul a -

- mi - e me vient sou - vent pi - tiez

et re - mem - bran - ce.

Here a trouvère song seems well on the way to becoming a rudimentary polyphonic composition and it is surely the vogue for polyphony in Parisian circles which lies at the heart of the change in performing aesthetic which we have been discussing. For men such as Johannes de Grocheio, 'high' musical art achieved its altitude by exploiting the savant technique of polyphony, not by using a High Style in words and music as had been the custom in the monophonic tradition. (Grocheio had some idea of what a High Style meant in terms of trouvère song, but it is revealing that he overdoes things in his attempts to capture its ethos; when he places the High Style song in a half-romantic world of princes, kings and noblemen he is using his imagination as much as his judgement to describe a repertory all but dead in his lifetime.) Grocheio's ears must have been full of the sounds of polyphonic forms such as the motet, perhaps the most admired form of music-making in thirteenth-century Paris. The friction of the motet, with its multiple texts and strong dissonances, was enough to scour away the old monophonic decorum, for when viewed in terms of that decorum the motet takes on a highly subversive appearance: it joins a new High Style in music to the old Lower Styles of poetry.

There is a good deal of poetry in the motet corpus which would be quite at home in a High Style trouvère song. This, for example:[40]

> Or voi je bien qu'il mi
> couvient descouvrir a celi
>   qui lonc tens
> m'a tenu en joie, cum fins amans
> doit estre joians,
> qui tout adés est a bien faire entendans
> et estables et celans,
> se je ne vuill a toute honor estre faillans
> et amer mesdisans
> comme povre truans...

> Now I clearly see that I must confess to her who has kept
> me in joy for so long, like a true lover who always
> intends to do good, and is constant and discreet, ought
> to feel, unless I want to lack all honour and, like a
> miserable wretch, love slander....

There is too much chiming of rhymes here, perhaps, for the true High Style *chanson* of the trouvères, but the diction and sentiment would do well enough for that genre. To a very large extent, however, motet poetry in the vernacular draws upon the idioms of the *pastourelle* and the simple refrains often associated with rondeaux. It presents us with a mass of Lower Style characteristics: diminutives in *-ete (amourete, flourete, joliete, pucelete, praëlete,* and many more); short lines with chiming rhyme-sounds ('Je sui joliete,/ doucete/et plaisans/jone pucelete...'); the exclamations which express strong passion but leave no room for feeling to be explored ('Dieus! hé! plus n'irai?'); the direct and desperate address to the beloved ('lady, with clasped hands I beg your mercy'); allusions to stereotyped narrative situations, especially those involving marriage ('I would sing out of sheer pleasure for the one that I have loved, but she has a new husband who has stopped me from seeing her'), and the easy pastiche of the *pastourelle* manner:[41]

> Par un matinet l'autrier
> m'aloie esbenoiant;
> si com m'aloie tous sous pensant,
> Marotele vi seant
> les un sentier ...

> The other morning I went out seeking pleasure, and as
> I was going alone, lost in thought, I saw Marotele
> seated beside a path ...

The list of Lower Style characteristics in vernacular motet verse might easily be extended, but it is already long enough to show that one of the most characteristic techniques of the motet is to mix the old Lower Styles of poetry with the new musical High Style of written polyphony. When a poem reaching after the poetic High Style of the trouvères was incorporated into a motet, the musical idioms and techniques laid upon it could be much the same as for a light-hearted love-song or a little *pastourelle*. This may also help to explain why the pattern of High and Low Styles, so important, I suggest, in the twelfth and earlier thirteenth centuries, began to be effaced in Paris and its environs during the body of the thirteenth. It was torn by the hard edge of the new polyphony and finally fell away.

6

The carole

They serve the Devil with their voices as
they sing, with their hands as they lead one
another, and with their feet as they move in
a circle. Whence their dance is called the
Devil's mill.

Anonymous, *Collatio de coreis*[1]

I

The last five chapters have followed a chronological path from the first Old
Provençal sources of the twelfth century to the music treatises of Grocheio
and Jerome of Moravia, compiled in Paris towards the end of the thirteenth
century. The aim of the three chapters which follow is to investigate some
special repertories which do not press to be included in a chronological
pattern but do demand separate treatment so that their distinctiveness may
emerge.

These repertories are special in various ways. The first comprises the
public dance-songs, or *caroles* (Latin *coreae*), which were sung in popular
festivities as well as at court. Although the musical remains of these dances
are relatively scarce, a great deal of evidence survives pertaining to the way
in which they were presented and performed, and in the eyes of contemporary social commentators the *carole* simply *was* secular music in the North, not
the highbrow forms of trouvère song or the savant forms of conductus and
motet. The *carole* therefore presents a particularly striking case of the iceberg
problem which meets us everywhere in medieval music: the forms which
dominate our view of secular music-making in twelfth- and thirteenth-
century France are those which survive, but the view of contemporaries was
dominated by material which has left relatively little trace.

The second repertory comprises monophonic conducti. The texts of these
songs, which are in Latin rather than the vernacular cultivated by the
trouvères, range over many subjects including religious devotion and social
satire and they cannot be placed within the scheme of High Style and Lower
Styles which has guided us in Chapters 1–5. Furthermore, the monophonic
conductus is a largely northern and—in some measure—Parisian repertory,

and for this reason also it demands separate treatment.

Finally, there is the *lai*. Of all the medieval song-forms this is undoubtedly the one with the most complex history and terminology. I have deliberately placed this enigmatic genre last to emphasise (what the reader will already have discerned) that the problem of instrumental involvement in courtly monody is a very long way from being finally solved and requires much further research.

Of these three repertories it is the *carole* that deserves pride of place, for the surviving poetry and music of the *carole* have many points of contact with the Lower Styles of poetry discussed in Chapters 2–4. The *carole* is also one of the most colourful forms of medieval song and the one whose performing dimension can be most fully captured; a wealth of sources—sermons, treatises on the Vices, manuals of confession, for example—have things to reveal about this 'Devil's mill'.

II

When the moralists of the thirteenth century turned their gaze upon secular music their vision was filled with the spectacle of public dances, or *caroles*

Figure 8 A carole *accompanied by a fiddle. Reference as for Figure 7. The picture illustrates Judges 21:21 (*filias Silo . . . ducendos choros . . .*).* *Reproduced by permission.*

(Figure 8). These dances seem to have flourished in every region of life, from the village churchyards to the aristocratic halls, and churchmen inveighed against them throughout the thirteenth century. So abundant are the references to these *caroles* and *coreae*, and so meagre are the moralists' references to élite music such as courtly monody or the motet,[2] that *coreae* deserve to be placed at the centre of our picture of secular music in thirteenth-century France.

Beyond the walls of aristocratic residences and castles these dances, celebrated during spring and summer,[3] were public festivals in a world where almost all the daylight hours were given over to manual labour. To judge by the quantity of harangue directed against them from the pulpit and confessional they loomed large in the lives of country people and city-dwellers, just as they did at court during the great festivals of Christmas and Pentecost.[4] In both the popular and courtly manifestations of the *corea* (which should not, perhaps, be too sharply distinguished), the dancers prepared themselves in advance with fresh clothes and floral garlands for their foreheads; once the *corea* was under way and the performers, linking hands, began to move in a circle to the left,[5] the dance became a public event where there could never be too many participants or spectators ('the more who participate', comments an anonymous preacher, 'and the more who watch, the merrier it is').[6] In the eyes of many contemporary moralists the result of all this dancing and crowding was to produce a grotesque parody of the Church's liturgy in which the singers who led the dance were anti-priests:[7]

> Item in chorea habet diabolus sacerdotem cantantem
> et clericum respondentem et quasi omnes horas fecit
> cantari per vicos et plateas; et sicut sacerdos mutat
> vestimenta quando debet celebrare, sic isti quando
> debent choreas ducere ... et loco officii Dei faciunt
> officium diaboli, ad quam conveniunt plures quam ad
> officium Dei, et diutius expectant, quia prolixius
> est officium et quandoque tota nocte et amplius, et
> magis devote et virilius serviunt diabolo quam Deo. ...
> Item contra sacramentum ordinis faciunt, quia tali
> servitium impendunt diabolo quale clerici Deo, ut
> habetur. Sed et per cantus earum cantus ecclesiasticus
> contempnitur; quoniam enim deberent interesse vesperis
> intersunt choreis.

> In a *corea* the Devil has a priest who sings and a cleric who
> serves, and he [the Devil] causes almost all the hours to be
> sung through the streets and roadways. And just as a priest
> changes his clothes when he must celebrate, so they who
> must lead *coreae* do ... and in place of the Office of God
> they celebrate the Office of the Devil, to which many

more people come than the Office of God and spend more
time because the Devil's Office is longer (and at one
time or another can last the whole night or more). They
serve the Devil much more devotedly and keenly than
God.... In this they sin against the sacrament of ordination,
because they busy themselves in just such a liturgy to the
Devil as clerics perform to God, as has been said. And
through the music [of the women who dance *coreae*] the
music of the Church is brought into disdain, for when they
should be at Vespers they are present in *coreae*.

This diabolic liturgy was celebrated in aristocratic courts as well as in
'streets and roadways'. Old French fiction is replete with references to such
courtly dances known by the Old French equivalent of *corea*: *carole*. Jean
Renart, for example, describes several scenes where courtiers go carolling,
complete with the text of the songs to which they dance:[8]

Main a main...
devant le tref, en un pré vert,
les puceles et li vallet
ront la carole commenciee.
Une dame s'est avanciee.
vestue d'une cote en graine,
si chante ceste premeraine:

C'est tot la gieus, enmi les prez,
Vos ne sentez mie les maus d'amer!
Dames i vont por caroler,
remirez vos braz!
Vos ne sentez mie les maus d'amer
si com ge faz!

Hand in hand... before the tent, in a green pasture,
the maidens and young men have begun the *carole*. A lady
has come forward in a scarlet dress and sings this [song]
to begin... [song follows]

Here Jean Renart has captured the ethos of the thirteenth-century *carole*. His
dance is the very epitome of the primaveral quality of *jeunesse*, for it is
performed in a green pasture by maidens and young men; it expresses the
elegant and carefree movement of people who, in Jean Renart's imagination, are held in an idealised state of candid and insouciant youthfulness.

This emphasis upon youth traversed all classes of society where *caroles*
were performed. As manifested in these dances the courtly cult of *jeunesse*
drew nourishment from festivals in the towns and villages where the public
dances were mostly performed by *mulieres et iuvenes*—by women and young

men.[9] The primaveral ethos of the *caroles* also attracted the young students in the schools. '[I was] a merry and amorous leader of *coreae* and master of dances in wooded places', says the theologian Henri Bate; 'such things are not inimical to the student life, especially amongst the young.'[10]

To judge by a wealth of literary testimony, *coreae* were usually danced to songs which the dancers provided for themselves. The writings of thirteenth-century preachers and theologians are laden with bitter invectives against these *cantus* and *cantilene* which drew young husbands away from their wives and seduced serving girls away from their households.[11]

III

Some degree of instrumental involvement in *coreae* seems to be suggested by pictorial sources (Figure 8) and by several passing references in the writings of thirteenth-century theologians. Just as the Israelites danced to instruments when they had crossed the Red Sea, argues Honorius Augustodunensis, so the faithful 'still use musical instruments in their ring-dances' (Appendix 3:48). In a comparable passage Guillaume d'Auvergne mentions how dancers perform *coreae* 'making a clamour and springing . . . to the sounds . . . of musical instruments' (*ibid.*, 45).

Here we seem to be dealing with luxurious evidence: pictures, references in romances, harangues from the pens of moralists and passing references in theological treatises and encyclopedias. Yet none of the specific sources cited so far has clarified the question of whether the songs performed in *coreae* were accompanied by instruments, or whether there were certain kinds of *corea* which were performed to the music of instruments alone. Depictions of these dances, for example, are not usually endowed with sufficient detail to reveal whether any of the participants are singing as they move. Similarly, it is uncertain whether the *coreae* mentioned by Honorius Augustudonensis ('which the faithful still [perform with] musical instruments') are accompanied dance-songs or just dance-pieces played upon instruments.

At this point Johannes de Grocheio's evidence is of great interest. He is our principal witness to the musical character and performance practice of the thirteenth-century *corea*; the striking feature of his account is that he draws a clear distinction between purely vocal and instrumental *coreae*. Grocheio's term for the pieces performed during these dances is *ductia*, no doubt because of the Latin idiom *coreas ducere*, 'to lead [i.e. to dance] *coreae*'.[12] He distinguishes a vocal and an instrumental form. From his descriptions we learn that the vocal *ductia* began and ended with a refrain and that between the refrains there lay poetic material with some lines sharing the forms and rhymes of the refrain.[13] These details are confusing at first, and there are more: from Grocheio's description of the rondeau (*rotunda vel rotundellus*) we may deduce that the added material in the vocal *ductia* had different melodic material from the refrain. Bewildering though these details may be, they gradually resolve into a description of a virelai like this one:[14]

	melodic scheme	rhymes
Hé! aloete,	A	a
joliete,	B	a
petit t'est de mes maus.	C	b
S'amor venist a plesir	d	c
que me vousissent sesir	d	c
de la blondette,	a	a
saverousete,	b	a
j'en fëusse plus baus.	c	b
Hé! aloete,	A	a
joliete,	B	a
petit t'est de mes maus.	C	b

In the light of Grocheio's description of the vocal *ductia* the crucial lines here are 3–4: *S'amor venist a plesir/que me vousissent sesir*; in accordance with virelai form, this couplet introduces new melodic material and new rhymes not found in the refrain. This seems to be the kind of piece which Grocheio had heard 'sung in *coreae* by young men and girls'.

Grocheio's instrumental *ductia*, however, displays a different musical form. Its function is exactly the same as that of its vocal counterpart ('the *ductia* excites the soul of man to move ornately... *in coreis*'),[15] yet while the vocal type appears to have been cast in the mould of a virelai, the instrumental *ductia* consists of paired melodic sections with open and closed endings, so following this form (compare Music example 9):

A	open
A	closed
B	open
B	closed
C	open
C	closed etc.

Thus Grocheio's account of *corea* music reveals a fissure between vocal and instrumental usage. According to his report, vocal and instrumental *corea* melodies were identical in name and function but were quite distinct in their form (and therefore, presumably, in the choreographies which were used with them).

If we widen our field of view to take in the references of moralists and preachers we find further sign of a divide between *coreae* performed to songs on the one hand and performed to instrumental music on the other. For example, Albertus Magnus legislates that *coreae* are not evil in themselves, 'whether they be done with song *or* with musical instruments' (Appendix 3:47), and since this judgement appears in the context of a treatise on confession and penitence (a genre of writing which demanded close attention to distinctions in behaviour) it is tempting to give some weight to Albertus's reference to *coreae* performed to songs *or* to musical instruments.

A comparable separation of voices and instruments meets us in a theological encyclopedia by another contemporary of Grocheio, Guillaume d'Auvergne. In his *De Universo*, composed between 1231 and 1236, Guillaume discusses the question of whether there are *coreae* in heaven amongst the blessed and offers this description of earthly *coreae* (Appendix 3:45):

> You see, moreover, men and women leaping with
> the joy they find in this kind of sport [i.e. dancing in
> *coreae*], making a clamour, springing, wishing to
> fit the form of their movements to the music of
> songs, or of musical instruments, to the best of their
> ability.

'To the music of songs or of musical instruments': there are many references to *caroles* in Old French epics and romances which point in the same direction as the passages by Albertus Magnus and Guillaume d'Auvergne. I have not found a reliable reference to the instrumental accompaniment of a vocal *carole* anywhere in Old French narratives of the twelfth and thirteenth centuries,[16] only a few doubtful examples where it is impossible to establish whether singing is involved (see Appendix 3:31 and 34–5). Almost all of the references to courtly *caroles* seem to describe a purely vocal entertainment which courtly amateurs provide for themselves without the help of minstrels.[17]

There are two vernacular sources which may help us clarify the role of instruments in vocal *corea* music a little further. We have already seen that one of the songs performed to instrumental accompaniment in Jean Renart's romance of *Guillaume de Dole* is a rondeau, *C'est la jus en la praele*, sung to a minstrel's fiddle. This is the kind of song which often figured in courtly *caroles*—as many passages in *Guillaume de Dole* testify.[18] Indeed the minstrel who accompanies the song had promised, earlier that day, that he would bring his fiddle to the gathering 'if we are to have *caroles*'.[19] Yet in the event there is no reference to dancing when *C'est la jus en la praele* is performed.

This scrap of evidence may suggest that refrain-songs such as *C'est la jus en la praele*, although not habitually accompanied when performed as part of a populous *carole*, could be accompanied when performed as solo songs. At all times such songs must have been closely associated with the alternatim style of performance dictated by the *carole* (where, so it seems, a soloist often sang the added sections while the company performed the refrain),[20] and it is possible to understand why musicians should have wished to reinforce these pieces when performing them in a solo context—perhaps with the instrument doubling the refrains.

There is a sign that this is indeed what happened in the thirteenth-century romance of *Claris et Laris*. At one point in this text knights and ladies listen to a minstrel in the open air:[21]

> La escoutoient bonement
> .I. conteor, qui lor contoit
> Une chançon et si notoit
> Ses refrez en une viele,
> Qui assez iert et bonne et bele.

> There they listened attentively to a minstrel, who sang
> them a song and performed the refrains on his fiddle which
> was both good and beautiful.

This *chanson* with its refrains may be a rondeau or some similar form. This is suggested by certain features in the poet's description of the scene, for the minstrel performs *En mi ... d'une praierie* which is near *la rive de mer*; both of these phrases are key registral terms in the thirteenth-century repertory of rondeaux and simple refrain songs. Compare the following incipits of lyrics quoted in Jean Renart's *Guillaume de Dole*:[22]

> C'est la jus *en la praele*
> C'est la gieus *en mi les prez*
> Sor la *rive de mer*
> Tout la gieus, *sor rive mer*

This is not to claim that the author has scattered clues to the nature of the minstrel's song here and there in his account of its performance, but only that his imaginative apprehension of this musical scene is impregnated with poetic formulae which suggest that the *chanson* is a monophonic refrain-song, perhaps a rondeau or virelai. These few lines may be our only guide to the way in which such lyrics were performed as solo songs with instruments during the thirteenth century.

7

The monophonic conductus

'This boy knew how to play a fiddle ... he was familiar with (and willingly sang) all kinds of monophonic songs in diverse languages....'

Henri de Malines, *Nativitas magistri*
Henrici Mechliniensis

I

According to his own account, Henri de Malines, theologian and graduate of the University of Paris, was 'most willing to sing all kinds of monophonic songs (*cantiones vulgarium*) in diverse languages' when he was a young man.[1] Since Malines lies midway between Brussels and Antwerp it is likely that some of these songs *in diversis linguis* were in Flemish; others were probably in French, the universal language of courtliness, and some perhaps in Latin, a language which Henri wielded to good use throughout his distinguished career as a theologian. In the minds of such *clercs* as Henri—men who mingled Latin and vernacular in their sermons, produced French translations of Latin treatises, and naturalised a host of Latin words into the vernacular—the distinction between Latin and vernacular lyric cannot always have been a firm one. Johannes de Grocheio, for example, basing his views upon Parisian custom, classifies all non-liturgical monophonic songs together as *musica vulgaris* (compare Henri's *cantiones vulgarium*) and does not even raise the issue of language; what matters in his eyes is whether a piece is savant (i.e. polyphonic), or whether it is intended for use in church.

Indeed Grocheio provides clear evidence that Parisian musicians of c1300 assimilated the High Style trouvère song in the vernacular to Latin song; some Parisians apparently called the trouvère productions *simplices conducti*, 'monophonic conducti'.[2] In adopting this terminology the Parisians were assimilating a genre whose history has little connection with their city—the trouvère *chanson*—to one whose story gathers around the banks of the Seine—the monophonic conductus. It was an obvious assimilation to make, for both forms were characterised by their monophonic and predominantly syllabic or mildly melismatic melodies, their usually strophic form and their use of rhyme. The resemblances between the two forms would have been conspicuous to *clercs* who enjoyed both kinds of music—men such as the 'masters and students' perhaps, who, according to Grocheio, admired trouvère songs in the High Style and amongst whom there must have been many connoisseurs of Latin song.[3]

Since we have Grocheio's authority that High Style trouvère songs could be associated with the fiddle in late thirteenth-century Paris, it seems likely that Latin monophonic songs may have been performed in the same way since both could so easily be bracketed together as *simplices conducti*. This is only an inference, of course, but a few fragments of evidence suggest that monophonic conducti may have been associated with instruments as early as the first decades of the thirteenth century. As early as *Le Roman de la Violette* (probably 1227–9) the term *conduis* is used to denote music played by jongleurs upon their fiddles,[4] and although this is a flimsy basis for a generalisation about the performance of the monophonic conductus repertory it may at least be said that the word *conduis* undoubtedly passed into Old French from contemporary Latin usage and may therefore have retained some specialised meaning.

A more intriguing passage is contained in Gautier de Coinci's *Miracles de Nostre Dame* where Gautier gives his version of the famous miracle whereby the Virgin caused a candle to descend upon the fiddle of a minstrel who went from church to church singing her praises (Appendix 3:12 and 37). Having told this story Gautier takes the opportunity to admonish the ecclesiastical singers of his day:[5]

> La clere vois plaisant et bele,
> Le son de harpe et de vïele,
> De psaltere, d'orgue, de gygue
> Ne prise pas Diex une figue
> S'il n'a ou cuer devocïon.

> A clear, pleasing and beautiful voice, the sound of
> harp, fiddle, psaltery, organ and *gygue*—God does not
> hold them worth a fig unless there is devotion in the
> [musician's] heart.

This passage implies that there was some kind of music, involving voices and instruments, which was ostensibly devotional but failed in that object if the musicians performing it were defective in faith or conscience. This music is unlikely to encompass the secular *pastoreles*, *sonnés* and *chançonnetes* which Gautier so often condemns as trivial and unworthy of educated men. However, it may well have included the

> . . . chans piteuz et doz
> Et les conduis de Nostre Dame

which Gautier deemed proper musical fare for gatherings of learned men.[6]

The Notre Dame conductus repertory, both monophonic and polyphonic, incorporates a large hoard of devotional *conduis*, including 39 *conduis de Nostre Dame* (to borrow Gautier's phrase), 16 pieces in praise of various saints, 43 for Easter and 62 for advent and Christmas.[7] The monophonic items may represent the music which Gautier had heard sung and accompanied by musicians who (in his judgement) sometimes forgot their devotional purpose and revelled in their artistry. Gautier would probably have considered instrumental accompaniment appropriate for *conduis de Nostre Dame* (or for any devotional conductus), to judge by the zest with which he tells the story of the minstrel at Roc-Amadour who sang to the Virgin Mary and accompanied himself on his fiddle (Appendix 3:37).

To return to the artistic parity between the trouvère *chanson* and the monophonic conductus, it seems likely that (at least in Parisian circles) Latin conducti would sometimes have been performed in much the same way that their vernacular counterparts were treated by a *bonus artifex in viella*. An instrumental accompaniment based upon the practice of fifthing, such as we reconstructed for trouvère monody in Chapter 5, certainly looks at home when placed above many conducti:[8]

Example 17

II

So far we have dealt with the conductus in the general terms which are all that the fragmentary state of the evidence allows. However, our last musical example carries us to a collection of pieces within the monophonic corpus where the likelihood of instrumental involvement in some performances seems strong: the Latin rondeaux in the eleventh fascicule of the Florence manuscript.

There are sixty of these pieces, most of them in some kind of rondeau form and provided with bold and ingratiating musical settings.[9] For the most part their poetic forms and musical style are closely related to those of vernacular dance-songs such as we meet in Jean Renart's *Guillaume de Dole*. Compare the following song, for example, with *C'est la jus en la praele*, which Jean Renart describes as being performed to a fiddle (see above, pp. 34–5):[10]

Nicholaus inclitus,
Laudet omnis spiritus,
Factus est divinitus
Presul cum letitia;
Laudet omnis spiritus
Gubernantem omnia.

Example 18

The eleventh fascicule of the Florence manuscript opens with a historiated initial which shows clerics with linked hands; to judge by other thirteenth-century illustrations (Figure 8) they are dancing a *corea* or *carole*. This accords with the lyrico-choreographic forms of these Latin rondeaux and with various references to singing and dancing within some of their texts:[11]

Vocis tripudio	With vocal dance
Psallat hec concio	let this company sing.

A further link between the world of the secular *corea* and these Latin rondeaux is established by the frequent references in the Latin poems to 'floral joy', 'floral festivities' or 'new flowers':[12]

Expellant tedium	May these floral festivities
Prestent solatium	Expel care,
Festa floralia.	and may they grant solace.

Cesset labor studii.	Let the labour of study cease!
In hoc floralia gaudio	In this floral joy
Floris renovatio	the renewal of the flower
Lusus est incitatio.	is an incitement to play.

On one level these references to flowers and floral entertainments need no explaining: they express the eternal link between dancing in the open air and the return of spring. Yet there is probably more to these 'floral joys' than primaveral imagery; they evoke the use of flowers for garments and bodily ornaments which was such a characteristic feature of *coreae*. In what may be the longest and most detailed reference to secular musical life in any non-musical work of the thirteenth century, Guillaume Peyraut inveighs against the use of floral garlands by women dancers, taking his text from a mighty passage in Revelation 9:7 ('the shapes of the locusts were like unto horses prepared for battle, and on their heads it was as if they had crowns of gold'):[13]

> Hoc pertinet ad ornatum quem habent tales mulieres
> in capitibus, et insinuatur quod ornatos quos iste
> mulieres deferunt in capitibus quos adquisierunt
> a suis amasiis sint quasi corone multiplici triumpho
> quem habuit diabolus per eas. . . . Sic solent strenui
> milites in thorneamentis in capitibus equorum suorum
> coronas ponere de floribus.

> This relates to the adornment which such women
> have on their heads, and it implies that the
> adornments which these women bear on their heads,

89

and which they have got from their lovers, are like
garlands of manifold triumph which the Devil has
won through them ... just as bold knights are
accustomed to place crowns of flowers on the
heads of their horses in tournaments.

Such floral garlands placed upon the forehead were regarded by many
moralists as a sin against the sacrament of confirmation, the sign of the cross
being replaced by the sign of the Devil. One anonymous casuist even breaks
into the vernacular to express his hatred of them:[14]

... faciunt contra sacramentum confirmationis quia
in fronte signum crucis suscepunt tanquam empte
Christi sanguine, in choreis vero, signo crucis abiecto,
signum diaboli pro eo posuerunt, scilicet signum
venalitatis in capite quod *gerlond* dicitur.

... [dancers in *coreae*] sin against the sacrament of
confirmation because they have taken the sign of the
cross upon their forehead as a sign that they are
bought by the blood of Christ; in *coreae*, however,
they put aside the sign of the cross and replace it
with the emblem of the Devil, that is the sign of
lechery which is called 'garland'.

Clerics, students and other *litterati* able to read and write Latin also took
part in these *coreae*. In his reminiscences Henri de Malines candidly admits
that in his younger days he was an enthusiastic *corearum ductor*, or leader of
coreae, while a sermon preached at St Victor in 1230 by Pierre de Bar-sur-
Aube records how newly-elected Masters of the University of Paris arranged
great festivities in which their friends would 'lead *coreae* through the streets
and highways'.[15]

But it was not only in Paris that clerics and men of (some) Latin learning
showed their appetite for *coreae*. In the middle years of the thirteenth century
Odon Rigaud, archbishop of Rouen, visited many ecclesiastical foundations
in Normandy and the records he kept reveal how popular were *coreae* with
men who, in his judgement, should have known better. At St Yldevert
(Seine-Inférieure) he found 'clerics, vicars and even chaplains conducting
themselves in a dissolute and scurrilous way on certain feast-days, especially
that of St Nicholas, leading *coreae* through the streets and making *le vireli*',
while at the priory of Villarceaux (Seine-et-Oise) he found members of the
community dressing up 'in secular clothes ... and leading *coreae* with secular
persons'.[16]

It is possible that some of the lighter Latin rondeaux in the Florence
manuscript were intended for performance in contexts such as these. Some
of them may be pious contrafacta of secular dance-songs intended to provide

literate men whose appetite for *coreae* could not be suppressed with material which would not pollute their throats, but many of them are more spirited than spiritual and surely reflect the ebullience of a young student population ('let the labour of study cease!') for whom the distinction between Latin and vernacular lyric was not always conspicuous.

The performing-traditions of the vernacular *coreae* are therefore our best guide to the performance of these Latin rondeaux. I tentatively suggest that these songs were sung unaccompanied when performed as populous dance-songs (the picture which opens the rondeau fascicule in the Florence manuscript does not show instrumentalists, for what that may be worth). Yet they are likely to have been often accompanied when they were performed as solo songs—customarily, perhaps, by a single instrument.

8

The *Roman de Horn* and the lai

What leaf-fring'd legend haunts about thy shape?

Keats, *Ode on a Grecian Urn*

I

In Chapter 1 we encountered what is probably the most striking reference to accompanied performance anywhere in medieval literature. It is a passage in the Anglo-Norman *Roman de Horn* (c1170) where the hero sings something called a *lai* to the harp. It is worth looking at again:[1]

> Lors prent la harpe a sei,   qui'il la veut atemprer.
> Deus! ki dunc l'esgardast   cum la sout manïer,
> Cum ces cordes tuchout,   cum les feseit trembler,
> Asquantes feiz chanter   asquantes organer,
> De l'armonie del ciel   li poüst remembrer!
> Sur tuz homes k'i sunt   fet cist a merveiller.
> Quant ses notes ot fait   si la prent a munter
> E tut par autres tuns   les cordes fait soner:
> Mut se merveillent tuit   qu'il la sout si bailler.
> E quant il out (is)si fait,   si cummence a noter
> Le lai dont or ains dis,   de Baltof, haut e cler,
> Si cum sunt cil bretun   d'itiel fait costumier.
> Apres en l'estrument   fet les cordes suner,
> Tut issi cum en voiz   l'aveit dit tut premier:
> Tut le lai lur ad fait,   n'i vout rien retailler.

> Then he took the harp to tune it. God! whoever
> saw how well he handled it, touching the strings
> and making them vibrate, sometimes causing them to
> sing and at other times join in harmonies,
> he would have been reminded of the heavenly harmony.

This man, of all those that are there, causes most
wonder. When he has played his notes he makes the
harp go up so that the strings give out completely
different notes. All those present marvel that
he could play thus. And when he has done all this
he begins to play the aforesaid *lai* of Baltof, in
a loud and clear voice, just as the Bretons are versed
in such performances. Afterwards he made the strings
of the instrument play exactly the same melody as he had
just sung; he performed the whole *lai* for he
wished to omit nothing.

These lines are tokens of an ardent imagination. Horn checks the tuning
of the harp by plucking the strings melody-wise (*chanter*) and chord-wise
(*organer*).[2] When he has finished these testing flourishes (*Quant ses notes ot
fait*) he begins to retune it, making the strings give out completely different
notes (. . . *si la prent a munter / E tut par autres tuns . les cordes fait soner*), and then
sings the *lai* composed by Baltof, son of the king of Brittany, 'just as the
Bretons are versed in such performances'. After this he repeats the music of
what he has just sung upon the harp (*Apres en l'estrument . fet les cordes suner /
Tut issi cum en voiz . l'aveit dit tut premier . . .*).

However we may choose to interpret it, this remarkable description of
something called a *lai* being performed by a courtly amateur is one of the
most detailed references to vocal-instrumental delivery that the Middle
Ages have left us; it is an important witness to performing techniques such
as the elaborate tuning-preliminary (which seems to be half preparation and
half performance in this case) and the alternatim use of voice and
instrument. Yet it is the nature of the music being performed which has
brought these lines from the *Roman de Horn* to the pages of countless
musicological books and articles,[3] for by calling Horn's piece a *lai* the author
seems to steer us directly towards one of the most impressive and rewarding
repertories of medieval song. For the troubadours and trouvères a *lai* was a
specific lyric form, of most ambitious design, in which each subdivision of
the text had its own metrical form and musical setting. Two verses of the
anonymous French *Lai d'Aélis* of the thirteenth century will show the
expansiveness of *lai* design:[4]

I En sospirant trop de parfont
   Atendrai le confondement
   Ke les grans destreces me font
   K'en mon cuer font lor fondement,
   Et li pensers ki me confont,
   Par quoi sospir parfondement;
Je ne sai s'il est folie ou s'il est sens:
En amer me font gaster Amors mon tens.

93

Nuit et jor sospir et plor quant me porpens;
Sospirer cele me fait a cui je pens.
Diex m'otroit ke ce ne soit sor son deffens!
Morir quic se de li n'ai secors par tens.

Example 19

II France deboinaire,
    De ta grant franchise
    Ne porroit retraire
    Nus en nule guise.
    Coment porroit faire
    Mes cuers nul servise
    Ki te peüst plaire?
    Ice me devise:
    Ne te puis plus taire
    Le mal ki m'atise;
    Ne m'i fai contraire:
    Je t'aim sans faintise.

Example 19 (contd)

At first sight the harping passage of the *Roman de Horn* seems such a vivid and detailed piece of writing that the idea of questioning its verisimilitude barely arises in our minds, and part of its apparent fidelity to contemporary life lies in the detailed information it seems to provide about the performance of lyric *lais* such as the *Lai d'Aélis*.

Yet a search through Old French literature soon reveals that this harping episode is not unique. Indeed there are passages in other romances which are so similar to the musical episode in the *Roman de Horn* that the extract quoted at the beginning of this chapter begins to look like a complex literary convention. The key elements in this convention are

(1) the courtly hero/heroine who plays the harp and who
(2) sings/composes works called *lais*
(3) as part of a tale richly endowed with what might be called 'Celtic mystique'—the charisma of Arthurian Britain and all ancient Celtic realms (especially Cornwall, Brittany and Ireland).

Here, for example, is Iseut performing a *lai* in Thomas's *Tristan* of c1170:[5]

Ysolt chante molt dulcement,
La voiz acorde a l'estrument.
Les mains sunt beles, li lais buens,
Dulce la voiz e bas li tons.

Iseut sings very sweetly,
attuning her voice to the instrument.
Her hands are beautiful, the *lai* good,
her voice is sweet and the music soft (?low).

In its twelfth-century versions the Tristan legend is perhaps the keenest evocation of that legendary Celtic past, 'scented with the forests and sea-breezes of Brittany and Cornwall', which fascinated the medieval European imagination for several centuries.[6] Iseut is a princess of Ireland (we recall that Horn performs his *lai* in the chamber of an Irish princess) and the story of her tragic love for Tristan moves between Brittany, Ireland and Cornwall (where Marc, Iseut's husband, is king).

Here is another *lai* passage, this time from the romance of *Galeran de Bretagne* (the title itself is significant). The hero, Galeran, is teaching his lady-love how to play a *lai* that he has just composed:[7]

'Fresne,' said Galeran, 'I have tried out my skill with a new *lai* and I am very keen to teach it to you at once'.... 'Begin,' said Fresne, 'then I will harp and learn the *lai* on my instrument.' Then he began to play, and she listened, studying the way he cast his fingers on the strings. When he had listened to the notes he tuned them with his tuning key so that they were perfectly accorded. The words and the music were sweet, and he sang and played the *lai* until she knew both the words and the tune; then she tuned her silver-stringed harp to the *lai*.

Taking these references together we can begin to see the harping episode in the *Roman de Horn* in a fresh light. The passage where Horn sings a *lai* to the harp—at first sight such an arresting and seemingly idiosyncratic piece of writing—now appears to activate a complex narrative motif in which there are a number of stable elements: the musician is always a protagonist or an important person in the story; he or she is a courtly amateur; the instrument which they play (in a most accomplished manner) is the *harpe*; the pieces which they perform are called *lais*; the stories in which these protagonists appear are fraught with the romance of the ancient Celtic realms of the North.

II

The history of this complex motif deserves a study to itself and lies beyond the scope of this book (although we shall glance at it towards the end of this chapter). What matters here is that the term *lai* is part of the motif. Does this reveal anything about the performance of pieces such as the *Lai d'Aélis* (Example 19)?

It can be said at once that in all cases where a romancer gives examples of what he means by the *lais* which his heroes perform, the pieces presented are never polymorphous lyric works such as the *Lai d'Aélis*. Two romances compiled during the first decades of the thirteenth century will suffice to demonstrate the point: *Guiron le Courtois* and the *Tristan en prose*. These two works continue the hero-harpist tradition which we encountered earlier in the *Roman de Horn* and in *Galeran de Bretagne*, for they both contain scenes (shrouded in Celtic mystique) where something called a *lai* is performed to the harp by some virtuoso courtly amateur. In *Guiron le Courtois* the poetic texts of these pieces are inserted into the narrative, and in some manuscripts of the *Tristan en prose* these lyric insertions may even appear with their music.

A case in point is provided by a passage from *Guiron le Courtois*. Here the author tells how the first ever *lai* came to be composed. It seems that Meliadus, king of Leonois and the father of Tristan, has returned home to his kingdom where he languishes for love of the queen of Scotland. The extract is well worth quoting *in extenso*:[8]

> King Meliadus did not forget his love, and when he was back in Leonois he was so unsettled that he did not know what to say for himself. He was so deeply in love he thought he would die. He composed songs about his love which he sang night and day, and it was this which gave him most comfort in this affair. What shall I say? He suffered for a long time from this love which he did not dare confess to any man in the world. Eventually, he composed a poem about his love which was more wondrous and subtle than anyone had ever composed before, and he set this poem to music such that it might be sung to the harp (*et sor celui dit troue chant tele que len puet chanter en arpe*), for there was no man in all the world at that time who

knew more of harping than he, or who was a more accomplished composer of music and notes. Meliadus called this poem which he composed for the love of his lady *lays*, as a sign that he wished to leave all other music. And you may be sure, all and some, that this was the first *lai* which was ever sung to the harp. Before Meliadus no *lai* had ever been composed, nor was any *lai* composed after Meliadus until Tristan [son of Meliadus] began to sing and compose *lais*.

When the king had composed the *lai* he began at once to harp it before one of his knights in whom he placed great trust (for he had been raised with him as a child). This knight was also a skilled harpist and he sang very well in the manner of that country. When the knight heard the *lai* he praised it greatly, and as he had never heard such a poem he asked the king what it was called. The king said: 'It is called *lai*. I know indeed that you have never heard tell of such.' Then he began to explain why he had called it *lai*.

[The knight, learning that Meliadus loves the queen of Scotland, offers to go to perform the *lai* before the queen at Arthur's court]:

'. . . I will go to [Arthur's] court and carry this new *lai* with me; when I see the queen of Scotland I will sing and harp it, and when she hears it she will surely ask who the composer may be; I promise you that I will say my piece to her then and will advance your cause, never fear . . .'. When the king heard this plan he agreed to it, for he was convinced that what the knight had said was the best plan. Once the knight had learned how to harp and sing the *lai* he departed from Leonois.

[Having arrived at the court of Arthur the knight is taken by Gauvain to where the ladies of the court are sitting by a river, singing and playing instruments]:

Among them was the queen of Scotland . . . there were a few knights there. With them was a harper who harped a song that a knight of north Wales had only recently composed. A lady named Orgayne sang the song while the harper played. . . . Then up comes Sir Gauvain, bringing with him the knight from Leonois. Because they all knew him [Gauvain] to be a man of excellent breeding they rose at once to greet him and received him most honourably, making him sit amongst them with the knight from Leonois. As soon as the queen of Scotland saw the knight she recognised him. . . . The lady called Orgayne recognised him also. She had stopped her singing when the two knights approached, and once they were seated the ladies said to her: 'Finish what you have begun for us.' Orgayne replied at once: 'I will not sing unless you ladies agree to command whomsoever I choose to sing when I have finished my tale and my song.' Smiling, they replied at once saying: 'We promise you that, on the understanding that it will not be Milady the queen of Scotland who is here.' 'In the name of God,' said Orgayne, 'it is not at all the queen that I am thinking of or whom I seek.'

[Orgayne finishes her song and asks that the knight from Leonois should sing]:

The knight, who wished for further entreaty than that of the lady Orgayne alone, replied that he had no skill in singing. All the ladies then entreated him, and when he saw that they (and the knights who were there) pressed him so intently, he replied: 'Then give me the harp', and they passed it to him at once. When he had settled himself he began to look upon the queen of Scotland so that she noticed his attention. When he had tuned the harp to the best of his ability, and according to the music that he wished to play, he began his song and his *lai* at once . . .

Several manuscripts of *Guiron le Courtois* give the text (but not the music) of this *lai*: it is a long love-poem in monorhymed quatrains, beginning:[9]

Dame, a vos icestui lay mant;
Fait l'ai senz vostre comant.
A vos tuit me recomant;
Autre Deu ge ne demant.

This poem is very similar to many of the so-called *lais* inserted in various manuscripts of another great prose romance, the *Tristan en prose*. The majority of these *lais*, some of which have survived with their music, are composed of monorhymed quatrains with a melodic scheme aabc (the melody being more or less exactly repeated for each stanza).[10] In one instance a *lai* given the title *Lay voir disant* is prefaced by a picture of a harper playing the piece to King Mark at Tintagel (Figure 9). The first stanza runs:[11]

Example 20

It is apparent that these 'Arthurian' *lais* in quatrains are quite distinct from lyric *lais* such as the *Lai d'Aélis* (Example 19) in their form. The essence

Figure 9 *A harpist performs the* Lay voir disant *before Mark, king of Cornwall. From a thirteenth-century copy of the* Tristan en prose. *Paris, Bibliothèque Nationale, MS fr.776, f.271v. Reproduced by permission.*

of the lyric *lai* is that each subdivision of the text has its own metrical form and its own melody, but the stanzas of the 'Arthurian' *lais* are built on the opposite principle: they are isometric and are all set to the same melody.

These 'Arthurian' *lais* are something of a mystery. They have often been compared with the Ambrosian hymn,[12] and when they are supplied with music they are usually laid out in the manuscripts like liturgical hymns in an antiphonal: with music for every verse (Figure 9). These *lais* might also be compared with some of the earliest narrative poems in the French language. The eleventh-century *Passion* of Clermont-Ferrand, for example, is composed throughout in quatrains of octosyllables, and was clearly intended to be sung, for the first verse is provided with musical notation:[13]

Hora vos dic vera raizun
de Jesú Christi passïun:
los sos affanz vol remembrar
per que cest mund tot a salvad.

Compare the eleventh-century *Saint Alexis*, composed in five-line stanzas
of decasyllables:[14]

Bo[e]ns fut li s[i]ecles   al tens anciënur,
Quer feit i ert   e justise ed amur,
S'i ert creance,   dunt or(e) n'i at nul prut;
Tut est muez,   perdut ad sa colur:
Ja mais n'iert tel   cum fut as anceisurs.

It is possible that such stanzaic, narrative poetry lasted into the twelfth
and thirteenth centuries amongst professional entertainers singing songs of
the lives of saints and of the deeds of secular heroes. Perhaps this is the
background of the 'Arthurian' *lais*.[15]

As a coda to *Guiron le Courtois* and the *Tristan en prose* there is a passage
from the thirteenth-century romance of *Sone de Nausay* which also offers a
description of a *lai* being accompanied on the harp by a courtly amateur,
and where the text of the composition is also given. This poem seems to
reinforce our picture, for while it is not an 'Arthurian' *lai*, it is definitely not
a lyric *lai* either:[16]

Dist Papegais: 'Dont escoutes,
Et si se taise vos barnés'.
Li bons rois le gierfaut rechoit
Et Papegais en piés estoit.
Lors li fu sa harpe aportee
Li mieudre c'ains fu atempree.
Et Papegais si bielle estoit,
Que cascuns s'en esmierveilloit.
Et quant ot la harpe saisie,
Au roi est errant repairie,
Se li dist: 'Sire, .I. lai orres
Qui tous est fais de verités.
Ensi est ma dame avenu,
Pour quoi nous sommes chi venu.
. . . . .
Le harpe fait primes sonner,
Toutes les cordes concorder.
Le lay de bouche commencha.
Oyes les vers, comment il va:
   'Gentilleche et pités, pries pour mi,
   Et si tenes compagnie a cest lai,
   Et si dires a mon tresdouch ami
   Premierement, quant mon cuer li donnai,

> Ā lui siervir mon cors abandonnai
> Si cuitement, ains riens n'i escondi.
> Et nonpourquant si fu en sa mierchi
> Pour le peür qu'en la nef presentai
> Et le meschief qu'en ses bras me pasmay.'

(Seventeen more stanzas follow, all identical in form to this one.)

> Papegais said: 'Then listen, and call your magnates
> to be silent.' The noble king takes the falcon and
> Papegais rose to her feet. Then her harp was brought
> to her, the best ever tuned. Papegais was so fair
> that everyone marvelled at her. And when she had
> taken the harp she went straight back to the king and said
> to him: 'Sire, you will hear one *lai* in which
> everything is true. So it went with my lady, and
> that is the cause of our coming here . . . First she
> made the harp sound and made all the strings
> agree. Then she began to sing the *lai*. Hear how
> the lines go: . . .'
> (song follows . . .)

The song performed in this extract, *Gentilleche et pités, pries pour mi* (not known from any other source) is a somewhat anomalous piece of work. It has a polished surface that catches many reflections of the High Style trouvère song: the isometric stanzas of decasyllabic lines; the illusion of an intense subjectivity (*A lui siervir mon cors abandonnai*) and exaggerated sensibility (. . . *qu'en ses bras me pasmay*); yet the resemblance to the classic song-form of the trouvères fades as the text unrolls to more than twice the length of a normal trouvère *chanson*.

We have seen that each of the harping episodes in the *Roman de Horn*, *Galeran de Bretagne*, *Tristan*, the *Tristan en prose* and *Guiron le Courtois* activates a complex narrative motif: the hero-harpist performing something called a *lai* in a scene charged with Celtic mystique. There seems no reason to doubt that these passages embody details of contemporary musical practice (the harpist tuning-up before his performance, for example), yet it is far from certain whether the details add up to a whole that reflects reality in the same direct way. These episodes are not so much snapshots of contemporary life as oil-paintings, touched and re-touched during many generations.

Yet this leaves a good deal to be explained. Why do we find these detailed harping episodes in Anglo-Norman and Old French narratives, and why are they so detailed?

Here we confront some wide-ranging questions about the way medieval narrators conduct their dealings with music. To begin with the obvious, these fictional tales must first be read on their own terms as stories; and stories, as Tolkien pointed out, are like soup in which many ingredients, some new, and some ancient, lie simmering together.[17] Indeed there are reasons for believing that the harping passages we have examined are a mixed broth of ancient and modern in which the stock is provided by a story-pattern already in existence by c500 AD: the story of Apollonius of Tyre.

III

Shakespeare's description of the Apollonius story as one that

> ... hath been sung at festivals,
> On ember-eves and holy-ales

is a fitting introduction to his own version of a tale which had enjoyed more than a millennium of popularity before *Pericles* was launched on the theatre-goers of Elizabethan London. It first comes into view as a Latin prose-tale, the *Historia Apollonii Regis Tyri*, probably composed c500.[18] This *Historia* was much read in the monasteries of Dark Age Europe and by c1000 had already been translated into English prose. The story tells how Apollonius, prince of Tyre, is forced to flee his homeland and is eventually shipwrecked and cast ashore at Cyrene. He dines with the king, and after the meal Apollonius plays the lyre so well that the princess of that land asks her father if she may take music-lessons from their guest. Here is the description of that performance as it runs in the Old English version of the Latin narrative:[19]

> Ða wearð stilnes and swige geworden innon ðare healle.
> And Apollonius his hearpenaegl genam and he tha
> hearpestrengas mid craefte astirian ongan and thare hearpan
> sweg mid winsumum sange gemaegnde. And se cyngc silf
> and ealle the thar andwearde waeron micelre staefne cliopodon
> and hine heredon. . . . Soðlice mid thy the thaes cynges dohtor
> geseah thaet Apollonius on eallum godum craeftum swa wel
> waes getogen, tha gefeol hyre mod on his lufe.

> Then there was stillness and silence in the hall.
> Apollonius took his tuning-key (*hearpenaegl*) and then
> began to stir the harpstrings with skill and to mingle
> the sound of the harp with joyful singing. And the
> king himself and all those who heard him called out with
> great cries and praised him. . . . Truly, when the king's
> daughter saw that Apollonius was so well versed in all
> noble skills she began to fall in love with him.

Here, if anywhere, is material which may help to establish a literary tradition for the harping episode in the *Roman de Horn*. Here is that same eye for instrumental technique ('Apollonius took his tuning-key and then began to stir the harpstrings with skill') and that same interest in the manner of the performance ('[he mingled] the sound of the harp with joyful singing'). In the Old English version of the Apollonius story, as in the *Roman de Horn*, the musician is a courtly amateur who astonishes his royal listeners with a harp (*hearpe* in the Anglo-Saxon and *harpe* in the *Roman de Horn*).

A closer look at the resemblances between the story of Apollonius and the *Roman de Horn* leads to a discovery: in many respects they are the *same* story. In both tales the hero leaves his native land in a boat, having been driven from his homeland; he sets off at the mercy of the waves with no idea where he will come aground. He then arrives in a foreign land and impresses his foreign hosts with his accomplishments. Eventually he has a chance to amaze a royal company by the excellence of his string-playing. Every listener is lost in admiration as the hero performs, but it is the king's daughter who is most struck by his talents and she asks that he may become her music-teacher.

We can make still more of these resemblances if we turn to the story which, in many ways, is the *fons et origo* of the harping mystique which runs through French chivalric literature: the tale of Tristan. Here again we find many of the same narrative motifs as have now become familiar from the *Roman de Horn* and the story of Apollonius:[20]

APOLLONIUS OF TYRE	TRISTAN	ROMAN DE HORN
Apollonius flees into exile	Tristan, wounded, resolves to go to Ireland to be cured by Iseut	Horn exiled from his homeland by pagan invaders
He sets off in a boat	He sets off in a boat	He is set adrift in a boat
He arrives in a strange land	He arrives in a strange land	He arrives in a strange land
which is Cyrene	which is Ireland	which is Ireland
He conceals his identity	He conceals his identity	He conceals his identity
He distinguishes himself by his string-playing at the royal court of Pentapolis	He distinguishes himself by his *harpe*-playing at the royal court of Ireland	He distinguishes himself by his *harpe*-playing at the royal court of Ireland

APOLLONIUS OF TYRE	TRISTAN	ROMAN DE HORN
with an instrument passed from hand to hand	—	with an instrument passed from hand to hand
The daughter of the king wishes to have him as her music-teacher	The daughter of the king wishes to have him as her music-teacher	The daughter of the king wishes to have him as her music-teacher

If the resemblances between the *Historia Apollonii Regis Tyri* and certain elements of the *Roman de Horn* are striking, the parallels between the tale of Apollonius and the medieval legend of Tristan are even more arresting. In an important article Delbouille has shown that the Apollonius legend was well-known in twelfth-century France and that it exerted a powerful influence upon the development of literary fiction in the vernacular.[21]

It is universally accepted that many elements in the Tristan story are of Celtic—perhaps Cornish—origin,[22] yet there can be little doubt that many details of the Tristan story are derived from the tale of Apollonius, including the detail of Tristan's skill as an instrumentalist, an element for which no convincing Celtic analogue has yet been found.[23] The result of this confluence of story traditions was therefore a hero-harpist charged with the potent Celtic mystique which bewitched medieval listeners and readers for three centuries. As a glance at the story of Apollonius shows, this complex of story motifs allowed for some passing description of performance practice ('Apollonius took his tuning-key and then began to stir the harpstrings with skill'). This set of story motifs is the generating cell of every *lai*/harp passage in Old French fiction, and the history of the set—how it originated and came to exist as we find it—probably lies with the history of stories rather than with the history of music and performance practice. There are non-musical explanations for the emergence in twelfth-century French literature of (1) a protagonist who is a courtly amateur string-player, (2) whose chosen instrument is the harp, which he plays in a virtuosic way and (3) whose story unfolds in a Celtic world.

Those 'non-musical' explanations probably lie with what might be called 'metaphorical' realism: the realism which emerges when a network of story motifs which a culture has inherited from the past becomes a means of confronting current interests or anxieties. The motif of the hero-harpist was successful, I suggest, because it provided the means for mediating contemporary interest in the figure of the trouvère; many of the harper-heroes in Old French literature are composers (Horn is perhaps the most striking example).

On a deeper level the hero-harpist motif might be interpreted as a mediation of the relationship between music and the far-reaching mental changes which we generalise as the twelfth-century Renaissance. It is on the basis of this kind of interpretation that I drew upon the *Roman de Horn* in Chapter 1. While many of the musical details in that romance are probably realistic in a directly referential way (the composition of a song by a noble; the excitement at court which a new song causes, and so on), the frame which holds these details together—the motif of the hero-harpist—existed in all its essentials long before the trouvères.

The question remains of how the word *lai* became involved with this complex of narrative motifs. Here the answer may lie in the distinctively Celtic mystique of the hero-harpist, for as early as the twelfth century the word *lai*—at least in northern France—seems to have been charged with a powerful Celtic aura of its own. From around 1150 narrative literature in France and the Anglo-Norman realm begins to speak of *lais de Bretaigne*, and these references have caused a considerable amount of confusion. The story seems to begin with a legend that the Celtic Britons—the inhabitants of Brittany and of the British Isles before the English—were accustomed to compose works called *lais* to commemorate notable events which had taken place amongst them. This legend is embodied in a famous collection of narrative poems by the twelfth-century poetess Marie de France, who claims to be recounting certain notable events which gave rise to the composition of these *lais* amongst the ancient Britons.[24]

The reality behind this legend is unknown but may not be difficult to reconstruct, for there can be no doubt that a host of professional instrumentalists and story-tellers of Celtic extraction were active in France and England during the twelfth century; how else are we to explain (1) the huge fund of stories set in named areas of Wales, Scotland, Cornwall and Ireland which seem to have been available to French romancers in the second half of the twelfth century,[25] and (2) the many loose references to instrumentalists from *Bretaigne* to be found in twelfth-century fiction? It is easy to imagine these Celtic story-tellers—anxious, like all medieval narrators, to assert that they had the 'true' story—claiming that their stories, songs and instrumental pieces were actually derived from commemorative compositions produced in the very days of the ancient Britons themselves; there was no better way for professional entertainers to exploit the vogue for stories laden with the mystique of the ancient Celtic realms of the North. If, as is generally believed, the word *lai* is of Celtic origin, then there is little difficulty in explaining how that term became attached to the legend of these commemorative compositions.

Is this perhaps how the myth of the *lais de Bretaigne* was born? No minstrel, whatever his speciality, could afford to ignore the popularity of narrative material (such as the stories of King Arthur) charged with Celtic mystery, and the involvement of many kinds of entertainers in disseminating such stories—singers, narrators, string-players, and so on—may explain why it is almost impossible to form a clear impression of what the *lais de Bretaigne* mentioned by Marie de France and other authors actually comprised. It was in the interest of twelfth-century entertainers to keep the mythology of the ancient *lai* vague and mysterious; one minute a fiddler might wish to exploit it, the next, perhaps, a singer-narrator or a professional reader carrying a book of written stories.

Given the aura of Celtic mystery surrounding the term *lai*, it was inevitable that it should be drawn into the harper-hero motif which was itself so richly endowed with that aura. Since most of the harper-hero stories in Old French literature are actually set in Ancient Britain (the story of Tristan, for example), then a *lai* (in the sense 'an ancient composition of the Celtic Britons before the coming of the English') was the obvious thing for them to perform. When romancers actually quote the *lais* which their protagonists perform, the songs in question are never polymorphous lyrics *like the Lai d'Aélis* (Music example 19). However puzzling it may seem— and in some ways it seems very puzzling indeed—we should probably draw a firm distinction between pieces like the *Lai d'Aélis* and Music example 20; it was the latter that was directly involved in what might be called the *lai*-harp motif. It is possible, however, that pieces like the *Lai d'Aélis* were sometimes accompanied to give them a certain 'Celtic' glamour, especially in view of the close relationship between the *lai* and the *descort* (see above).

PART 2
PERFORMANCE PRACTICE

Our foreheads felt the wind and rain.
Our youth returned, for there was shed
On spirits that had long been dead,
Spirits dried up and closely furled,
The freshness of the early world.

Matthew Arnold, *The River*

9

Open-string instruments: tunings and techniques

> ...a small kind of tinkling which symbolised
> the aesthetic part of a young lady's education.
>
> George Eliot, *Middlemarch*

I

In Part 1 of this book I attempted to reconstruct an artistic tradition for the use of instruments in courtly monody. The purpose of Part 2 is to explore certain technical characteristics of instruments which bear directly upon the character of the accompaniments they would be able to provide—especially tuning-patterns and the use of drones or other heterophonic techniques.

It seems advisable to include every major kind of medieval instrument in this survey and yet the evidence for the use of plucked instruments in any kind of troubadour or trouvère song seems very slight. Time and time again it is the words *viella, viele* and *viola* which appear in sources that refer to the accompaniment of the voice and it would be no injustice to the evidence to devote the whole of this part of the book to bowed instruments. Nonetheless it would be hazardous to deny the possibility that open-string instruments participated in the performance of monophonic songs and I have therefore included them here.

One of the first thirteenth-century theorists to bring his Latin down to the level of wood and strings is the Englishman Amerus, whose *Practica Artis Musice* was completed in 1271. Amerus writes that a semitone[1]

> ...minor est tono voce et spacio, quod manifeste
> patet in musicis instrumentis. Ponatur quod quelibet
> littera gamme ponitur in corda sicut contigit in psalterio
> et cythara et huiusmodi instrumentis; et ubi due corde sunt
> propiores, ibi est semitonus, et alie corde equedistantes
> sunt toni.

> ... is less than a tone as may be clearly seen in musical
> instruments. Let a diagram be put down in which each letter
> of the gamut has a string, just as happens in the
> *psalterium* and *cythara* and with instruments of this kind;
> and where two strings are placed closer together there is a
> semitone, and the other strings which stand apart at equal
> intervals describe tones.

In the manuscripts of Amerus's treatise these comments on the *psalterium* and *cythara* (probably the pig-snout psaltery and the pillar harp) are accompanied by a drawing which does little to carry out the author's instructions. In the Bamberg manuscript, for example (Figure 10), only the semitones a-b-♮-c are marked with the corresponding strings 'placed closer together'; other semitone steps, such as E-F, are not indicated. Amerus's diagram seems to imply that open-string instruments were tuned diatonical-ly in the 1270s, and as late as the fifteenth century the *basic* tuning of a harp seems to have been a diatonic series.[2] The word 'basic' deserves to be italicised since it is tempting to believe that the increasing use of *musica ficta* in vocal music during the fourteenth century is likely to have exerted some pressure upon instrumentalists to adapt their tunings accordingly.

Several vernacular sources of the thirteenth century suggest that this did happen, at least amongst harpists. The hero-harpist romances examined in Chapter 8 often mention the hero's tuning-preliminary before playing, and while this 'tuning' motif can be traced as early as the *Gesta Herewardi* written by Richard of Ely between c1109 and 1131 (where the hero, Hereward, 'most skilfully tunes the strings' before playing),[3] it is tempting to assume that the hero-harpist romances embody a contemporary view of scordatura as one of the most telling signs of an expert harpist. There are several such tuning passages in the thirteenth-century *Tristan en prose*, one of the most widely-read chivalric romances of later-medieval France. At one stage in the narrative Iseut harps a *lai* in her chamber and is overheard by a harper who then offers to play her a *lai* himself. Iseut invites him to perform it and the harper begins by re-tuning the instrument, even though it has just been played by Iseut:[4]

> ... pren ceste harpe et lacorde a ta uolente selonc
> le cant de tes uers ... li harperes ... le commence a
> atemprer selonc ce kil sauoit kil couenoit au
> cant kil uoloit dire.

> ... take this harp [said Iseut], and tune it according
> to the music for your lines ... the harper ... then began
> to tune it according to what he knew would be necessary
> for the music he was about to perform.

Another reference to such scordatura occurs when a harp which has already been used by a young girl is passed to Tristan so that he may show what he knows of harping:[5]

Mesire Tristrans prent la harpe et le conmence
a atemprer a sa maniere et a sa guise. . . .

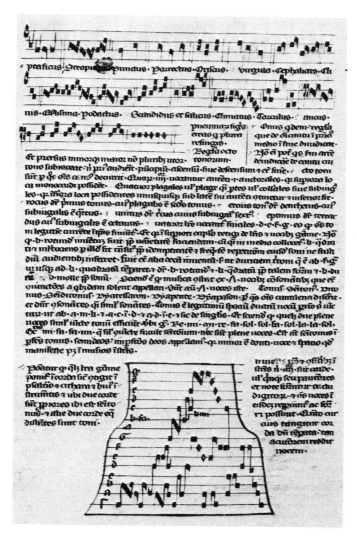

Figure 10 *Diagram of a pig-snout psaltery from Amerus,* Practica Artis Musice. *Bamberg, Staatsbibliothek, MS Misc.Lit. 115, f.74v. Reproduced by permission*

> Tristan takes the harp and begins to tune it in his
> way and after his fashion. . . .

Here is the familiar motif of the harper-hero who discards the tuning which a previous player has used; we remember Thomas's *Roman de Horn*. Yet the author of the *Tristan en prose* is even more determined than Thomas to stress the close relation between the hero's tuning-preliminary and the uniqueness of his musical skill; Tristan does not just re-tune the instrument artfully, he does so *a sa maniere et a sa guise*: in his way and after his fashion.

On another occasion it seems that two adjustments are involved. Tristan arrives with Hector before the house of Bréhus and is led before a young girl who sings beautifully. Tristan sings a *lai* which he composed himself, preparing for the performance by setting the harp 'according to the music which he wished to perform': *selonc le cant quil uoloit dire*.[6] Tristan announces the piece and then 'he begins it when he has tuned the harp another time': *il le conmenche adont quant il a la harpe atempre autre fois*.[7]

In the Vienna manuscript of the *Tristan en prose* we have the melodies for most of the *lais* performed in these scenes, but unfortunately they do not take us further forward.[8] The music of the *lai* which the harper-messenger performs for Iseut *(A vous, Amours, ains c'a nului)* reveals nothing about the messenger's use of scordatura since it is a simple diatonic melody which might be played on any set of strings set to a major scale.[9] Nor does the music reveal what may have been involved when Tristan tuned *a sa maniere et a sa guise*; the piece which Tristan re-sets for *(La u joe fui dedens la mer)* can be played with exactly the same diatonic arrangement as the piece which has just been performed *(Apres chou que je vi victoire)*.

Yet while they reveal little in precise terms, these passages from the *Tristan en prose* are telling insofar as they suggest a willingness on the part of aristocratic readers in thirteenth-century France and England to scrutinise the opening moments of a hero-harpist's performance and to imagine him setting the instrument in an artful and individualistic way: '. . . he begins to tune the strings above to those below' *(commence a acorder les cordes desus a celes desous)*; 'he accords some strings to the demands of others so that those below reply to those above in true sound and true accord' *(acorder les unes cordes a la raison des autres si que celes desous respondent a celes desus en droit son et en droit vers)*.[10] These references may not tell us much about the tunings used by thirteenth-century harpists, yet the way in which the romancers consistently associate exceptional harping-gifts with scordatura and individual settings (rather than with rapidity of execution, for example, or with complexity of embellishment) is most suggestive and may well be a window onto contemporary harping.

So may a remarkable passage in the *Lumiere as Lais* ('Light to the Laity'), a religious poem in Anglo-Norman which was completed at Oxford in 1267 by one Pierre of Peckham.[11] Pierre's attention turns to harping when he compares the condition of Man living in charity with the well-tuned strings of a harp. The motif is a common one in medieval literature, but Pierre's material is distinguished by the large amount of technical detail which it contains. It begins:[12]

Coment l'em deit temprer la harpe

Ky deyt harpe dreyt temprer,
Pur fere la en acord suner,
Les cordes couient si adrescer
Ke chescune acorde a sun per,
Solum dreyte proporciun.
Ke le oreylle iuge en le sun,
E sulum le art k'est troue
E par art de musike proue,
Ke deus acordent en diapason,
E deus en diatessaron,
E deus ausi en dyapente ...

How one should tune the harp

He who wishes to tune the harp aright
And make it sound harmoniously
Must arrange the strings
So that each one agrees with its fellow
According to true proportion.
Let the ear judge the sound
Both according to skill
And according to the demonstrable laws of music,
So that two accord in an octave
And two in a fourth
And two in a fifth ...

This is the work of a knowledgeable author who can deploy technical terms such as *dyapente, diatessaron, diapason, meyne* (for the theorists' *mese*), *espace* (for *spatium*) and *proporciun* (for *proporcio*) with confidence. For the most part it is dull in the extreme, but Pierre has one interesting detail to report:[13]

Les regards puet em chaunger,
Par tuens diuersement temprer,
E par diuers ordeynement
De semitoens diuersement.
Par la quele veie e nature
En harpe est la diuerse temprure.
Mes coment ke turne le curs
As treys touz jours auerunt recurs:

> Cume diapente, diapason
> Ensemble od diatessaron.

> One may change the settings
> By tuning different notes,
> And by different arrangements
> Of variously placed semitones.
> By this means
> There is diverse tuning in the harp.
> But wherever it may turn
> There will always be need of three:
> The fifth and the octave
> Together with the fourth.

Even though this use of *regards* to mean 'settings' cannot be documented (it may be a harpers' usage, something we would not expect to find recorded in the dictionaries)[14] Pierre's general meaning is clear: the basic diatonic sequence can be changed '... by different arrangements/Of variously placed semitones'.

Pierre may be speaking of chromatic adjustments, but not necessarily so: diatonic playing may demand a great deal of tuning-variation if a player wishes to play in different registers. Imagine ten strings of a thirteenth-century harp set to produce a major-scale sequence:

strings	1	2	3	4	5	6	7	8	9	10
intervals		T	T	S	T	T	T	S	T	T

If the player of a harp arranged in this way wished to play a melody with what we would describe as a minor character, and also wished to play it from the fourth string of his instrument upwards (perhaps in order to accompany a singer who wished to perform at that pitch), he would move from tuning (1) below to tuning (2):

(1) strings	———————————————	4	5	6	7	8	9	10
intervals			T	T	T	S	T	T

(2) strings	———————————————	4	5	6	7	8	9	10
intervals			T	S	T	T	S	T

For the harpist (who would not perform an infinite number of adjustments such as this, but only those which suited his particular needs and repertory) the retuning operation would involve a complex synchronisation of memory, hearing and touch: automatic movements whose rapidity and fluency were a measure of his experience and technique (and which listeners greatly admired, to judge by the evidence of the romances). Since this kind of adjustment only creates a new stepwise pattern of tones and semitones, it does not move outside the diatonic setting described by Amerus. Such diatonic arrangements and adjustments are sufficient to accommodate virtually all the written music which has survived from the period 1100-1300.

None the less there must have been some instrumentalists in the thirteenth century who needed more shelving for their musical ideas than could be borne by a row of diatonic strings. Those who wished to play written polyphony, for example, would sometimes have found a need for both f and f♯ (to employ modern concepts and terminology) so that they could play fifths over both b♭ and b♮ (two more notes they would often have required in the same piece). To employ medieval concepts and terminology: they would have needed to insert *ficte musice* into the *recta* notes of their tunings.

So it is suggestive that several fourteenth-century theorists appear to have considered *musica ficta* to be particularly necessary for musical instruments.[15] The anonymous author of the *Summa Musice* records that some instrument-makers were accustomed to insert a semitone on musical instruments between G *sol re ut* and F *fa ut*, while others placed one between G *sol re ut* and a *la mi re*; these adjustments, he comments, are chiefly made on 'that instrument which is called the organ', which seems to allow the possibility that similar *ficta* additions may have been made to such instruments as the harp and psaltery.[16]

A few decades later Jacques de Liège remarks that on some instruments, especially the organ, the tone may be divided almost everywhere (*quasi ubique*) into two unequal semitones, 'so that more music may be accomplished there and more harmonies and polyphony (*discantusque*), but this is of no profit in the music of the human voice'.[17] Here there is an explicit link between *musica ficta* and polyphony. For singers, *musica ficta* was intangible: something which they had been taught to conceptualise and then to execute in a certain way; but for the harpist, psaltery-player or organist every *ficta musica* was concretised as a separate string or an individual pipe that had to be planned for by makers (the *artifices* mentioned in the anonymous *Summa Musice*) and then absorbed into playing-technique. Whence, presumably, the theorists' awareness of the special importance of *musica ficta* to instrumentalists. A singer did not build extra semitones into his voice; every conceivable adjustment was present and waiting to be elicited by correct notation. The special emphasis which the theorists place upon the usefulness of *ficte musice* to organists is understandable since ecclesiastical organists were no doubt sometimes required to accompany choral singing and to play written polyphony upon their instruments.[18]

It is impossible to determine which *ficte musice* were most often employed by thirteenth-century string-players; nor can we assess how extensive their use of *ficte musice* may have been, save to say that a completely chromatic tuning (to use modern concepts and terminology) is perhaps unlikely to have been used. What can be said, however, is that the most literate instrumentalists are likely to have paid close attention to what we would now call temperament when they used semitone adjustments. Jacques de Liège reports that instrumentalists divided the tone into two unequal semitones, implying that literate players were careful to maintain the Pythagorean distinction between the major and the minor semitone.[19]

There is an appreciable difference between the two intervals; expressed in the convenient form of cents (one hundredths of a tempered semitone) it amounts to 24 cents, nearly a quarter of the modern tempered semitone. The most common *ficta musica* of the thirteenth century, f♯ (to use modern terms and concepts again), is a minor semitone (90 cents) away from the g above. Since Gothic musicians regarded the semitone as the 'condiment' of music it is unlikely that they would have been careless with such delicate spices.[20] We may imagine that an octave of harp or psaltery strings tuned by a trained musician with *ficta* semitones placed between c and d and f and g might have sounded something like this (the numbers indicate cents):

114		90		204		90		114		90		204	204		90	

C	C♯	D	E	F	F♯	G	a	♮	c

II

Once tuned, the strings of an instrument become a trellis to shape the florescence of the player's invention. The harp and psaltery offered the medieval player an elaborate lattice of strings with considerable scope for interlacing his music. It is possible to imagine a medieval harpist or psaltery-player producing drones with the lower strings, for example, having perhaps assigned a particular course, or courses, to that function (compare the special drone-pipe of the thirteenth-century organ, the *bordunus organorum*).[21] Psaltery-players would have come into their own with the technique of flourishing a melody with parallel intervals in the manner of improvised *organum*; once they had tuned the unison pairs of their double-courses into octaves or fifths they could produce thickened volutions of sound from their standard playing-technique.

This is all speculation, of course; yet there is scattered and fragmentary evidence that all of these techniques may have been exploited by medieval harpists and psaltery-players. We begin with the word *bourdon*. When used in connection with parts of instruments in the thirteenth century its meaning usually lies in the area of 'something which produces an unvarying

118

note, drone'. Thus the bagpipe's drone was termed *bourdon* and the drone-pipe of an organ was a *bordunus organorum*; the lateral, unstopped strings of fiddles were *borduni*.[22] In some cases the term *borduni* lingered well into the Renaissance; we find the bottom course of the lute named *bordon* in late fifteenth-century Spain, for example,[23] and the lowest string of the dulcimer named *bourdon* in seventeenth-century France.[24]

So it may be significant that the lowest strings of the harp appear to have been called *bourdons* in thirteenth-century French (or Anglo-Norman, to be precise). Let us turn back to Pierre of Peckham's *Lumiere as Lais*. Pierre relates that the harp may be tuned in various ways with differing patterns of tones and semitones; yet however diversely it is tuned, he continues, there will always be a need for the octave, fifth and fourth:[25]

> Kar saunz ices ne purra mie
> En harpe estre sun de armonie.
> Les essais e les burduns
> De ces treis unt ausi les suns.

> For without these there cannot
> be any harmonious sound in the harp.
> The *essais* and the *burduns*
> also exhibit these three sounds.

The terms *essais* and *burduns* are presumably intended to cover the whole string band from high to low, and as all known usages of bourdon-words display the idea of deepness, the *burduns* are presumably the lower strings and the *essais* the higher ones.[26] Everything which we know about the application of bourdon-words to components of instruments in Pierre's lifetime suggests that the lowest strings of the harp acquired the name *burdun* because they were (or had once been) used for drone-playing.

A few crabbed words squeezed into the margin of a copy of Alain de Lille's *Anticlaudianus* may help us trace these harp-bourdons a little further. Alain tells how *Natura* desires to make a perfect man and how *Prudentia* is sent to Heaven as an ambassador to obtain a soul for him. Journeying through Air and amidst the Music of the Spheres, she hears the 'celestial cythara', sounding so softly 'that it performs the function of a string lying lower' (.. *neruique iacentis/Inferius gerit illa uicem* ...).[27] At this point a fifteenth-century copy of the text in the library of Balliol College, Oxford, has an important annotation:[28]

> corde ordinate in inferiore parte cithare que dicitur bordon
> *neruique iacentis*

> of the string called *bordon* which is arranged in the lower
> part of the cithara.

In accordance with prevailing medieval usage this *cithara* with its *bordon* may be a pillar-harp.[29]

If harpists used drone-strings (at least in the twelfth and thirteenth centuries) then two references to open-string playing from that period gain something in force and clarity. In his *Topographia Hibernica* of 1185–8 Gerald of Wales gives a striking account of the string-playing skills of the Irish. The musicians of Ireland, Gerald relates, 'play quite freely the tinklings of the thinner strings along with the duller sound of the thicker one' (*sub obtuso grossioris chordae sonitu, gracilium tinnitus licentius ludunt*).[30] This reference to 'a thicker [string]' in the singular may be nothing more than a stylistic flourish adorning the simple thought: 'they make the deep strings accompany the higher ones'. Gerald's writing is full of such plain earthenware as this, fired to a high glaze by rhetoric. But in this case his meaning may be made of finer matter for he had almost certainly heard Irish harping,[31] and his 'thicker string' with its 'deep sound' might conceivably be a drone-bourdon accompanying the melody in the treble.

There may be an echo of such a bourdon-technique in an unpublished psalm-commentary now in the Bodleian Library at Oxford, and probably dating from the twelfth or thirteenth century. Here an anonymous commentator steps outside accepted traditions of describing the Psalmist's *cithara* and records that ' ... two hands are used in playing the *cithara*; one hand continually (*iugiter*) plucks the lower strings; the other hand plucks the higher strings, not continually, but at intervals and in turn' (*non iugiter sed vicissim et interpollatim*).[32] There is no escaping the firmness of the author's distinction between lower strings which are plucked continually and higher ones which are plucked intermittently. Perhaps the lower strings are drones, plucked constantly to accompany the higher strings which are touched 'at intervals and in turn' as they are used for melody.

A drone, firmly planted, can provide a player with the trunk of a technique, but it is melody that ramifies his art. It will never be known how medieval harpists and psaltery players executed their tunes, what graces and ornaments they used, what tricks of phrasing they employed. Here and there a poet, busy about some other matter, allows us to glimpse a little of what has been lost in oblivion; the author of *Galeran de Bretagne*, for example, mentions a melodic style (or playing technique?) called 'Saracen notes',[33] but nothing is known of them. However, amongst these poetic references a few fragments of evidence suggest some use of parallelism and improvised heterophony. The *Sermones* of the twelfth-century German satirist Sextus Amarcius incorporate a luxuriant description of a performance upon the *chelys* (?lyre)[34] where Sextus even notices the material from which the strings are made (see Appendix 4:8). Fortunately his eye for detail also extends to the performer's technique: as the musician delivers a programme of narrative songs (or declaimed poems?) he 'repeatedly adjusts the melodious strings in fifths' (*Ille fides aptans crebro diapente canoras*).[35] This sounds like a tuning-prelude, but 'adjusts' may not be the best translation for *aptans*;

perhaps 'he accommodates/harmonises the melodious strings' would be better (the minstrel has already done his preliminaries—including, presumably, his tuning—a few lines earlier). Some kind of fifth-based heterophony during performance may be implied.

We reach slightly firmer ground with the account of harping in the *Roman de Horn* of c1170.[36] Two verbs denote the techniques Horn deploys: *chanter* and *organer*. Among the surviving texts which may be regarded as part of Thomas's literary heritage there is only one other instance of this pair: in Wace's *Brut* (1155). The occasion is a liturgical celebration during King Arthur's plenary court at Caerleon: [37]

> As processiuns out grant presse,
> Chescuns d'aler avant s'engresse.
> Quant la messe fu comenciee,
> Ke le jur fu mult exalciee,
> Mult oïssiez orgues suner
> E clers chanter e organer,
> Voiz abaissier e voiz lever,
> Chanz avaler e chanz munter;
> Mult veïssiez par les mustiers
> Aler e venir chevaliers;
> Tant pur oïr les clers chanter,
> Tant pur les dames esgarder,
> D'un mustier a l'altre cureient
> . . . . .

> There was a great press of people at the procession as
> each one pushed forward. When the mass
> (which was especially solemn for that occasion) was
> begun, you might have heard much noise of organs and
> clerics *chanter e organer*, voices raised and lowered,
> music mounting up and falling down; you would have
> seen the knights coming and going between the churches,
> running from one to the other both to hear the clerics
> singing and to look upon the ladies.

Here is the corresponding passage in Wace's source, Geoffrey of Monmouth's *Historia Regum Britannie:*[38]

> Postremo processione peracta . tot organa tot cantus
> in utriusque fiunt templis . ita ut pre nimia dulcedine
> milites qui aderant nescirent quod templorum prius
> peterent . Cateruatim igitur nunc ad hoc. nunc ad illud
> ruebant.

> Afterwards, when the procession was over, so many *organa*,
> so many chants are accomplished in both churches that

121

because of the great sweetness of the music those knights
who were there did not know which church they should enter
first. They flocked in crowds, first to this one and then to
the other.

Geoffrey's *organa* are probably to be interpreted as polyphonic liturgical pieces rather than as pipe-organs ('*organa* ... are accomplished' seems an unidiomatic way to say 'organs are played'). Wace certainly does add a reference to pipe-organs as he renders the passage (*Mult oïssiez orgues suner*) but then goes on to mention the clerics who *chanter e organer*. If his verb *organer* means simply 'to play the organ' then he is repeating himself ('you might have heard much noise of organs and of clerics singing and playing the organ'); I think it more likely that *chanter* and *organer* refer to vocal music—as both Geoffrey of Monmouth's meaning and Wace's subsequent lines ('voices raised and lowered') suggest. *Chanter* would then denote the performance of plainchant and *organer* the singing of liturgical polyphony. This might suggest that Thomas's opposition of *chanter* and *organer* distinguishes monophonic melody (*chanter*) from some kind of heterophonic accompaniment (*organer*). As was the case with the poem of Sextus Amarcius, this passage leaves us with a lingering suspicion that Thomas is describing some kind of tuning-preamble (where *organer* might denote the simultaneous sounding of strings in octaves and fifths to tune them). However, Thomas's text discourages us from drawing a firm distinction between tuning on the one hand and performance on the other. His account of harping reminds us of certain non-Western playing traditions such as that of the north-east African *krar*, a bowl-lyre, whose player 'carefully checks and rechecks the accuracy of the tuning ... often making minor corrections while simultaneously playing partially improvised sequences based on the melodic phrase of the song'.[39]

III

We have been concentrating on the harp where the material is richest. But what of the members of the zither family—the psaltery, the *rota*, the *medius canon* and the rest?

The *psalterium* was of passing interest to some of the music-theorists since it had a string for every note and therefore lay within the conceptual field of traditional music-theory. The *Speculum Musice* of Jacques de Liège, for example, contains several passages in which various matters of musical mathematics and acoustics are explored through the *psalterium* ('if the string of a psaltery is touched with a quill in a deliberate or accidental way ...').[40] Some theorists may even have compiled treatises on the proportions of psaltery strings, for Engelbert of Admont seems to refer to such essays in his treatise.[41] No such work is known to survive. The closest we come to a treatise *de brevitate et extensione chordarum psalterii* is a brief passage in Amerus's *Practica Artis Musice* of 1271 where there is mention of the *psalterium* as an instrument which has a string for every letter of the gamut and an accompanying diagram shows a schematic psaltery of the familiar pig-snout form (see above, p.112 and Figure 10). This would seem to point to a diatonic tuning.

This meagre information from the theorists can be supplemented with some extracts from Petrus de Abano's *Expositio problematum Aristotelis*, begun in Paris and completed at Padua in 1310.[42] Abano's work is extremely valuable for the precise and unique information which it provides about the number of strings used on the *cythera, zigga, rubeba, medius canon* and *rota*. He does not describe their tunings, but by collating his information with the evidence of Amerus we may hazard a reconstruction of the dispositions of the open-string instruments.

We pass over the *cythera* (4 strings) which is presumably the gittern or the citole, the *zigga* (4 strings) which is probably a bowed instrument, and the *rubeba* (2 strings), which is undoubtedly the bowed instrument described by Jerome of Moravia (see below, p.126). This leaves the *medius canon* and the *rota*, both open-stringed instruments. The *medius canon* must be a form of psaltery related to the *qānūn*; Abano says that it has 64 strings, which is exactly the number recorded for the *qānūn* by the fourteenth-century Persian treatise *Kanz al-tuḥaf*.[43] The *rota* is the triangular zither with strings on both sides of the soundbox (Figure 11); according to Abano this double string-band was an archaic feature, and comprised 22 strings in each band, making a total of 44.[44] In addition to these figures Abano mentions other string-totals without specifying the instruments to which they belong:

Figure 11 The rota. Note the double row of tuning-pegs and the position of the player's hands. The double string-band of the rota is mentioned in the early fourteenth century by Petrus de Abano. Twelfth-century sculpture from Surgères.

123

medius canon	64
rota	22+22
unspecified	28
unspecified	44

This is valuable information—there is almost nothing like it elsewhere—but Abano goes further. He remarks that some of these string-totals are reducible to a certain number of *notiores*, 'more notable' strings. These are his figures:

28	reduce to	7 *notiores*
44	reduce to	11 *notiores*
64	reduce to	16 *notiores*

Each of the numbers in the left-hand column is divisible by 2 and by 4, suggesting that these instruments, whatever they may be, are equipped with double or quadruple courses. Assuming for a moment that they are double-course, we arrive at the figures of 14, 22 and 32 courses for each instrument. In contrast, the numbers of 'more notable' strings in the right-hand column have no common denominator (in two cases, 7 and 11, they are not divisible at all). I assume that the left-column gives a census of the *strings* on each instrument while the right-hand column lists the 'more notable' *courses*:

14 double courses have 7 'more notable' courses

22 double courses have 11 'more notable' courses

32 double courses have 16 'more notable' courses

In each case, therefore, half of the courses are classified as *notiores*.

Abano reveals this information in the process of explaining how strings were added to the ancient Greek lyre. The core of that instrument, according to Abano, was a scalar sequence efgabcde, whose notes were 'more essential than the others' on the instrument (*ceteris essentialiores*).[45] The instrument grew around these 'more essential' strings as notes were added above and below them. By applying a diatonic tuning to the figures given by Abano we arrive at an approximate disposition for the *medius canon* and *rota*.

As for the playing-techniques of psalteries, we learn almost nothing from medieval writers. Yet there is some suggestive post-medieval evidence to be harvested from the pages of Mersenne's celebrated *Harmonie Universelle* of 1635. Mersenne gives a fairly detailed account of a *psalterion* which is a small hammer dulcimer, but in the text he records that it may be played with a quill (or with the fingers) and it is therefore a relative of the medieval psaltery in more than name.[46] The drawing displays one striking feature: the lowest string, which stands on bridges of its own, is tuned a fourth below the next string. In the text Mersenne calls this low string a *bourdon*. Now many Gothic illustrations of psalteries, from all periods and places, show players with one finger extended over the lowest course (or courses) of their instruments;[47] this posture suggests that they may be plucking just such *bourdons* as are shown in Mersenne's diagram of the *psalterion*.

There is one more detail in Mersenne's account of the *psalterion* which may be a relic of medieval practice. He records that the courses may sometimes be tuned in octaves together with fifths and fifteenths 'to augment the harmony'.[48] If such parallel harmony was acceptable in the dulcimer-playing of seventeenth-century France (and Mersenne seems to have admired the *psalterion*), it is not likely to have been shunned in the Middle Ages when the technique of parallel organum was still cultivated by some liturgical singers.[49] It is tempting to build on Mersenne's evidence and try a very tentative reconstruction of a possible Gothic psaltery-tuning after this fashion. As the player's quill plectra elicited a ringing sound from the metal strings, and as the melody moved in parallel fifths over a drone (which may itself have been compounded from unisons and fifths), the psaltery's sound-picture would have been a colourful one and a world away from the silvery thread of melody which we may hear in our mind's ear upon first seeing images of psalteries in medieval manuscripts and carvings.

10

Jerome of Moravia and stopped-string instruments

For wise he was, and many curious arts,
Postures of runes and healing herbs he knew.

Matthew Arnold, *Balder Dead*

I

Jerome of Moravia's chapter on fiddles opens with the *rubeba*, an instrument whose Arabic name and single pair of strings suggest a relationship with the modern *rabab* of Morocco. In Jerome's lifetime we find this instrument depicted in one of the celebrated *Cantigas* manuscripts, probably produced in Seville c1275. At this date the *rubeba* may only just have reached as far north as Paris (for the term *rubebe* first appears in Parisian vernacular sources around 1270)[1] and Jerome seems very keen to define the *rubeba* ('a musical instrument played with a bow ...') as if it were unfamiliar to his readers.

According to his account the two strings of the *rubeba* were tuned a fifth apart—another link with the Moroccan *rabab*—allowing the player to produce a full octave without using the weak fourth finger (although Jerome allows that it may be used to produce a ninth note). He is quite explicit that once the little finger has been employed the *rubeba* can ascend no further and the technique of changing position is nowhere envisaged in his chapter.

The *viella* or five-stringed fiddle comes next (Figure 7), a much more versatile instrument which has not one tuning but three:[2]

1	D	Γ	G	d	d
2	D	Γ	G	d	g
3	Γ	Γ	D	c	c

That is, in modern letter-notation (relative pitch):

1	*d*	*G*	*g*	*d'*	*d'*
2	*d*	*G*	*g*	*d'*	*g'*
3	*G*	*G*	*d*	*c'*	*c'*

In tuning 1 the d-course, which Jerome calls the *bordunus*, runs to the side of the fingerboard and cannot be stopped by the fingers.

Tuning 1

The syntax of the first tuning is perhaps that the *G* and *g* strings form an octave pair while the two *d'* strings make a unison double-course:

$$d \qquad Gg \qquad d'd'$$

Viewed in this way the tuning looks like a simple fifth *g–d'* which has been heaped-up (1) by doubling the *g* an octave lower, and (2) by filling in that octave step with *d*. It is an accretion of ideas and devices that suggests a vital and generative playing-tradition. The tradition stipulated five strings for the *viella* (the number mentioned by Elias of Salomon); in this first tuning the five-string set has been formed into three courses, each of which is the focus of a separate idea: a unison pair, an octave pair, and a single string running to the side of the fingerboard which may be plucked with the thumb as well as bowed. Each of these ideas represents a distinct design upon sound and it is this which makes Jerome's treatise so engaging; few other writings take us to that part of the medieval string-player's mind where sounds were imagined and then sought after.

What did thirteenth-century fiddlers hear in their mind's ear which brought them to this tuning? A comparison with the modern violin may be instructive here. The four courses of a violin do not represent different designs upon sound, but one design: each course is single; each is planned to blend in sonority with the others and each stands the same distance away from its fellow. In addition, the violin's tuning is not chordal (a pile of fifths produces cacophony) but is designed to produce a single line passing smoothly from string to string without any disjunctions in the quality of the sound—only a pleasing rise in brilliance as the melody moves to higher strings and an increasing warmth and vibrancy as it falls to lower ones.

The fundamental contrast between the modern violinist and the thirteenth-century *viellator* is therefore that the violinist generally thinks in terms of pure monophony whereas his medieval predecessor cultivated devices that would produce both melody and heterophony: auxiliary noises clustering around any tune he played. This distinction, a measure of the great difference between the thirteenth-century fiddler's ear and the modern violinist's, is clearly embodied in the tunings of the two instruments: the *viella* chordal, the violin melodic. The accordatura of the *viella* points to the thirteenth-century fiddler's distinctive tendency to think of his art in terms of simultaneously sounding strings.

The next important contrast is that whereas the violinist seeks a certain homogeneity and continuity, the medieval fiddler who used Jerome's first tuning was apparently looking for disjunctions. This tuning unloads three different colour-making devices upon five strings, and each device is used once only: unison pair, octave pair, and *bourdon*. As the player crossed from course to course, from *Gg* to *d'd'* and back again, his melody would comprise a series of parallel octaves one moment and a chain of reinforced unisons the next. The mixture of harmonics in the tune would be constantly, and abruptly, changing. And there would be a further disjunction in that all the notes played upon the double course *Gg* would set up an octave-ambiguity leaving the ear uncertain as to where the melody was located, high or low. Once the player shifted to the top course *d'd'* this ambiguity would be suddenly (but only temporarily) resolved as the octave doubling dropped away, leaving two strings sounding in a powerful, perhaps even strident unison.

To these disjunctions would be added a third: the percussive, plucked drone of the *bordunus*.

The purpose of these devices was presumably to create an impression of density, changeability and abundance with just five strings: to confuse the ear's awareness of what was actually happening by setting up the kind of *brouillard sonore*, 'sonorous mist', so beloved of non-Western string-players in many traditions and[3]

> ... often intensified by the attachment of additional strings (sympathetic strings on the sitar), special resonators (huge calabashes on the vina) or responsive buzzers or bells ... metal rings to the strings, blurring the sound but ... giving greater projection.

The character of this first tuning might therefore be said to be more heterophonic than polyphonic, for although there is nothing in the arrangement which would actually prevent a player from performing a line in a written polyphonic composition if he wished, the tuning seems to have been primarily designed to create disjunctions that thread a texture of auxiliary noise through monophonic melody.

Tuning 3

At this point it will be helpful to jump to Jerome's third tuning, which carries this heterophonic tendency further still. The arrangement of the strings is probably:

$$GG \quad d \quad c'c'$$

Here a disjunction is introduced by the leap of a seventh between the middle *d* course and the top pair *c'c'*. In terms of post-medieval concepts of bowed string-playing this seems an outlandish gap, but Jerome's first tuning has prepared us for such a thing. Here the thirteenth-century fiddler seems to be pushing for heterophony even at the expense of the facility which, in post-medieval bowing, is so important: the ability to produce a smooth melodic line throughout a generous compass. In the first tuning we saw Jerome's *viellator* arranging his five strings into two double courses and a lateral bourdon; in this third arrangement the fiddler seems to be thinking of all five strings as one large, humming block. In the disposition *GG d c'c'* the leap of a seventh between *d* and *c'c'* makes little sense if we think of a *viella* tuned in this way as a primarily melodic instrument; why should any fiddler who wished to play melodies running from course to course have set a seventh between some of his strings? With the first-position resources of the period a player could reach to *g* or perhaps to *a* on the *d* course, leaving him with a gap of a fourth or minor third between those stopping positions and the next open course *c'c'*. Surely we would do better to see this tuning as a constant drone-chord *GGd* with a melodic facility of a fifth (provided by the top string) running over it.

Such a tuning would have been ideal for the short melodic fragments of the *chansons de geste* which seem to have loomed large in the repertory of French professional *viellatores* during the thirteenth century.[4] The sole-surviving example of a *chanson de geste* melody (possibly the music for a form of the epic of *Girart de Roussillon*)[5] spans only a fourth and would therefore be suited to performance on a *viella* tuned in Jerome's third manner:

Example 21

Au – di – gier, dit   Raim – ber – ge,   bou – se vous di.

More than any other information we have about the tuning of medieval instruments, Jerome's third accordatura highlights the distance which separates modern notions of string-playing from medieval ones. It shows how the *viellator*'s tendency to think in terms of simultaneously sounding strings could go so far as to allow the melodic scope of five strings to wither down to the scope of only one string: a fifth. Self-accompaniment, through heterophony, is the priority.

Tuning 2

Jerome's second tuning is an exception to all this, and it may be some confirmation of the interpretations we have offered so far that Jerome also saw it as an arrangement requiring some special comment. In this tuning the strings produce the same notes as in tuning 1 save for the top string, which lies a fourth higher:

$$d \qquad Gg \qquad d' \qquad g'$$

This second tuning, says Jerome, 'is necessary for secular and all other kinds of songs, especially irregular ones, which frequently wish to run through the whole hand'.[6] As we have already seen above (p.65), this is a problematic remark, for it may be doubted whether there are any pieces of thirteenth-century music in existence which run through the *whole* gamut, a compass of two octaves and a sixth.

Now we move from uncertain ground to the most dangerous terrain. After the strange landscape of tuning 3 (*GG d c'c'*) with its small shoot of melody in a bed of drones, tuning 2 (*d Gg d' g'*) seems to bring us home to country that we recognise. It has a wide compass (two octaves and a fifth when the top string is fingered) and therefore appears to have been shaped by the concern for playing melody through a generous compass which has characterised much art-bowing since the Renaissance; it puts us in mind, perhaps, of a round-bridged *viella* where all strings may be played individually in the interests of clear, smooth melody, as on a violin.

Yet is this necessarily an accurate view of Jerome's tuning? Consider the arrangement and 'pitch' of the strings. This second disposition has often been presented as a continuously ascending series *G d g d' g'*, while Jerome's use of gamma to denote the lowest string of the set (nominally equivalent to *G*) has prompted the view that the bottom of some thirteenth-century fiddles actually sounded in the region of modern *G* at the bottom of the bass clef—or even lower.[7] But this is probably a false picture of Jerome's instrument. To take the pitch question first, if Jerome had called the lowest string anything other than gamma he would have been unable to record the stopped pitches of tuning 2. That tuning spans two octaves and a fifth; a tone less than the *musica recta* gamut. If Jerome had started mid-way in the gamut, for example, he would have exhausted the notational signs available to him before he reached the ceiling of the instrument's compass.

As for the order of the courses, Jerome says that the first four strings produce the same notes as in tuning 1 (*d Gg d' ...*) save that the top string is tuned to *g'* and the *d bordunus* is allowed to run over the fingerboard so that it may be stopped; he is quite explicit about these details and so it seems that tuning 2, like tuning 1, is re-entrant.[8]

What of the *G* and *g'* strings? Do they form an octave course as they seem to do in tuning 1? In all probability they do. The open strings of tuning 2 span two octaves $(G\text{–}g')$, more or less the limit of what seems to have been attainable with medieval gut on instruments such as the *viella* where all the strings must be of the same length.[9] Much further than this and players would have had to endure constant breakages at the top together with poor tone and tuning instability at the bottom. It seems likely therefore that the tone of the G in tuning 2 *d G g d′ g′* would have been only just satisfactory, and in this tuning, where all the strings were used melodically, would probably have required the reinforcement which it also receives in tuning 1 (where it is doubled at the octave) and in tuning 3 (where it is doubled at the unison). We seem to have been led away somewhat from the idea of this tuning as a vehicle for melody or even sonority.

When the *viellator* ran through the compass of his instrument it would have sounded like this (relative pitch):

Example 22

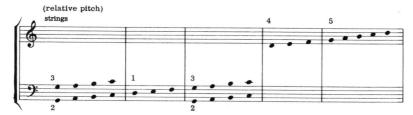

Jerome's three *viella* tunings imply at least two different instruments. It is obvious that 3 *GG d c′c′* could not be established with the same set of strings as 1 *d Gg d′d′*. The same may be said of 1 and 2:

$$
\begin{array}{ll}
1 & d \quad Gg \ d'd' \\
2 & d \quad Gg \ d' \quad g'
\end{array}
$$

Although the first four strings of each arrangement are tuned in the same way, and while the replacement of the lateral *d* bourdon used in tuning 1 back on the fingerboard for tuning 2 would be only a minor operation, a fiddler who wished to pull the top *d′* string of tuning 1 up a fourth to *g′* for tuning 2 would encounter problems of string-breakage and tuning instability. This does not prove, of course, that players did not sometimes create tuning 2 out of tuning 1, but it might have made their lives easier to carry a second *viella*.

II

A crucial determinant of a bowed instrument's technique is its bridge.[10] If it is round, as on a violin, then the player can bow each string individually; if it is entirely flat, he must bow all the strings at once. Whence an insuperable problem: we know very little about the bridges of medieval bowed instruments.

Bridges are often shown in pictorial sources, but it is very doubtful whether this material will ever provide enough accurate and trustworthy evidence to serve as a basis for reconstructing thirteenth-century fiddle-technique. The problem is not simply that medieval artists must often have been ill-informed about technical minutiae such as fiddle-bridges; it is also that a flat-topped bridge can be turned into an effectively round one by cutting string-slots of graded depth.[11] This simple fact vitiates much of the iconographical evidence which has been brought into the debate concerning round and flat bridges on medieval fiddles. (Iconographers will find this a harsh judgement, but they will be the first to admit that very few pictorial sources are precise enough to incorporate such a detail as this.)

Jerome's evidence throws a little light on this problem for his chapter clearly points to the use of heterophonic, self-accompanying devices (especially the drone) which would be well-served by having all the strings lying in a single plane or, perhaps better, in a slight arc. Tuning 3 *GG d c'c'* seems hardly intelligible unless we interpret it as a drone-block *GGd* with a melody running above it, while tunings 1 and 2 are completely concordant: each forms a consonant chord without a third, suggesting that the bow is intended to touch several strings at a time. Tunings like these, mixing fourths and fifths, are not the most advantageous ones for melodic playing (compare the violin's neat pile of fifths), but they are ideal for the kind of polychordal execution where the player uses only the 'home key' of his instrument (in this case *g*, to use modern concepts and terminology) and is therefore always safe to fill out his melody by brushing adjacent strings. I suspect that many thirteenth-century fiddlers played in this way, and it is doubtful whether many of them can have shared the modern notion of a 'tune': a melody abstracted from its accompaniment and from the reflexes of eye and hand necessary to play it on a particular instrument.

What happened when thirteenth-century *viellatores* played was presumably something like this: the five strings were disposed in a slight arc so that players could sound all five at once by applying some pressure to the bow, or choose them individually or in pairs by bowing delicately; with the five strings arranged in this way an appreciable number of combinations would be possible and melodies would be embedded in a constantly changing 'drone'.

III

We have lingered long with the *viella*, but what of other fingerboard instruments: the lutes, gitterns and citoles? A few scraps of evidence suggest that they may have been tuned and played in ways comparable to the practices of *viellatores*. We have already seen that the author of the *Summa Musice* records that fingerboard instruments 'are tuned in the consonances of octave, fourth and fifth, and by putting down their fingers the players of these make tones and semitones for themselves ...'.[12] This certainly sounds like the kind of tuning which Jerome describes, and the advantages to a medieval lutenist or gittern-player of a tuning mixing octaves, fourths and fifths to produce some kind of accordatura are obvious. Everything we have said about the fiddler's wish to turn his instrument into a heterophonic, self-accompanying resource might also be applied to players of plucked fingerboard instruments.

Here the evidence of certain sixteenth-century lute-duets, where one lute plays a constant drone to accompany the florid melody of another, is most suggestive. These pieces may well be a relic of medieval practice[13] and the same might be said for the drone-tunings which some of them employ. In the light of these pieces a tuning such as *d a d' g'* (which accords with the evidence of the *Summa Musice* and of some sixteenth-century lute sources)[14] seems a possibility for Gothic lutes, gitterns and citoles. By stopping the top course a tone above the nut, the player would produce a full accordatura of *d a d' a'*. The gap of a fourth between the top two courses breaks the accordatura but is none the less ideal for drone-playing; it is comfortable for the player to have a finger or two on the fingerboard when the full drone is produced—to hold down the drone, as it were—rather than to find his left hand suddenly redundant every time a sweep of all four strings is required.

The obscurity which surrounds these plucked instruments only emphasises the nimbus of light around the *viella*, the reigning instrument in the second feudal age. In the thirteenth century the *viella* found its way into almost every area of intellectual life: the sermon; the music-treatise; the psalm commentary; the gloss upon Aristotle; the romance. No instrument came more readily to the mind of a thirteenth-century author in search of a comparison or figure of speech. A passage from a treatise on composing sermons by the Franciscan friar Thomas Waleys provides my favourite example. Waleys tells of a Master of Theology whose sermons were always greeted with great applause, and who loaned a copy of one of his sermons to a lesser man eager for the same success. The borrower preached it only to find that he evoked lukewarm response from his hearers. He returned to the *magister* and asked why he had not achieved an equal success, and the master, looking for a delicate way to point up the other's failings as a preacher, replied:[15]

'My dear friend, I loaned you my *viella*, but you do not have the bow with which I touch its strings.'

11

Conclusions: voices and instruments

The High Style troubadour and trouvère song

The main thesis of this book has been that our understanding of the role of accompaniment in courtly monody must be based upon a sense of genre. It has not generally been recognised by musicologists that there are many aspects of troubadour and trouvère song which may be profitably approached from the point of view of genre (e.g. the question of rhythm; see above, p.16 and Figure 2).

Although the evidence pertaining to the use of accompaniment in these repertories is very fragmentary and will only permit the most tentative conclusions, there does seem to be a pattern in the evidence which survives. It suggests that the High Style song (Music examples 1, 2, 6, 7, 10, 15 and 16), the summit of the lyric genre system in both Old Provençal and Old French, was originally associated with performance by solo voice alone. During the thirteenth century in France this 'Occitan' ethos was weakened, to be replaced by a more liberal use of instruments with the rise of a written tradition of trouvère monody and the emergence of a class of string-playing *clercs*, especially in Paris.

It is consistent with this picture that the evidence from twelfth-century Occitania also points to instrumental involvement in two genres which can be contrasted with the High Style song: the *dansa* (where the contrast is one of form and ethos, although the tone of *dansa* poetry comes increasingly close to that of High Style poetry as the thirteenth century draws to a close), and the *descort* (where the contrast is a far-reaching one of form). The evidence for instrumental participation in the *dansa* runs from the last decades of the twelfth century through to the *Doctrina de Compondre Dictats*, probably from the close of the thirteenth. There is also good evidence for instrumental involvement with the *descort*. Whether this 'involvement' comprised an accompaniment to sung performances of these lyric genres, or whether it was restricted to instrumental performance of their melodies, is not clear at present.

134

The *lai*

As far as can be discerned, the references to accompanied *lais* in romances such as the *Tristan en prose* do not refer to the polymorphous lyrics which musicologists (following an established usage in both Old and Middle French) now call *lai* (Music example 19). In those cases where it can be established what a romancer means by *lai* (i.e. when the song in question is quoted, either as a song with music or simply as a poem without notation), the *lai* is usually a strophic song in quatrains of a kind scarcely found outside the romances (Music example 20).

Dance-songs

Refrain songs which could be performed for dancing such as the *dansa* (Music example 8) and *rondet* (example 5) seem to have been closely associated with accompaniment both in Occitania and France. However, instruments do not appear to have been much used when songs of this order were performed for the populous *corea*.

The *pastourelle*

The genre of the *pastourelle* in both north and south seems to occupy an interesting middle position between the High and Lower Styles. The *pastourelle* is almost invariably narrative, and shares a great deal of its lyric registration with simple dance-songs (the outdoor setting with rustic girls and shepherdesses; diminutive suffixes in *-ette*, and so on). As we have seen, the *Leys d'Amors* associate the *pastorela* with a melodic style which should be a 'little more fast and lively' than that of the chief High Style forms, the *vers* and *canso*, and the music of some French *pastourelles* is full of the conspicuous melodic patternings and short-range repetitions which we have associated with instruments; the celebrated *pastourelle* by Moniot d'Arras, *Ce fut en mai*, for example, which tells in its opening stanza how the poet heard a *viele* in the woods, is effectively an *estampie* with two *puncta* in its musical form. This is an exceptional piece, perhaps, yet there seems good reason to believe that *pastourelles* may often have been accompanied.

Monophonic conducti

In all probability the performing traditions of these pieces were never closely involved with the decorums of the High Style song. Accompaniment may well have been used on a regular basis.

135

Techniques of performance

Most accompaniment seems to have been provided by solo instrumentalists. In Jean Renart's *Guillaume de Dole*, for example, accompaniment for the voice is almost invariably provided by a solo fiddle, and there is no firm evidence that mixed groups of string, wind and percussion performed in courtly monody. Even references to small ensembles of related (or of the same) instruments are rare (see above, p.30, and Appendix 3:5 (last reference) for two notable exceptions). In the unique manuscript of the *Doctrina de Compondre Dictats* the *dansa* is said to be accompanied 'by instruments' (*ab esturmens*), yet even here there is doubt, for it seems that the scribe originally wrote *esturment* in the singular.[1]

This conclusion may be widened momentarily into a proposition that much—perhaps most—monophonic music of combined voices and instruments was provided by solo musicians in the twelfth and thirteenth centuries. To turn from Old French literary evidence to the account books of the English royal court, for example, is to encounter a similar picture of solo minstrelsy. As Richard Rastall has pointed out in an important study:[2]

> *Bas* instruments were generally used for solo minstrelsy,
> judging by the many gifts to single *bas* minstrels recorded
> in the various account books. . . . We who live in an age of
> concerted music might be surprised that so much solo music was
> heard in the Middle Ages. Household accounts show that
> harpers (who probably sang very often), players of the
> various bowed instruments, bagpipers . . . taborers and
> trumpeters could all produce acceptable entertainment
> on their own.

This predominance of solo minstrelsy has important repercussions for playing-techniques. An instrumentalist who must perform alone will often require his instrument to have some self-accompanying facility so that, when he plays, the skein of melody will be woven together with some kind of auxiliary noise. The context in which medieval string-playing was usually conducted therefore implies some use of heterophonic devices.

This is exactly what we find in Jerome of Moravia's treatise on fiddles. As we saw in Chapter 10, Jerome's tunings suggest that as late as the final decades of the thirteenth century, *viellatores* used drone-accompaniments to their own playing and generally conceived of their own technique in terms of simultaneously sounding strings. We have found similar signs of polychordal thinking (often involving drones) in relation to plucked fingerboard instruments, the harp and psaltery. In all probability, therefore, drones were a resource used by medieval string-players of all levels of attainment.

At the same time there is evidence for accompaniment in parallel intervals. In some clerical circles vocal 'organum' of this kind continued to be used as an impromptu means of decorating chant until at least the close of the thirteenth century and there can be little doubt that it was used by some instrumentalists in secular contexts. Jerome of Moravia's advanced fiddle technique is essentially a rationalised parallel procedure analogous to (and probably based upon) the contemporary vocal practice of fifthing, and as late as the seventeenth century we find Mersenne recommending that the strings of the dulcimer/psaltery may be tuned in perfect consonances 'to augment the harmony'. This may well be a relic of medieval practice.

Alternatim

In addition to techniques of simultaneous participation it is apparent that solo singer/instrumentalists sometimes organised their performance on an alternatim basis—not surprisingly, since these musicians had only three colours at their disposal: voice alone, instrument alone, and voice and instrument together.

There are references to such alternatim performance scattered here and there in medieval literature and we must go far afield to find them. The most famous, needless to say, is the passage incorporated in the *Roman de Horn* of c1170 (see above, p.5), where Horn sings and then performs exactly what he has sung upon his harp. At about the same time Gerald of Wales describes how a band of horsemen travelled with a fiddler and singer going before them 'who replied to the notes of the song on his fiddle in an alternatim fashion' (*cantilenae notulis alternatim in fidicula respondentem*).[3] This is reminiscent of a passage in the Old French romance of *Claris et Laris* where a minstrel sings a refrain-song and doubles the refrains upon his fiddle (see above, p.84). A further reference to alternatim practice—and a most striking one—appears in a thirteenth-century gloss on Martianus Capella; here a procedure adopted by minstrels (*joculatores*) is described: 'while they play their instrument, they stay silent; and while their instrument is silent, they sing' (*dum instrumentum suum tangunt, silent; et dum silet instrumentum suum, cantant*).[4]

There is ample evidence that such alternatim procedures sometimes took the form of preludes and postludes. Johannes de Grocheio reveals that when fiddlers performed High Style songs they were accustomed to tack a postlude on the end which they called *modus*.[5] This is a well-known reference, but there is another, less familiar allusion to this practice in a treatise on the virtues and vices, *Le Somme le Roi* (1279), compiled by friar Laurent at the request of Philippe III; here Laurent compares his own prologue to the Lord's Prayer to *une entrée de viele*, a fiddle prelude.[6] The use of such preludes on the harp is abundantly attested in the *Tristan en prose*.[7]

Tessitura

To judge by pictorial sources (a treacherous source of information in this context, admittedly), most stringed instruments of the twelfth and thirteenth centuries must have played in a tessitura very roughly equivalent to that of the modern violin or viola. The history of instrumental compass from c1300 to c1500 is one of expansion downwards—the development being particularly clear in the case of the lute which began its life in the West with four courses (thirteenth and fourteenth centuries), then changed to five (most of the fifteenth century) and then to six (the end of the fifteenth century). Given what is known of the string materials available to medieval lutenists, it seems unlikely that this increase in string numbers was accompanied by a significant movement upward in pitch for the top strings; it may be that the top strings of a fourteenth-century lute lay in much the same pitch-range as the top strings of a sixteenth-century lute of comparable string-length (and equipped with comparable strings). Roughly speaking we may suppose that the prevailing tessitura of much twelfth- and thirteenth-century string-playing was probably ranged upwards from the *c* at the bottom of the viola, perhaps (and I think this more likely) only from somewhere in the region of *g* at the bottom of the violin.

Turning now to the human voice we find that the music theorists of the thirteenth and fourteenth centuries usually give (more or less) two octaves as the compass of the voice.[8] Putting aside the delicate (and probably unanswerable) question of whether the falsetto voice was cultivated in the performance of troubadour and trouvère song,[9] and restricting our attention (as the theorists do) to the male voice, we may propose something in the region of *F–f'* as roughly corresponding to the two-octave span which the theorists give as the compass of the *vox humana*.

If these are tolerably accurate assessments of vocal and instrumental tessitura then it is plain that male voices and stringed instruments (which we have placed at around violin or viola pitch) overlapped for about an octave: roughly speaking, *f–f'*. This means that many stringed instruments would possess many notes which lay too high for voices to reach—and this is what certain theorists say.[10] A tentative conclusion would therefore be that any accompaniment which stringed instruments offered to the performance of lyric songs by male voices is likely to have lain in the same tessitura as the voice (our crude calculations show that 'fundamental' drones would have been feasible) or to have lain above it—perhaps doubling at the fifth (as in Jerome of Moravia's advanced fiddle technique) or at the octave.

Appendix 1

Terminology of musical instruments

The first historians of medieval instruments found themselves in the position of Adam in the Garden of Eden. Around them lay a new world of pictures and carvings populated by a mass of instruments all waiting to be named, and like living creatures these instruments seemed to exist in an almost infinite variety of species. Amongst the fiddles, for example, some were oval-bodied or pear-shaped while others were almost square, or shaped like a boat; there were some with only one string while others had as many as five; some were played on the left shoulder and others on the right; some seemed to be tiny and smaller than modern violins, while others looked quite large and bigger than modern violas.

Adam had the freedom to invent new names for the creatures in his world but the early historians of medieval instruments faced a more difficult task. They were to choose from names that were already in existence in contemporary literature—names that were little more than labels that had long ago fallen off their parcels. What did Old French *vïele* mean, for example, and did it mean the same as Middle English *fithele*? If so, for how long? Did *vïele* mean that same instrument when it appeared in Latin as *viella*?

Many questions of this kind had to be confronted, but most pressing of all was the task of determining whether medieval writers used their instrument-terminology in a precise way, or whether they often allowed one thing to have two names and one name to denote two things.

The general view today seems to be that medieval instrument-terminology was confused:[1]

> As the Latin terms for antique and obsolete or
> obsolescent instruments continued to be used, their
> significance was gradually lost and the old word was
> bestowed on a new instrument or on one whose name was
> unknown ... and, with the introduction of vernacular terms
> or of new instruments, *confusion was compounded* [my italics].

There is surely a danger here that we will assume medieval instrument-terminology to have been confused merely because we find it confusing. The most useful question to ask is therefore probably this: why have we become confused?

Firstly, we have not always been sensitive to the nature of the sources. Consider, for example, the following table of instrument-names compiled from John Palsgrave's *Lesclarcissement de la Langue Francoyse* of 1530; it has been said that this table carries 'confusion to the point of ridicule':[2]

Croude an instrument	rebecq
Croudar	ieuevr de rebecq
Fyddell	rebeq
Fydlar or crouder	rebecquet
Rebecke an instrument of musyke	rebec
I fyddell	Ie ieoue du rebecq
Can you fydell and playe	Scauez vous iouer du
upon a tabouret to?	rebecq et sus le tabouryn
	aussi

Palsgrave renders three English words (*croude*, *fyddell* and *rebecke*) with a single French term (*rebecq*). One explanation is that all of these nouns were employed willy-nilly in the sixteenth century: hence the proposition that speakers of the time had carried 'confusion to the point of ridicule'. Yet there is another explanation: that Palsgrave believed, and was right in believing, that the single French word *rebecq* would serve the Englishman in all situations where, at home, he might have used either *croude*, *rebecke* or *fyddell*. This workmanlike approach to definition is almost universal in popular language dictionaries and phrase-books of all periods. Here is a table comparable to the one based on Palsgrave, compiled from a modern authoritative dictionary of French:

Do you wear shorts?	portez-vous des culottes?
Tights	culottes
Tights or knickers	culottes
Do you wear breeches or shorts?	portez-vous des culottes
	ou des culottes?

Here the single French word *culotte(s)* is equated with four English words: 'shorts', 'tights', 'breeches' and 'knickers'. Certainly the table could be improved: *un short* is now acceptable French usage and 'knickers' would perhaps be better rendered as 'culottes de femme'. Yet what the list gives is enough for many purposes and there is no confusion amongst English-speakers as to what the words 'shorts', 'tights', 'breeches' and 'knickers' mean. In the same way there is no feeling amongst French-speakers that *culotte* is a vague or imprecise term. It is easy to imagine how a Frenchman equipped with this table alone might have difficulties in an English clothes-shop and become very confused indeed, but that confusion would result from a mismatching of verbal resources between English and French, and not from deficiencies in the resources of each language.

The second reason why medieval instrument-terminology often appears confusing is that some influential writers have dealt lightly with some important distinctions: of language (English is not the same as French; vernaculars are not the same as Latin); of date (an eighth-century word is not the same as a thirteenth-century one); and of usage (learned, bookish, or Latinate usage is not the same as day-to-day spoken usage). Let one example from a classic English work suffice. In his *Old English Instruments of Music* Galpin reproduces a drawing of a lyre from an Anglo-Saxon psalter of c1030–50 now in Cambridge University Library (Galpin's plate 38). Here are three references to the illustration from his text:[3]

> in an Anglo-Saxon Psalter of the early part of the
> eleventh century . . . the bowed *Cruit* is seen in the
> hands of Asaph
>
> *Crowd*—early 11th century (Cambridge)
>
> . . . Asaph is playing on the bowed *Rotte* (the *Crwth* or *Crowde*)

This is a remarkable muddle in which *cruit, crowd* (and *crowde*), *rotte* and *crwth* are all used to denote the same instrument. *Cruit* is an Old Irish word. *Crwth* is its Welsh cognate, not recorded before the thirteenth century. *Rotte* is recorded in northern European Latin as early as the sixth century and *rote* is its Old French relative, not recorded until the twelfth century. As for *crowd(e)*, this is a Middle English borrowing of Welsh *crwth* not recorded before c1300. None of these words can be shown to have existed in Anglo-Saxon.

Finally, the considerable diversity of both the instrument-names (as they are recorded in texts) and of the instruments (as they are shown in pictures) goes far to confuse us. This richness in the material has often been emphasised—indeed it has been over-emphasised and the time has come to redress the balance. As for the names, once we have discounted variations of spelling within one language (thus, for example, Middle English *fithele, vydele, fethele,* and so on) and gathered cognates together from various languages (*fithele, vielle, fidula, vyhuela, viola,* for example) it is the consistency of the names, and not their diversity, which strikes us. Many of them can be reduced to a stable skeleton of two or three consonants present in virtually all the recorded European languages of the Middle Ages, but fleshed out with vowels in different ways in the different tongues. The 'fiddle' words listed above, for example, all seem to be generated from something like this (where asterisks denote the variable vowels, and brackets enclose any part of the skeleton which may be dispensed with):

$$f/v * (d) *1 *$$

Similarly, 'psaltery' words look something like this:

$$s * (1)t * r *(n)$$
$$f/v * (d) *a 1 *$$

whence Middle English *sautrye*, Old French *psalterion*, Old Castilian *salterio*, Middle High German *psalterium*, and so on. Most of the major instrument terms of the later Middle Ages appear to have been international ones.

It is often supposed that the typological diversity of medieval instruments would have made accurate use of terminology impossible, but there seems little to recommend this view. A modern analogy may be helpful. Since the 1930s 'guitars' have proliferated in almost every conceivable shape and size (makers of electrified instruments have been particularly inventive); 'guitars' have been built which are arrow-shaped, rectangular and lyre-shaped as well as figure-of-eight-shaped in the traditional design; they have been strung with metal and plucked with artificial fingernails or with a plectrum, and strung with bare and wound nylon and played with the fingers; 'guitars' have been built in both 6 and 12 string forms; equipped with round soundholes, with f-shaped soundholes like a violin, with flat bellies, and with curved bellies like a cello; some types have been built with electronic pickups. Although epithets are sometimes used to distinguish these various types of guitar ('folk', 'jumbo', 'electric', 'Spanish', 'acoustic', and so on), all these instruments are readily identified by speakers of modern English as 'guitars', without any sense of confusion. Could not the same thing have happened in the Middle Ages?

But the most important point is that when we assemble the sources that reveal the names which specific instrument-types bore in the Middle Ages we find evidence of considerable consistency in usage. In the remainder of this appendix I have assembled some of the most detailed and revealing sources (principally drawings of instruments with their names written by them). What emerges from this list is that there were certain pan-European traditions of nomenclature which lasted throughout the later Middle Ages.

Terminology: selective list of sources before c1350

Labelled illustrations

This category embraces drawings in which names are written next to the pictures of the instruments named, or where the drawings are inserted, like diagrams, into texts which have instruments as their subject.

It is important to distinguish illustrations of this kind from pictures in which instruments figure as part of a scene that is a response to something described in a text. In illustrations of that kind there is always a danger that

the pictorial material is only a partial or imperfect response to the text—
because the artists have relied upon stock pictures in model books, for
example, or because of inattentiveness to what the text actually says.

1   Petrus de Palude/Nicholas Trevet, commentary upon Psalm 150
    (Figure 6). The *cithara* and *psalterium*. This text, which was designed to
    carry illustrations, appears in the psalm-commentaries of the Domini-
    cans Petrus de Palude and Nicholas Trevet. Both commentaries
    achieved wide circulation and therefore there are numerous (illus-
    trated) manuscripts of the commentary upon Psalm 150.[4] The illus-
    trations show little variation, although there are clear signs that some
    artists wished to bring the pictures closer into line with the instruments
    of their own region.[5]

2   Marginal drawings accompanying Jehan des Murs's *Musica Speculativa*,
    in Paris, Bibliothèque Nationale, MS Lat. 7378A, f.45v.[6]

3   Marginal drawings accompanying Alain de Lille's *De Planctu Naturae* in
    Brussels, Bibliothèque Royale, 21069, ff.39r and 39v.[7]

4   Albumasar. Numerous manuscripts including Paris, Bibliothèque
    Nationale, MS Lat.7330, f.12v and London, British Library, MS
    Sloane 3983, f.42v.[8]

5   Joachim of Fiore, *Psalterium Decem Chordarum*. The manuscripts of this
    early thirteenth-century allegorical treatise on the *psalterium* usually
    contain diagrams of the instrument.

6   Marginal drawings accompanying a psalter-commentary in Oxford,
    Bodleian Library, MS e.Mus.15, f.43r.

7   Drawing of *Musica* with labelled instruments (*organistrum*, *lira* and
    cithara) in the *Hortus Deliciarum* of Abbess Herrad of Hohenbourg.
    Now destroyed.[9]

8   Drawing of four labelled instruments (*organistrum*, *lyra*, *cythara anglica*
    and *cythara teutonica*). From a late twelfth- (or early thirteenth-) century

manuscript destroyed in the fire at Gerbert's monastery of St Blaise in 1768 but copied by him before the catastrophe. Probably produced in the same scriptorium (or from the same models) as number 7.[10]

Illustrations of references in texts

9   The Sloane Bestiary (British Library, MS Sloane 3544, f.43r). A reference to the way in which dolphins 'crowd together and swim towards any *symphonia*' is illustrated with a painting of a figure playing a rectangular hurdy-gurdy in a boat.[11]

10   Guillaume de Deguilleville, *Le Pèlerinage de la vie humaine*. There are numerous manuscripts of this fourteenth-century allegory, many of which contain an illustration showing Latria with an organ, horn and a *psalterion* which, in all the manuscripts about which I have information, is shown as a pig-snout psaltery.[12]

Descriptions or revealing allusions

11   *Summa Musice*

12   Amerus, *Practica Artis Musice*

13   Jerome of Moravia, *Tractatus de Musica*

14   Elias of Salomon, *Scientia Artis Musice*

15   Petrus de Abano, *Expositio problematum Aristotelis*

Identifications

In this section the labelled illustrations inventoried above are listed by number.

Fiddle names

The available evidence shows that Old French *viele*, and its Latin offspring *viella*, were principally used to denote bowed instruments.[13] The names *viele* and *viella* are usually associated with five strings (3 [p.20], 12 [p.79], 13 and 14 [pp.20 and 26]), although Amerus, in a general reference to fingerboard instruments, mentions 'four or five or less' (12 [p.79]). Source 1 is the only text to mention the possibility of equipping a *viella* with up to seven strings (see above, p.57). The body-shapes of these instruments reduce to two main types: the ovoid, where there is a firm distinction between neck and body, and the piriform, where the body and neck blend into one another. It seems likely that the names *viele/viella* straddled this morphological boundary (and also the boundary between the tri-chordic and pentachordic traditions of stringing). It is possible, however, that the piriform instruments often attracted the name *gigue* (see below). This leaves the tri-chordic octoform fiddles played in the lap, very common in pictorial sources before c1300. In source 4 (Paris MS), such an instrument (and a piriform fiddle) is labelled *viola*. It would seem, therefore, that the *viele, viella, viola* complex covered most (perhaps all) bowed instruments before 1300.

Rebec names

Although the term *rebec* is recorded before 1300[14] it is primarily a late-medieval word. Old French texts show forms closer to their Arabic parent *rabab*. Jerome of Moravia describes the *rubeba* as a bi-chordic bowed instrument (13) and Abano lists the *rebeba* as a two-stringed instrument (15, *Particula* 19, problem 3). The guiding factor in the use of names built upon r–b stems would seem to have been smallness. Jerome of Moravia's introductory remarks imply that the *rubeba* is smaller than the *viella*—and not simply because it has only two strings (13, p.88, lines 4–5). In the fifteenth century Gerson writes of the biblical *symphonia* that 'some think the *symphonia* to be the *viella*, or *rebecca*, which is smaller',[15] while Tinctoris describes the *rebecum* as 'very small' (*valde minus*) in his *De Inventione et Usu Musicae*.[16] The term *rubebe* does not appear in Old French sources until c1270,[17] and Jerome of Moravia seems to have regarded the *rubeba* as an instrument which might be unfamiliar to his readers. The word therefore belongs to the very end of our period and the sources suggest that it generally denoted a two-stringed bowed instrument, played in the lap.

Gigue names

Renaissance usage points to bowed instruments, and the same meaning is clearly implied for Middle High German *gyge* in *Der Busant* (Appendix 4:26). Abano's statement that the *ziga* has four strings points to a fingerboard instrument. In source 4 (Sloane MS), the words *Giga vel lira* are written above a pillar-harp (only *giga* appears in the Paris manuscript). However, *lira* is written in a later hand in the Sloane manuscript and may be an

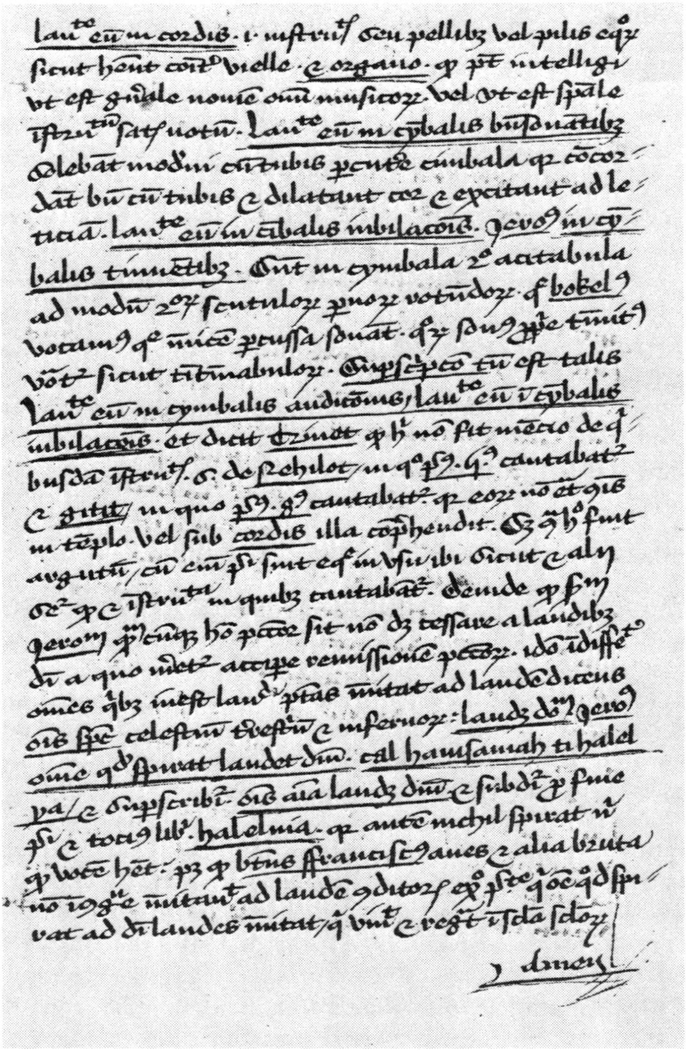

Figure 12 *The English Franciscan, Henry of Cossey, on the string-materials of the* viella. *Cambridge, Christ's College, MS 11, f.251v. Reproduced by permission.*

attempt to supply the more common (or the correct) Latin term for the harp. *Giga* might then belong to the hurdy-gurdy nearby, which has no label, or to the gittern, which is also unlabelled. The latter suggestion accords with the gloss *Hec giga: getyrne* in a fifteenth-century English Nominale.[18] As Laurence Wright has shown, the gittern was a piriform short lute so there is no difficulty in assuming that the term often (usually?) denoted piriform bowed instruments during the Middle Ages.

Lute names

There is almost no medieval evidence apart from Amerus (12, p.97). There can be no doubt, however, in view of usage in virtually all the vernaculars of Renaissance Europe (and in medieval/modern Arabic) that terms such as Old French *luthz* generally denoted a plectrum-plucked short-lute with a vaulted back and turned-back pegbox. As Wright has shown, the gitterns of the Middle Ages were very similar to the lute in form, but smaller. It is tempting to believe, therefore, that size may have been one of the factors defining the use of lute names in the Middle Ages, a 'lute' before 1300 being generally larger than anything one would call a 'gittern'.

Gittern names

Wright has convincingly demonstrated that these names referred to short-lutes, generally with a vaulted back and sickle-shaped pegbox.

Citole names

In the same article Wright demonstrates that these names were customarily applied to plectrum-plucked short-lutes, often shown with holly-leaf shaped bodies and 'thumb-hole' in the neck.

Psaltery names

There are numerous thirteenth- and fourteenth-century sources in which the Latin word *psalterium* and French *psalterion* (in various forms and spellings) are associated with 'pig-snout' psalteries (1: see Figure 6), 2, 3, 5 (some manuscripts) and 10 (a large body of illustrations). Earlier manuscripts of source 5, the *Psalterium Decem Chordarum* of Joachim of Fiore, show trapezoidal instruments with single, central soundhole.[19] This seems to be the form required by Joachim's allegory and therefore represents one kind of *psalterium* that he knew. Pig-snout instruments are not often found in pictorial sources before 1200, whereas trapezoidal instruments are common (Figure 14).[20] This suggests that in the twelfth century, *psalterium*, and its vernacular scions, was usually applied to trapezoidal instruments, but in the thirteenth century came to denote at least two types of instrument when the pig-snout form (whose origins are obscure) was disseminated.

Rotta names

Steger has drawn attention to the Moissac cloister sculpture of shortly before 1100 where a triangular harp-zither is labelled *rota*. Two new pieces of evidence can now be adduced, both of which support Steger's contention that this was the kind of instrument which (at least in the Gothic period) bore forms of the name *rota*. Source 4 (Paris manuscript) shows what is probably a triangular zither, labelled *rota*. This has almost certainly been copied from an earlier manuscript or a pattern-book and its relation to fourteenth-century usage might be questioned on those grounds. However, Petrus de Abano states that the *rota* he knew had two string-bands—a description which fits the structure of triangular harp-zithers as revealed with particular clarity in the romanesque sculpture of France (see Figure 11).

Harp names

Harp names have changed their meaning since late Antiquity. The philological and archaeological evidence suggests that the lyres used by some Germanic peoples during the Dark Ages bore the name *harp* before the advent of the pillar-harp in the medieval West.[21] The name 'harp' must have been slowly grafted onto the pillar-harp, perhaps from the eighth century on (the chronology of events here is almost completely obscure). In some areas of Europe where the old northern lyres continued to be used into the Gothic period the name 'harp' may often have been retained—as suggested, for example, by certain Scandinavian carvings which interpret the *harpa* of the Gunnarr legend as a lyre.[22]

The meaning of *harpa* in an eleventh-century text such as the *Ruodlieb*, for example, therefore remains uncertain; both lyre and pillar-harp are possible, and we can only speculate how many other possibilities there may be. By the Gothic period, however, the evidence from France (where plucked lyres do not appear to have been used later than the twelfth century) points directly to the pillar-harp as the instrument denoted by Old French *harpe* (the illustrations in certain manuscripts of the *Tristan en prose*, for example.)

LATIN TERMS

The histories of Latin terms such as *cithara* and *lyra* in the Middle Ages are complex and have drawn forth some very detailed research.[23] Here it is only possible to draw the outlines of these histories.

Cithara

In Classical Latin the term *cithara*, a borrowing from Greek, was reserved for various forms of lyre (and, perhaps, of harp). This is the usage transmitted, for example, by Boethius's *De Institutione Musica*, where it is clear that the *cithara* is an instrument with a string for every note. *Cithara* could also be used in a general sense, as revealed in Isidore of Seville's discussion of stringed instruments in the *Etymologiae* (3:22). There *psalteria, lyrae* and other instruments are described as different species of *cithara*.

These two traditions persisted throughout the Middle Ages. It is tempting to believe that many medieval authors who use the term *cithara* (and especially poets) have no more specific meaning in mind than 'a stringed instrument' (for the general sense see source 8). Yet during the Gothic period there existed a powerful tradition which associated *cithara* with the word 'harp', in its various forms in different vernaculars, and with the pillar-harp. In England this tradition can be traced as early as the eighth century and from 1200–1500 it flourished (see, for example, sources 1, 3, 6 and 7,) although it had to compete with *lira* (sources 2 and 4 (British Library MS)).

Yet there are clear signs that this 'open-string' tradition was not the only one which influenced the use of *cithara* in Medieval Latin. As early as the fourth century there are references to *citharae* with four strings.[24] This seems rather a small string-total for a Late Antique lyre, so these *citharae* may be fingerboard instruments.

The history of fingerboard instruments in Dark Age Europe is so obscure that it is impossible to trace this use of *cithara* into the Gothic period with any precision. What is clear, however, is that by 1200 plucked instruments were in use in the West bearing names ultimately derived from Latin *cithara* (e.g. *gittern* and probably also *citole*). With the increasing acceptance of vernacular-derived terminology in medieval Latin the form *(h)arpa* became an acceptable—although far from universal—way of referring to the pillar-harp; as a result *cithara*, so often associated with harps, sometimes became attached to gitterns and citoles whose vernacular names were so similar to *cithara*. This is what seems to happen in Abano (15) where the *cythera* is said to have four strings, and in source 2, where the *chytara* (sic) is shown as a citole.

Lira

Although this word is found in Latin sources throughout the Middle Ages, it does not seem to have enjoyed anything more than a sporadic existence in Old French. The 'open-string' tradition which exerted such an influence upon the use of *cithara* in the Middle Ages also controlled the senses of *lira* to some extent, whence the word is sometimes found in association with pillar-harps. Two manuscripts of c1200, both illustrated in the region of Alsace, show the *lira* as single-string bowed instruments (7 and 8). These two sources are closely related.[25] One of them is the celebrated *Hortus Deliciarum* of Herrad of Hohenbourg and it has long been recognised that some illustrations in this (now destroyed) manuscript show signs of Byzantine influence. It may be no coincidence, therefore, that the bowed instruments in these pictures are strikingly similar to the modern Pontic *lira*. There is very little evidence to suggest that this use of *lira* was widely disseminated during the Gothic period. The same may be said of the usages whereby *lyra* (in various forms) was applied to the hurdy-gurdy and the lute; I find no evidence that these traditions were established during our period.

Symphonia

During the Gothic period, *symphonia* and its vernacular offsprings was a general name for hurdy-gurdies (regardless of size or of whether played by one or two men).[26]

Organistrum

A general name for hurdy-gurdies (regardless of size or of whether played by one or two men) but generally confined to areas of High and Low German speech.[27]

Appendix 2

Selective typology of musical references in French narrative fiction to 1300

The aim of this appendix is to establish a context for the many brief extracts from long narrative works which will be presented in Appendix 3. Appendix 2 describes some of the most important genres of musical reference in Old French fiction and is based upon the following texts:

Romances

Amadas et Ydoine
Athis et Prophilias
Attila
Beaudous
Le bel inconnu
Blancandrin et l'orgueilleuse d'Amour
La chastelaine de Vergi
Le chevalier au lion (Yvain)
Le chevalier de la Charrete
Li chevaliers as deus espees
Claris et Laris
Cligés
La confrere d'amours
Le conte du Graal (Perceval)
Le court d'amours
Durmart le Gallois
Eledus et Serene
Eracle

Erec et Enide
Escanor
L'estoire del Saint Graal
L'estoire de Merlin
Fergus
Floire et Blancheflor
Floriant et Florete
Galeran de Bretagne
Gautier d'Aupais
Gille de Chyn
Gligois
Guillaume d'Angleterre
Guillaume de Dole
Guillaume de Palerne
Guiron le courtois
Hunbaut
Ille de Galeron
Ipomedon
Jehan et Blonde
Joufroi de Poitiers
Kanor
Le lai d'Aristote
Le livre d'Artus
Le livre de Lancelot del Lac
La manekine
Meraugis de Portlesguez
Les mervelles de Rigomer
La mort le roy Artus
Narcisus
Partonopeu de Blois
Peliarmenus
Philomena
Piramus et Tisbé
Prose Tristan (read in Vienna 2542)
Protheslaus
Robert le Diable
Le roman d'Auberon
Le roman de Laurin
Le roman de Silence
Le roman de Thèbes
Le roman de Troie
Le roman de la Violette

Epics

Aiol
Aliscans
Ami et Amile
Anseïs de Carthage
Anseÿs de Metz
Auberi le Bourgoin
Aye d'Avignon
Aymeri de Narbonne
La bataille Loquifer
Boeve de Haumtone
Brun de la Montagne
La chanson d'Aspremont
La chanson de Godin
La chanson de Guillaume
La chanson des quatre fils Aymon
Le charroi de Nimes
La chevalerie d'Ogier de Danemarche
La chevalerie Vivien
Couronnement de Louis (verse redactions)
Doon de Maience
Doon de Nanteuil
Doon de la Roche
Les enfances Guillaume
Les enfances Renier
Les enfances Vivien
L'entree d'Espagne
Fierebras
Floovant
Florence de Rome
Folque de Candie
Garin le Loheren
Gaufrey
Gaydon
Gerbert de Mez
Girart de Roussillon
Girart de Vienne
Godefroid de Bouillon
Gormont et Isembart
Gui de Bourgogne
Hervis de Metz
Hugues Capet
Huon de Bordeaux
Jehan de Lanson

Jourdain de Blaye
Macaire
Maugis d'Aigremont
Moniage Guillaume (verse redactions)
La mort Garin le Loherain
Les Narbonnais
Otinel
La prise de Cordres et de Sebille
Prise d'Orange (verse redactions)
Raoul de Cambrai
Le roman d'Aquin
Le roman du comte de Poitiers
Le siège de Barbastre
Tristan de Nanteuil
Voyage de Charlemagne
Yon

The 'Reviewing' Register
(a generalised view of a multifarious activity)

1 The feast

1.1 Essentially a listing of the musical (and other) entertainments offered at some courtly function,

1.2 usually a feast, and therefore in the hall,

1.3 and in this context often clearly signalled by some formulaic reference to the termination of the meal, often with *Quant*... or *Apres*...

> *Quant les tables furent levees*...
> *Quant les tables ostees furent*...
> *Quant cho vint apres mangier*...
> *Apres disner i eut*...
> *Apres mengier*...

1.4 The occasion of the feast is often a royal marriage (under the influence of *Brut* lines 10543ff and *Erec et Enide*, lines 1983ff).

1.5 The doings of professional entertainers, especially instrumentalists and singers, loom very large in these lists of entertainments at feasts. Many such lists are mainly strings of instrument-names (a rhetorical procedure acknowledged in Geoffrey de Vinsauf's *Poetria Nova* (c1200)).

1.6 However, many lists also include references to the doings of courtiers, primarily dancing (see 2.1–13), tale-telling, and (for the men) the playing of chivalric sports (such as fencing and jumping). In this case there may be moments of focus on specific activities.

1.7 There is a single, stable literary purpose for almost all such material: it emphasises the luxury and abundance of the scene whilst reinforcing the image of the court as a stable point of departure and point of return for all 'romance experience'.

1.8 In accordance with this fixity of purpose there is a fixity of technique. Syntax is highly stereotyped and built of paratactic formulae, including the following, where (in the first four examples) a cultivated vagueness of sense—suggesting a feast so magnificent that it all but defies description in discursive terms—is intensified by anaphora and asyndeton:

li uns	*VERB*	*li autres*	*VERB*
cil	*VERB*	*cil*	*VERB*
li alquant	*VERB*	*li plusor*	*VERB*
la ot........		*la ot........*	

la oïssiez...
la peüssies oïr...

1.9 The total effect of the entertainment and its music is often expressed by the formula

grant joie/noise (de)mener

1.10 The formulae in 1.8 may introduce references ranging from a couplet to a dozen lines. There are other formulae allowing narrators to signal the presence of music in a single line, including:

(et) VERB et VERB (et) VERB cil jongler

Cantent et notent, vïelent chil jongler	*Hervis de Metz 569*
Cantent et harpent, vïelent cil jongler	*Hervis de Metz 7929*
e cantent et vïelent et rotent cil jugler	*Voyage de Charlemagne 413*
e cantent et vïelent et rotent cil geugler	*Voyage de Charlemagne 837*

2 *The carole*

Après disner i eut vïeles,
Muses et harpes et freteles,
Qui font si douces melodies,
Plus douces ne furent oïes.
Après coururent as caroles.
Ou eut canté maintes paroles.   *Jehan et Blonde 4761—6*

2.1 A dance performed by courtly amateurs and often mentioned in FEAST passages (1.1–10), often as an entertainment taken up when

155

the company tires of the music offered by minstrels, or when the celebrations are carried beyond the hall and into the open air.

2.2 *Carole* references therefore often follow the material inventoried in 1.1–10 (as in the example from *Jehan et Blonde* quoted above).

2.3 The dance is often performed outdoors

2.4 to songs which the courtiers sing for themselves

2.5 and which may be accompanied by the instrumental music of minstrels.

2.6 Sometimes, but not frequently, the *caroles* seem to be purely instrumental and provided by minstrels (few texts can be securely interpreted to have this meaning).

2.7 The *caroles* are performed by a mixed company of men and women

2.8 or by women alone

2.9 and are especially associated with young girls (in numerous references the young girls are said to dance *caroles* while the young men indulge in chivalric sports such as fencing).

2.10 As implied by 2.3, the ethos of the *carole* is predominantly 'pastoral', and it is associated with the freshness and candour of youth. Whence *caroles* are particularly associated with the younger (and perhaps probationary) members of courtly society and are often danced by *puceles, puceletes jouvenceles, meschines, escuiers, bachelers* and *vallets*.

2.11 *Carole* (verb *caroler*) is the most common word for dancing, although *danser, treschier* and *baler* are also used.

2.12 In the tradition of lyric insertion established by Jean Renart's *Guillaume de Dole* some thirteenth-century romances give the texts (and occasionally the music) of these *caroles*, a degree of explicitness that carries such references away from the Reviewing Register towards the Focusing Register.

2.13 Occasionally the *carole* seems to take the form of a joyous train of courtiers, both male and female, moving across the open country. Here the genre blends with the SINGING PARTY genre (3.1–6).

3 The singing party

A genre embracing several classes of reference where courtiers entertain themselves, often as part of a feast when the meal is over and some (or all) of the courtiers have tired of the minstrels.

3.1 In a group, indoors (in hall or chamber), or outdoors, courtiers sing

3.2 and dance *caroles* (never in the chamber)

3.3 and perhaps tell stories or read romances (the key verb being *conter*).

3.4 The entertainment may be mixed with references to chivalric sports

3.5 and may take place indoors or (perhaps more often) outdoors.

3.6 Large *caroles* danced outdoors to the singing of courtiers often blur with the motif of the journey or formal progress enlivened by instrumental music.

The 'Focusing' Register
(a particularised view of a specific activity)

4 Singing on horseback

Boefs si en mounte le palefrei corser...
Tretot en chantaunt comence a chivacher

Boeve de Haumtone 863–5

4.1 Outside the CAROLE (2.1–13) and the SINGING PARTY (3.1–6) the courtly amateur rarely sings except when riding (for the singing of *lais* to the *harpe* see 5.1–9). The hero or some other important character (generally male) sings having just mounted his horse, or

4.2 sings during the course of a journey on horseback.

4.3 His song is commonly described as a *son*.

4.4 He may be holding a hunting bird.

4.5 Sometimes he is alone

4.6 and sometimes with others who sing with him (in which case the genre may blur with the SINGING PARTY, 3.1–6).

4.7 By singing, the hero expresses his fine state of mental and physical health (in epics before the late-twelfth century)

4.8 and also his courtliness and amorousness of bearing (in romance, and in many of the later epics).

4.9 There may also be a powerful suggestion (at least in epic) that the singing protagonist is enjoying his last moments of light-heartedness before some disaster, and even that his singing is an expression of a false sense of security.

Quant Gui l'entent, si ist de son donjon,
En sa compengne son senechal Milon,
Ostes et Dreues, qui sont si compangnon.
Es mulez montent, qui furent au perron,
A l'ostel vindrent trestuit chantant un son,
Et li frere se drecent.

Les Narbonnais 1000–5

Ferraus repaire et vait notant .I. son,
Et Amaufrois disoit .I. lay breton.

Gaydon 7778–9

Jolyvement chauntaunt comence a
chevacher.

Boeve de Haumtone 1144

Parmi .I. bois s'en vont [no baron] chantant
Et molt grant joie demenant.

Claris et Laris 15319–20

Gilles et tout si compeignon
Vienent cantant une chanchon.

Gille de Chyn 533–4

> ...*vient [.i. chevalier] .i. esprevier paisant*
> *Et .i. noviel sonet cantant.*

Mervelles de Rigomer
15199–200

> *Aallars et Guichars commenceront .i. son,*
> *Gasconois fu li dis et limosins li ton,*
> *Et Richars lor bordone belement par desos;*
> *D'une grande huchie entendre les puet on.*
> *Ainc rote ne viele ne nul psalterion*
> *Ne vos pleüst si bien comme li troi baron.*

La chanson des
quatre Fils Aymon
6599–6604.

5 The lai/harp complex

5.1 A courtly amateur
5.2 who is invariably a protagonist or an important character in the narrative, is a gifted harpist,
5.3 and harps pieces, in public, called *lais*,
5.4 and can usually compose them,
5.5 and often sings them to his/her own accompaniment.
5.6 There is a slot for some technical description of the performance, usually a tuning procedure.
5.7 The tale in which the courtly harper appears will normally have a 'Celtic' setting (Brittany, Cornwall, Wales; Arthurian Britain is a particular favourite)
5.8 and the harpist will often be in disguise when he performs (or travelling incognito). This does not usually apply if the character is female.
5.9 If not a major protagonist of the tale the harpist will often be the messenger and ally of a protagonist, carrying the *lai* as a message or commemoration on the protagonist's behalf to one in a foreign realm for whom the *lai* has some special significance.

6 The solo performance

6.1 A solo musician, often a minstrel, performs. If a courtly amateur, then he/she is usually
6.2 a courtly amateur disguised as a minstrel for some purpose
6.3 or a character wrongly brought up as a minstrel following some tragedy, subterfuge or treachery following his birth,
6.4 or a character within the LAI/HARP COMPLEX (see 5.1–9).
6.5 If the solo performer is an instrumentalist, or a singer/instrumentalist, then the instrument will generally be a *viele* unless the reference falls within 5.1–9.
6.6 If the solo musician is a vocal performer without an instrument then he is usually a narrator of saints' lives or epic tales.
6.7 The genre provides a slot for some passing reference to what the

musician plays (which may or may not be filled), and narrators seem to have been free to fill the slot as they wished.

6.8   A special sub-genre of references to courtly, amateur instrumentalists centres upon the private musician/retainer of Charlemagne in epic tradition (*Chanson de Guillaume* and *Aye d'Avignon*).

7 Courtly accomplishment

Many epic and romance heroes are praised for their accomplishments and education which are often itemised in detail.

7.1   In both Epic and Romance chivalric skills and sports (jousting, fencing, leaping, etc.) predominate in the lists of male accomplishments, and the main arts of peace are chess and draughts.

7.2   It is exceptionally rare for a male to be praised for an ability to sing or to read. References to a hero having mastered the 'vii ars' are also very rare, though rather more frequent in connection with women.

7.3   Outside of 5.1–9 (and of texts relating to Aristotle's education of Alexander) it is almost unknown for a male to be praised for instrumental skills; exceptions are *Florimont*, which is related to the Alexander material, the *Roman de Horn* and *Eracle* where, in both cases, the ability to play the *harpe* is presented as a skill cultivated by the nobility of the past.

7.5   In accounts of female education and accomplishment both singing and playing are sometimes mentioned, and perhaps the seven Liberal Arts.

Appendix 3

Literary references relating to the involvement of stringed instruments in French and Occitan monody

Most of the following references are taken from Old French and Old Provençal literature, together with certain Latin writings produced in France and Occitania during the time of the troubadours and trouvères. Since Catalonia shared in the troubadour culture of Occitania, several Old Catalan sources are included (items 15 and 19–21). One Old Spanish text has been included (item 4), since it offers the fullest description of a performing ensemble which occurs time and time again in the following texts: fiddle and voice.[1]

The list is restricted to passages bearing upon the performance of lyric repertory, and references belonging to the lai/harp complex are omitted (see the selective typology in the previous appendix, section 5.1–10, and Chapter 8).

The ideal reference for our purposes is one which specifies that a certain kind of song is being accompanied by a certain kind of instrument. A corpus of such references would provide a solid basis for investigating the performance practice of twelfth- and thirteenth-century music, but unfortunately very few of the passages gathered here provide clear information of this kind. Most of them are indecisive for one or more of the following reasons:

1   It is impossible to establish what kinds of songs are being performed.
2   It is impossible to determine whether (a) instrumental or (b) accompanied-vocal performance is being described.
3   When the texts mention voices(s) and instruments(s) together they are not sufficiently explicit in delineating relations of space and time for us

to conclude that voice(s) and instruments(s) are performing simultaneously and in the same place.

Just as it may be impossible to establish the precise meaning of nouns such as *chanson* and *vers* so it is difficult to determine the meaning of certain verbs. Every medieval poet had learned from his Bible that Jubal was the father of those who 'sing in organs' (*cantant in organis*), and the meaning 'to play an instrument' certainly lies within the range of Old French *chanter* (see items 14 and 36) as it does of Old French *dire* and medieval Latin *cantare* (compare *cantare cum lira* in item 14). It is no surprise to find the verb *cantar* ('to sing') reinforced with *de boca* ('with the mouth'), in the Provençal romance of *Flamenca* (item 5, line 319).

So it is that we often cannot determine the meaning of a musical reference with any precision. But it is also the case that many of the references may have no 'precise' meaning. On one level this is a matter of usage: medieval authors were free to employ words such as *chanson* and *vers* in a more broad and generous way than modern scholars. On a deeper level it is a question of the quality of thought which medieval writers, especially narrators, brought to the task of writing about music. Virtually none of the sources gathered here were written to impart the kind of information we are seeking from them. The romancers, for example, were rarely interested in describing musical performances in any detail (the material belonging to the lai/harp complex, examined in Chapter 8, is an exception here) and the romancers often describe performances with formulaic phraseology and an inert imagination that does not so much *refer* ('there was a fiddler who accompanied a singer performing a dance-song') as gesture towards an idea ('there was entertainment'). When referring to music, the romancer's fundamental technique was a kind of excited inventory, as if everything were seen through the eyes of a participant glancing from side to side in some lavish aristocratic hall, taking in the many different kinds of entertainment which he sees (or saw over a period of time). This listing technique is fundamental to the romancer's engagement with music because the flamboyance and luxury of aristocratic life are a preoccupation of romance; one way of emphasising the magnificence of an occasion was to amass brief references to the musical entertainment on offer there. Many of the musical passages in romance are generated by associations of this kind and therefore this listing manner is a pervasive one (see items 2, 3, 5 (lines 593–607), 24, 25, 26, etc.). Such lists of instruments and songs accompany the very first glimmers of French romance with Wace's *Brut* of 1155, a text where the technique is shown in its most rudimentary form ('there was A, B, C. . .'):[2]

Mult peüssiez oïr chançuns,
Rotruenges e novels suns,
Vïeleüres, lais de notes,
Lais de vïeles, lais de rotes. . . .

Sometimes the list may be built around verbs rather than nouns ('the one does A, the other does B...'), as in *Flamenca* (item 5):

> L'uns viola[1] lais de Cabrefoil,
> E l'autre cel de Tintagoil;
> L'us cantet cel dels Fins Amanz,
> E l'autre cel que fes Ivans.
> L'us menet arpa, l'autra viula;
> L'us flaütella, l'autre siula;
> L'us mena giga, l'autre rota;
> L'us diz los motz e l'autrels nota...   600–7

> One plays the *lai* of Cabrefoil on the *viola*, and the other
> the *lai* of Tintagoil; one sang the *lai* of the Fins Amanz,
> and another the *lai* which Yvain composed. One brought the
> *arpa*, another the *viula;* one plays the *flaütella*, and
> another whistles; one brings the *giga* and another
> the *rota*; one gives out the words and another puts the music
> to them.

This listing technique is an efficient way of referring to things in a distributive way ('the *lai* of Cabrefoil... the *lai* of Tintagoil') but it does little to establish relationships between things. Time and time again such references leave us wondering whether the voices and instruments mentioned are to be understood to be performing together, or separately, and this uncertainty extends far beyond the realms of *chanson de geste* and romance (see items 3, 19, 20, 24, 25, 26, 29, 30, 31, 34, 38 and 39). In some cases it is probably a critical indecorum to give such close attention to the question of what any given writer 'may have meant', for he may have meant nothing beyond 'there was playing and singing'. Some such dilution of aim is clearly signalled by the poetic theorist Geoffrey de Vinsauf (fl. c1200), who advises novice poets to adorn their verses with lists of instruments if they wish to draw out a description of a feast into something elaborate and 'poetic'.[3]

The stereotyped diction of these lists is another sign of a dilution of sense. In *Hervis de Metz*:

> Cantent et notent, vïelent chil jongler.
> The minstrels sing, play and fiddle.

where the poet is describing a *noces* in a grand palace.[4] As we read through the romance it becomes increasingly difficult to believe that there is any solid sense behind the façade of these words. This same line appears three times elsewhere in the text (lines 189, 6841, 9065)—or rather four times if we include this slight variation upon the basic scheme at line 7929:[5]

> Cantent et harpent, vïelent cil jongler.

A variant also appears in another epic, the *Voyage de Charlemagne*:[6]

> e cantent et vïelent et rotent cil jugler
> e cantent et vïelent et rotent cil geugler

In other words these lists are, in some measure, formulaic: they are composed of pre-set pieces of language, the common property of poets working within Old French epic tradition, designed to present a conventional scene or action within fixed metrical constraints.[7] (See Appendix 2:1.1–10.)

It is a measure of the simplicity and syntactical poverty of many narrative references to music that punctuation is rarely a crucial issue in determining the meaning of a passage. Indeed the only instance in this appendix where choice of punctuation appears to be crucial is Gerbert de Montreuil's *Le Roman de la Violette* (item 33), where Gerbert offers a passage which stands quite outside the 'distributive list' tradition.

Amidst the ambiguities and uncertainties certain general conclusions may be drawn:

1 The evidence is overwhelming that the preferred instruments for accompanying the voice in twelfth- and thirteenth-century France and Occitania were bowed instruments. This suggests at least a measure of standardisation and convention in performance practice: the same type of solo instrument seems to have been used, time and time again. There is no firm evidence for the accompaniment of any medieval courtly monody by the bands of mixed string, wind and percussion instruments which have figured so prominently on recordings and on the concert platform during the last twenty years. The Old Spanish *Libro de Apolonio* (item 4) suggests that such fiddle-accompaniment was a highly-prized and subtle art.

2 There is abundant evidence for the accompaniment of dance-songs. See items 2 (the Provençal *dansa*); 3 (?again the *dansa*); 9 (again the *dansa*). Item 13 presumably describes instrumental music since there is no mention of singing.

3 There is also good evidence for the instrumental accompaniment of love-songs (whose identity cannot be precisely established from the texts). See items 22 and 29.

Sources from Occitania or perhaps relating to southern French practice

Verse narratives

1 Anon *Daurel et Beton*

2   Anon *Jaufre*
3   Anon *Canso de la Crosada*
4   Anon *Libro de Apolonio* (Old Spanish)
5   Anon *Flamenca*
6   Arnaut Vidal de Castelnaudary *Guilhem de la Barra*

Troubadour lyrics

7   Peire d'Alvergne *Deiosta.ls breus jorns*
8   Guillem Ademar *Chantan dissera si pogues*
9   *Senher n'Aymar, chauzes de tres baros*

Old Provençal prose

10   *Vidas*
11   *Razos*

Miscellaneous Latin sources

12   *Miracles of Our Lady of Roc-Amadour*
13   Gervase of Tilbury *Otia Imperialia*
14   Boncompagno da Signa *Rhetorica Antiqua*

Treatises on poetry (including Catalan and Italian)

15   ?Jofre de Foixà *Doctrina de Compondre Dictats*
16   Francesco da Barberino *Liber Documentorum Amoris*
17   Guillem Molinier *Las Leys d'Amors* (a version in prose)
18   Joan de Castellnou *Compendi*

Ramon Llull

19   *Libre de Contemplació en Deu*
20   *Libre de Meravelles*
21   *Libre d'Evast e d'Aloma e de Blanquerna*

Sources from northern France

Verse narratives

22   Anon *Ami et Amile*

23 Anon *Claris et Laris*
24 Anon *Doon de Nanteuil*
25 Anon *Du vilain au buffet*
26 Anon *Florence de Rome*
27 Gautier de Tournai *Gille de Chyn*
28 Jean Renart *Guillaume de Dole*
29 Anon *Hervis de Metz*
30 Anon *L'atre perilleux*
31 Anon *La chanson des quatre fils Aymon*
32 Messire Thibaut *Le Roman de la Poire*
33 Gerbert de Montreuil *Le Roman de la Violette*
34 Anon *Le Roman des Sept Sages*
35 Anon *Le Roman du Comte de Poitiers*
36 Anon *Les Deux Bourdeurs Ribauds*
37 Gautier de Coinci *Les Miracles de Nostre Dame*
38 Huon de Meri *Le Torneiment Anticrist*
39 Anon *Macaire*

Music theorists

40 Elias of Salomon *Scientia Artis Musice*
41 Jerome of Moravia *Tractatus de Musica*
42 Johannes de Grocheio *De Musica*

Treatises on confession or on the vices and virtues

43 Thomas de Chobham *Summa Confessorum*
44 Guillaume Peyraut *Summa de Vitiis et Virtutibus*
45 Guillaume d'Auvergne *De Universo*
46 Guillaume d'Auvergne *De Viciis et Peccatis*
47 Albertus Magnus *Commentary upon the Sentences of Peter Lombard*
48 Honorius Augustodunensis *Gemma Anime*

Petrus de Abano

49 *Expositio problematum Aristotelis*

The numbers in square brackets after the narrative extracts refer to the typology of literary material presented in Appendix 2

Sources from Occitania

Verse narratives

1 ?12c *Daurel et Beton*

Source: A.S. Kimmel, ed., *A Critical Edition of the Old Provençal Epic* Daurel et Beton (Chapel Hill, 1971). See above, pp.20ff., and add the following:

> 'Senher, Daurel ay nom, e say motz gen arpier,
> E tocar vihola e ricaman trobier . . .' 84–5

'My lord, my name is Daurel and I know how to harp words in a pleasing way, and how to play the fiddle and compose in a cunning (?noble) way . . .'

> Pueis [Daurel] pres l'arpa, a .ii. laisses notatz
> Et ab la viola a los gen deportat;
> Sauta e tomba, tuh s'en son alegratz. 1208–10

Then Daurel took the harp and played two *laisses* and pleased his audience with the fiddle; he dances and tumbles, all are delighted by him.

> Qua[n]t ac .vii. ans Beto sap gen violar
> E tocar citola e ricamen arpar
> E cansos dire, de se mezis trobar. 1419–21

When Beton was seven years old he knew how to fiddle in a noble fashion and harp nobly, and how to sing *cansos* and compose unaided.

See also 1941ff (where the piece sung by Daurel to Beton's fiddling appears to be in the style of epic rather than lyric).

2 ?c1170 *Jaufre*

See above, p.22.
[1]

3 c1228 *Canso de la Crosada* (anonymous continuation)

Source: E.Martin-Chabot, ed., *La Chanson de la Croisade Albigeoise*, 3 vols., Paris (1931–61), 2, p.98, line 46.

A banquet is described which does not lack

... jotglars e las viulas e dansas e cansos

[1]

4   13c   *Libro de Apolonio*

Source: G. Battista de Cesare, ed., *Libro de Apolonio* (Milan, 1974).

Several stanzas of this Old Spanish romance contain what may be the fullest account of fiddle-accompanied singing in medieval literature. The text leaves us in no doubt that simultaneous participation of voice and instrument is taking place, but reveals little about the kind of music which is being performed. As always, this is primarily a problem of terminology; although the following passages have received much attention (from Spitzer, Devoto and Artiles among others),[8] our knowledge of musical terminology in Old Spanish is too fragmentary to permit much more than a guess at the author's meaning in most instances. Yet the text is valuable as an indication that the author thought of accompanied singing as a subtle and highly nuanced art. Devoto's study considers almost all previous literature on the subject and takes full account of the mass of scholarly conjecture which has accumulated around these passages.

The *Libro de Apolonio* is ultimately based upon the *Historia Apollonii Regis Tyri* of c500. It exists in two recensions, *RA* (c500) and *RB* (somewhat later). Passages of the Latin which shed light upon the interpretation of the Old Spanish text are given below. The most important musical episode of the Latin romance is set at the court of King Archistrates of Pentapolis when Apollonius is entertained by the singing and playing of the king's daughter. In *RA* the princess sings and accompanies herself:[9]

> Puella vero iussit sibi afferri liram. At ubi accedens cepit, cum nimia dulcedine vocis cordarum sonos, melos cum voce miscebat.

> The girl commanded the *lira* to be brought to her. And when she took it she mingled the melody of the string-music with her singing with surpassing sweetness of voice.

Apollonius is dissatisfied with the girl's playing and asks for the instrument. Then he performs for the company; in the words of both *RA* and *RB*: 'he mingles his modulated voice in song with the strings' (*Miscetur vox cantu modulata cordis*). The author of the *Libro de Apolonio* probably worked from a version of the story in which the wording of this episode left no doubt about the simultaneous participation of voice and instrument: he had only to follow it to produce a clear reference to instrumental accompaniment. Yet this hardly detracts from the interest of the following passages. They are full of technical terminology (none of which appears to have any precedent in

Latin Apollonius tradition), suggesting that the author's imagination is engaging with contemporary performance practice.

The princess begins to play:

> 178 Aguisósse la duenya,   fiziéronle local;
>   tenpró bien le vihuella   en un son natural,
>   dexó cayer el manto,   paróse en un brial;
>   començó una laude,   omne non vio atal.

> The girl prepared herself and they made room for her; she tuned
> the *vihuella* well to a natural accord, let fall her mantle and
> was left in her gown; she began a *laude*, none had ever heard the
> like.

Lexical problems: the reference to tuning the *vihuella* ... *en un son natural* is tantalising (for previous conjectures as to the meaning of the phrase see Devoto, *op. cit.*, pp.305ff). Forms of the adjective *natural* occur as a description for music twice elsewhere in the poem (427b and 495b, the former in a reference to fiddling; see below). In each case *natural* forms the rhyme-word, as here, which may suggest a relatively weak meaning for the term ('pleasing', perhaps?), but some technical sense may be involved, at least in the above stanza. A *natural* tuning might conceivably be an accordatura of perfect intervals akin to the ones described by Jerome of Moravia.

The term *laude* (Devoto, *op. cit.*, pp.297ff) presents an intractable problem. It may mean little more than 'song', although this sense is not recorded in the available dictionaries of Old Spanish (such as they are). A connection with Italian *lauda* (and, for that matter, with Old French *lai*) is possible.

> 179 Fazía fermosos sones,   fermosas debailadas;
>   quedava a sabiendas   la boz a las vegadas,
>   fazía a la viuela   dezir puntas ortadas,
>   semejava que eran   palabras afirmadas.

> She made beautiful melodies and beautiful *debailadas*; at times
> she skilfully softened her voice and made the *viuela* give out
> masterly *puntas*, it seemed that [voice and instrument] were
> united utterances.

Specific details from the HISTORIA: according to *RA* the princess's voice and instrument sounded together in marvellous harmony (quoted above).

Lexical problems: the noun *debailadas*, which occurs again at 189b, is a mystery (Devoto, *op. cit.*, pp.311ff, lists previous conjectures). In various forms the term also appears in the *Libro de Buen Amor* of Juan Ruiz (where it is also associated with the fiddle) and in the *Libro de Alexandre:*[10]

Libro de Alexandre	MS P	2118b	*dulçes deballadas*
	MS O	1976c	*dolçes de las baȳlas*
Libro de Buen Amor	MS S	1231a	*dulçes de vayladas*
	MS T	1231a	*dulçes baylares*
	MS G	1231a	*dulçes vayladas*
Libro de Apolonio		179a	*fermosas debailadas*
		189b	*debayladas*

In various places this table of forms seems to show the influence of Old Catalan *balar*, 'to dance' (whence, presumably, the *deballadas* of *Alexandre* 2118b), and of Old Spanish *bailar*, 'to dance' (cf. Old and Middle French *balade*). It is tempting to translate the *debailadas* of the *Libro de Apolonio* as 'dance-like melodies', or something similar. This has often been proposed (see Devoto, *loc. cit.*, and Spitzer, p.370).

Puntas is a term that is elsewhere used for the music of instruments in Old Spanish,[11] but not, perhaps, in a technical sense (compare Grocheio's use of *punctum* to denote the sections of the instrumental *stantipes* and *ductia*).[12]

> 180   Los altos e los baxos   todos d'ella dizíen.
>   La duenya e la viuela   tan bien se abiníen
>   que.l teníen a fazannya   quantos que lo veíen.
>   Fazía otros depuertos   que mucho más valíen.

Both those of higher and of lower rank spoke of her. The girl and the *viuela* accorded so well together that all those who saw her were astonished. She then showed her skill in even more excellent ways.

Specific details from the HISTORIA: the astonishment of the courtiers. In *RA:*[13] *Omnes convive ceperunt mirari dicentes: 'Non potest esse melius, non esse dulcius plus isto, quod audivimus.'*

Apolonio does not join in the general praise for the princess's performance; in his judgement she does not have a perfect command of the art (183c). The princess replies to this charge that Apolonio should 'sing a *lauda* on the *rota* or on the *giga*' himself (184c) now that he has disparaged her own performance:

> 185   Non quiso Apolonio   la duenya contrastar:
>   priso una viuela,   sópola bien tenprar;
>   . . . .

188 Alçó contra la duenya   un poquiello el çejo.
     Fue ella de vergüenza   presa un poquellejo.
     Fue trayendo el arquo   egual e muy parejo,
     abés cabíe la duenya   de gozo su pellejo.

189 Luego fue levantando   unos tan dulçes sones,
     doblas e debayladas,   temblantes semitones:
     . . . .

185 Apolonio did not wish to contradict the girl: he took
a *viuela*—he knew how to tune it well enough!

188 He raised his face a little towards the girl. She was a
little taken aback with embarrassment. He drew the bow in even
and similar strokes, and the princess was beside herself with
joy.

189 Immediately he played such sweet melodies, *doblas e
debayladas*, with quivering semitones . . .

Specific details from the HISTORIA: None. In *RA* the performance of
Apollonius is described very briefly: *Atque ita facto silentio 'arripuit plectrum
animumque accomodans arti'. Miscetur vox cantu modulata cordis.*

Lexical problems: All in 189b. The meaning of *doblas e debayladas* is obscure
(for the latter see the note on 179a above; see also Devoto, *op. cit.*, p.313f).
On the basis of usage in Latin (and in Old and Middle French) *doblas* might
be translated 'in octaves', and might then refer to the kind of effect that
would result from Jerome of Moravia's fiddle-tunings with octave strings. A
connection with sixteenth-century Spanish *redobles*, 'diminutions' is also
possible. The *temblantes semitones* are a mystery (trills? vibrato?). The author
of the *Libro de Alexandre* mentions *el plorant semiton* in connection with
instrumental music, a usage which may be based upon the use of *plango* in
contemporary Latin music-theory to denote the insertion of *ficta* semitone
adjustments into the *musica recta* gamut.

A further reference to fiddling and singing occurs when the dispossessed
daughter of Apolonio is earning her living as a minstrel. She takes her *vïola*
to the market square:

426 . . . .
     Priso una vïola   buena e bien tenprada
     e sallió al mercado   vïolar per soldada.

427 Començó unos viesos   e unos sones tales
     que traíen grant dulçor   e eran naturales.
     . . . .

428   Quando con su vïola   hovo bien solazado,
        a sabor de los pueblos   hovo asaz cantado ....
       ....

... She took a fine *vïola* that was well tuned and went to the market to earn money by fiddling.

She began to perform words and music that were 'natural' and very sweet ....

When she had well entertained the people with her *vïola* and had sung very much to their taste ....

Specific details from the HISTORIA: in both *RA* and *RB* the princess plays the *lira*; the former mentions her *facundia sermonis*, the latter her *facundia oris*.

Lexical problems: the pairing of *viesos* and *sones* in 427a recalls a troubadour usage of the twelfth century (*vers e.l so*, 'words and the music'), whence the translation offered here. See also Devoto, *op. cit.*, pp.295ff. On *natural* see the note on 178b above. In the following the musician is again Tarsiana, daughter of Apolonio:

495   ....
     movió en suo vïola   un canto natural,
     coplas bien assentadas,   rimadas a senyal.
     Bien entindié el rey   que no lo fazíe mal.

... she played a *natural* song on her *vïola* with well-set stanzas/verses with clear rhyme. The king [Apolonio] saw that she did it by no means poorly.

Specific details from the HISTORIA: at this point in the Latin Tarsiana sings a song whose text is given in full, but there is no reference to string-playing.

Lexical problems: the puzzling term *natural* makes another appearance. 'In a natural hexachord'? It is perhaps unwise to press for a technical intepretation of this sort (see note on 178b above).
[6]

5 c1250 *Flamenca*

Source: M.J.Hubert and M.Porter, eds, *The Romance of Flamenca* (Princeton, 1962).

A great festivity at the court of Lord Archimbaud:

> Li juglar comensan lur faula,
> Son estrumen mena e toca
> L'us e l'autres canta de boca.   317–19

The minstrels begin their narration; one brings up his
instrument and begins to play it while the other sings.

My translation assumes that *faula* < *fabula*, and that this passage
describes the performance of accompanied narratives.

A further passage runs:

> Apres si levon li juglar:
> Cascus se volc faire auzir.
> Adonc auziras retentir
> Cordas de manta tempradura.
> Qui saup novella violadura,
> Ni canzo ni descort ni lais,
> Al plus que poc avan si trais.
> L'uns viola[l] lais de Cabrefoil,
> E l'autre cel de Tintagoil;
> L'us cantet cel dels Fins Amanz,
> E l'autre cel que fes Ivans.
> L'us menet arpa, l'autra viula;
> L'us flaütella, l'autre siula;
> L'us mena giga, l'autre rota;
> L'us diz los motz e l'autrels nota . . .   593–607

After [the meal] the minstrels arise; each one wished
to make himself heard. There you would have heard strings
resounding in many tunings. He who knew some new fiddle-tune
or a *canso* or *descort* or *lais* pressed forward as best he could.
One plays the *lai* of Cabrefoil on the *viola*, and the
other the *lai* of Tintagoil; one sang the *lai* of the Fins
Amanz, and another the *lai* which Yvain composed. One brought
the *arpa*, another the *viula*; one plays the *flaütella*, and
another whistles; one brings the *giga* and another the
rota; one gives out the words and another puts the music
to them.

These are the opening lines of a remarkable passage in which the author
draws up a long list of heroes from Classical, biblical and Arthurian story,
all of whom supposed to have figured in the songs sung by the minstrels
at the wedding of Lord Archimbaud and Flamenca. The mention of *lais* of

Cabrefoil, Tintagoil and *Fins Amanz* is surely designed to make the scene recede into that mysterious and remote 'Celtic' past where so many of the favourite stories of the twelfth and thirteenth centuries are located, and to give the passage a distinctively narrative, 'French' feel.

This long passage ends:

> L'us diz lo vers de Marcabru,
> L'autre comtet con Dedalus
> Saup ben volar, e d'Icarus
> Co[n] neguet per sa leujaria.
> Cascus dis lo mieil[z] que sabia.
> Per la rumor dels viuladors
> E pel brug d'aitans comtadors,
> Hac gran murmuri per la sala.   703–10

> One sang the *vers* of Marcabrun, and another sang
> of how Dedalus knew well how to fly, and of Icarus
> who was drowned for his recklessness. Each one told
> his tale to the limit of his skill. What with the hum
> of the *viula* players and the noise of so many storytellers there
> was a great noise in the hall.

Is there some relation between 'the *vers* of Marcabrun' and 'the hum of the *viula* players'?

The romance of *Flamenca* also contains a reference to the performance of a *dansa* at court by two hundred fiddlers. No mention is made of singing (lines 716ff).
[1]

6   1318   Arnaut Vidal de Castelnaudary: *Guilhem de la Barra*

Source: P.Meyer, ed., *Guillaume de la Barre*, SATF (Paris, 1895), line 635.

A reference to minstrels with *lors bals e lors esturmens*. These *bals* are surely identical with the *bals* described in nearby Toulouse by Guillem Molinier in the *Leys d'Amors* (see item 17): instrumental dance-tunes to which words could be added to make an instrumentally accompanied dance-song.
[1]

Troubadour lyrics

7   ?1149–?1168   Peire d'Alvergne: *Deiosta.ls breus jorns*

Source: Paris, Bibliothèque Nationale MS fr.22543 *(R)* f.6r.

The second and final tornada of this poem begins:

> Sest uers sabra son pes uiolar adrics
> ques daluernhe . . .

'Audrics will know how to fiddle this *vers*, I think, which is by [Peire] d'Alvergne.'

Deiosta.ls breus jorns is preserved in ten manuscripts in addition to MS *R*, and none of those which I have examined support *R*'s version of the first line of the tornada. Since there seems no reason to privilege *R*'s reading it is unlikely that the above represents Peire's original text. Peire presumably wrote something like this (A.del Monte, *Peire d'Alvernhe : Liriche* (Torino, 1955), p.72):

> En aquest vers sapcha vilans, Audrics,
> que d'Alvergne manda c'om ses dompneis
> no val ren plus que bels malvatz espics.

Audrics, through this song let every churl know that [Peire] d'Alvergne claims that a man without a love-service to perform is worth no more than a withered ear of corn.

The most that can be said is that one Provençal scribe of c1300 was prepared to let a song by Peire d'Alvergne leave his desk with a call for accompaniment contained in its final tornada.

8 ?1195–1207 Guillem Ademar: *Chantan dissera si pogues*

Source: Paris, Bibliothèque Nationale MS fr. 856 (C), f.163r.

This *canso* is preserved only in MS C where the second tornada reads:

> Peironet ab nullet apren
> lo uers a dir azaut e clar
> que me fai albis sospirar
> quar midons en mos bratz non tenc.

Peironet, learn to sing this song with *nullet* pleasingly and with a clear voice, and say that Albi makes me sigh because I have never held my lady in my arms.

The poem was first published by Appel (*Provenzalische Inedita* (Leipzig,

1890), pp.114–16) who tentatively proposed that the mysterious *nullet* might be an error for **viulet*, 'small fiddle' (he compares Middle French *violete*, 'fiddle'). The opening lines of this tornada might then be translated: 'Peironet, learn to sing this song with a small fiddle pleasingly and with a clear voice ...'. Yet Middle French *violete* does not appear to be recorded before the fifteenth century (Appel's example is taken from the early sixteenth-century chronicle of Philippe de Vigneulles), and *viulet* is not attested in Old Provençal. K. Almqvist (*Poésies du Troubadour Guilhem Adémar* (Uppsala, 1951), pp.116–17) retains the MS reading, construing *nullet* as the name of a second minstrel ('Little Nobody', as it were) who is being addressed together with Peironet.

9 1196 *Senher n'Aymar, chauzes de tres baros*

See above, pp.22–3.

Old Provençal prose

10 13c *Vidas*

Source: J.Boutière and A.H.Schutz, *Biographies des Troubadours*, 2 ed. (Paris, 1973), pp. 252–4 (Elias Cairel), 311–13 (Pons de Capdoill) and 408–9 (Perdigo).

These celebrated 'Lives' of the troubadours account for 101 individuals, roughly a quarter of the known troubadours. Most of the 'Lives' probably date from the later thirteenth century. It is universally acknowledged that these texts contain a great deal of romantic fiction, much of it based upon the poems themselves rather than upon any external information.[14]

Three troubadours in the Vidas are said to have been fiddlers:

Elias Cairel
fl. first decades of the 13c.
According to his Vida (version of MSS AIK): *Elias Cairels ... fetz se joglars ... Mal cantava e mal trobava e mal violava e peichs parlava, e ben escrivia motz e sons*, 'Elias Cairel ... became a minstrel .... He sang badly and composed badly and fiddled badly and spoke even worse, and wrote words and melodies well.' MS H omits the reference to the fiddle and gives a different assessment of Elias's abilities (Boutière/Schutz, p.254). The idea that Elias was a minstrel may have been developed from his tenso *N'Elias Cairel, de l'amor* (see H. Jaeschke, ed., *Der Trobador Elias Cairel* (Berlin, 1921), p.134).

175

Pons de Capdoill
Pons appears in documents up to 1220.
According to his Vida Pons *sabia ben trobar e violar e cantar* 'knew well how to compose and to fiddle and to sing'. There is a passage in a poem by Pons which may have given rise to this reference (Max von Napolski, ed., *Leben und Werke des Trobadors Ponz de Capduoill* (Halle, 1879), p.52) where the poet tells his lady that no music of instruments, including *viulas*, 'counts for anything compared with the solace you can bring'.

Perdigo
fl. late 12c, early 13c.
According to his Vida Perdigo *saup trop be violar e trobar* 'knew very well how to fiddle and how to write songs'. This information is probably based upon the *partimen* listed here as item 9.

Only 3 of the 101 troubadours commemorated in the Vidas are said to have been fiddlers, but as the compilers of the Vidas often had little (or no) information beyond what they could glean from a literal-minded reading of the poems this is not a revealing figure. A third of the troubadours with Vidas are said to have been *joglars*, and since instrumental skills were fundamental to the livelihoods of most musical minstrels it is likely that many troubadours could play an instrument of some kind (for the case of an aristocratic troubadour who played the *viola*, unknown to the Vida compilers, see item 13).

11 13c *Razos*

Source: as for item 10, pp.465–6

The Razos, probably composed at about the same time as the Vidas, explain the circumstances in which various troubadour songs were composed (or the reasons why they were composed, which often amounts to the same thing). One of the most famous is devoted to *Kalenda maya* by Raimbaut de Vaqueiras (Music example 10), a poem apparently devised to fit the melody of an estampie played by two French players of the *viola* *(aquesta stampida fu facta a las notas de la stampida qe.l jo[g]lars fasion en las violas)*. The *Razo* text neither says nor implies that Raimbaut's song was performed to instrumental accompaniment.

Miscellaneous Latin sources

12 1171 *Miracles of Our Lady of Roc-Amadour*

Source: E.Albe, ed., *Les Miracles de Notre-Dame de Roc-Amadour au XIIe siècle* (Paris, 1907), pp.128ff.

An extract from a story telling how the Virgin caused a candle to light upon the fiddle of a minstrel who played devoutly before her image at Roc-Amadour. The story also appears in Gautier de Coinci's *Miracles de Nostre Dame* (item 37) and in the *Cantigas de Santa Maria* (Cantiga 8) of Alfonso el Sabio. A related story of a similar miracle at Arras crops up here and there, the most interesting instance from the musical point of view being the anonymous *Dit des Taboureurs* of the thirteenth century.[15]

> ... Petrus Iverni, de Sigelar ... ex more veniens ad
> ecclesias, post orationem quam Domino fundebat,
> tangens cordas vidule, laudes Deo reddebat. Qui,
> cum esset in basilica Beate Marie Rupis Amatoris,
> diuque psallendo fidibus requiem nullam daret, sed
> modulatis vocibus interdum instrumento concordans,
> sursum respexit: 'Domina, inquiens, si tibi vel filio
> tuo Dominatori meo organica placent cantica ...

> ... Peter Iverni, from Sigelar ... coming to churches
> according to his custom, after the prayer which he
> poured out to the Lord, gave praises to God touching
> the strings of his fiddle. When he was in the church
> of Saint Mary of Roc-Amadour he was hymning upon his
> strings for a long time without rest, but harmonising
> with musical notes on his instrument the while he raised
> his eyes aloft, saying: 'Lady Mary, if my playing pleases
> you or the Lord your Son ....'

The crucial passage *modulatis vocibus ... instrumento concordans* presumably means 'harmonising with musical notes on his instrument' (i.e. with *vox* in its usual technical sense of 'note'). I assume that Peter is singing to his own accompaniment.
[elements of 6]

13   c1211   Gervase of Tilbury : *Otia Imperialia*

Source: Shelagh Grier, *The Otia Imperialia of Gervase of Tilbury: a critical edition of Book III, with introduction, translation and commentary* (D.Phil. Thesis, University of York, 1981), 1, pp.232–4.

This passage may be based upon an eye-witness report of a troubadour performing. Gervase of Tilbury married a relative of Imbert d'Aiguières, archbishop of Arles 1191–1202, and his marriage brought him the *palatium* where the events which he describes here took place. Gervase's mother-in-law was probably the source of the story. Gervase was appointed marshall of Arles by the emperor Otto IV (addressed in the parentheses below), but the date of the appointment is unknown. He probably settled there in 1190. The flamboyant protagonist of this story, Giraldus de Cabreriis, is probably the Catalan troubadour Guiraut de Cabreira.[16]

> XCII   DE EQVO GIRALDI DE CABRERIIS
> ... Erat temporibus nostris in Catalonia miles
> nobilissimis ortus natalibus, militia strenuus,
> elegantia gratiosus, cui nomen Giraldus de
> Cabreriis ... Erat miles in iuuentute sua, iocundus,
> hylaris, musicis instrumentis plurimum instructus,
> a dominabus inuidiose desideratus. In palatio nostro
> (quod ex uestri munere uestraque gratia ad nos
> rediit per sententiam curie imperialis, princeps
> excellentissime, propter ius patrimoniale uxoris
> nostre), in presentia pie memorie Ildefonsi, illustris
> regis quondam Aragonensis, et socrus nostre, que
> singulari laude precellebat inter dominas sui
> confinii, necnon in conspectu multorum procerum,
> miles sepe dictus uiolam trahebat, domine chorum
> ducebant, et ad tactum cordarum equus incomparabilibus
> circumflexionibus saltabat.

> CONCERNING THE HORSE OF GIRALDUS DE CABRERIIS
> ... There was in our own time a knight in Catalonia
> of very high birth, dashing in warfare and gracious
> in manners, whose name was Giraldus de Cabreriis ....
> This knight was in the flush of youth, charming,
> lively, highly skilled on musical instruments, and
> madly desired by the ladies. In our palace (which
> came into our possession as a result of your generosity
> and kindness, by the ruling of the imperial court, Your
> Excellency, in accordance with our wife's right of
> inheritance) in the presence of Alfonso of pious
> memory, the late renowned king of Aragon, and our
> mother-in-law, who excelled among the ladies of her
> connection in her matchless repute, and in the
> sight of many princes, too, the knight I have been
> speaking of used to play the fiddle: the ladies led
> the dance, and at a touch of the strings the horse
> used to frolic with extraordinary capers.

Gervase does not say whether Guiraut (or the ladies for whom he played the *viola*) sang as he played dance-music. In view of the conclusions reached in

Chapters 2–4 it is revealing that this unique glimpse of a troubadour playing an instrument should reveal him as a fiddler of dance-music. [elements of 6]

14 b.1215 Boncompagno da Signa: *Rhetorica Antiqua*

Source: L.Rockinger, ed., *Briefsteller und Formelbücher* (Munich, 1863), p.163.

One of the most widely-circulated medieval treatises on the art of letter-writing. A passage is devoted to letters of recommendation for various minstrels (including a section on composers, *inventores cancionum*, which praises the troubadour Bernart de Ventadorn). One recommendation for a string-player, entitled *De liratore vel symphonatore*, asserts that the subject of the letter *nouit cantare cum lira et tangere mirabiliter simphoniam*, 'knows how to sing with [play upon?] the *lira* and touch the *simphonia* most expertly'.

Treatises on poetry

15 end 13c ?Jofre de Foixà: *Doctrina de Compondre Dictats*

See above, pp.40ff.

16 1310 Francesco da Barberino: *Liber Documentorum Amoris*

Source: F.Egidi, ed., *Francesco da Barberino Documenti d'Amore*, 4 vols (Rome, 1905–27), 2, p.263.

> Consonium antiquitus dicebatur omnis inventio
> verborum que super aliquo caribo, nota, stampita, vel
> similibus componebantur, precompositis sonis.

> *Consonium* was the word used of old to denote every
> poetic composition devised to fit the pre-existing tune
> of any *caribo, nota, stampita* or some similar melody.

This definition recalls the story of Raimbaut de Vaqueiras (item 11) and the *bals* as described in the *Leys d'Amors* (see above, p.43). Barberino is describing the practice of putting words to a pre-existing instrumental tune.

17 1333–40 Guillem Molinier: *Las Leys d'Amors* (A)

See above, pp.40ff.

18 14c ?first quarter Joan de Castellnou: *Compendi*

Source: J.M.Casas Homs, *Joan de Castellnou Obras en Prosa, 1, Compendi de la coneixença dels vicis en els dictats del Gai Saber* (1969), *passim.*

As far as instruments are concerned Joan de Castellnou's treatise contains the same material as the *Leys d'Amors* (both verse and prose redactions) almost verbatim.

Ramon Llull

19 c1272 Ramon Llull: *Libre de Contemplació en Deu.*

Source: *Ramon Llull, Obres Essencials,* 2 vols. (Barcelona, 1957 and 1960).

Llull spent many years at the University of Paris and must have known the monophonic song-culture of both northern France and Occitania, together with the largely Provençal-derived art of the Catalan troubadours.

Com hom se pren guarda de ço que fan los joglars

1 . . . L'art, Sènyer, de joglaria començà en vós a loar e en vós a beneir; e per açò foren atrobats estruments, e voltes, e lais e sons novells, ab què hom s'alegràs en vós.

2 Mas segons que nosaltres veem ara, Sènyer, en nostre temps tota l'art de joglaria s'és mudada, car los hòmens qui s'entremeten de sonar estruments e de ballar e de trobar, no canten ni no sonen los estruments, ni no fan verses ni cançons sinó de luxúria e de vanitats d'aquest món.

3 Aquells, Sènyer, qui sonen los estruments e qui canten de putaria e qui loen cantant aquelles coses qui no són dignes d'ésser loades, aquells són maleits, per ço com muden l'art de joglaria de la manera per què l'art s'atrobà en lo començament. E aquells, Sènyer, són benauiriats qui en los estruments e en les voltes e.ls lais s'alegren e.s deporten en la vostre laor e en la vostre amor e en la vostre bonea; car aquells mantenen l'art segons ço per què fo començada.

5 Si los hòmens, Sènyer, se prenien guarda de mal que.s segueix per los joglars e per los trobadors, ni com lurs cantars e lurs estruments contenen vils obres de poc profit, ja no serien los joglars ni.ls trobadors tan bé acollits ni tan bé emparats com són.

6   Per los estruments que.ls joglars sonen, e per les novelles
raons que atroben e que canten, e per los novells balls que fan
e per les paraules que dien, és oblidada, Sènyer, la vostre
bonea . . . .

13   Força e vertut, e sentetat, e granea, e benedicció e noblea
sia coneguda ésser en vós, sènyer Déus, car molt he gran
desig que veés joglars vertaders qui loassen ço qui fa a loar e
blasmassen ço qui fa a blasmar; e encara he, Sènyer, desig que
null hom no sabés trobar ne cantar ni sonar null estrument, si
doncs no era servidor e joglar de vera amor e de vera valor, e
que fos sotsmès e amador de veritat.

22   Senyor ver Déus, qui us encarnàs en nostra dona sancta
Maria per tal que recreàssets l'humanal linatge; nós veem,
Sènyer, que los joglars ballen e canten e sonen estruments
davant los hòmens, per tal que ells moven a alegre e a plaer de
lur cantar e de lur ballar e dels estruments que sonen . . . .

23   Si los joglars, Sènyer, per art e per subtilea que han,
saben concordar la nota e.l ball e les voltes e.ls lais que fan
en los estruments, ab la nota que imagenen en lo cor, com pot
ésser aquesta meravella, Sènyer, que ells no saben obrir lur
cor a loar-vos . . . ?

[In the following translation those Catalan terms whose precise meaning is
not obvious are inserted in square brackets after the English equivalent
which I have chosen for them.]

How one should be wary of the doings of minstrels

1   The art of minstrelsy, Lord, began in praising and in
glorifying you, and it was for that purpose that instruments
were invented, and dances [*voltes*] and songs [*lais*] and new
melodies with which men rejoice in you.

2   But, as we may now see, Lord, in our time all the art of
minstrelsy is changed, for those who apply themselves to playing
upon instruments, to dancing and to composing neither sing, nor
play their instruments, nor compose poems or songs save on the
subject of lust and the vanity of this world.

3   Such minstrels, Lord, as play upon instruments and sing of
wantonness, praising in their singing such things as are not
worthy of praise; such are damned, for they pervert the art of
minstrelsy away from the purpose for which it was founded in
the beginning. But those minstrels, Lord, who rejoice and take
delight with their instruments, dances and songs in your praise,

love and goodness are blessed, for they preserve the art of
minstrelsy as it was first established.

5   If Mankind could only beware of, Lord, the evil which ensues
from minstrels and composers and how their songs and instruments
are wretched and useless things, then these minstrels and
composers would not be so readily welcomed and accepted as they
are.

6   Through the instruments that the minstrels play and the new
poems which they compose and sing, through the new dances that
they devise and the things which they say, your goodness is
forgotten, Lord . . . .

13   Might and virtue, holiness, greatness and blessedness and
nobility may be known to be in you, Lord, for I greatly desire that
you might see true minstrels who praise those things which are to be
praised and decry those things which are to be decried; and I further
desire that no man should be able either to compose, sing, or play
any instrument if he be not a servant and minstrel of true love and
true worth, and a subject and lover of truth.

22   Lord, True God, who became incarnate in Our Lady Saint
Mary so that you might renew the race of Mankind! We see, Lord,
that minstrels dance, sing and sound instruments before men, so
that they move them to joy and pleasure with their singing and
dancing and with the instruments which they play . . . .

23   Since minstrels, Lord, through the art and skill which they
possess, can harmonise the music, dances [*ball e les voltes*] and
songs [*lais*] which they perform on their instruments with the music
which they imagine in their hearts, how does this wonder come
about that they do not know how to open their hearts to praise you
. . . ?

Like the moralistic diatribes of every age, this one generalises and
exaggerates its subject. The language and tone of these passages do not
suggest that Llull is engaging with a specific musical milieu (that of Paris,
for example, or of Parma where he compiled the *Libre de Contemplació en Deu*).
He twice refers to *trobadors* (section 5) and uses *atrobar* and *trobar* to denote
the art of composing songs (sections 2, 6 and 13), but this Provençal-derived
terminology does not establish that he is referring to such courtly or
sophisticated milieux of southern France and Catalonia as may have
fostered songs of the Old Provençal tradition during the last decades of the
thirteenth century. Llull mentions composition in these extracts because he
is concerned with the moral responsibilities of those who make music—both
of those who compose and of those who merely play. Within this scheme
trobador seems to mean little more than 'composer' in the most general sense.

Llull makes little attempt to distinguish *joglars* from *trobadors*. He does not seem interested in drawing a moral distinction between them, and while he employs *trobador* in the sense 'composer', he also speaks of *joglars* 'who compose and sing new poems' (*joglars ... per les novelles raons que atroben e que canten ...*). He is content to bundle together all the skills of musical entertainers—composing, singing, playing instruments, dancing—and his references to 'minstrels and composers [with] their songs and instruments' are perhaps too casual to be truly informative.

20   *Libre de Meravelles*

Source: as **19,** 1, p.381.

> Dementre que lo rei e la regina manjaven, joglars anaven
> cantant e sonant estruments per la sala amunt e avall ....

> While the king and queen were eating, minstrels went to
> and fro in the hall singing and playing their instruments ....

21   ?1283–5   *Libre d'Evast e d'Aloma e de Blanquerna*

Source: as **19,** 1, pp.221 and 225–6.

Chapter 76 (p.221) tells how a cleric passed a tavern where there were many rascals and wretches 'who were drinking in the tavern, singing, dancing and sounding instruments' (*los quals bevien en la taverna, e cantaven, e ballaven, e sonaven estruments*). He entered the tavern and began to dance with them, singing a song about the Virgin Mary. Llull gives the text: a strophic song of two stanzas (inc: *A vós, dona verge santa Maria*) with one tornada and apparently without a refrain.

A further passage runs:

> Esdevenc-se un jorn que dementre menjava un cardenal,
> en sa cort venc un joglar molt bé vestit e arreat,
> e fo home de plaents paraules e bell de persona,
> qui cantava e sonava esturments molt bé. Aquell
> joglar havia nom Joglar de Valor .... Com lo cardenal
> hac menjat, e lo joglar cantà cançons e cobles
> que l'emperador havia fetes de nostra dona santa Maria
> e de valor, e sonà esturments en los quals faïa los
> balls e les notes que l'emperador havia fetes a honor
> de nostra Dona. Molt fo plaent a oir e a escoltar lo
> joglar e sos esturments ....

> It happened one day that, while a certain Cardinal was dining, there came to his court a minstrel who was very well arrayed and adorned; he was a man of pleasing speech and personable, and he sang and played upon instruments very skilfully. This minstrel was called 'the Minstrel of Virtue' .... When the Cardinal had dined, the minstrel sang songs and poems which the emperor had composed in honour of Our Lady St Mary and of virtue, and he sounded his instruments, playing the *balls* and tunes which the emperor had made in honour of Our Lady. It was most pleasing to hear this minstrel with his instruments ....

By associating instruments with a genre named *balls* Llull parallels the evidence of Molinier's *Leys d'Amors* (item 17) and Arnaut Vidal de Castelnaudary's *Guilhem de la Barra* (item 6). It is tempting to see this account of a minstrel performing pieces which 'the emperor had composed in honour of Our Lady St Mary' as an allusion to the *Cantigas de Santa Maria*, some of which were apparently composed by King Alfonso el Sabio of Castile and Leon.

Sources from northern France

Verse narratives

Few of the following texts can be accurately dated and they are therefore presented here in alphabetical, rather than chronological, order.

22 *Ami et Amile*

Source: P.F.Dembowski, ed., *Ami et Amile* (Paris, 1969), lines 2325–6. See also above, pp.31ff and items 24 and 38.

Lubias and twelve of her knights go to hear mass at Mont St Michel with a minstrel riding before them:

> Devant li vait uns jouglers de Poitiers
> Qui li vielle d'ammors et d'ammistié.

> Before her goes a minstrel from Poitiers
> Who fiddles for them of love and devotion.

In the romance of *Guillaume de Dole* by Jean Renart a famous song by the troubadour Bernart de Ventadorn is described as a *son Poitevin*, where the

meaning would seem to be something approaching 'a song from [?north-west] Occitania'. The above passage may perhaps refer to an Occitanian musician.
[6]

23 1268 *Claris et Laris*

See above, pp.84–5.

24 *Doon de Nanteuil*

Source: P.Meyer, 'La chanson de Doon de Nanteuil: Fragments Inédits', *Romania* 13 (1884), p.21. See also above, pp.31ff. and items 22 and 38.

At a feast:

> Le jor y ot tant rotes et vielle atrempée,
> et chançons poitevines y ot mout distintées.

> That day many a *rote* and *vielle* was tuned, and many a *chançon poitevine* was uttered.

On the meaning of *poitevine*, see item 22.
[1:5]

25 *Du vilain au buffet*

Source: A. de Montaiglon and G.Raynaud, eds, *Recueil Général et Complet des Fabliaux des XIIIe et XIVe Siècles*, 3 (Paris, 1878), p.204.

> L'uns fet l'ivre, l'autres le sot,
> Li uns chante, li autres note,
> Et li autres dit la riote,
> Et li autres la jenglerie;
> Cil qui sevent de jouglerie,
> Vielent par devant le conte . . . .

> One [minstrel] imitates a drunkard, another a half-wit,
> one sings, another plays an instrument; one keeps up a flow
> of patter, another of ribaldry; those who are skilled in
> minstrelsy play their fiddles before the count . . . .

The line *Li uns chante, li autres note* ('one sings, another plays an instrument')
seems to have been a stereotyped formula; compare *Flamenca* (item 5) line
607, and *Joufroi de Poitiers*:[17]

> Li uns note, li autre conte

[1]

26 13c *Florence de Rome*

Source: A Wallensköld, ed., *Florence de Rome*, 2 vols (Paris, 1907 and 1909),
2, p.126.

Milon, son of the king of Hungary, and one of the *persecuteurs* of Florence of
Rome, is entertained whilst in prison:

> Milles fut tot par lui, noblement comme sire,
> En la plus haut tor que l'en peüst eslire;
> Fables et chansonettes la font devant lui dire,
> Harper et vieller, conter romans et lire.

> Milon was all alone in noble state like a lord,
> in the highest tower that could be found; [his
> captors] command stories and songs to be performed
> before him, with music of *harpe* and *vielle*, and reading
> and relating of romances.

[elements mostly 1]

27 ?1230–40 Gautier de Tournai: *Gille de Chyn*

See above, p.30, and add:

> La lor cantoit .I. son nouvel
> Uns menestrex en la viele.

> There a minstrel sang them a new song on the *viele*.

[6]

28 c1228 Jean Renart: *Guillaume de Dole*

See Chapter 3, *passim*.

29 ?c1250 *Hervis de Metz*

See above, p.31.

30 ?mid-13c *L'atre perilleux*

Source: B.Woledge, ed., *L'atre perilleux* (Paris, 1936), lines 6639–44.

Celebrations after the wedding of King Arthur and Guinevere (a familiar setting: compare Wace, *Brut*, lines 10543ff and Chrestien de Troyes, *Erec et Enide*, lines 1983ff):

> Cil jougleour de pluisors terres
> Cantent et sonent lor vieles,
> Muses, harpes, orcanons,
> Timpanes et salterions,
> Gigues, estives et frestiaus
> Et buisines et calemiaus.

Minstrels from many countries sing and play their *vïeles* etc.
[1]

31 12c *La chanson des quatre fils Aymon*

Source: F.Castets, ed., *La chanson des quatre fils Aymon* (Montpellier, 1909).

> Grant joie i ot le jor el palais honoré;
> Asses i ont vallet et chanté et joé 1765–6

> There was great rejoicing that day in the noble palace; the valets
> both sang and played there aplenty ....

Old French narrative poets occasionally mention singing and playing in the same breath—usually, as here, with casual syntax which suggests that they had no more precise meaning in mind than is captured in the above translation (compare *La Prise de Cordres et de Sebille* 2097–8: *Cant ot mangié cil chevalier nobile/Jugleor chantent et vïelent et tinbrent*).[18]
[1]

An army of Christian knights makes merry to the astonishment of Saracens camped nearby:

> Lor loges an covrirent et par tot alumerent.
> Puis dancent anviron, de bon quer [quarolerent];

Li jugleor viellent, li harpeor harperent,
Li donzel anvoissi par de devant chanterent.   15766–9

They covered their quarters and lit candles everywhere.
Then they dance around them and [caroled] in high spirits;
the minstrels fiddle, the harpers played their harps,
and the light-hearted young squires sang before the tents.

[elements of 2 and 3:4]

32   Messire Thibaut: *Le Roman de la Poire*

Source: F.Stehlich, ed., *Messire Thibaut, Li Romanz de la Poire* (Halle, 1881),
lines 1140–1.

During a great celebration:

Cil jongleor en lor vieles
Vont chantant cez chançons noveles.

The minstrels go singing [playing?] new songs on their
vieles.

[1]

33   Gerbert de Montreuil: *Le Roman de la Violette*

Source: D.L.Buffum, ed., *Le Roman de la Violette ou de Gerart de Nevers*, SATF
(Paris, 1928), 1400ff.

The following passage has often been cited as firm evidence that the ability
to accompany oneself on an instrument was regarded as an exceptional skill
during the Middle Ages.[19]
    The immediate narrative context of the extract is as follows. The hero of
the romance, Gerart de Nevers, returns to Nevers disguised as a minstrel to
see how things stand now that the traitor Lisiart is installed there. Gerart is
shown into the hall and called upon to fiddle. He is wet and exhausted from
travelling and so replies that he would gladly warm himself and eat before
he performs. 'To the devil with your hesitation!' sneers Lisiart. Hearing this,
Gerart springs forward and begins tuning his *vïele*, complaining that a
minstrel's life is a hard one, for the more cold and miserable he is, the more
often his masters command him to sing and sit in a draught. In Buffum's
edition his plaint continues as follows:

'Faire m'estuet, quant l'ai empris,
Chou dont je ne sui mie apris:
Chanter et vïeler ensamble.'
Lors commencha, si com moi samble,
Con chil qui molt estoit senés,
Un ver de Guillaume au court nes,
A clere vois et a douch son:
      Grans fu la cours en la sale a Loon [etc.]

'Since I have undertaken it I must do that which I am not at
all taught to do: sing and play the *vïele* together.'
Then, as it seems to me, he began a laisse from [the
chanson de geste] of Guillaume au court nez, like one who was
well-skilled in such matters, with a clear voice and a sweet
sound [a laisse of 22 lines follows].

It is this version of the text which has been cited as evidence that self-accompaniment (or, at least, self-accompaniment with a *vïele*) was regarded as an advanced skill in the thirteenth century. Yet why should Gerart say (whether to the company or himself) that he cannot sing and fiddle at the same time? A glance at the Old French text shows that choice of punctuation may have a decisive effect upon the meaning of this passage, and since the two earliest manuscripts of the romance have no punctuation at this point, we are free to experiment.[20] A period after *apris* in the second line alters—indeed reverses—the sense:

'Faire m'estuet, quant l'ai empris,
Chou dont je ne sui mie apris.'
Chanter et vïeler ensamble
Lors commencha, si com moi samble,
Con chil qui molt estoit senés,
Un ver de Guillaume au court nes,
A clere vois et a douch son.

'Since I have undertaken it I must do that which I am not at
all taught to do.' Then, as it seems to me, he began to both
sing and fiddle a laisse from [the *chanson de geste*] of
Guillaume au court nez, like one who was well-skilled in
such matters, with a clear voice and a sweet sound.

Here the implication that it is difficult to sing and fiddle at the same time has vanished; when Gerart says he must do something 'which I am not at all taught to do' he now seems to be saying in a covert way that he is not a minstrel but a count, forced for a moment to act as a minstrel—*Chou dont je ne sui mie apris.*

And there is one further possibility. One of the four MSS of *Le Roman de la Violette* (Buffum's MS C of the early fifteenth century) gives a text in which the third and fourth lines of the extracts quoted above are transposed.[21] Here is Buffum's text with the transposition made:

> 'Faire m'estuet, quant l'ai empris,
> Chou dont je ne sui mie apris.'
> Lors commencha, si com moi samble,
> Chanter et vïeler ensamble . . . .

> 'Since I have undertaken it I must do that which I am not at
> all taught to do.' Then he began, so it seems to me, to
> fiddle and sing at the same time . . . .

With this transposition—which may possibly represent the authentic text[22]—the reference to Gerard's difficulty in fiddling and singing together seems to vanish. For the practice of self-accompaniment by fiddlers, see items 12 and 46.
[6]

34 *Le Roman des Sept Sages*

Source: J.Misrahi, ed., *Le Roman des Sept Sages* (Paris, 1933), lines 697–8.

An emperor's triumphal return:

> Li jougleour vont vïelant
> Et les borjoises karolant . . . .

> The minstrels go fiddling and the townswomen carolling . . .

[2]

35 *Le Roman du Comte de Poitiers*

Source: B.Malmberg, ed., *Le Roman du Comte de Poitiers* (Lund, 1940), lines 1364–5.

A description of a festivity at court. According to a common pattern in such descriptions the young squires busy themselves with fencing and similar sports, the old men play chess, and the young girls entertain themselves with dancing:

Avec le deduit des puceles
Estoit li dous sons des vïeles.

With the diversions of the girls was the sweet sound of
fiddles.

Probably a reference to dance-music, perhaps dance-songs (compare
Appendix 2, 2:8–9).[23]

36 *Les Deux Bourdeurs Ribauds*

Source: E.Faral, ed., *Mimes Français du XIIIe siècle* (Paris, 1910), p.101.

The poem mocks the stereotyped and boastful patter of professional
minstrels:

Ge sui jugleres de viele;
Si sai de muse, et de fretele,
Et de harpe, et de chifonie,
De la gigue, de l'armonie:
Et el salteire et en la rote
Sai je bien chanter une note.   29–34

I am a minstrel of the *viele*; I know how to play
the *muse*, the *fretele*, the *harpe*, the *chifonie*,
the *gigue* and the *armonie*: and I know how to sing
a melody well on the *salteire* and *rote*.

37 c1218–1236   Gautier de Coinci: *Les Miracles de Nostre Dame*

Source: V.F.Koenig, ed., *Les Miracles de Nostre Dame par Gautier de Coinci*, 4
vols (Geneva and Lille, 1955–70).

Gautier de Coinci was a trained musician and a keen observer of secular
song-styles. Several of the lyric insertions in *Les Miracles de Nostre Dame* are
witty and perceptive parodies of contemporary genres such as the *pastourelle*.
One of these lyric insertions begins:

Ma vïele
Vïeler vieut un biau son
De la bele
Qui seur toutes a biau non,

> En cui Diex devenir hom
> > Vout jadis,
> Dont chantent en paradis
> Angle et arcangle a haut ton.
> > > III, p.300, 1–8

> My *vïele* wishes to play a new melody about the beautiful one
> whose reputation exceeds all others in fairness, in whom
> God long ago wished to become a man, of which angels and
> archangels sing with loud voice in Paradise.

It is tempting to construe the first two lines of this poem as a call for instrumental (specifically fiddle) accompaniment. But there is another reason why Gautier may have wished to name the *vïele* twice in these eight lines. In the preface to the first book of the *Miracles* he proclaims:

> Or veil atant traire ma lire
> Et atemprer veil ma vïele,
> Si chanterai de la pucele
> Dont li prophete tant chanterent . . . .
> > > I, p.22, 56–9.

> Now I wish to take up my *lire* forthwith, and I shall tune my
> *vïele*; I will sing of the maiden of whom the prophets
> have sung so often . . . .

Here, once again, is Gautier invoking his *vïele*, and we scarcely need the signal provided by the word *lire* in the first line of the extract to realise that Gautier is drawing upon more than a millennium of Latin literary tradition in which literate poets present themselves as string-playing bards. Whence Statius:

> . . . nunc tendo chelyn satis arma referre
> Aonia et geminis sceptrum exitiale tyrannis . . . .

> Now I tune my lyre only for the singing of Aonian arms and
> of the sceptre fatal to both tyrants . . . . (*Thebaid*, 1:33–4)

Whence also the poeticisms, which abound in medieval Latin verse, whereby a 'lyre plectrum' stands for the poet's tongue or his pen, and playing (or tuning) the lyre becomes a high-style periphrasis for 'writing poetry'.

Yet there is another layer of meaning in Gautier's announcement that he will 'tune his fiddle' to sing of the Virgin: the layer of Christian biblical commentary whereby the stringed instruments mentioned in the psalms were allegorically related to aspects of Christian spirituality. [*Oratio*] *est lyra nostra*—'prayer is our lyre', says St Jerome in his commentary upon the psalms, and the idea is common enough in medieval Latin hymnody:[24]

> Lyra laudis formet sonum,
> Laudet Blasium patronum,
>   Nec obstet desidia.

One passage in the *Miracles* reveals how imagery such as this lay close to the surface of Gautier's mind. Having recounted the miracle of the candle which descended onto a minstrel's *vïele* at Roc-Amadour (cf. item 12) he emphasises the importance of inner as well as outward effort in the performance of devotional music by 'our priests, cantors, clerics and monks':

> ... quant la bouche bien s'esforce,
> Li cuers se doit si resforcier
> Et si les cordes renforcier
> De sa vïele et si estendre
> Que li clers sonz sanz plus atendre
> Au premier mot s'en voist et mont
> Em paradys lassus amont.
> Lors est a Dieu leur chançons bele.
> Mais pluiseur ont tele vïele
> Qui tempre et tart est destempree
> Se de fort vin n'est atempree.
>
>   IV, p.184, 220–30.

> ... when the mouth is working hard the heart should so
> strive, and so press upon the strings of its *vïele*, and so
> tune them up, that with the first word the bright sound
> ascends without delay to Paradise. Then their singing is
> pleasing to God. But there are many [liturgical singers] who
> have such a *vïele* that will go out of tune all the time
> unless it is tuned up with strong wine.

Here liturgical singers are presented figuratively as fiddlers whose *vïele* is their heart. For Gautier, therefore, the *vïele* is an emblem both of the poetic muse (*atemprer veil ma vïele*) and of Christian spirituality and communication with God. To return to the lyric *Ma vïele*: when Gautier announces that his *vïele* wishes to play a new song I take him to mean that his Christian devotion and his poetic muse (two aspects of his art that he would surely not have distinguished in these terms) are newly inspired.

Gautier's telling of the Roc-Amadour miracle incorporates several references to simultaneous singing and fiddling by the minstrel-hero of the tale, Pierre de Sygelar:

La vïele prent de rechief,
Vers l'ymage lieve le chief,
Si chante si bien et vïele
N'est sequence ne kyrïele
Qu'escoutissiez plus volentiers,

IV, p.178, 77–81.

... sa chançon, sa melodie
Recommencié a de rechief
· · · · · · · · · · · ·
La bouche chante et li cuers eure.

ibid. p.180, 122–3; 128.

He takes his *vïele* again and raises his eyes towards the
statue [of the Virgin]; he sings and fiddles so well that
there is no sequence or kyrie that you would have heard more
gladly ... he began once more his song and his music ... his
mouth sings and his heart rejoices.

38   soon after 1233   Huon de Meri: *Le Torneiment Anticrist*

Source: M.O.Bender, ed., *Le Torneiment Anticrist by Huon de Meri* (University
of Mississippi, 1976), p.71.

After a feast:

Cil jougleor en pes esturent;
S'unt vieles e harpes prises:
Chançons, lais, sons, vers e reprises
E de geste chanté nous ont.
Li chevalier Antecrist font
Le rabardel par grant deduit.
Li autres Antecrit deduit
En sons gaçons et aveirgnas.
· · · · · · · · · · · ·
Li chevalier, tuit se coucherent.
Cil jougleur lur vielerent
Por endormir sons poitevins.

482–9; 493–5

The minstrels rose to their feet and took up *vieles* and
harpes, then they sang us *chançons, lais, sons, vers,*
reprises and *chansons de geste*. The knights of Antichrist
dance the *rabardel* with great delight; another entertains
Antichrist with melodies from Gascony and the Auvergne ....

The knights all went to bed. The minstrels fiddled Poitevin
melodies for them to help them sleep.

[1:5]

39 *Macaire*

Source: M.Guessard, ed., *Macaire*, Les Anciens Poètes de la France (Paris,
1866), lines 58–61.

This French *chanson de geste* survives only in a Franco-Italian version:

> La çentil dame estoit en son verçer,
> Cun mante dame s'estoit à deporter;
> Si se fasoit davanti soi violer,
> E una cançon e dir e çanter.

> The noble lady [the wife of Charlemagne] was in her
> orchard and was entertained with many other ladies; she
> commanded the fiddle should be played before her and that a
> song should be sung.

[6]

Music theorists

40 1274 Elias of Salomon: *Scientia Artis Musice*

Source: Gerbert, *Scriptores*, 3, p.61.

On the ways in which *musica falsa* can arise:

> Quarto accidit ob defectum et negligentiam boni musici,
> qui quando videt falsam notam, non corrigit, nec redigit
> in luculentam notam et concordem. Item incidit in
> contagionem falsae musicae, quicumque plangit F. vel G.,
> c. vel d. quae nullo modo debent neque patiuntur plangi,
> ut in palmae natura et figura continetur .... Et hoc contingit
> in pluribus, quia ignorans cantor ignorat scientiae naturam,
> quam potest videre in palma, et habilitare vocem suam ad
> cantandum cantum, qui cum instrumento ligneo, cum viella
> optime, cantaretur.

> [*Musica falsa*] arises in a fourth way from the failure and
> neglect of a good musician who, when he sees a false

195

note, does not correct it or bring it back to beauty and
concordance. Again, he falls into the contagion of *musica
falsa* who puts a semitone between *F* or *G*, or *c* or *d* which
should never have a semitone placed between them so that
[the music] may be contained within the form and content of
the [Guidonian] hand . . . . And this arises in many instances,
because an ignorant singer does not know the nature of the
learning that he can see in the hand, nor can he adjust his
voice to singing a song which should be sung with a
wooden instrument—with a *viella* best of all.

It seems that instrumentally-accompanied *cantus* is involved here, but what
is this *cantus* and what kind of musician is meant by *cantor*? The music may
be secular song of some sort (since it is instrumentally-accompanied), but it
is conceivable that Elias is referring to forms of para-liturgical chant akin to
certain types of secular song (hymns, perhaps, or sequences). The *cantores* in
question are presumably clerical singers of some kind with a duty (not
always discharged) to learn the Guidonian hand, but Elias may be using the
term *cantor* to cover all musicians without formal training. As for the music
involved, whatever it may be, it is difficult to understand why it *should* be
sung with a musical instrument, best of all with a *viella*. Is it because that is
the most artistic kind of performance for the music invoked? Because singers
liable to make errors in the placing of semitones can sing correctly when
accompanied by an instrument?

41   ?c1300   Jerome of Moravia: *Tractatus de Musica*

See above, pp.64ff.

42   c1300   Johannes de Grocheio: *De Musica*

Source: E.Rohloff, ed., *Die Quellenhandschriften zum Musiktraktat des Johannes de
Grocheio* (Leipzig, 1972).

In describing the musical forms used by the Parisians of his day Grocheio
distinguishes two kinds of music made by the human voice, *cantus* and
cantilena, each with three sub-divisions:

CANTUS
cantus gestualis
cantus coronatus
cantus versualis

CANTILENA
rotunda vel rotundellus

stantipes
ductia

We shall return to the meanings of these terms; what matters here is Grocheio's statement that accomplished fiddlers normally include all of these musical forms in their repertory:

> Bonus autem artifex in viella omnem cantum et cantilenam
> et omnem formam musicalem generaliter introducit. (p.136)

> A good fiddler generally performs every
> kind of *cantus* and *cantilena*, and every musical form.

What are these *vocal* forms which any good fiddler can generally perform? To begin with the *cantilena* group:

> CANTILENA
> rotunda vel rotundellus
> stantipes
> ductia

Each genre in this group has a refrain (*Responsorium vero est, quo omnis cantilena incipit et terminatur*). Within the group the terms *rotunda* and *rotundellus* seem to have both a general and a precise sense: Grocheio says that some people use these two words to denote any *cantilena*, whereas 'we' (presumably the Parisians of his day) confine the terms *rotunda* and *rotundellus* to a refrain-song having the same melody for its refrain as for its verses: a description which fits the rondeau. The *stantipes*, to judge by its name, is an estampie. The *ductia* is described as a choric dancing-song, light and brisk.

The identification of the three kinds of *cantus* poses a delicate problem.

> CANTUS
> cantus gestualis
> cantus coronatus
> cantus versualis

The *cantus gestualis* is certainly the epic narrative, or *chanson de geste*. But what of the *cantus coronatus* and the *cantus versualis*? Van der Werf has proposed that Grocheio's account of these types is so imprecise as to be almost useless, but this is a harsh judgement.[25] Let us look again at what the theorist has to say:

> Cantus coronatus ab aliquibus simplex conductus dictus
> est. Qui propter eius bonitatem in dictamine et cantu
> a magistris et studentibus circa sonos coronatur, sicut
> gallice *Ausi com l'unicorne* vel *Quant li roussignol*. Qui
> etiam a regibus et nobilibus solet componi et etiam coram

regibus et principibus terrae decantari, ut eorum animos
ad audaciam et fortitudinem, magnanimitatem et liberalitatem
commoveat, quae omnia faciunt ad bonum regimen. Est enim
cantus iste de delectabili materia et ardua, sicut de
amicitia et caritate, et ex omnibus longis et perfectis efficitur. (p.130)

Cantus versualis est, qui ab aliquibus cantilena dicitur
respectu coronati et ab eius bonitate in dictamine et
concordantia deficit, sicut gallice *Chanter m'estuet quar
ne m'en puis tenir*, vel *Au repairier que je fis de
Prouvence*. Cantus autem iste debet iuvenibus
exhiberi, ne in otio totaliter sint reperti.... (p.132)

The *cantus coronatus* is called a simple [i.e. monophonic]
conductus by some, which is crowned amongst musical
compositions by masters and students on account of
its excellence in text and music, examples being the
French songs *Ausi com l'unicorne* or *Quant li roussignol*.
It is customarily composed by kings and nobles and
usually performed before kings and princes of the land
so that their minds may be moved to boldness, hardiness,
magnanimity and liberality, all of which things are
conducive to good government. This kind of song deals
with pleasing and demanding themes such as friendship
and love, and it is entirely made from perfect longs.

The *cantus versualis* is called by some a *cantilena* with
respect to the *cantus coronatus*, for it lacks its
excellence in poetry and concord, examples being
the French song *Chanter m'estuet quar ne m'en puis
tenir*, or *Au repairier que je fis de Prouvence*. This kind of
song should be performed for young people, so that
they may not fall completely into idleness ...

These definitions are clear and coherent if we think in terms of the register of
the songs involved. A survey of Grocheio's description of song-forms
suggests that two registrations underlie what he has to say, and I shall call
them the *cantilena* register and the *cantus* register. The *cantilena* register is the
lower, for it is associated

(1) with the refrain (all of Grocheio's *cantilene* have refrains);

(2) with dance (although Grocheio only mentions dancing with reference
to the *ductia*, we know from other sources that the rondeau and estampie,
Grocheio's other *cantilene*, were often used for dancing, though this may
not have been Parisian practice);

(3) with the entertainment of the young (this is specified for all Grocheio's
cantilene).

In contrast the *cantus* register is higher (at least as far as it embraces lyric rather than the narrative *cantus gestualis*, or epic), because it is headed by the *cantus coronatus*, a kind of song which Grocheio validates in almost every possible way:

    (a) its music and poetry are excellent;

    (b) it deals with delightful but demanding subject-matter (*de delectabili materia et ardua*);

    (c) it is normally composed by the highest in the land and

    (d) it is usually performed for them;

    (e) it does not have a refrain (all the *cantilene* do);

    (f) it is not associated with young people.

This lyric registration may be represented diagrammatically:

Cantilena register	*Cantus* register
rondeau *ductia* *estampie*	*cantus coronatus* *cantus versualis*
refrain	no refrain (or at least refrain is not a crucial signal of this register)
composers not mentioned	*cantus coronatus* associated with royal and noble composers
performed for/by the young	*cantus coronatus* performed for royalty and nobles but *cantus versualis* should be performed by/for the young
not associated with any special subject matter	*cantus coronatus* deals with material which is delightful yet demanding
associated with dance (only *ductia* is explicitly associated with dance in the treatise)	no reference to dance

There is a differentiation within the *cantus* register, for the *cantus coronatus* is clearly superior to the *cantus versualis*. The *cantus versualis* (a) lacks the excellence of the *cantus coronatus* in text and concord (?music ?rhyme),[26] and is (b) performed for the diversion of the young rather than for the delectation of the great. We can now see that this last comment about the proper audience for the *cantus versualis* is a suggestive one once we have understood Grocheio's sense of lyric registration; in his terms, to say that a song should be performed for the young is equivalent to saying that its registration has a tendency to sink towards the *cantilena* register where every type of lyric is performed for the young. Hence Grocheio is being perfectly consistent—*pace* Van der Werf—when he says that the *cantus versualis* is called a *cantilena* by some persons.[27]

What, then, are the *cantus coronatus* and the *cantus versualis*? The *cantus coronatus* has been repeatedly linked with the handful of songs in trouvère manuscripts which are marked with a crown or with the words *chançon couronnée*, and with the practice of the Puis whereby the composers of winning songs were crowned and their songs copied down with an appropriate marking.[28] Yet while there is no doubt that such prize-songs were often called *chançons couronnées*, this term also appears in certain texts where the meaning 'a prize-winning song at a Pui' seems somewhat out of the way. When the thirteenth-century theorist Anonymous 2 says that *musica falsa* is used 'for the sake of beauty, as in *cantinellis coronatis*', it seems unlikely that he is referring to prize-songs;[29] no doubt winning songs were often successful because they were judged to have more musical beauty than their competitors, but can such winning songs have been so markedly characterised by their use of semitone adjustments that a music theorist could hold them up as a telling example of musica ficta? Surely Anonymous 2 must be referring to some broader category?

The same may be said of two further literary references to the *chançon couronnée*, both of which appear to have gone unnoticed up to now:

(1) In the anonymous *Complainte Douteuse* of the thirteenth century a lover announces that he will sing *iceste chançon coronee* as a message to his lady, and one stanza of an (otherwise unknown) song follows, beginning *Paine d'amors e li maus que j'en trai*.[30]

(2) In the Anglo-Norman *Geste de Blancheflour e de Florence* the poet enters a garden and hears a variety of musical instruments (a conventional motif in love-gardens) together with the *chaunceon corounée*.[31]

Surely these two poets—and Anonymous 2—are referring to a certain genre of song, rather than to certain individual songs distinguished by the happy fate of having won a competition? This genre of song must surely be the *grand chant courtois*, as the examples of *cantus coronatus* cited by Grocheio suggest (one a song of Thibaut de Navarre, and the other perhaps the lyric *Quant li roussignol* attributed to the Chastelain de Couci and to Raoul de Ferrières).[32] In other words, *cantus coronatus/chançon couronnée* in its general sense was a thirteenth-century term for distinguishing the most elevated and excellent form of trouvère song.

What, then, is a *cantus versualis*? I suggest that this is Grocheio's term for songs which did not aim at the highest quality (or did not achieve it), yet which belonged above the *cantilena* register. In other words the distinction between *cantus coronatus* and *cantus versualis* was not so much a formal contrast as an aesthetic one for Grocheio: a *cantus versualis* was simply not as excellent as a *cantus coronatus* when viewed in terms of style, content, characteristic milieu, function and ethos—in terms of register. Small wonder, then, if modern scholars comparing Grocheio's examples of the *cantus coronatus* and the *cantus versualis* have been unable to discern significant differences between them. Is our understanding of thirteenth-century taste in love-lyric so fine that we can reconstruct the judgements of contemporaries as to what made a poem excellent as opposed to merely fine? Jean de le Mote's *Le Parfait du Paon* gives us some idea of what was involved in judging a song's claim to be a *chançon couronnée* during the lifetime of Grocheio: one had to watch for little faults in the use of language (*faus ronmant*), momentary tautologies (*redicte en sens*), failures to achieve the true High-Style of the best courtly lyric (*Li mot ne sont pas haut mes il sont bien plaisant*) and so on.[33] These may well be some of the criteria which Grocheio has in mind when he says that the *cantus versualis* lacks the excellence of the *cantus coronatus* in 'text and concord'. The songs which he cites as examples of each genre may look more or less alike to us, but it does not follow thereby that Grocheio had no valid reason for distinguishing them in the way that he does.

Treatises on confession or on the vices and virtues

43   c1216   Thomas de Chobham: *Summa Confessorum*

Source: F. Broomfield, ed., *Thomae de Chobham Summa Confessorum* (Paris and Louvain, 1968), p.292.

The strongest manuscript tradition gives this work to Master Thomas of Chobham (Surrey), who is sometimes described simply as sub-dean, sometimes sub-dean of Salisbury. Yet although this manual for confessors was probably compiled by an Englishman and in England, Chobham's account of minstrels (from which the following excerpt is taken) resembles passages in other manuals, some of which are probably French.[34] His immediate source was probably Peter the Chanter's *Summa de Sacramentis*,[35] but the following passage on instrumentalists who perform secular songs does not seem to have a counterpart in Peter's *Summa*.

De histrionibus

   ... Est etiam tertium genus histrionum qui habent
   instrumenta musica ad delectandum homines, sed
· talium duo sunt genera. Quidam enim frequentant

publicas potationes et lascivas congregationes
ut cantent ibi lascivas cantilenas, ut moveant
homines ad lasciviam, et tales sunt damnabiles. . . .

Concerning minstrels

. . . There is also a third kind of minstrels who
use musical instruments to delight their hearers,
but there are two kinds of these. Some frequent public
drinking-places and wanton gatherings so that they
may sing lecherous songs there to move the minds of
men to lechery, and these are damnable . . . [the second kind
of minstrel with instruments comprises those who sing
of the lives of saints and of the deeds of magnates]

44 b1249/50   Guillaume Peyraut: *Summa de Vitiis et Virtutibus*

Source: Oxford, Bodleian Library MS Lyell 12 (English, late 13c), f.32r.

De auditu cantilenarum

Sequitur de auditu cantilenarum amatoriarum et
turpiloquiorum et instrumentorum musicorum. Auditus
cancionum valde timendus est. Unde Ecclesiasticus .ix.
ubi sic legitur: cum saltatrice ne scis assiduus
nec audias illam ne forte pereas in efficacia illius.
Ad auditum turpiloquiorum possumus referre quod dicit
apostolus: corrumpunt bonos mores colloquia prava.

Musica eciam instrumenta multum sunt timenda. Frangunt enim
corda hominum et emolliunt et ideo per verbum Sapientis
essent frangenda.

Concerning listening to songs.

Here follows a section on listening to songs of
love, to unclean words and to musical instruments.
Listening to songs is an activity which is greatly
to be feared. Whence Ecclesiasticus 9[:4] where it
says: 'do not cultivate the company of a
dancing-girl, and do not listen to her, lest you
may perish through her charms'. As far as concerns
listening to unclean words we have the testimony of the
Apostle [I Cor. 15:33]: 'corrupt speech destroys good
morals'.

Musical instruments are also much to be feared. They
break and soften the hearts of men; therefore let them
be shattered according to the word of Solomon.

Peyraut's use of Ecclesiasticus 9:4 ('Do not cultivate the company of a
dancing-girl') shows that, like many moralists of the thirteenth century, he
associates the morally damaging effects of love-songs with the public
dances, or *coreae*, often held on liturgical feast-days and frequently performed in churchyards. Peyraut is giving us, in other words, the moralist's
perspective on the kind of festivity described by Johannes de Grocheio: the
occasions when 'girls and young men in festivals and in great gatherings'
performed refrain forms—often for dancing—such as the rondeau *Toute sole
passerai le vert boscage* and the *ductia* beginning *Chi encor querez amoretes*. Peyraut
clearly thinks of instrumental music as something to be condemned in the
same breath, together with the 'unclean words' (*turpiloquia*) which countless
medieval moralists associate with these public dances. For the possibility
that the dance-songs performed on these occasions were sometimes
instrumentally accompanied, which may be implied here, see the following
passage and items 45–8.

In a long section on *coreae*, full of references to contemporary life, Peyraut
recounts the story told in Gregory's *Dialogues* of a man who appeared before
the door of a rich lord, leading an ape and playing cymbals as he cried: 'alas!
alas! this unfortunate is dead.'[36] When the rich man left his house later that
day he was killed. Peyraut comments:

Quale est hoc nisi hominem morti condempnatum cum
choreis et instrumentis musicis ad tormentum suum
ire? Ad mortem suam cantando et letando vadunt qui
choreas ducunt.

What is this if not a man condemned to go to his death
with dancing and with the sound of musical instruments?
Those who lead *choreae* go singing and rejoicing to their
death.

45   1231–6   Guillaume d'Auvergne: *De Universo*

Source: Guillaume d'Auvergne, *Opera Omnia* (Venice, 1591), II, p.704.

[From a section concerning the possibility that there may be dances
(*choreae*) in the after-life]:

Vides insuper viros, et mulieres, per gaudijs huiusmodi
dissilientes, strepentes, saltantes, et sonis cantilenarum
aut musicorum instrumentorum quam possunt effigiatione
motuum concordare conantes.

You see, moreover, men and women leaping with
the joy they find in this kind of sport [i.e. dancing in
choreae], making a clamour, springing, wishing to
fit the form of their movements to the music of
songs, or of musical instruments, to the best of their
ability.

46   Guillaume d'Auvergne: *De Viciis et Peccatis*

Source: Oxford, Bodleian Library, MS Bodley 281 (Canterbury, first half of
the 15c), f.139r-v.

[On human skills that involve many faculties at the same time]:

Similiter se habet in citharizante seu viellante qui
simul et movet pollicem et digitos multos et tangit
nervos cum archu movens archum multipliciter, audit
etiam sonos multos simul ut sciret quam consonanciam
resonarent, cantat et ore proprio et gesticulatur toto
corpore.

It is the same for him who plays the *cithara* or the
fiddle: at the same time he moves his thumb and many
fingers, touching the gut-strings with the bow and
moving the bow in many different ways; also, he hears
many sounds at the same time so that he may know what
consonance they are producing; and moreover he sings
with his own mouth and moves with his whole body.

This is a clear reference to self-accompaniment by fiddler or (?) harpist. The
passage seems worth including here not only because of the unambiguous
reference which it contains to instrumental accompaniment of the voice but
also for the evidence it provides that string-players, specifically fiddlers,
sometimes accompanied themselves (compare items 12 and 33).

47   Albertus Magnus: *Commentary upon the* Sentences *of Peter Lombard*

Source: A. Borgnet, ed., *Beati Alberti Magni Opera Omnia*, 29 (Paris, 1894),
p.633.

In the celebrated *Sentences* of Peter Lombard there is a brief discussion of the
Sacrament of Penance which enjoins that penitents should absent themselves from all kinds of entertainments (4:xvi). In his commentary upon this

section Albertus marshals Scriptural and patristic authorities which both support and contradict the Lombard's ruling, then offers the *solutio* from which the following extract is taken:

> Responsio. Dicendum, quod choreae et hujusmodi ludi,
> sive fiant cantu, sive instrumentis musicis, secundum
> se non sunt mali, sicut ultimo per auctoritates probatum
> est. . . .

> Solution. It is to be said that *choreae* and games
> of this kind, whether they be done with song or with
> musical instruments, are not evil when judged according
> to their own natures, as has just been proved by the
> authorities cited. . . .

48   12c   Honorius Augustodunensis: *Gemma Anime*

Source: PL 172, cols. 587–8 (compared with Oxford, Bodleian Library, MS Bodley 196 (English, c1300), f.42r).

An extract from a chapter entitled *De choro* (i.e. the liturgical choir and its arrangement). Honorius is surely describing the performance-style of twelfth-century ring-dances in this passage: the dancers sing and move in a circle, hold hands one moment and clap the next, and stamp their feet—all, apparently, to the accompaniment of instruments:

> *Chorus* psallentium a chorea canentium exordium sumpsit,
> quam antiquitas idolis ibi constituit, ut videlicet
> decepti deos suos et voce laudarent, et toto corpore
> eis servirent. Per *choreas* autem circuitionem voluerunt
> intelligi firmamenti revolutionem: per manuum complexionem,
> elementorum connexionem: per sonum cantantium, harmoniam
> planetarum resonantium: per corporis gesticulationem,
> signorum motionem: per plausum manuum, vel pedum strepitum,
> tonitruorum crepitum. Quod fideles imitati sunt, et in
> servitium veri Dei converterunt. Nam populus de mari
> Rubeo egressus choream duxisse, et Maria eis cum tympano
> praecinuisse, et David ante arcam totis viribus saltasse,
> et cum cithara psalmos cecinisse legitur. Et Salomon
> cantores circa altare instituisse dicitur, qui voce,
> tubis, organis, cymbalis, citharis, cantica personuisse
> leguntur. Unde et adhuc in choreis musicis instrumentis uti
> nituntur, quia globi coelestes dulci melodia circumferri
> dicuntur.

The *chorus* of praising singers is derived from the
dancing-chorus of singers which the men of ancient times
established before their idols so that the heathens
might worship their Gods both with their voices and
with their entire bodies. By the circling motion of
their *choreae* they wished to symbolise the revolution of the
heavens; by the linking of hands, the inter-relationship
of the Elements; by the sound of singers, the harmony
of the resounding planets; by the gesticulation of the
body, the movement of the constellations; by the
clapping of hands or the stamping of feet, the crashing
of thunder. The faithful have imitated this and turned
it to the service of the true God, for we read that the
Israelites led a ring-dance having crossed the Red Sea, and
that Miriam sang before them with her drum; David danced
with his men before the ark and sang the psalms with a
cithara. Solomon is said to have instituted singers
around the altar who sang songs with voice, with *tubae*,
organa, *cymbala* and with *citharae*. Whence [the faithful]
still use musical instruments in their ring-dances, for the
celestial bodies are said to be borne around by sweet
melody.

Petrus de Abano

49 1310 Petrus de Abano: *Expositio problematum Aristotelis*

Source: *Expositio problematum Aristotelis* (Mantua, 1475), part 19, problem 9.

Petrus de Abano's commentary upon Aristotle's *Problems* was begun in Paris
and completed at Padua in 1310. This passage may be the only sustained
discussion of instrumental accompaniment to survive from the twelfth and
thirteenth centuries. The following extract gives Aristotle's text (as it
appears in the Latin translation cited by Abano), followed by Abano's
commentary:

> *Propter quid delectabiliter unitatem cantus*
> *audimus si quis ad fistulam aut lyram cantat*
> *et ad cordas, et eundem cantum cantant utrobique.*
> *Si enim ad hoc magis idem potius oportebat ad*
> *multos fistulatores, et adhuc delectabiliter*
> *esse. Aut quia adipiscens manifestius intentionem*
> *magis quando ad fistulam aut lyram quando vero ad*
> *multos fistulatores aut lyras multas non*
> *est delectabile propter id quod destruit melodiam.*

Quare cum delectatione audimus cantum unitum, seu
in unum coniunctum, ut si quis cantat in fistula
vel lira, et universaliter in cordis ceu in
psalterio, canone et huiusmodi instrumentis ex
cordis multis compositis, dummodo utrobique cantet
eundem cantum (quoniam si unus cantus seu dantia
fieret instrumento, et alius voce canentis etiam,
in illo non consurgeret propter dissonantiam
delectatio). Deinde. *Si adhuc*. Quasi arguit in
contrarium dicens quod si huiusmodi delectatio
contingat propter unitatem cantus et ydemptitatem,
tunc oportebit magis delectari cum quis cantabit
cum multis fistulantibus vel lirantibus, cum magis
videantur super unum opus unitari vel plures
trahentes navim unitantur ut melius trahant.
Deinde. *Aut quia*. Solvit dicens causam esse quia
cum aliquis cantat signanter intentionem et maneriem
cantus, magis unitatur vox cum sono instrumenti quam
quando cantaret in diversis instrumentis etiam eodem
cantu utrobique exeunte. Et hoc quia in cantu quedam
reservantur proportiones ut dicetur commensurate,
quibus observatis iocunda consurgit armonia quod quidem
corrumpitur et indelectabilis redditur cum cantans
ad multa cantaverit instrumenta. Quod autem inductum
est in contrarium prius non valet, quia licet multi
possint idem cantare, non tamen eodem modo. Non
enim solum requiritur ydemptitas ex parte illius qui
cantatur et cuiuslibet cantantis ad se ipsum, ymo
unuscuiusque et ad alium ad omnes, ita quod ex omnibus
resultent proportiones debite in cantu. Quod autem
subiecit de tractu navis non huic simulatur dicto
quoniam plurimi possunt simul idem ut navim eodem
modo et tempore trahere ut audientes vocem rectoris
navis; non autem talis unitas potest in cantu
plurium observari armonico cum eum ex pluribus
et contrariis oporteat constituere in unum tandem redditur
quod fit impossibile pluribus entibus vocibus et
instrumentis.

[Aristotle]:

*Why do we hear a solo song with more pleasure if anyone
sings it to a fistula or lyra, and to strings, and yet
the same song is sung on both sides? If it is more
pleasing in this way the same thing should ensue even
more when there are many fistula players, and be yet more
delightful. Could it be that the design of a song is more
clearly expressed when it is sung to a fistula or lyra,*

*for when it is sung to many fistula players and lyra
players it is not delightful and the melody is destroyed?*

[Petrus de Abano]:

Why is it that we listen to solo music (or to music which
has been united into a whole) with more pleasure if it is
sung to a *fistula* or *lira*, and upon strings in general,
either to the *psalterium*, the *canon* and to instruments of
this kind comprising many strings, if the same music is
performed on both sides (for if one music or setting be
given to the instrument and another be given to the voice
there will arise no pleasure on account of the resulting
discord)? Then: *Si adhuc.* Here it is as if [Aristotle]
argues to the contrary saying that if this kind of pleasure
arises from the unity and oneness of the music, then we
should be even more delighted if anyone sings to the music
of many *fistula* or *lira* players when they might thus be
seen to be all the more united in a common task like many
united to row a boat so that it may be rowed the better.
Then: *Aut quia.* [Aristotle] answers the question saying
the reason is that when one delivers the design and
musical character of a song in a distinct manner
then the voice is more unified to the sound of a
[single] instrument than when the song is sung to diverse
instruments giving out the same music. This is because
there are certain relationships (*proportiones*) which must
be preserved in music if a song is to be performed in a
well-adjusted manner; when they are preserved, the
pleasantness of the music springs forth, and it is only
corrupted and made unpleasant when it is sung to many
instruments. What has been said above to counterbalance this
does not hold [i.e. the argument that if our pleasure in
accompanied song comes from the unity of voice and
instrument then our pleasure should be increased by adding
more instruments and thus increasing the unanimity
displayed], for even if many might perform the same thing,
they cannot perform it in the same way. Not only is
unanimity required in terms of the music which is performed,
and in terms of the singer being consistent with himself, it
is required from everyone, so that the necessary
relationships in the music are preserved by all. What was
said about the rowing of a ship does not hold here, for
while many may row a ship in time together and in the
same manner as they listen to the voice of the ship's
commander, this kind of unanimity cannot be achieved
in music produced by many when it is constituted from
various and contrary elements and yet is performed as

one (which is impossible to achieve if there are many voices
and instruments).

For other discussions of accompaniment in Abano's commentary see
Problems 39 and 43. This material is very closely based upon Aristotle's text
and may have no independent value as a source of information about early
fourteenth-century practice.

Appendix 4

String-materials in the Middle Ages

Why wilt thou examine every little fibre of my soul,
Spreading them out before the sun like stalks of flax to dry?

William Blake, *The Four Zoas*

I

When we speak of the vocal 'cords' which produce the human voice we acknowledge the expressive power of musical strings; there is no finer metaphor for the part of us which is musical and which best expresses our thoughts than the tensed filaments of a musical instrument. The comparison is a suitable one, for the musical personality of a chordophone resides in its strings: to paraphrase William Blake, they are the fibres of its soul. In terms of timbre and articulation the difference between strings of gut, metal, horsehair and silk is considerable; a song accompanied by (let us say) a fiddle strung with horsehair would present a very different acoustic experience to the listener from one performed to a fiddle strung with gut or metal. To establish the kind of string-material associated with each medieval instrument is therefore to bring the sound-pictures of medieval song into sharper focus.

Little has been done to determine which medieval instruments were strung with gut, which with metal, and so on. Yet there is an abundance of literary evidence bearing upon this topic and waiting to be sifted. The purpose of this appendix is therefore to sketch the outlines of medieval stringing traditions with the aid of a modest (and mostly new) corpus of written material. Since the craft of building and maintaining musical instruments hardly ever commanded written record during the Middle Ages we must rely upon passing references in a wide variety of texts for our information.[1] The backbone of this appendix is formed from allusions in Latin commentaries upon Psalm 150; the injunction *Laudate eum in chordis* often drew forth a mention of string-materials in these texts as a prelude to some appropriate allegory. In one case, a commentary by Bruno the Carthusian (5; these numbers refer to the list at the end of this appendix), there is even an allusion to the process of manufacturing gut-strings (Figure 13). As we might expect from the brief survey of Bible-commentary presented in Chapter 5, the friar-commentators active around 1300 are particularly valuable witnesses. We may include here a note upon psaltery materials in the monumental encyclopedia *De Proprietatibus Rerum*, compiled by the English Franciscan Bartholomaeus (18).

During the thirteenth century musical theorists began to take a passing interest in the physical and musical properties of instruments, and in some cases this included the substances with which they were strung. The anonymous *Summa Musice,* for example, the only music treatise which deserves to be placed beside Jerome of Moravia's *Tractatus de Musica* for the diligence with which it considers instruments, reviews the range of materials in use towards the end of the thirteenth century and, in doing so, provides the earliest reference to silk strings in the medieval West (20).[2]

A problem of terminology meets us everywhere. The difficulty is particularly apparent in the case of terms denoting metals. There are standard dictionary definitions of words such as *aes* ('bronze') and *orichalcum* ('brass'), but the precise meaning of these terms at any given time and place in the Middle Ages is a question for metallurgists and cannot be considered here. There is no guarantee that the *aes* of some thirteenth-century writer in France is necessarily the same as the *aes* of Cicero or Pliny. The problem is compounded by the likelihood that many medieval writers deploy such terms in a loose fashion by applying them indifferently to any yellow-looking metals which were not gold.

A brief survey of the terms and phrases associated with string-materials will help to clarify what can be achieved with these literary sources:

Gut

Latin   cordas ... intestinales (20)
            cordas de ... intestinis (23)
            intestinas ... chordas (3)
            chorda ... de nervo (27)
            corda siccatur et tenditur ... et caro hominis ... (13)

            corium mortui animalis (7)
            intestine animalium (9:2)
            ex intestinis mortuorum animalium (10)
            pellibus (25)

            de pellibus mortuis (22)
            de pellibus mortuorum animalium (14)

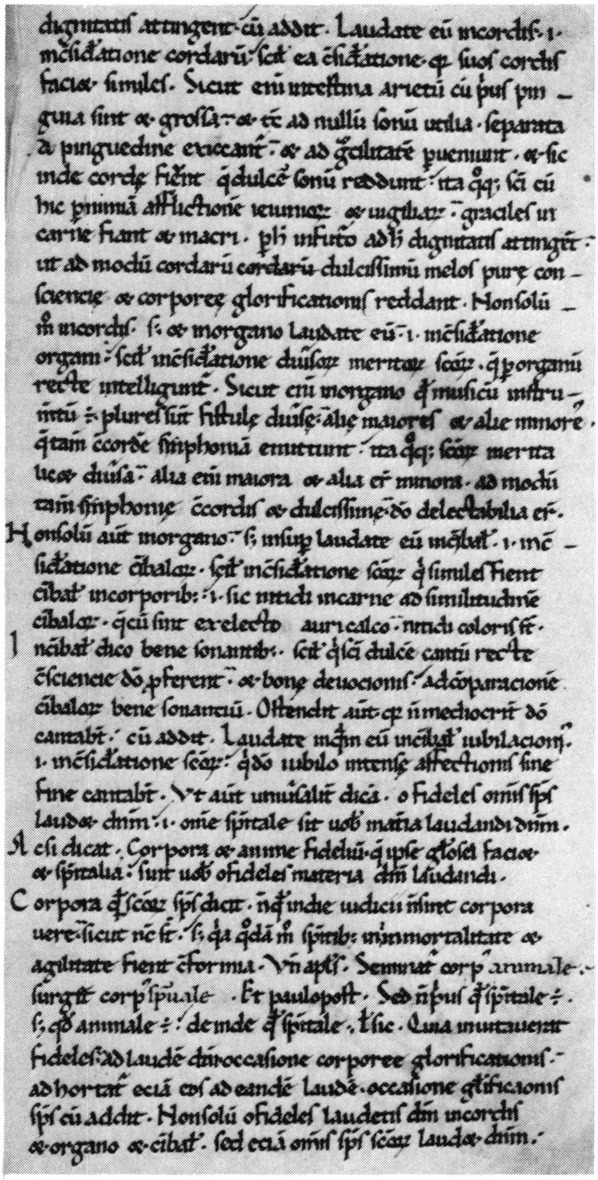

Figure 13 *An allusion to the process of manufacturing gut strings in the psalm-commentary of Bruno the Carthusian (the passage begins at line 3). See Appendix 4:5. Grenoble, Bibliothèque Municipale, MS 341, f.379r. Reproduced by permission.*

cordarum vel intestinis (2)
intestina arietum (5)

ex interioribus ovium (1)
de ovium intestinis factis (18h)
intestina ovium (17)
de intestinis ovium (18:1)
de intestinis ovis (18:2)
de visceribus ovium (18g)
viscera [of sheep] (4)
de intestinis pecoris (12)

de intestinis luporum (18:1)
de intestinis lupi (18:2)
lupina chordula (18i)
de visceribus lupi (18g)

de corio (11)
corium mortui animalis (7)

vervecum . . . extis (8)

seu pellibus vel pilis equorum (25)

Middle French	les menues cordes de boyaux (28)
	boyaulx des brebis (18c 1 and 2)
	boyaulx de loup (18c 2)
Old High German	indarmum (2)
Middle High German	shäfes darm (21)
Middle English	schepis guttis (18e 1 and 2)
	roopis [of sheep-gut] (4b)
	wolfes guttes (18e 1 and 2)

Metallic

Latin	cordas . . . metallinas (20)
	chorda . . . de metallo (27)
	aeneis . . . chordis (11)
	corde . . . argentee (24)
	cordule . . . de argento (18:3)
	cordas de ere (23)
	cordule de auricalco (18:3)

Middle French	fil darchal (18c 3)
	fil dargent (18c 3)
	d'argent (15)
	de fin or (16)
Spanish	plata (18d 3)
	laton (18d 3)
Middle English	latoun (18e 3)
	siluer (18e 3)
Middle Dutch	latoen (18f 3)
	siluer (18f 3)

Silk

Latin   chordas . . . sericinas (20)

Middle High German   mit syden seiten (26)

Horsehair

Latin   seu pellibus vel pilis equorum (25)

Gut

Although Classical Latin offers certain distinct meanings for the words *intestina* ('gut'), *nervus* ('sinew'), *exta* ('the larger internal organs') and *viscera* ('entrails in general') it seems best to translate them all by the generalising English word 'gut', for it is usually impossible to establish whether any more definite meaning is involved. Accordingly, there are many references in this appendix which will bear no more precise translation than 'gut string(s)' or something similar.

Some texts offer more precise information. Sheep-gut is mentioned as early as the fifth century in the psalm commentary of Arnobius Junior (1) and continues to be mentioned throughout the Middle Ages more often than any other type of gut string (4, 12 (where the animal, which I take to be a sheep, is called *pecus* rather than *ovis*), 17, 18:1 and 2 (plus derivatives), 21). Ram gut is mentioned in the psalm-commentary of Bruno the Carthusian (5) and there is one reference to string made from the dyed gut of a wether (8).

The terms *corium* and *pellis* pose a delicate problem. Strictly speaking both should be translated 'skin' or 'hide' or 'leather', yet there are reasons for assuming that they refer to strings of gut. The earliest use of *corium* appears in Pseudo-Haymo of Halberstadt's commentary upon Psalm 56:9: '[The Psalmist] says *chitara* to represent mortification [of the flesh], for in the Passion Christ was stretched on the cross like the *corium* of a dead animal' (7). This version of the common allegory that the stretched strings of David's instruments pre-figured the bodily sufferings of Christ reveals little by itself and it may be that 'leather' or 'hide' is the appropriate translation here. Yet it is noteworthy that several other psalm-commentaries which mention strings from 'an animal' or 'a dead animal' (this phrase is something of a formula) use *intestina* rather than *corium*:[3]

Chorde sunt intestine animalium (9:2)
ex intestinis mortuorum animalium (10)

The equation *corium* = gut is reinforced by the report in item 11, the *Topographia Hibernica* (1185–8) of Gerald of Wales, that the Irish play upon 'bronze' strings as opposed to strings made of *corium*. Since this observation is embedded in a passage whose purpose is to contrast the musical talents and customs of the Irish with those prevailing in the Anglo-Norman milieu of Gerald's readers, it seems likely that the *corium* which (by implication) everyone except the Irish uses is the fundamental string-material of the Middle Ages: gut.

The term *pellis* ('skin', 'hide') occurs only twice: once in an anonymous set of glosses on the psalms (14) where strings are said to be made *de pellibus mortuorum animalium*, and once in a tantalising gloss in the psalm-commentary (25) by the English Franciscan, Henry of Cossey, where the phrase 'Praise him upon strings' is glossed in this way:

id est instrumentis seu pellibus vel pilis equorum
sicut habent communiter vielle

that is, on instruments either with *pellibus* or with the
hairs of horses such as fiddles generally have.

Is this a reference to fiddles strung with leather? It is impossible to be certain. On balance the evidence for the use of leather strings on the art-instruments of the Middle Ages seems slight.

Horsehair

But the interest of Henry of Cossey's psalm-commentary does not end there for his gloss upon Psalm 150 seems to say that horsehair strings were 'generally' (*communiter*) used on the leading art-instrument of the thirteenth century, the *viella*. It is surprising to find the *viella* associated with a string-material which has been excluded from the tradition of Western art-music since the Renaissance, yet I suspect that Cossey's allusion to 'instruments ... with the hairs of horses such as fiddles generally have' can only be reasonably construed as a reference to strings of horsehair. It is conceivable that he is referring to the *bow* of the fiddle rather than to its strings, but that is unlikely; there seems no reason to mention bows in a gloss to a phrase which calls the faithful to praise God upon strings. Cossey could look back on a millennium of Christian tradition in which that call had often been glossed with a reference to string-materials followed by some appropriate allegory. It is certain that horsehair strings were employed in Wales in the fourteenth century and it is by no means impossible that they were sometimes used on the *viella*.[4]

Silk

There are only two references to silk strings, both of c1300. The Middle High German romance *Der Busant* (26) mentions them in connection with a spectacularly lavish fiddle which is decorated with gold and ivory, whilst the author of the *Summa Musice* (20) merely lists *cordas...sericinas* together with gut and metallic strings. The passage from *Der Busant* strongly suggests that strings of silk were regarded as a luxury commodity at the end of the thirteenth century, but until more references are found it will be impossible to establish how widely they were used.

Metallic

Only two of the references to metallic strings fail to mention specific material (they are: *cordas...metallinas* in item 20 and *chorda de metallo* in item 27). All of the remaining sources employ terms for which dictionaries of both classical and medieval Latin offer distinct meanings: *orichalcum* ('a form of brass or similar alloy'), *electrum* ('silver-gold alloy'), *argentum* ('silver'), *aes* ('copper, bronze or brass') and the adjective *aeneus* ('bronze, or other alloy of copper'). The variable meanings of these words even in classical Latin (where *aes* may denote at least three different alloys) and the likelihood that most of the medieval writers who employed them used them loosely, suggest that it is not safe to lean too heavily upon dictionary definitions for words such as these. Perhaps the most satisfactory way to deal with these references is to sort them into two categories: 'metal strings' and 'precious metal strings'. The justification for this classification is that when a medieval author refers to *aes*, for example, it is usually impossible to establish whether he means anything more precise than 'a yellowish looking metal'; but it seems reasonable to suppose that words denoting the precious metals gold or silver will have been chosen and employed with more discrimination.

The foundation for our knowledge of metal stringing in the medieval instrumentarium is laid by the English Franciscan friar, Bartholomaeus Anglicus. In his encyclopedia *De Proprietatibus Rerum* ('On the Properties of Things'), completed c1250, Bartholomaeus notes that strings of the *psalterium* are made *de auricalco et etiam de argento*: from 'latten' and also from 'silver' (18:3). I choose the translation 'latten' for *auricalco* since this is how the term is rendered in the vernacular translations of Bartholomaeus's work (18c, d, e and f).[5] The metal (and precious metal) stringing of the *psalterium* is confirmed almost two hundred years later by the French theologian Jean de Gerson; in his *Tractatus de Canticis* of c1426 Gerson records that the *psalterium* has *chordulas vel argenteas vel ex electro*, strings of 'silver' or of 'silver-gold alloy', while in his *Collectorium super Magnificat* of 1428 the strings are said to be made *ex auro vel auricalco*, from 'gold' or 'brass' ('latten'?).[6] No other stringed instruments of medieval France and England are associated with metallic stringing in our texts.

II

Several details now fall into place which allow us to sketch the outlines of medieval stringing traditions.

Firstly, Jean de Brie's *Le Bon Berger* (28) of 1379 recommends that gut-strings are best for '*vielles, harpes, rothes, luthz, quiternes, rebecs, choros, almaduries, symphonies, cytholes* and other instruments that one makes to give sound by means of the fingers and of strings'. This is a very comprehensive remark and few fourteenth-century instruments seem to be excluded from its range. One is missing, however: the *psalterion*, presumably because it was habitually strung with metallic material as attested by Bartholomaeus Anglicus and Jean de Gerson.[7]

Secondly, all the medieval evidence pertaining to the string-materials of stringed-keyboard instruments (which surely began life as mechanised psalteries, borrowing a good deal of psaltery technology) shows that they were strung with metallic materials. This supports the assumption that there was a long tradition of equipping psalteries with such strings.

The picture that emerges from the texts is therefore clear (although it can scarcely be complete): virtually all of the art-instruments of the Middle Ages were associated with gut stringing, although horsehair seems to have been sometimes used on the *viella* (and, no doubt, on some other instruments). Psalteries seem to have stood directly outside this tradition in that they were associated with metal stringing.

Here it may be possible to narrow down what is meant by 'psaltery', since it seems that there was at least one major family of zithers, the triangular harp-zither, or *rota* (Figure 11), which was associated with gut stringing; this tradition is mentioned in two sources widely separated in date (12 and

28). When Gerson speaks of the metallic strings of the psalterium there can be little doubt that he means a pig-snout psaltery of a familiar Gothic type (Figure 6),[8] and to judge by the evidence of illustrations where the term *psalterium* (or some vernacular form of the word) is accompanied by a drawing, the same might be said for Bartholomaeus Anglicus and Jean de Brie.

What of the chronology of metallic strings in the West? When were they introduced? This appendix offers some tantalising clues to how these questions might be answered. The earliest reference to metallic stringing on the list is contained in Gerald of Wales's account of Irish musicianship (11). This report, based on Gerald's own experience, was written during the period 1185–8, and it implies that the Irish were exceptional for the way they placed metallic stringing at the centre of their instrumental traditions.

The next references to metallic strings seem to maintain this 'Celtic' association: two Old French romances composed in the first decades of the thirteenth century: *Galeran de Bretagne* (15) and the Vulgate *Merlin* (16). *Galeran de Bretagne* mentions a harp which is strung with 'silver' (*argent*),[9] but the Vulgate *Merlin* goes one better and presents a harp with strings of 'thin gold' being played by the wizard himself in disguise. Arthur is holding a great feast, and on the second day he, Guinevere, and all the other kings and queens (of whom there are twelve present) wear their crowns; in the midst of the festivities a blind minstrel enters the hall; he is beautifully dressed and all marvel at him. As he walks amongst the tables he plays *j lai breton*:[10]

> ... ot vne harpe a son col qui toute estoit dargent
> moult ricement ouuree et les cordes estoient de fin
> or . et auoit en la harpe de lieus a autres pieres
> precieuses. ...

> ... he had a *harpe* around his neck which was richly worked
> all over with silver and the strings were of fine gold,
> and there were here and there on the harp precious
> stones. ...

The evidence of *Galeran de Bretagne* and the Vulgate *Merlin* is both mysterious and suggestive. Both texts mention precious-metal strings, and in each case the instrument so equipped is a *harpe*. But these two passages share a good deal more than that. In both of them the harp is used to play (or accompany) a Breton *lai*, and both works belong in the stratum of medieval French Romance which owes much to Celtic—especially Irish— story material.

The significance of this Celtic link is that Ireland has a long tradition of metal-strung instruments (we remember that Gerald of Wales remarks upon the Irish use of metal strings in the 1180s) and there are several references to them in Old Irish texts, some of them antedating both Gerald and our two romances. The evidence, fragmentary though it is, suggests that metallic stringing was used by Irish musicians in the twelfth century at a time when it was still regarded elsewhere as an exceptional material to employ (the fascinating question of how long the Irish had been using such strings awaits the attention of a specialist in Old Irish literature). It may then have passed into the Anglo-Norman and French realms with the Celtic musicians and story-tellers of whose activity in the twelfth century there is so much evidence. In these lands, however, metal stringing did not become established until the fifteenth century, for during the period 1250–1400 the literary evidence suggests that such strings were primarily associated with pig-snout psalteries.[11]

Tentative chronology of materials

Late Antiquity	1000	1200	1300	1400

Gut ——————————————————————————————————

                _Silk ——————————————————————

                     _Horsehair ————————————

             Metallic ——[psalteries] ——————————

String-materials in medieval texts

1   Arnobius Junior *In Psalmos*
2   Anon glossator
3   Walther of Speyer *Vita Sancti Christophori*
4   Wenrico *Conflictus Ovis et Lini*
5   Bruno the Carthusian *In Psalmos*
6   Pseudo-Remigius of Auxerre *In Psalmos*
7   Pseudo-Haymo of Halberstadt *In Psalmos*
8   Sextus Amarcius *Sermones*
9   Honorius Augustodunensis *In Psalmos*
10   Anon *In Psalmos*
11   Gerald of Wales *Topographia Hibernica*
12   Anon *Surgical Treatise*
13   Michael of Meaux *In Psalmos*
14   Anon *In Psalmos*
15   Anon *Galeran de Bretagne*
16   Anon *Merlin*
17   Anon *Secretum Philosophorum*
18   Bartholomaeus Anglicus *De Proprietatibus Rerum*
19   Guillaume d'Auvergne *De Viciis et Peccatis*

20 Anon *Summa Musice*
21 Hugo von Trimburg *Der Renner*
22 Nicholas de Gorran *In Psalmos*
23 Nicholas de Lyra *Postilla*
24 Petrus de Palude *In Psalmos*
25 Henry of Cossey *In Psalmos*
26 Anon *Der Busant*
27 Anon *Epistola cum Tractatu de Musica Instrumentali Humanaque ac Mundana*
28 Jean de Brie *Le Bon Berger*

Index to string-materials

Vernacular terminology (only the main terms are listed here)

FIDDLE NAMES
viella vielle viguela phiala fedele vedel

Gut	18:1, 18c:1, 18d:1, 2, 18e:1, 18f:1, 21, 28
Silk	26
Horsehair	25

REBEC NAMES

rebecs

Gut	28

GIGUE NAMES

gige

Silk	26

LUTE NAMES

luthz

Gut	28

GITTERN NAMES
guisterne ghytaern guitarra quiterne

Gut   18c:1, 2, 18d:1, 18f:1, 2, 28

CITOLE NAMES
cythole

Gut   28

PSALTERY NAMES
psalterion psalterio sautry [psalterium]

Metallic   18:3, 18c:3, 18d:3, 18e:3, 18f:3

HARP NAMES
harp(e) (see also *cithara* and *lira*)

Gut   4b, 18e: 1, 2, 28
Metallic   15, 16 (both under Celtic influence)

ROTTA NAMES
rotta rothes

Gut   12, 28

SYMPHONY-NAMES
symphonies [symphonia]

Gut   28

Latin terminology

CITHARA

'pillar-harp' with varying degrees of likelihood

Gut	4, (?)7, 10, 11 (of British Celts), 13 (?harp without pillar), 14, 18:1, 2, 22,
Metallic	24

CITHARA

'lyre'?

Gut	1, 4, (?)7

LIRA

'pillar-harp'?

Gut	17

LYRA

'lyre'?

Gut	4

PSALTERIUM

'rotta'?

Gut	4, 6, 9:1

PSALTERIUM

'psaltery' (probably pig-snout)

Metallic	18:3, 18f:3

CHOROS

'*string-drum*' (?)

Gut   28

CHELYS

'*lyre*' (?)

Gut   8

1   433–9   Arnobius Junior: *In Psalmos*

Source: Arnobius Junior, commentary upon Psalm 146:7 in Karlsruhe, Badische Landesbibliothek MS 184, f.124v. The *cithara* may be a lyre.

> . . . *psallite ei in cithara.* Cithara habet lignum crucis, habet cordas ex interioribus ovium, habet ex Evangeliis plectrum. . . .

> '. . . *praise Him upon the cithara.* The *cithara* has wood in the cross, it has strings from the intestines of sheep, and it has a plectrum from the Gospels. . . .'

2   9c   *Anonymous glossator*

Source: E. Steinmeyer and E. Sievers, *Die Althochdeutschen Glossen,* 1 (Berlin, 1879), 154:31/2. A common medieval word-play lies behind this gloss, between *cordis* construed as a genitive singular ('of a heart') on the one hand, and as an ablative plural ('upon strings') on the other.

cordarum	herzono
vel intestinis	indarmum

'of hearts or on gut-strings'

3   c982–3   Walther of Speyer: *Vita Sancti Christophori*

Source: K. Strecker, ed., *Vita Sancti Christophori* in MGH, *Poetae Latini Medii Aevi,* V, 1 (Leipzig, 1937), p.32, line 217.

...intestinas percussit pectine chordas

'...he struck the gut strings with a plectrum'

4 ?b c1088   Wenrico: *Conflictus Ovis et Lini*

Source: M. Haupt, ed., in *Zeitschrift für Deutsches Altertum*, 11 (1859), lines 307–10. The *lyra* is perhaps the round lyre of northern and central Europe, the *cithara* may be a pillar-harp and the *psalterium* a rotta. The following lines form part of a speech by the sheep:

> ...viscera corpore nostro
> dulcem dant usum deliciis hominum.
> quadam divina resonat dulcedine chorda
> apte iuncta lyrae, psalterio, citharae.

> '...the intestines in our body give sweet enjoyment
> for the delight of Man. The divine string resounds
> with sweetness suitably joined to the *lyra*, the
> *psalterium* and the *cithara*.

Compare:
4b (c1440) John Lydgate, *Horse, Goose and Sheep* (ed. M.Degenhart, *Münchener Beiträge zur romanischen und englischen Philologie*, 19 (1900), pp.66–7), lines 379 and 383.

> Of the shepe is cast awey nothyng:
> ......
> For harpe stringes his roopis serue echeoon.

Compare also item 28

5 b 1101   Bruno the Carthusian: *In Psalmos*

Source: Bruno the Carthusian, commentary upon Psalm 150:4 in Grenoble, Bibliothèque Municipale MS 341, f.379 (Figure 13).

> *Laudate eum in cordis*, id est in consideratione
> cordarum, scilicet ea consideratione qua suos
> cordis faciet similes. Sicut enim intestina
> arietum cum prius pinguia sint et grossa, et tunc
> ad nullum sonum utilia, separata a pinguedine
> exiccantur, et ad gracilitatem perveniunt, et
> sic inde corde fierent, que dulcem sonum reddunt,
> ita quoque sancti cum hic per nimiam afflictionem

ieiuniorum et vigiliarum graciles in carne fiant,
et macri, per hoc in futuro ad hoc dignitatis
attingent ut ad modum cordarum dulcissimum melos
pure consciencie et corporee glorificationis
reddant.

'Praise him upon strings', that is with a meditation
upon what considerations [the Psalmist] wishes to
liken to strings. For just as the guts of rams (which
are first thick and fatty and hence no use for making
sound) are separated from the fat, dried, and made thin
so that strings may be made from them, so it is with the
saints when they become thin and lean of flesh after
immeasurable trials of fasting and vigils, so that they
come to a state of excellence in which, like strings, they
give out sweetest melodies of pure conscience and of
beatification of the body.

6 ?12c Pseudo-Remigius of Auxerre: *In Psalmos*

Source: Pseudo-Remigius of Auxerre, commentary upon Psalm 32:2 (PL
131:306).

In psalterio decem chordarum psallite illi . . . .
Chorda . . . primum extenditur, deinde siccatur,
et post torquetur. Ita et nos si volumus fieri
tale instrumentum Deo per similitudinem, extendere
nos debemus, crucifigentes carnem nostram cum vitiis
et concupiscentiis. Siccare nos debemus, id est,
a carnalibus desideriis subtrahere; torqueri
etiam debemus, id est, tormenta aliunde illata
patienter tolerare . . . .

'Praise him on the *psalterium* with ten strings . . . .'
The string [of the *psalterium*] is first stretched, then
dried and then twisted. Similarly, if we wish to be made
into a likeness of such an instrument for God we must
stretch ourselves, crucifying our flesh with its vices and
desires. We must wring ourselves dry, that is, by drawing
ourselves away from fleshly appetites; we must also twist
ourselves, that is, patiently bear torments . . . .

7 12c Pseudo-Haymo of Halberstadt: *In Psalmos*

Source: Pseudo-Haymo of Halberstadt, commentary upon Psalm 56:9 in

Oxford, Bodleian Library, MS Bodley 737, f.100r. Written in the twelfth century (in France?).

> *Chitaram* dicit propter mortificationem, quia in
> passione extensus fuit in ligno, sicut corium mortui
> animalis.

> [The Psalmist] says *chitara* to represent mortification
> [of the flesh], for in the Passion Christ was stretched on
> the cross like the hide of a dead animal.

8 c1100 Sextus Amarcius: *Sermones*

Source: K.Manitius, ed., in MGH, *Quellen zur Geistesgeschichte des Mittelalters, VI. Band, Sextus Amarcius Sermones* (Weimar, 1969), pp.74–5. I borrow the translation of P. Dronke (*The Medieval Lyric*, revised edition (London, 1978), p.28) save that I have retained the instrument-name *chelys* whose meaning is uncertain.

> Ergo ubi disposita venit mercede iocator
> Taurinaque chelin cepit deducere theca.
> Omnibus ex vicis populi currunt plateisque,
> Affixis notant oculis et murmure leni
> Eminulisque mimum digitis percurrere cordas,
> Quas de vervecum madidis aptaverat extis . . . .

> A minstrel was brought in, his fee arranged; he took
> his *chelys* out of a leather case, and people rushed
> in from the streets and courtyards. Watching intently,
> murmuring admiration, they see the artist run his fingers
> over the strings made from the dyed gut of a wether.

9 early 12c Honorius Augustodunensis: *In Psalmos*

Source: (1) Honorius Augustodunensis, *De figura psalterii* in Vienna, Nationalbibliothek, Cod. Vindob. 927, f.lv, and (2) commentary upon Psalm 150:4 in Cod. Vindob. 928, f.188.

> (1) *De figura psalterii*. Psalterium, quod Christum et
> Ecclesiam concinit, forma sua corpus Christi exprimit. Dum
> enim inferius percutitur, superius resonat, et corpus
> Christi, dum ligno crucis percutitur, divinitas per miracula
> resonat. Delta, ad cujus formam psalterium fit, quarta in

ordine alphabeti notatur, et corpus Christi quattuor
elementis compaginatur: sive Ecclesia, corpus ejus, quattuor
Evangeliis edificatur. Exprimit eciam psalterium formam
hominis, qui constat ex superiori et inferiori, corpore
videlicet et anima, qui debet inferius percutere, id est
corpus suum affligere ieiuniis et orationibus ut sic suum
possit reddere dulce melos Domino . . . . Chorda exsiccatur,
torquetur, extenditur; ita homo debet a carnalibus
concupiscenciis exsiccari, virtutibus torqueri, karitate
extendi, quia nulla operacio valet sine karitate . . . .

In its form the *psalterium*, which joins Christ and the
Church, symbolises the body of Christ. For while it is
beaten from below, it resonates from above, and the body of
Christ resounded wondrously while it was beaten with
the wood of the cross. The letter Delta, in whose form the
psalterium is built, is the fourth letter of the alphabet,
and the body of Christ was made from four elements—or
[the significance may be that] the Church, which is his
body, is built upon the four Gospels. The *psalterium* also
symbolises the form of Man, which consists of a higher and a
lower [part], that is, the body and the soul, which Man must
beat from below, that is, try his body with fasts and
prayers, so that he may render a sweet melody to God . . . .
A string is dried, twisted, and then stretched; so must
Man dry himself from fleshly desires, be plaited with
virtues and stretch himself with love, for nothing
is of any worth without love . . . .

(2) *Laudate eum in cordis et organo.* Chorde sunt intestine
animalium exsiccata et attenuata, dulciter sonancia, et
designant internas cogitaciones iustorum, vigiliis et
ieiuniis exsiccatas, et sancta meditacione attenuatas,
dulcissimum melos pure consciencie resonantes.

'Praise Him upon strings and the *organum.*' Strings are the
dried and stretched intestines of animals which give sweet
music, and they symbolise the inner thoughts of the just,
dried with vigils and fasts, and stretched with holy
meditation, giving the sweetest music of pure conscience.

10 ?12c Anonymous: *In Psalmos*

Source: Anonymous, commentary upon Psalm 32:2 in Oxford, Bodleian
Library, MS Bodley 860, f.48v-9. Written in the thirteenth century in
England.

Cithara reddit sonum ab inferiori, et habet cordas
factas ex intestinis mortuorum animalium.

The *cithara* gives its sound from below, and it has strings
made from the intestines of dead animals.

Figure 14 *Gerald of Wales on the string-materials used by the Irish, Scots and Welsh. British Library, MS Royal 13 B.viii, f.26. English, c1200.*

11 1185–8 Gerald of Wales: *Topographia Hibernica*

Source: J.F.Dimock, ed., *Giraldi Cambrensis Topographia Hibernica*, Rolls Series 21:5 (London, 1867), pp.153–5. See Figure 14.

From an account of the musical instruments of the Irish. Gerald travelled to Ireland with Prince John in 1183-4; on the whole he formed a low opinion on the Irish (*omnes eorum mores barbarissimi sunt*) whilst admiring their string-playing. He describes their style of performance and then widens his range of reference momentarily to include the Welsh and Scots. The instrument-names he uses are *cithara* and *tympanum* (Ireland), *cithara, tympanum* and *chorus* (Scotland) and *cithara, tibia* and *chorus* (Wales). *Chorus* and *tibia* probably denote wind instruments and can therefore be passed over. The *cithara* and *tympanum* of the Irish may be the pillar-harp and the instrument known in Old Irish sources as *tiompán* (whatever it may have been);[12] various forms of lyres and harps (some of the former perhaps bowed) may lie concealed under the names of the Scottish and Welsh instruments. It is possible that *cithara* means 'pillar-harp' each time it appears. After mentioning the instruments of the Celtic peoples of Britain Gerald points out that 'they [i.e. the Irish, but possibly also the Scots and Welsh; the context is not clear] use metallic strings'.

The translation given here is based, for the most part, on the one offered in Hibberd, 'Giraldus Cambrensis'.

> *De gentis istius in musicis instrumentis peritia incomparabili.*
> In musicis solum instrumentis commendabilem invenio
> gentis istius diligentiam. In quibus, prae omni natione
> quam vidimus, incomparabiliter instructa est. Non enim in
> his, sicut in Britannicis quibus assueti sumus instrumentis,
> tarda et morosa est modulatio, verum velox et praeceps,
> suavis tamen et jocunda sonoritas.
> Mirum quod, in tanta tam praecipiti digitorum rapacitate,
> musica servatur proportio; et arte per omnia indemni, inter
> crispatos modulos, organaque multipliciter intricata, tam
> suavi velocitate, tam dispari paritate, tam discordi
> concordia, consona redditur et completur melodia.
> Seu diatesseron, seu diapente chordae concrepent, semper
> tamen a B molli incipiunt, et in idem redeunt, ut cuncta sub
> jocundae sonoritatis dulcedine compleantur.
> Tam subtiliter modulos intrant et exeunt; sicque, sub
> obtuso grossioris chordae sonitu, gracilium tinnitus
> licentius ludunt, latentius delectant, lasciviusque
> demulcent, ut pars artis maxima videatur artem velare,
> tanquam 'Si lateat, prosit; ferat ars deprensa pudorem'.
> ....
> Notandum vero quod Scotia et Wallia, haec propagationis,
> illa commeationis et affinitatis gratia, Hiberniam in
> modulis aemula imitari nituntur disciplina. Hibernia

quidem tantum duobus utitur et delectatur instrumentis;
cithara scilicet, et tympano. Scotia tribus; cithara,
tympano et choro. Wallia vero cithara, tibiis et choro.
AEneis quoque utuntur chordis, non de corio factis
[*var:* AEneis quoque magis utuntur chordis quam de corio
factis]. Multorum autem opinione, hodie Scotia non tantum
magistram aequiparavit Hiberniam, verum etiam in musica
peritia longe praevalet et praecellit. Unde et ibi quasi
fontem artis jam requirunt.

Among these people I find a commendable diligence only
in musical instruments, on which they are more skilled
than any nation we have seen. For among them the execution
is not slow and solemn as it is with instruments in Britain
to which we are accustomed, but it is rapid and lively,
although the sound is soft and pleasant.
It is astonishing that with such a rapid snatching of the
fingers, the musical proportion (*proportio*) is preserved,
and with art unimpaired in spite of everything, the melody
is finished and remains agreeable, with such smooth
rapidity, such unequal equality, such discordant concord,
throughout the varied intervals (*crispatos modulos*) and the
many intricacies of the part-music (*organaque ... intricata*).
Whether the strings sound [are tuned in?] fourths or fifths,
they always start from B flat and return to it so that
everything ends with the charm of a pleasant sonority.
So carefully do they enter and leave the melodies
(*modulos*); thus, along with the duller sound of a
thicker string, they boldly play the tinklings of the
thinner ones, the more their concealed art delights them,
the more luxuriously they caress the ear so that
the greatest part of their art seems to conceal the
art, as though 'if art is hidden, that is to its credit;
if revealed, it is to its shame'.
....
It is to be observed that Scotland and Wales—the former
by virtue of trade and affinity, and the latter by
propagation—strive in practice to imitate Ireland in their
melodies. Ireland uses and takes delight in two
instruments: the *cithara* and the *tympanum*, Scotland in
three, the *cithara*, *tympanum* and *chorus*, and Wales in
the *cithara*, *tibia* and *chorus*.
Moreover they [just the Irish? or the Scots and Welsh also?]
play upon 'bronze' strings (*Aeneis ... chordis*) rather than
strings made of gut [*var:* they play upon 'bronze' strings
more than strings made of gut]. In the opinion of many
people, Scotland has not only equalled her mistress,
Ireland, in music, but today excels and surpasses her by

far. For this reason people look upon her now as the
fountain of the art.

12   12c   Anonymous: *Surgical Treatise*

Source: K. Sudhoff, *Beiträge zur Geschichte der Chirurgie im Mittelalter*, Part 2
(Leipzig, 1918), p.136.

This section forms part of the treatment for a wounded man prior to the
compounding of a medicine.

> Si quis vulneratus fuit, antequam faciat aliquam
> medicinam, accipiat cordam rotte, que facta est
> de intestinis pecoris, et ligetur ea ad collum cum
> dominica oratione et postea non morietur.

> If anyone has been wounded, before making a medicine,
> take the string of a *rotta* made from the intestines
> of sheep and tie it round his neck with the Lord's
> Prayer and afterwards he shall not die.

13   b 1199   Michael of Meaux: *In Psalmos*

Source: Michael of Meaux, commentary upon Psalm 97:5–6 in Oxford,
New College, MS 36, f.54r-v. Written in the late fourteenth century.

> *Psallite domino in cithara.* In cithara duo sunt ligna,
> superius et inferius; inferius concavum, superius
> solidum. Inter hec tenduntur corde, quibusdam clavis
> deorsum tendentibus, quibusdam sursum trahentibus.
> Superiores clavos plectrum torquet, ad inferiores
> cordas. Corde digitis percusse sonant. Moraliter.
> Duo ligna sunt due cruces. Inferius lignum, crux
> carnis; superius, crux mentis. Crux carnis est afflictio
> in corpore; crux mentis, compassio in corde. Inferius
> lignum solidum non est, quia omne quod in carne est,
> dolet; si consciencie bone gaudium tollitur foris speciem
> doloris habet, sed intus veritatem non habet, et ideo
> vacuum est. Superius lignum solidum est quia dolor mentis
> ad intima penetrans monstrari potest, fingi non
> potest. Corda est corpus quod tenditur et maceratur
> inter penam corporis et dolorem mentis. Inferior
> clavus est timor, superior amor, quia timore caro
> configitur, amore animus vulneratur: illa ne ad mala
> moveatur, iste ut ad bona sensificetur. Plectrum

est gratia que affectum cordis apprehendens ad se
trahit et ad superiora ire facit. Corda siccatur et
tenditur ut sonum reddat, et caro hominis a malo
mundatur primo, post in bono excitatur. Ibi est exsicata,
hic tensa. Siccatur per abstinentiam, tensa est per
pacientiam. Inferiores clavi rotundi sunt, superiores
solidi, quia timor circumspectus debet esse, amor
perfectus.

'Praise the Lord on the cithara.' In the *cithara* there
are two wooden parts, the upper and the lower; the lower
part is hollow and the upper part is solid. Between
these two stretch the strings, some having been tuned
to lower notes and some to higher. The tuning-key tightens
the upper pegs and [tightens] the strings at the lower
[pegs]. The strings sound when struck with the fingers.
Now follows the spiritual interpretation. The two wooden
parts are two crosses; the lower wooden part is the cross
of the flesh, and the upper is the cross of the mind. The
cross of the flesh is bodily affliction, and the cross of
the mind is compunction in the heart. The lower wooden
part is not solid because all that is made of flesh
grieves; if the joy of good conscience is taken away it
has the outer form of grief but it has no truth within
and therefore it is hollow. The upper wooden part is solid
because grief of the mind penetrating to the inmost part
may be shown but not contrived. The string is the [human]
body which is stretched and made lean between suffering
of the body and grief of the mind. The lower peg is fear,
the upper love, because flesh is pierced by fear and
the mind is wounded with love: the former, so that flesh
may not be moved to evil, the latter, so that the mind may
be sensitive to good. The tuning-key is grace which,
grasping the desire of the heart, draws it to itself
and brings it to a higher passion. The string is dried
and stretched so that it may give sound, and the flesh
of man is first washed pure from sin, and then stirred
towards good. There it is dried, here stretched; dried,
through abstinence, and stretched through endurance.
The lower parts of the peg are round, the upper parts
solid [square?], because fear must be circumspect, and
love perfect.

This appears to be a description of a triangular harp without pillar:

CITHARA

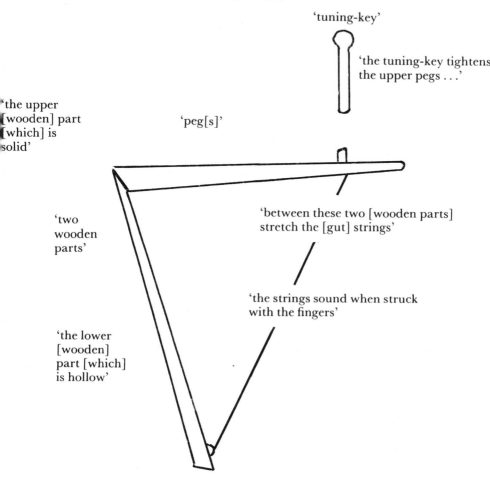

'tuning-key'

'the tuning-key tightens the upper pegs ...'

'the upper [wooden] part [which] is solid'

'peg[s]'

'two wooden parts'

'between these two [wooden parts] stretch the [gut] strings'

'the strings sound when struck with the fingers'

'the lower [wooden] part [which] is hollow'

14 12c/13c Anonymous: *In Psalmos*

Source: Anonymous, commentary upon Psalm 32:2 in Oxford, Bodleian Library, MS Hatton 37 f.49r. Written in the thirteenth century in England. See above, p.120.

> *In Cythara*. Nota. Cithara sonum reddit ab inferiori, caro autem inferior pars est hominis. Hinc est quod per citharam caro significatur. Item, cythare corde

de pellibus mortuorum animalium fieri solent; hinc est
quod per cytharam carnis mortificatio exprimitur. Item,
cytharando duabus manibus operamus: una manu cordas
inferiores iugiter tanguntur; altera non iugiter sed
vicissim et interpollatim cordas superiores.

'[Praise the Lord] on the *cithara*'. Note. The *cithara*
gives sound from below and flesh is the lower part of
Man. Hence it is that the *cithara* symbolises flesh.
Again, the strings of the *cithara* are usually made from
the guts [literally: 'skins'] of dead animals; hence it is
that the *cithara* stands for mortification of the flesh.
Again, we employ two hands in playing the *cithara*: one hand
perpetually plucks the lower strings; the other plucks the
higher strings, not continually, but at intervals and in
turn.

15   c1230   Anonymous: *Galeran de Bretagne*

Source: L. Foulet, ed., *Galeran de Bretagne* (Paris, 1925), lines 2320f. See
above, p.96.

16   early 13c   Anonymous: *Merlin*

Source: H.O.Sommer, *The Vulgate Version of the Arthurian Romances, 2, Lestoire
de Merlin* (Washington, 1908), p.408. See above, p.218.

17   ?13c   Anonymous: *Secretum Philosophorum*

Source: Cambridge, Trinity College, MS 0.1.58, f.92v, written in the
fifteenth century in England.

The *lira* may be a pillar-harp.

Ad faciendum cordas lire
Cum autem volumus facere cordas lire ... recipe intestina
ovium et lava ea munde et pone ea in aqua vel in lexivia per
dimidium diem vel plus usque caro se separet leviter a
materia corde que est similis quasi nervo. Post depone
carnem de materia cum penna vel cum digito mundo. Post pone
materiam in lescivia forti vel rubio vino per 2 dies. Post
extrahe et sicca cum panno lineo et iunge 3 vel 4 simul
secundum quantitatem quam volueris habere et atturna ea

usque sufficiat. Et extende ea super parietem et permitte sicare. Cum atuem siccata fuerit recipe ea deorsum et pone ea in loco non nimis humido nec nimis sicco, quia propter nimiam siccitatem de facili rumpuntur, et sic propter humiditatem. Et postea ea reserva.

When we wish to make strings for the *lira* . . . take the intestines of sheep and wash them cleanly, then place them in water or lye for half a day or more until the flesh comes away easily from the material of the string which is like a sinew. Then take the flesh from the material cleanly with a quill or with a clean finger. Next, put it in strong lye or red wine for two days. Then take it out and dry it with a linen cloth and join 3 or 4 together according to the quantity that you wish to have, then twist them until it is enough. Next, extend it over a wall and allow it to dry. When it is dry, take it below and put it in a place that is neither too humid nor too dry, because excessive dryness easily destroys them—as does dampness. Then keep them for use.

18   c1250   Bartholomaeus Anglicus: *De Proprietatibus Rerum*

Source: Oxford, Bodleian Library, MS Bodley 749 (2771), written c1370–80 (in England?).

References 1 and 2 appear to draw upon semi-proverbial lore (cf. 18g–18i below). Reference 3 may be original to this text. The English equivalents of *viella, cithara* and *psalterium* given by John of Trevisa in 1398 are respectively: *fedele, harpe* and *sautry* (see below 18e).

1   f.122r . . . corde facte de intestinis luporum in viella
vel in cithara cum cordis factis de intestinis ovium eas
destruunt et corrumpunt.
2   f.245r . . . cordula facta de intestinis lupi adiuncta
cordis cithare factis de intestinis ovis eas destruit et
corrumpit . . .
3   f.281r Psalterium . . . Fiu[n]t autem optime eius cordule de
auricalco et etiam de argento.

1   . . . strings made from the intestines of wolves [put] on
a *viella* or on a *cithara* with strings made from sheep-gut
destroy and corrupt the sheep-gut strings.
2   . . . a string made from the intestines of a wolf

placed beside sheep-gut strings on a *cithara* destroys
them.
3 *Psalterium* . . . its strings are best made from 'latten' and
also from 'silver'.

LATER VERSIONS AND DERIVATIVES:

18b (c1300) Aegidius of Zamora, *Ars Musica* (M. Robert-Tissot), ed.,
Johannes Aegidius de Zamora Ars Musica, AIM, CSM 20 (1974) repeats
Bartholomaeus's material on instruments almost verbatim.

18c (1372) Jean Corbechon, *La Proprietaire des Choses* (quoted from
edition of Lyon, 1491/2). A French translation, with interpolations,
undertaken at the request of Charles V of France. Corbechon follows his
source closely (but note that he renders Bartholomaeus's *cithara* as *guisterne*
and not as *harpe*, the translation chosen by Corbechon's English contemporary,
John of Trevisa. See below, 18e.)

1 nv^v . . . la corde qui est faicte des boyaulx des
brebis quant on les mect ensemble en une vi[e]lle ou
en une guisterne . . .
2 2ij . . . toute la nature du loup est contraire a la brebis
entant que qui mettroit en une guisterne une corde faicte
des boyaulx de loup entre les cordes faictes de boyaulx
de brebis elle les mengueroit et corromproit.
3 Bvij Les meilleures cordes qui soyent pour le
psalterion sont de fil darchal ou de fil dargent.

18d (1375–1425) Vinçente de Burgos, *El libro de las propriedades de las
cosas* (quoted from the edition of Toulouse, 1494).

1 Evij The wolf- and sheep-gut strings are placed on
the *viguela o guitarra*.
2 lliij^v the story is repeated and the instrument is a
vihuela.
3 ppiij^v the best strings of the *psalterio* are made from
plata o de laton.

18e (1398) John of Trevisa, *De Proprietatibus Rerum* (M.C.Seymour,
general editor, *On the Properties of Things: John Trevisa's translation of
Bartholomaeus Anglicus*, De Proprietatibus Rerum: *A Critical Text*, 2 vols
(Oxford, 1975), 1, p.606; 2, pp.1224 and 1392).

1 . . . strenges imaad of wolfes guttes ido and iput in a
fedule othir in an harpe among strenges imade of schepis
guttis . . . corrumpith strengis imade of guttis of
schiepe . . .

2   And so I haue yradde in a booke that a strenge ymade
of a wolues gutte ydo among harpestrenges ymade of the
guttes of scheep destroyeth and corrumpeth hem . . .
3   Strynges of the sautry beth best ymade of latoun or
of siluer.

In the printed edition of 1495 *lute* is substituted for *fedele* in reference 1 (see
OED sv *String* sb. 3a).

18f   Anonymous, *Van den Proprieteyten der dinghen* (quoted from the edition of
Haarlem, 1485).

1   3iij^v   the wolf- and sheep-gut strings are placed on the
ghytaern and *vedel*.
2   Miij^v   the story is repeated and the instrument is a
ghyteern.
3   EEiiij^v   the best strings for the *psalterium* are made
from *latoen* and from *siluer*.

The story of the wolf-gut strings appears to have been proverbial. Compare,
for example, the following three texts:

18g   (c1256–60)   Albertus Magnus, *De Animalibus* (H.Stadler, ed., *Alberti
Magni De Animalibus,* in *Beiträge zur Geschichte der Philosophie des Mittelalters*, 15
and 16 (1916 and 1921), 16, p.1411).

. . . cordae de visceribus ovium factae cum cordis de
visceribus lupi factis permixtae non sonant.

. . . strings made from the intestines of sheep mixed with
strings made from the intestines of wolves do not sound.

18h   (b ?c1340)   Armand de Belvézer, *Sermones* (quoted from *F. Armandi de
Bellovisu . . . Sermones plane divini assumptis ex solo Psalterio Davidico thematis*
(Lyon, 1525)).

cxj   If a string made *de luporum intestinis* is put
onto *aliquo instrumento musico cum chordis de ovium
intestinis factis* it will destroy them.

18i   (1425)   John   Amundesham,   *Annales   Monasterii   Sancti   Albani*
(H.T.Riley, *Annales Monasterii Sancti Albani a Johanne Amundesham*, 2 vols,
Rolls Series 28 (London, 1870–1), 1, p.208).

An extract from questions put by the Abbot to the priors of the cells which reveals the semi-proverbial character of the notion that wolf-gut strings can destroy strings made from the guts of sheep, or will not accord with them.

> ... nunquid in concordi claustralium cithara, aliqua
> fuerit lupina chordula quae non convenit cum caeteris.

> ... whether anyone has been the wolf-string which does not
> accord with the others in the harmonious *cithara* of the
> monks.

19 Guillaume d'Auvergne: *De Viciis et Peccatis*

See Appendix 3:46.

20 1274–1312 Anonymous: *Summa Musice*

Source: St Paul in Kärnten, Archiv des Benediktinerstiftes, Cod. 264/4, f.4. Early fifteenth century.

The *cythare* are probably pillar-harps, while *vielle* and *phiale* are presumably various kinds of fiddle (or they may be synonyms). *Psalteria* would then cover psalteries, *monocordium* the monochord (the text is probably too early for any more exotic meaning such as 'clavichord'), while *simphonia seu organistrum*, possibly synonyms in this author's vocabulary, cover hurdy-gurdies. The *chorus* may be a string-drum.

> Cordalia sunt ea que per cordas metallinas, intestinales
> vel sericinas exerceri videntur; qualia sunt cythare,
> vielle et phiale, psalteria, chori, monocordium, simphonia
> seu organistrum, et hiis similia.

> Stringed instruments are those which are seen to
> operate with strings of metal, gut or silk; such are
> *cythare, vielle* and *phiale, psalteria, chori, monocordium,*
> *simphonia* or *organistrum*, and others like these.

21 1296–1313 Hugo von Trimburg: *Der Renner*

Source: G.Ehrissman, ed., *Der Renner von Hugo von Trimburg*, 4 vols (Tübingen, 1908–11), 1, lines 12441–50.

Von tanzen

Wenne sant Gregôrius der heilige man
Sprichet, als ich gelesen hân,
Daz riuten and eren bezzer sî
Denne der dem tanze wone bi.
Sôgetân spil ist tugende hagel:
Swenne einer mit eines pferdes zagel
Strîchet über vier shäfes darm,
Daz im sîn vinger und sîn arm
Müeder werden denne ob si hêten
Einen ganzen tac unkrût gejeten.

Concerning dancing

For St Gregory, the holy man, said, as I have read, that it
is better to do manual agricultural labour than to go
dancing; that kind of play is injurious to virtue. Whenever
a man bows with a horse's tail over four sheep-guts let his
fingers and arms be as tired as if he had been weeding all
day.

22 c1300   Nicholas de Gorran: *In Psalmos*

Source: Nicholas de Gorran, commentary upon Psalm 70:22, in Oxford,
Bodleian Library, MS Bodley 246, f.187v, written early in the fifteenth
century in England.

In cithara. id est in carnis mortificacione. In
cithara enim sunt corde de pellibus mortuis . . . .

On the cithara: in mortification of the
flesh. For on the *cithara* there are strings made
of dead guts . . . .

23 c1320   Nicholas de Lyra: *Postilla*

Source: Nicholas de Lyra, commentary upon Psalm 150:4, in Oxford,
Bodleian Library, MS Laud misc. 152, f.71v.

Laudate eum in cordis; in instrumentis habentibus
cordas de ere seu intestinis.

'Praise Him upon strings'; that is, on instruments
having strings of 'bronze' or gut.

24 b 1326 Petrus de Palude: *In Psalmos*

Source: Petrus de Palude, commentary upon Psalm 80:3 in Troyes, Bibliothèque Municipale, MS 144, volume 2, f.2v. The illustrations which accompany Petrus's commentary upon Psalm 150 show that he understood the *cythara* to be a pillar-harp.

> .xv. corde exiguntur ut bene sonet cythara: vii dona
> et quatuor cardinales virtutes et tres theorice
> et humilitas que custos est aliarum ... hii sunt .xv. gradus
> psalmorum, .xv. stadula quibus distat Bethania et Ierusalem
> [secundum] Jo[hannem] .xi. Iste corde debent esse argentee,
> id est de sacro eloquio fundate, et quinto corda brevior
> est et magis extensa; tanto altiorem et dulciorem sonum
> reddit. Humilitas autem abreviat cordam et fervor extendit eam.

> Fifteen strings are required if a [mystical] *cythara* is to
> sound well: the Seven Gifts, the Four Cardinal virtues, the
> Three Contemplations and Humility which is the defender of
> them all ... these [fifteen mystical strings] are also the
> fifteen Gradual Psalms and the fifteen furlongs between
> Bethania and Jerusalem according to John 11. These strings
> should be made of silver, that is, forged from Holy Writ,
> and the fifth string is shorter and under greater tension so
> that it gives a higher and sweeter sound. Humility shortens
> the string and passion for the Divine stretches it.

25 b 1336 Henry of Cossey: *In Psalmos*

Source: Henry of Cossey, commentary upon Psalm 150:4, in Cambridge, Christ's College, MS 11, f.251v, written in England in the fifteenth century (Figure 12).

> Laudate eum in cordis; id est instrumentis seu pellibus
> vel pilis equorum sicut habent communiter vielle.

> 'Praise Him upon strings'; that is, on instruments
> either with guts or with the hairs of horses such as
> fiddles generally have.

26 early 14c Anonymous: *Der Busant*

Source: Moscow, Central'niy gosudarstvenniy arkhiv drevnikh aktov, Fond no. 181, ed. hr. 1405, f.74v–75.

This MS was not used in the edition of F.H. von der Hagen, *Gesammtaben-teuer* (Stuttgart and Tübingen, 1850), 1, p.348, lines 397–411.

Da hiβ er ym bereydèn
Mit syden seiten
Ein fedele erzuget wol
Als sie ein furst foren sal.
Der korper gezieret,
Das lijt gebrieuieret
Mit golde vnd mit gesteine
Von edelm hellfen beyne.
Hinder dem swebet ein palmat siden
Borte; sie waz an allen orten
Mit gulden borten vber leit.
Alsus die gige wart bereit.
Die nagel woren guldin.
Der gygen sag von syden fin
Gewircket wol mit bylden clar.

Then he commanded a fine fiddle with silk strings to be prepared for him as if it were for a prince to use; the body decorated, the neck inlaid with gold, precious stones and noble ivory. Below the neck there hung a band of soft silk; the fiddle was all adorned with golden (?) braid of silk. Thus the *gige* was made. The pegs were golden, and the fiddle-bag seemed to be of fine silk embroidered with beautiful pictures.

27 ?13c Anonymous: *Epistola cum Tractatu de Musica Instrumentali Huma-naque ac Mundana*

Source: J.Smits van Waesberghe, ed., *Adalboldi Episcopi Ultraiectensis Epistola cum Tractatu de Musica Instrumentali Humanaque ac Mundana*, DMA A.II (Buren, 1981), pp.15 and 16. In a brief (and rudimentary) discussion of the properties of strings the author mentions strings *de metallo* ('of metal'), *de nervo* ('of gut') and *de nervo vel filo* ('of gut or of ?sinew').

I include the following, which lies beyond the period covered by this book, since it offers such full information:

28 1379 Jean de Brie: *Le Bon Berger*

Source: P. Lacroix, *Le Bon Berger* (Paris, 1879), p.35.

No medieval manuscript copy of this work is known to exist; the text survives only in printed abridgements of the sixteenth century (Lacroix reprints the edition of Paris, 1541). Of the instrument-names used, *vielles, harpes, luthz* and *rebecs* may probably be taken in their usual senses. The terms *quiternes* and *cytholes* may be taken in the senses proposed for them by Wright ('Medieval Gittern and Citole'). The *choros* may be string-drums and the *symphonies* are surely hurdy-gurdies. The word *almaduries* (which looks like a borrowing from Arabic) is a mystery. Jean de Brie is discussing the contrasting natures of the wolf and the sheep.

> Les menues cordes des boyaux bien lavez, séchez,
> tors, rez, essuez et filez, sont pour la mélodie des
> instrumens de musique, de vielles, de harpes, de rothes,
> de luthz, de quiternes, de rebecs, de choros, de
> almaduries, de symphonies, de cytholes et de aultres
> instrumens que l'on fait sonner par dois et par cordes.

> The fine sinews of [sheep-] gut well washed, dried,
> twisted, scraped, wiped and spun are used for musical
> instruments: *vielles, harpes, rothes, luthz, quiternes,*
> *rebecs, choros, almaduries, symphonies, cytholes* and other
> instruments that one makes to give sound by means of the
> fingers and of strings.

Notes

Preface

1   I have assumed throughout this book that the High Style songs of the troubadours and trouvères *were not generally* performed in 'modal' or any directly comparable system of fixed rhythm, but were delivered in something approaching the 'declamatory' rhythm proposed by Van der Werf (*Troubadours and Trouvères*). Van der Werf's proposals are beginning to find favour amongst specialists in courtly monody (see, most recently, Switten, *Cansos*). There are also strong arguments in favour of the isosyllabic style of delivery recently defended by John Stevens (*'Grande Chanson Courtoise'*).

Introduction

1   Lacurne de Sainte-Palaye, *Histoire Littéraire des Troubadours*, especially 1, pp.43, 378 and 428 (the biographies of the troubadours who are credited with the ability to play the fiddle in the *Vidas*). For sixteenth-century interest in the trouvères and the performance of their works see Fauchet, *Recueil*, pp.72ff.

2   Bec, *La langue Occitane*, pp.91ff.

3   Mansi, *Concilia, passim*. These volumes have provided a solid foundation for much twentieth-century work on medieval minstrelsy. For two classic cases see Waddell, *Wandering Scholars*, pp.244ff, and Faral, *Les Jongleurs*, Appendix 3, items 3, 5, 6c and *passim*.

4   See in particular Percy, *Reliques*, 1, xv-xxiii; 3, i-xxiv, and Ritson, *Ancient Songs*, i-lxxvi.

5   *Op. cit.*, 2, p.13 and 1, p.428.

6   Burney, *A General History of Music*, 2, p.233.

7 Parker, 'Troubadour and Trouvère Songs', p.203. Compare the similar approach in Le Vot, 'Interprétation musicale', p.17. For the older literature see, for example, Levy, 'Musikinstrumente', and Nef, 'Instrumentenspiel'.

8 Van der Werf, *Troubadours and Trouvères*, p.20.

9 See Appendix 3, *passim*.

Chapter 1: Epic and Romance

1 On the change from Epic to Romance and its significance see Southern, *The Making of the Middle Ages*, pp.209ff; Vinaver, *Rise of Romance*; Hanning, *The Individual in Twelfth Century Romance*. See also Morris, *Discovery of the Individual* and Benton, 'Consciousness of Self'. For an encyclopedic guide to the presentation of manhood in Old French epic up to 1250 see Combarieu du Grès, *L'idéal humain*, and for the place of music in the change see Page, 'Music and Chivalric Fiction'.

2 Pope, *Horn*, gives the text, and on the ethos of this poem (especially its relation to epic tradition) see Burnley, 'Roman de Horn'. While I agree with Burnley that Thomas takes a positive view of Horn, his claim that Thomas 'aimed . . . at heroic biography, at presenting . . . an example of traditional feudal and epic virtue' (p.395) is quite out of keeping with Horn's expert musicianship. Epic heroes never play instruments before the later thirteenth century, and even then only in a few isolated cases. On this question see Page, 'Music and Chivalric Fiction'.

3 Pope, *Horn*, lines 2830–44. This passage has often been quoted, translated and interpreted. See, for example, Handschin, 'Estampie und Sequenz', 1, pp.6ff; Reaney, '*Lais* of Guillaume de Machaut', pp.20ff; Bliss, *Sir Orfeo*, pp.xxix–xxx; Dobson and Harrison, *Medieval English Songs*, pp.87–8 (by far the most useful and reliable discussion).

4 For the interest in songs and their composers see Pope, *Horn*, lines 2788ff.

5 See Klaeber, *Beowulf*, 2105ff (where the musician may be the Danish king, Hrothgar), and below, Chapter 8, on the story of Apollonius of Tyre. The earliest appearance of a harper-hero in anything which might plausibly be called romance occurs in the *Ruodlieb*, a Latin verse-tale, probably of south-German origin and dating from c1050. For the text see Zeydel, *Ruodlieb*, p.110.

6 The qualification ('as interpreted by secular individuals') seems advisable as there may be an important distinction to be drawn between courtesy as a literate art of self-beautification practised by courtier clerics inspired by classical ideals of decorum, and courtesy as understood by (predominantly) illiterate secular persons at court and much more closely involved with sexual narcissism. See Jaeger, *The Origins of Courtliness, passim.*

7 This question is discussed further in Page, 'Music and Chivalric Fiction'.

8 Whitehead, *Chanson de Roland*, lines 281–5.

9 Pope, *Horn*, lines 1250 and 1255–7. Compare lines 1050ff.

10 Kimmel, *Daurel et Beton*, lines 1419–21 and 1564–77.

11 This contrast is most suggestively discussed in Murray, *Reason and Society*, pp.125–7.

12 Whitehead, *Chanson de Roland*, line 20.

13 *Ibid.*, lines 24–6.

14 Schultz-Gora, *Folque de Candie*, 2, line 9899.

15 *Ibid.*, line 12512.

16 Text in White, *La Conquête de Constantinople*, p.90. Compare p.69.

17 Text from Lecoy, *Guillaume de Dole*, lines 4120–40; music from the Chansonnier de l'Arsenal, p.179.

18 Text from Pattison, *Raimbaut d'Orange*, p.152.

Chapter 2 : The twelfth century in the South

1 Text and music from Van der Werf, *Extant Troubadour Melodies*, p.17*.

2 Gennrich, *Rondeaux, Virelais und Balladen*, 1, p.10. On this and associated genres see for example Bec, *La Lyrique Française*, pp.220ff; Delbouille, *Bele Aëlis*; Doss-Quinby, *Les Refrains*, and Le Gentil, *Guillaume de Dole*.

3 Marshall, *Linguistic and Literary Theory*, 2, pp.66–7.

4 Text in Bartholomaeis, *Insegnamenti pe' giullari*, pp.3ff.

5 *Ibid.*

6 *Ibid.*

7 For the text and music see Van der Werf, *Extant Troubadour Melodies*, p.227*.

8 *Ibid.*, p.220*.

9 For some of the evidence see, for example, Faral, *Les Jongleurs*, Appendix 3, item 91, and the testimonies of Albertus Magnus (Borgnet, *Beati Alberti Magni Opera Omnia*, 8, p.748), Thomas de Chobham (Broomfield, *Summa Confessorum*, p.292), Gerbert de Montreuil (Buffum, *Roman de la Violette*, lines 1400–29; see Appendix 3:33 of this book), and an anonymous thirteenth-century preacher quoted in Techener, *Description Raisonnée*, 1, p.273.

10 I am assuming here that the text dates from the middle decades of the twelfth century, as argued by Kimmel (*Daurel et Beton*), pp.34ff, although it may date from significantly later (c1200, perhaps?). For further material from this epic see Appendix 3:1.

11 Kimmel, *Daurel et Beton*, line 1173ff.

12 *Ibid.*, lines 1498–1505.

13 The meanings of *lais* in Old Provençal are discussed, with lavish documentation, in Baum, 'Troubadours et les lais'.

14 Text and music from Van der Werf, *Extant Troubadour Melodies*, pp.96*–7* (MS *R*).

15 For the relative chronology of these terms see Marshall, *Linguistic and Literary Theory*, pp.864ff.

16 *Ibid.*, p.889.

17 Text from Lavaud and Nelli, *Les Troubadours*, 1, lines 9811–14.

18 See, for example, the usage of Marcabrun in his famous *Pax in nomine Domini* (text and music in Van der Werf, *Extant Troubadour Melodies*, p.227* (line 2)). See also Marshall, *Linguistic and Literary Theory*, pp.669ff.

19 Text from Linskill, *Raimbaut de Vaqueiras*, p.140, lines 49–50.

20 For the surviving *descort* tunes see De la Cuesta, *Cançons dels Trobadors*, pp.402ff (*Qui la vi en ditz*, by Aimeric de Peguillan), and pp.531ff (*Ses alegratge*, by Guillem Augier Novella). There is some doubt about the structure of *Qui la vi en ditz*; Maillard ('*Lai lyrique*', p.125, n.28a) interprets it as two poems, the second beginning *Cilh qu'es caps e guids*. De la Cuesta, *op. cit.*, interprets it (correctly, in my view), as one poem.

21 Baum, 'Descort', p.97. On an important sub-division of the descort repertory see Marshall, 'Isostrophic *Descort*'.

22 There is some dispute as to whether the final *A* in this scheme represents the traditional form of the *dansa*. As pointed out above, the five surviving *dansas* with music (all anonymous) are preserved in a French chansonnier, the Manuscrit du Roi, and are thus both late and peripheral witnesses to the Occitan *dansa* tradition which reaches back to at least the mid-twelfth century. In one instance (here Music example 8) there can be no doubt that the final *A* is certainly intended, since the scribe has signalled it (the hint is not properly taken up by De la Cuesta (*Cançons dels Trobadors*, p.741). Perhaps the final *A* was a Gallicism. De la Cuesta lists all these *dansas* as virelais (save *Ben vòlgra, s'èsser pogués*, which he inventories as 'Dança, virelai'). For text and music of these pieces see his edition, pp.726–7 (*Amors, m'ard com fuoc amb flama*); pp.738–9 (*Ben vòlgra, s'èsser pogués*); pp.741–2 (*Dòmna, pos vos ai chausida*; here Music example 8); pp.805–6 (*Pos qu'ieu vei la fuèlha*), and pp.810–11 (*Tant es gaia et avinents*). For a meticulous handling of the descriptions of the *dansa* given by the poetic theorists see Marshall, *Razos de Trobar*, pp.138 and 141–2; *idem, Linguistic and Literary Theory*, 2, pp.904ff; Lewent, '*Dansa*', p.517.

23 The only significant troubadour who has left an important body of *dansas* (none of them surviving with music) is the Catalan Cerveri de Girona. Cerveri's work also includes some *estampidas* and is notable for the high proportion of late and traditionally minor forms which it includes.

24 For an edition of the full text see Riquer, *Guillem de Berguedà*, 2, pp.64ff. For further material on refrains in troubadour poetry (including refrains of this type) see Gorton, 'Arabic Words and Refrains', and Newcombe, 'The Refrain in Troubadour Lyric Poetry'.

25 Text from Suchier, 'Provenzalische Verse', p.513.

26 Field, *Raimon Vidal*, lines 1ff. and p.61. In what follows I paraphrase or

quote the text and translation in this edition.

27 *Ibid.*, lines 48ff and p.61.

28 *Ibid.*, lines 38–46, and p.61.

29 *Ibid.*, lines 52–3.

30 *Ibid.*, line 1245 and p.80.

31 Boutière and Schutz, *Biographies des Troubadours*, p.39.

32 *Ibid.*, p.33.

33 Field, *Raimon Vidal*, lines 1580ff and p.85.

34 *Ibid.*, lines 1020ff and p.76.

35 Whilst it would be impossible to deny the pervasive eroticism of much troubadour poetry, the distinctive excellence of this love-poetry at its best is that erotic desire and moral ardour coalesce in one passion which can only be felt by the refined heart. The tendency of the poetry to centre on words denoting moral prestige (*valors, pretz, onors*, and even the seemingly evanescent *joi* and *jovens*) gives many troubadour *cansos* a high moral tone which is partly responsible for the altitude of the 'High' Style.

36 Field, *Raimon Vidal*, line 108 and p.62.

37 *Ibid.*, lines 1580ff and pp.85–6.

Chapter 3 : The thirteenth century in the North

1 On the northern imitation of the southern *canso* and other genres see Bec, *La Lyrique Française*, pp.44–8.

2 Text from Vallerie, *Garin le Loheren*, line 11378. On the presentation of society in this romance, as contrasted with the later epic of *Hervis de Metz* (which we are about to use), see Noiriel, 'Chevalerie'.

3 Densusianu, *La Prise de Cordres*, lines 27–30.

4 The text is from Lecoy, *Guillaume de Dole*, lines 4653–9, and the music from Van der Werf, *Extant Troubadour Melodies*, p.78*. I have added

several editorial flats to Van der Werf's transcription. Notes in square brackets are those for which there is no syllable in Jean Renart's text of the song.

5   Text from Bartsch, *Romanzen und Pastourellen*, III, number 42.

6   For a catalogue of refrains and an attempt to define the corpus see Van den Boogaard, *Rondeaux et Refrains*. For further bibliography see Chapter 2, note 2.

7   The most recent edition is Lecoy, *Guillaume de Dole* (with a discussion of the date on pp.vi-viii). The poem contains detailed references to the area of Liège; see Lejeune, 'Principauté de Liège'. In what follows I shall suggest that Jean Renart has associated accompaniment with certain kinds of songs cited in his romance, but not with others. The method will be to establish the genres of the lyrics which are said to be accompanied, and then to look for a structure of resemblances between them in terms of metrical form, subject matter, function, and so on. To assume that this structure of resemblances is significant in some way relative to the issue of accompaniment is not quite the same as treating *Guillaume de Dole* as a 'mirror' of contemporary life and we are not required to ignore its idealising and romanticising impulses. No doubt many of the song-performances which Jean Renart describes (nobles singing High Style songs alone in their chambers, for example) are both romantic and contrived, as argued by Jung (*Roman de la Rose*).
   On the musical and lyrical material in *Guillaume de Dole* see especially Coldwell, 'Guillaume de Dole'; Bec, *La Lyrique Française*, pp.220ff; Delbouille, *Bele Aëlis*; Doss-Quinby, *Les Refrains;* Le Gentil, *Guillaume de Dole*. A little of the evidence offered by *Guillaume de Dole* is deployed by Parker, 'Troubadour and Trouvère Songs', pp.187–8, and by Kelly, *Medieval Imagination*, pp.239ff.

8   Lecoy, *Guillaume de Dole*, lines 1843–51.

9   *Ibid.*, line 2234. For the typology of the *chanson de toile* see Bec, *La Lyrique Française*, pp.107–19, and for some examples with music, Rosenberg and Tischler, *Chanter m'estuet*, items 9–11 and 108. On the use of the refrain in this genre see Jonin, 'Chansons de toile'.

10   Lecoy, *Guillaume de Dole*, lines 2247–52.

11   *Ibid.*, lines 2289–94.

12   *Ibid.*, lines 3419–30. Perhaps the only point of contact between this song and trouvère lyric is via the *Tournoiement des dames* of Huon d'Oisi

(see Gérold, *Musique au Moyen Age*, pp.86–8). Compare the materials in Pelaez, 'Tornoiement as dames de Paris'.

13 The association of instruments with Lower Styles clearly involves a link between instruments and narrative (as in *Bele Aiglentine*), a registration which is reinforced by the abundant evidence that Old French epics, the *Chansons de geste*, were often performed to instrumental accompaniment. See, for example, Faral, *Les Jongleurs*, Appendix 3, item 91, and the testimonies of Albertus Magnus (Borgnet, *Beati Alberti Magni Opera Omnia*, 8, p.748), Thomas de Chobham (Broomfield, *Summa Confessorum*, p.292), Gerbert de Montreuil (Buffum, *Roman de la Violette*, lines 1400–29; see Appendix 3:33 of this book), and an anonymous thirteenth-century preacher quoted in Techener, *Description Raisonnée*, 1, p.273.

14 See Appendix 3:13.

Chapter 4 : Late traditions in the South

1 The *Doctrina de Compondre Dictats* is edited in Marshall, *Razos de Trobar*, pp.95–8. For the arguments in favour of Jofre as the author see pp.lxxv–lxxviii, and on Jofre's knowledge of earlier troubadour poetry, pp.xciii–xcv. There is also an illuminating discussion of the treatise by Marshall, *Linguistic and Literary Theory*, 1, pp.274ff.

2 Marshall, *Linguistic and Literary Theory*, p.282.

3 Marshall, *Razos de Trobar*, pp.96 and 98.

4 *Ibid.*, p.98

5 Music from the Manuscrit du Roi, f.3v. For convenience I take the text from De la Cuesta, *Cançons dels Trobadors*, pp.741–2. There are several errors in De la Cuesta's representation of the original (mensural) notation.

6 The various versions and revisions of the *Leys d'Amors* are edited in Gatien-Arnoult, *Gay Saber*; Anglade, *Gay Saber*, and *idem*, *Leys d'Amors*. The earliest version is generally supposed to be the treatise published by Gatien-Arnoult, customarily labelled the 'A-text', but Gatien-Arnoult's text does not represent the earliest recoverable form of the Consistori's doctrines. When his edition is compared with the manuscript upon which it is based (Figure 3) it becomes clear that he arrived at his text by running together the work of the main hand with the

many annotations which surround it. The earliest recoverable form of the Consistori's doctrine therefore lies buried in Gatien-Arnoult's text amidst a mass of later accretions. For the purposes of this chapter I shall continue to cite the page numbers of Gatien-Arnoult's edition for convenience, although I shall quote directly from the manuscript (since there are numerous errors in the edition) and indicate when material is drawn from an annotation.

On the *Leys d'Amors*, with special reference to the material on music, see Gonfroy, 'Reflet de la *canso*'; Haynes, 'Music and Genre'; Hibberd, 'Estampie and Stantipes', pp.245–6 (n); Stevens, '*Grande chanson courtoise*', p.30. The outstanding treatment of the *Leys* in English is Marshall, *Linguistic and Literary Theory, passim,* but especially 1, pp.356ff and 2, pp.951ff.

As far as concerns the musical interests of the *Leys* compilers, it seems that the members of the Toulouse Consistori expected (or hoped) that some of the poems submitted to their first poetic competition would be accompanied by music. There are three grounds for accepting this view. Firstly, most of the references to musical settings in the earliest version of the *Leys* are found within the main text, not within the later annotations. This suggests that these musical prescriptions were part of the Consistori's 'teaching' from the very first, a view supported by the earliest treatise to issue from the Consistori, Raimon Cornet's *Doctrinal de trobar* of 1324, where there are also a few musical prescriptions (Noulet and Chabaneau, *Deux manuscrits Provençaux,* pp.210–11, lines 380ff.)

Secondly, the substance of the musical prescriptions in the earliest version of the *Leys* is preserved in the later versions B and C, which suggests that it retained some interest and importance throughout the period when the various texts of the treatise were being prepared. Indeed Joan de Castellnou (*Compendi de la coneixença dels vicis en els dictats del Gai Saber,* see Appendix 3:18) scrupulously borrows even the musical material in the annotations to the earliest version.

Thirdly, Molinier's account (in the C-text) of how contestants were summoned to the first competition, and his description of how the songs were to be judged, both suggest that he expected (or hoped) that music would sometimes be involved. See Anglade, *Leys d'Amors,* 1, p.9 (*Tug nostre major cossirier/E.1 pensamen e.1 dezirier/Son de chantar e d'esbaudir* ...), p.11 (*Et adonx auziretz chantar/E legir de nostres dictatz* ...), p.12 (... *requirem/Que.1 dit jorn qu'assignat havem/Vos veyam say tan gent garniz/De plazens sos e de bels ditz* ...). See also p.17 (*am gay so* ...), p.42 (*dansa ... am gay so* ...), and p.44 (... *motas acordansas/Fam de chansos, verses e dansas,/Am sos melodios e prims* ...).

The fact that the judges were expected to 'look over' (*vezer*) the entries (*ibid.,* p.14) rather than to hear them does not, in itself, indicate that the entries were expected to be without music. Compare the judging procedure in Jean de le Mote's *Parfait du Paon*, roughly contemporary with the Consistori's first competition; there the entries are also read over, yet it is quite certain that they have music (Carey, *Parfait du Paon*, 1052ff, and especially 1517–8, where the contestants 'solmise' their songs so that copies may be made).

7 Gatien-Arnoult, *Gay Saber*, p.350; Toulouse, Académie des Jeux Floraux, MS 500.007, f.41v.

8 *Ibid.*

9 On the changing sense of *vers* in the twelfth and thirteenth centuries see Marshall, *Linguistic and Literary Theory*, 2, pp.865ff and 951–2.

10 Gatien-Arnoult, *Gay Sabers*, p.338, MS f.40r (main hand).

11 *Ibid.*, pp.338–48, MS f.40r–41v (main hand in all cases).

12 *Ibid.*, p.346, MS f.41r (main hand).

13 On the registration of the *pastourelle* see Bec, *La Lyrique Française*, pp.119–36.

14 *Ibid.*, p.346, MS f.41r (main hand).

15 Marshall, *Razos de Trobar*, p.96.

16 From *La septime estampie real*, transcribed from the Manuscrit du Roi, f.177. Very little instrumental dance-music survives from the thirteenth century, and my generalisation about the idiom of instrumental music therefore takes in material surviving from before c1400. For a guide to further material see Arlt, 'Reconstruction', and Crane, 'On performing the *Lo estampies*'.

   Losses of instrumental music and instrument-related lyric genres have been severe. Only one Old Provençal *estampida* survives with its music (Music example 10), while the *bal*—the genre which the Consistori annotator considered particularly appropriate for instrumental accompaniment—has vanished without trace.

17 Text and music from Van der Werf, *Extant Troubadour Melodies*, pp.292*–293*. This song has been much discussed; see, for example, McPeek, 'Kalenda Maia'.

Chapter 5 : Paris

1 Field, *Raimon Vidal*, lines 158ff and p.63.

2   Gerbert, *Scriptores*, 3, p.282. For important new biographical infor-
    mation on Jehan des Murs see *Grove 6* sv Jehan des Murs.

3   For the intellectual and spiritual consequences of urbanisation in the
    twelfth and thirteenth centuries it would be hard to improve upon
    Little, *Religious Poverty* (with special reference to the friars) and Murray,
    Reason and Society, passim. On the forces affecting the relationship
    between minstrel and cleric during this period see Le Goff, *Temps,
    travail et culture*, especially pp.91f and p.100, and Casagrande and
    Vecchio, 'Clercs et jongleurs'.

4   Text in Rohloff, *Grocheio*, p.132. Further on ecclesiastical attitudes to
    dancing see Chapter 6.

5   London, British Library, MS Arundel 395, f.27v.

6   Material like the following, from the unpublished *Flores Psalterii* (?11c)
    attributed to Lietbertus of Lille, shows the way in which countless
    Bible commentaries deal with instruments:

*Psalmus enim pertinet ad bonam operacionem. Tympanum autem ad carnis
mortificacionem. Psalterium vero ad iocunditatem laudis. Cythara autem ad
confessionem humilitatis .... Accipe psalterium iocundum et canta letatus sum in
hiis que dicta sunt mihi. Adiunge cythara et dic Benedicam dominum in omni
tempore.*
(The psalm relates to good works, the *tympanum* to mortification of the
flesh, the *psalterium* to the pleasure of praise, the *cythara* to the admission
of lowliness .... Take up the pleasing *psalterium* and sing: 'I have
rejoiced in those things which have been said to me'. Join the *cythara* to
it and say: 'I will worship the lord for ever)'. (Oxford, Bodleian
Library, MS Bodley 318, f.128v.)

Here the literal sense has shrivelled up, but not so far that we cannot
see what it once was: the *tympanum* relates to 'mortification of the flesh'
because the skin of a drum is like the mortified flesh of a believer; the
psalterium is equated with the 'pleasure of praise' because its name is
connected with *psallendo*, 'praising', and so on. For surveys of references
to musical instruments in the writings of the Church fathers see Gérold,
Pères de l'Église, especially pp.123ff, 175ff, and 180ff; McKinnon, *Church
Fathers* and *idem*, 'Musical Instruments'.
    Vernacular instrument-terminology is very rare in Bible-commen-
taries and glosses compiled before the thirteenth century (I except here
the vernacular psalm-commentary of Notker Labeo and associated
glosses). In a search of published and unpublished commentaries upon
the Psalter the earliest instance I have found is in an eleventh-century

marginal note to the commentary of Remigius of Auxerre in Rheims, Bibliothèque Municipale, MS 133, f.221v: *cithara genus est musice artis que vulgo 'rota' appellatur.*

7   On the use of Hebrew sources see Smalley, *Study of the Bible*, pp.241ff., and Dahan, 'Interprétations juives'. The study of Hebrew did not make an immediate impact upon the glossing of instrument-names in Scripture, as may be judged from the psalm-commentary of one of the earliest Hebraists, Herbert of Bosham (London, St Paul's Cathedral, MS 2). Herbert's material on musical instruments is conventional and of no special interest.

   Among the friar-commentators who employed Hebrew material mention must be made of Nicholas de Lyra, whose monumental commentary upon the Bible contains several snippets of information about fourteenth-century instruments (mostly in the glosses on Daniel 3:5). I have consulted the text in Oxford, Bodleian Library, MS Laud misc. 152; see f. 71v (on metallic strings; see Appendix 4:23); ff.236r-v, on the *fistula* (a shepherd's pipe), *cithara* (harp) and *psalterium* (psaltery).

8   Douai, Bibliothèque Municipale, MS 45, volume 9, f.262v:

Sed quia Ysidorus, ethy[mologie] li[bro] 3, dicit quod psalterium habet lignum concavum unde redditur sonus a part superiori, et quod eius forma est secundum figuram littere grece que deltha dicitur, videtur quod psalterium antiquitus non fuerit illius forme cuius est nunc. Unde advertendum quod in instrumentis modernis omnia genera viellarum, quarum alique plures alique pauciores habent cordas, lignum concavum habent unde sonus redditur superius applicatum ad humerum sinistrum. Cuius corde dum sonant tractu virgule cordate, modulacio illius soni [MS: sonus] fit inferius tangendo cordas digitis manu [MS: manus] sinistre ut acucius vel gravius sonent. Convenit ergo psalterium cum viella in condicionibus duabus; una quod habuit lignum concavum unde redditur sonus superius; alia quod modulacio eius fiebat tactu digitorum inferius. Sed in tribus erat differencia. Primo in figura et forma, quia secundum Ysidorum formabatur ad modum littere delthe quam esse constat huius forme △, sed nullum inter instrumenta moderna memini me vidisse talis forme vel similis. Secunda differencia est in numero cordarum, quia nullum genus viellarum modernarum septenarium numerum cordarum transcendit, set psalterium vel .x. cordarum erat vel octo. Forte erat et tercia differentia, quia non tractu virgule sicut moderne vielle sed cum pulsu digitorum sonabat.

These drawings and their associated text appear to have passed through Dominican channels in the early fourteenth century, for we find them also in the psalm-commentary of Nicholas Trevet. For an example, see Page, 'Early Fifteenth Century Instruments', p.341.

9 This is the celebrated English Franciscan Roger Bacon:

> ... *si ipse* [*expositor*], *animo in aeterna suspenso, non possit his intrumentis uti, vocet saltem cum Elizaeo propheta, ut divinas revelationes devotius suscipiat, et totus in Deum efferatur.* ... *Nam licet non oportet propter scientiam scripturae quod habeat theologus usum cantus et instrumentorum et aliarum rerum musicalium, tamen debet scire rationem omnium istorum.* ...

> (... if the commentator, his mind set upon eternal things, cannot play these instruments, he may at least pray with the prophet Elijah that he may devoutly receive divine revelations and that all may be brought forth by God. ... Even if it is not actually necessary that the theologian, pursuing his studies of Scripture, should have any ability with song, instruments and other musical matters, he must nonetheless know the *ratio* of all these things. ...)

Brewer, *Roger Bacon*, pp.233–4 and Bridges, *Roger Bacon*, pp.236–7. Bacon's view of music is discussed in Adank, 'Roger Bacons Auffassung der Musica'; Bacon's example suggests another way in which literate and learned men could become interested in musical instruments: through experimental science and a fascination with *instrumenta* of all kinds. On this side of Bacon's activity see Kupfer, 'Father of Empiricism', and Fisher and Unguru, 'Experimental Science'.

10 Borgnet, *Beati Alberti Magni Opera Omnia*, 7, p.4. For other references to the *viella* see p.30 (upon the necessity of fiddling and other arts to the proper running of the state—a view which Johannes de Grocheio elaborates to produce his notably original *De Musica*), p.165a, and Volume 8, p.748. See also Stadler, *Alberti Magni de Animalibus*, 2, p.1293. Crombie (*Robert Grosseteste*, p.189) says that Albertus Magnus came under the influence of Grosseteste, first lecturer to the Franciscans at Oxford from 1229/30, later bishop of Lincoln, and a key figure in the history of experimental science in the West. There are striking references to contemporary instruments in the writings of several other friars connected with Grosseteste's 'circle', suggesting that, as in the case of Albertus, the friars' alertness to the properties of instruments often went hand in hand with an interest in Aristotelian science. One of these friars is the Franciscan Bartholomaeus Anglicus, whose celebrated encyclopaedia, *De Proprietatibus Rerum* (c1250), records that the strings of the *psalterium* 'are best made from "latten" and also from "silver"' (Appendix 4:18). Another of these friars is the Oxford Franciscan Roger Bacon, mentioned in the previous note, who seems to have become a member of Grosseteste's 'circle' by 1249.

11 Cited in Wright, 'Medieval Gittern and Citole', p.25.

12   Text in Page, 'German Musicians', p.194.

13   Text from Goldine, 'Henri Bate', pp.14–15, n.6.

14   On this clerical opposition to dancing see Chapter 6.

15   Text in Koenig, *Miracles de Nostre Dame*, 4, p.44, line 50.

16   Gerbert, *Scriptores*, 2, p.322.

17   Ruini, *Ameri Practica Artis Musice*, p.96.

18   Gerbert, *Scriptores*, 2, p.295. See also pp.296 and 327.
     Several further passages in the theorists relating to instruments and notation may be signalled here.
     Lambertus (Coussemaker, *Scriptorum*, 1, p.269) teaches his students how to read and write mensural notation 'so that any piece of music, however much it may have been diversified to the extreme, may be suitably made plain through [musical handwriting] in the manner of a fiddle' (*in modum vielle*)'. I suspect that Lambertus is here comparing the set of five musical staves used in thirteenth-century mensural notation to the five strings of the *viella*. He would then be saying that just as the fiddle's five strings can encompass the whole gamut (a point made with reference to the *viella* by Amerus, Elias of Salomon and Jerome of Moravia), so the trained musician can write all music, 'however much it may have been diversified to the extreme', on five staves (by learning how to move clefs and how to record any rhythm in mensural notation).
     The anonymous author of the *Summa Musice* (Gerbert, *Scriptores*, 3, p.214) deals with the various ways in which musical intervals are measured with *signa*. This term might best be translated 'ways of articulating' since the author's use of *signa* goes beyond the sense 'written marks' to embrace various non-scriptal ways in which intervals may be distinguished. This becomes plain when he points out that instruments articulate intervals in various ways according to their various properties (*Sed in sonoris musicae instrumentis diversimode se habent signa notarum secundum instrumenti proprietates diversas*). Thus wind-instruments such as the organ articulate them in sequences of tones and semitones, while fingerboard instruments articulate them in fourths, fifths and octaves and players must stop the strings to produce further distinctions. A singer, the author comments in a reference to the Guidonian hand, 'has the joints of the hand with differences of sound as a way of articulating' (*in manu ipsos articulos et sonorum differentias habet pro signis*). If this is the correct interpretation of the author's use of *signa* ('a way of laying out and articulating tones and semitones') then the

Summa Musice may not reveal anything about instruments and notation.

The most confusing and tantalising passage, however, is undoubtedly the one by Anonymous 4 (Reckow, *Anonymous 4*, 1, p.40) which records that *simplicia puncta* (principally ¶ and ■) are used 'in various kinds of music-books [and] in all and every kind of musical instrument' (*in quolibet genere omnium instrumentorum*). I can find no secure or convincing interpretation of this very important passage.

19   Text and translation in Page, 'Jerome of Moravia', pp.88–9.

20   *Ibid.*

21   *Ibid.*, pp.90–1.

22   Compare, for example, a fourteenth-century contrast between liturgical chant and *Irregularis autem dicitur cantus rusticanus sive laycalis...eo quod neque modis neque regulis constat* ('Irregular music [which] is called rustic or layman's music...in that it observes neither modes nor rules'; Gallo, *Tractatulus*, p.12).

23   For these arrangements see Chapter 10.

24   Rohloff, *Grocheio*, p.156.

25   Text and Music from Stäblein, *Hymnen*, p.36.

26   Rohloff, *Grocheio*, p.160.

27   For these interpretations see Appendix 3:42.

28   Rohloff, *Grocheio*, p.160.

29   On the interpretation of the *ductia* as a virelai see below, pp.81–2.

30   Gushee, 'Two central places', p.143.

31   Text in Page, 'Jerome of Moravia', p.92. It is possible that Jerome is paraphrasing material here which was originally independent of the main body of his account. He introduces the description of the advanced technique with the words *Quibus visis et memorie commendatis totam artem viellandi habere poteris arte usui aplicata* (*loc. cit.*). This is almost identical to a sentence appearing elsewhere in Jerome's treatise and which may well be 'a formula used to connect sections of two treatises that were originally independent' (Fuller, 'Theory of Fifthing', p.262, n.73).

32 *Ibid.*

33 Fuller, 'Theory of Fifthing'.

34 The musical examples are drawn from Fuller's study.

35 This brings out the core of my (reluctant) disagreement with Jerome's thirteenth-century annotator, Pierre de Limoges. Pierre sees Jerome's advanced technique as a self-accompanying one; I interpret it as a means of accompanying another instrumentalist or singer.

36 Melody from Van der Werf, *Troubadours and Trouvères*, p.123 (melody of MS K).

37 For a full account of Elias's recommendations see Dyer, 'Thirteenth Century Choirmaster'.

38 Borgnet, *Alberti Magni Opera Omnia*, 7, p.165:
Similiter viellatio bene suum habet ad harmoniam chordarum ex percussione conveniente: propter quod a multis bona fit viellatio, qui tamen rationem reddere nesciunt consonantis harmoniae: eo quod ex usu magis quam ab arte operantur.
(The art of fiddling comes into its own with harmony set up by skilled stirring of strings; on this account many succeed in the art of fiddling who cannot explain the rational basis of harmonious accord because their playing is based more upon practical experience than upon a scientific knowledge of music-theory.)

39 *Melodicus modus et lyratorum et fistulatorum, qui similiter ex usu solo melodias tonales in lyris et fistulis, et aliis instrumentis musicis contingunt et componunt, arti per naturam et usum quantum possunt appropinquantes, quia sicut dicit Aristoteles II Elementorum, multi sine arte faciunt ea quae sunt artis, et caet[era], sicut e converso multi ea, quae sciunt per artem, non possunt per usum.*
(The 'melodic' way [of teaching and learning music] is the one used by (?) harpists and (?) flautists, for they also perform and compose melodies on their harps, flutes and other musical instruments according to practical experience alone, coming as close to the exercise of truly scientific mastery as intuitive skill and practice will allow them to do, for as Aristotle says in the second book of the *Elements*, there are many who, without scientific mastery, accomplish the things which such mastery accomplishes. The converse is also true: there are many who cannot accomplish the things in practical terms of which they have scientific mastery.) Gerbert, *Scriptores* 2, p.289.

40 Text from Anderson, *Bamberg Manuscript*, p.xc.

41 *Ibid.*, p.ciii.

Chapter 6: The carole

1 Birmingham, University Library, MS 6/iii/19, f.103r. On this collection of *collationes* see d'Avray, *Preaching of the Friars, passim.*

2 For references to lyric in Old French sermons see Zink, *La Prédication,* pp.365ff; none of the passages cited seem to relate to the High-Style trouvère chanson. Latin sermons and devotional works generally have little to offer here, perhaps because references to trouvère song (as opposed to popular dance-song etc.) are very hard to spot. For some possible candidates see Guillaume d'Auvergne, *De Universo,* p.627 and a sermon by the Dominican Guido of Evreux (Oxford, Jesus College, MS E.8, f.13r). References to polyphony in sermons and moral or theological writings are very few. In the early fourteenth century Petrus de Palude inveighed against *motetti* in his commentary upon Psalm 32:2 (Douai, Bibliothèque Municipale, MS 45, volume 2, f.134r; there is no guarantee that polyphonic music is meant here) and Guillaume d'Auvergne mentions polyphonic songs with special admiration in his *De Universo* (p.996).

These references are as nothing, however, beside the encyclopedic treatment often accorded to *coreae.* The outstanding sources are the chapters on *coreae* in Guillaume Peyraut's *Summa de Vitiis et Virtutibus* (the passages cited in what follows are from Oxford, Bodleian Library, MS Bodley 457, ff.25r-28v). These chapters were often copied and excerpted during the later Middle Ages (for an elaborate fifteenth-century example see Oxford, Bodleian Library, MS Bodley 864, ff.146v-147v). Peyraut is also the main source for the (scanty) material on *caroles* in *Le Mireour du Monde* (Chavannes, *Mireour du Monde,* pp.76 and 162ff.; this text is often cited by Sahlin, *La carole médiévale,* pp.10, 32–3, *et passim,* whose coverage of the Latin source-material in sermons and treatises on the Virtues and Vices is sketchy).

Other important sources on the *corea* include London, British Library, MS Harley 3823, ff.372v–378v, and MS Royal 11 B.iii, ff.271v-272r. With the spread of treatises on penitence and confession in the thirteenth century the question of how many sins were involved in dancing *coreae* became a pressing one. The most interesting answers are often to be found in commentaries upon Peter Lombard's dictum (*Sentences,* IV:xvi) that the sinner should abstain from all amusements and entertainments during penance. Some of the thirteenth-century scholastics deal with the issue in a surprisingly indulgent way. See, for example, Albertus Magnus's discussion of the question (Borgnet, *Beati Alberti Magni Opera Omnia,* 29, pp.632ff). It is material such as this which lies behind Johannes de Grocheio's compassionate view that dancing in *coreae* is good for those who participate and can actually quell sexual lust (Rohloff, *Grocheio,* p.132). This is an opinion which would have staggered a moralist such as Guillaume Peyraut.

References to the character of *corea* music are scattered here and there in theological treatises and technical writings on music. See Borgnet, *op. cit.*, 29, p.633, for the remarks of Albertus Magnus, and for various comments in the writings of music theorists see Bragard, *Jacobi Leodiensis Speculum Musicae*, 6, p.216, and Gallo, *Johannis Boen, Ars Musicae*, p.18.

3 MS Royal 11 B.iii, f.272r: *a pascha usque ad autumpnum*, probably following Peyraut, f.26r, whose point is that this is the season when *coreae* 'chiefly hinder the church of God' (because they were often performed in churchyards and the singing of the dancers occasionally disturbed priests).

4 For the most part the abundant references to *coreae* in the Vices and Virtues literature refer to dances 'performed through the streets and roadways' (*per vicos et plateas*) rather than to the courtly occasions so often described in romances (see Sahlin, *La carole médiévale,* for a very generous selection of romance references).

5 This detail is mentioned by Peyraut (f.26v), and by many other writers (e.g. MS Harley 3823, f.375v). The importance which dancers (especially young girls) attached to performing *coreae* with fresh clothes is discussed at great length (and often with attention to picturesque details) by Peyraut and by the author of the treatise on *coreae* in MS Harley 3823, ff.372v–378v. On the floral garlands worn by the dancers see above, pp.89ff.

6 British Library, MS Arundel 395, f.58v: *quando plures sunt in chorea vel quando plures spectantes tanto est letior....*

7 MS Harley 3823, f.376r.

8 Lecoy, *Guillaume de Dole*, lines 507–19. For references to the songs performed for *caroles* see Birmingham, University Library, MS 6/iii/19, f.103v where they are described as *ro[ndellus] aut balatus*; Peyraut, f.25r (*audiunt cantus lascivie*), and f.26v (how women tempt men to dance with *cantus suavitate*).

9 MS Harley 3823, f.374v (*iuvenes et puellas*) and 376r (*iuvenes et iuvenculas*); Peyraut, f.27, *iuvenes...filie familias*. Compare also Grocheio (Rohloff, *Grocheio*, p.132): *in choreis a iuvenibus et a puellis.*

10 Goldine, 'Henri Bate', p.15, n.

11   Peyraut, f.27r.

12   Rohloff, *Grocheio*, p.132.

13   *Loc. cit.*

14   The line of reasoning here is that in Grocheio's classification the vocal *ductia* belongs to the class of *cantilene* whose distinguishing feature is that its members begin and end with a refrain (*Cantilena vero quaelibet rotunda vel rotundellus a pluribus dicitur, eo quod ad modum circuli in se ipsam reflectitur et incipit et terminatur in eodem*; 'Many call any kind of *cantilena* a 'rotunda' or 'rotundellus' because it turns in the manner of a circle and begins and ends in the same way'). Yet Grocheio prefers to reserve the terms 'rotunda' and 'rotundellus' for pieces whose 'parts' (*partes*) do not differ from the refrain in their music. In other words Grocheio's 'rotunda' and 'rotundellus' are what we are accustomed to call a rondeau, where the added lines have the same music as the refrain. The *ductia* must therefore follow a different scheme in that the music of the added lines differs from that of the refrain. The *virelai* seems to fit the bill neatly.

15   Rohloff, *Grocheio*, p.136.

16   Most references are ambiguous in some way. See, for example, Lecoy, *Guillaume de Dole*, lines 503ff; are the *vïeleors* in line 503 accompanying the *caroles* or do they provide a separate entertainment? See also Sahlin, *La carole médiévale*, pp.18–21 (where almost all of the texts cited with reference to instrumental participation date from the fourteenth century).

17   Sahlin, *op. cit., passim.*

18   Lecoy, *Guillaume de Dole*, especially lines 507ff.

19   *Ibid.*, line 1569.

20   Sahlin, *La carole médiévale*, p.23.

21   Alton, *Claris et Laris*, p.269, lines 9940–4.

22   Lecoy, *Guillaume de Dole*, lines 1846, 5440, 2523 and 4164.

Chapter 7: The monophonic conductus

1   For the full context of this passage see above, pp.59–60.

2 Rohloff, *Grocheio,* p.130.

3 *Loc. cit.: a magistris et studentibus circa sonos coronatur.* It is far from clear what is meant by *circa sonos coronatur* (literally '[the *cantus coronatus*] is garlanded around its notes [by Masters and students]'). These words have been interpreted to mean 'accompanied (*coronatur*) with other sounds (i.e. instrumentally)'; see Seay, *Johannes de Grocheo* [*sic*], p.16. I find this a somewhat forced interpretation but I have none better to offer.

4 Buffum, *Roman de la Violette,* lines 3089–90: *Cil jougleour vïelent lais/Et sons et notes et conduis.*

5 Koenig, *Miracles de Nostre Dame,* 4, p.186, lines 263–7.

6 *Ibid.,* 3, p.279, lines 366–7.

7 The figures are from Falck, *Notre Dame Conductus,* p.8.

8 Text and music from Marrocco and Sandon, *Medieval Music,* p.62.

9 These monophonic Latin rondeaux are edited in Anderson, *Notre Dame and Related Conductus,* 10.

10 *Ibid.,* p.XLVI.

11 *Ibid.,* p.XVI.

12 *Ibid.,* pp.XXVIII and XXIX.

13 Oxford, Bodleian Library, MS 457, f.25v.

14 London, British Library, MS Harley 3823, f.367v.

15 Davy, *Sermons Universitaires Parisiens,* p.248.

16 Cited in Aubry, *La Musique et les Musiciens,* entries for 22 August, 1263, and 9 July, 1249.

Chapter 8: The Roman de Horn *and the lai*

1 Pope, *Horn,* lines 2830–44. This text has already been fully quoted and translated above, pp.4–5; it is repeated here for convenience since it is the centrepiece of this chapter.

2 I adopt Harrison's interpretation of the performance-routine described in *Horn* (Dobson and Harrison, *Medieval English Songs*, pp.87–8).

3 The passage has often been quoted, translated and interpreted. See, for example, Handschin, 'Estampie und Sequenz', 1, pp.6ff; Reaney, *'Lais of Guillaume de Machaut'*, pp.20ff; Bliss, *Sir Orfeo*, pp.xxix–xxx; Dobson and Harrison, *Medieval English Songs*, pp.87–8.

4 Text and music from Jeanroy *et al.*, *Lais et Descorts*, pp.62–3 and 142.

5 Text from Payen, *Les Tristan en Vers*, p.171, lines 843–6.

6 On the mystique of this 'Matter of Britain' see, for example, Ollier, 'Utopie et Roman Arthurien', p.226.

7 Foulet, *Galeran de Bretagne*, lines 2278–81, 2295–301 and 2316–20. Foulet attributes this romance to Jean Renart, but this attribution has always been disputed and is now generally rejected. See Lindval, *Jean Renart*.

8 Translated from British Library, Additional MS 12228, ff.218r–222v.

9 *Ibid.*, f.222v.

10 For an account of the form of these *lais* see Fotitch and Steiner, *Tristan en prose*, pp.137ff.

11 Transcribed from Paris, Bibliothèque Nationale, MS fr. 776, f.271v.

12 Fotitch and Steiner, *Tristan en prose*, p.137.

13 D'Arco, *Passion*, p.95.

14 Rohlfs, *Sankt Alexius*, p.24.

15 Compare the remarks on stanza-form in Roques, 'Deux particularités métriques'.

16 Text from Goldschmidt, *Sone von Nausay*, pp.412ff, lines 15963–76 and 15979–91.

17 Tolkien, *Tree and Leaf*, *passim*, where the image is developed with characteristic insight and charm.

18 For the history of the Apollonius story see Kortekaas, *Historia Apollonii*,

pp.9f, and for an important account of the story's influence upon the emergence of romance in twelfth-century France see Delbouille, 'Apollonius de Tyr'. The Old French prose-version of the *Historia* is available in Lewis, 'Apollonius Romans'.

19 Text in Goolden, *Old English Apollonius of Tyre*.

20 The Anglo-Norman and Old French metrical versions of the Tristan story are edited and translated in Payen, *Les Tristan en Vers*. For material of musical interest from the Vienna 2542 text of the *Tristan en prose* see Maillard, 'Coutumes musicales'. The *Tristan en prose* was one of the most widely-read romances of the later Middle Ages, to judge by the number and chronological distribution of the surviving sources. For listings of manuscripts see Fotitch and Steiner, *Tristan en prose*, pp.130–6.

21 Delbouille, 'Apollonius de Tyr'.

22 For Celtic analogues of the Tristan legend see Schoepperle, *Tristan*, and most recently, Padel, 'Cornish background' and de Mandach, 'Tristan et Iseut'. Padel and de Mandach present very detailed arguments in favour of a Cornish origin for many elements of the Tristan story. As far as Tristan's musical accomplishments are concerned, most research has focused upon the 'Harp and Rote' episode. See Newstead, 'The Harp and the Rote' and Cluzel, 'Harpeur d'Irlande'. For a startlingly different view of the history of the legend see Gallais, *Tristan et Iseut*, where it is argued that many elements of the story are Persian in origin.

23 For attempts see Schoepperle, *Tristan, passim*.

24 For Marie's text see Ewert, *Lais, passim*.

25 Loomis, 'Oral Diffusion', p.52.

Chapter 9: Open-string instruments: tunings and techniques

1 Ruini, *Ameri Practica Artis Musice*, p.79. For further references to the tuning of open-string instruments in the theorists of this period see Reaney, *MS Oxford Bodley 842*, p.21 (a diagram of a *cythera per modum boycii*, that is, a diagram of Boethius's fifteen-note gamut imposed upon a drawing of a medieval pillar-harp); Anon, *Summa Musice* in Gerbert, *Scriptores*, 3, pp.214–15.

2 See, for example, the fifteenth-century English instructions for tuning a

harp printed in Handschin, 'Aus der alten Musiktheorie', pp.3–4. The text as it stands may need some correction yet there is no doubt that its instructions are a recipe for producing a diatonic tuning.

3 For the text see Hardy and Martin, *Lestorie des Engleis*, p.351. For a text of the *Gesta* with facing English translation see Miller and Sweeting, *De Gestis Herewardi Saxonis*.

4 Quoted from Vienna, Nationalbibliothek, MS 2542, f.113r.

5 *Ibid.*, f.416v.

6 *Ibid.*, f.485r.

7 *Loc. cit.*

8 The *lais* of the Vienna manuscript are edited in Fotitch and Steiner, *Tristan en prose*.

9 *Ibid.*, pp.150–1.

10 Vienna, Nationalbibliothek, MS 2542, f.356r.

11 For bibliography on this text see Page, 'String Instrument Making', p.64, n.60.

12 York Chapter Library, MS 16.N.3, f.112v.

13 *Ibid.*, f.113v.

14 See Godefroy, *Dictionnaire*, sv *regart*: 'Aspect, sorte, nature'.

15 These passages are assembled and discussed in Hibberd, 'Musica ficta'. In my view Hibberd tries too hard to smother the implication that the use of *ficte musice* was regarded by many music-theorists as particularly necessary for instrumentalists.

16 Gerbert, *Scriptores*, 3, p.221.

17 Bragard, *Jacobi Leodiensis Speculum Musicae*, 6, p.146.

18 Compare Coussemaker, *Scriptorum*, 2, p.441.

19 Bragard, *Jacobi Leodiensis Speculum Musicae*, 6, p.146.

20 Coussemaker, *Scriptorum*, 3, p.18.

21 For illustrations see Perrot, *Organ*, plates XXVII:2 and XXVIII:3.

22 Godefroy, *Dictionnaire*, sv *bordon*, 2; Tobler-Lommatzsch, *Altfranzösisches Wörterbuch*, sv *bordon; Mittellateinisches Wörterbuch*, sv 2* *burdo* 1; Page, 'Jerome of Moravia', p.90 (line 42).

23 Page, 'Fifteenth century lute', p.14.

24 Chapman, *Marin Mersenne*, p.225.

25 York, Chapter Library, MS 16.N.3, f.113.

26 The exact meaning of *essais* in this context is unknown. See Stone and Rothwell, *Anglo-Norman Dictionary*, sv *assai*, 'attempt'. The basic sense is presumably something like 'the testers', perhaps referring to certain strings which occupied a central position in any tuning procedure or in some such tuning prelude as is described in the *Roman de Horn.*

27 For the relevant section of the text in a modern edition see Bossuat, *Anticlaudianus*, IV, lines 345ff.

28 Oxford, Balliol College, MS 265, f.69v. I am most grateful to Dr Nigel Palmer of Oriel College, Oxford, for this reference. For an account of the manuscript see Mynors, *Catalogue of the Manuscripts of Balliol College, Oxford*, no. 265. I have no doubt that a comprehensive search through glossed manuscripts of the *Anticlaudianus* would reveal this same gloss in an earlier source.

29 On *harp/cithara* see Appendix 1.

30 For full text and translation see Appendix 4:11.

31 On the background to this text see particularly Gransden, 'Realistic Observation'.

32 Oxford, Bodleian Library, MS Hatton 37, f.49r.

33 Foulet, *Galeran de Bretagne*, line 1169.

34 See Appendix 4:8.

35 Manitius, *Sextus Amarcius, Sermones*, p.75, line 416.

36 For text and translation see above, pp.4–5.

37 Arnold, *Brut,* lines 10417–29.

38 Griscom and Jones, *Historia Regum Britanniae,* p.456.

39 Kebede, 'Bowl-lyre', p.386.

40 Bragard, *Jacobi Leodiensis Speculum Musicae,* 1, pp.70–1.

41 Gerbert, *Scriptores,* 2, p.328.

42 I am grateful to Ann Lewis of Keble College, Oxford, for drawing this source to my attention.

43 See Grove 6, sv *Qānūn.*

44 *Particula* 19, problem 3, and on the archaic character of the *rota* strung on both sides, problem 39.

45 *Particula* 19, problem 3.

46 For the diagram and a translation of the text see Chapman, *Marin Mersenne,* pp.224–6.

47 See, for example, Panum, *Stringed Instruments,* figures 119, 123 and 133.

48 Chapman, *Marin Mersenne,* p.224.

49 See Dyer, 'Thirteenth Century Choirmaster', for a study of Elias of Salomon's instructions (1274) on how to decorate liturgical chant by singing in parallel fifths, octaves and twelfths.

Chapter 10: Jerome of Moravia and stopped-string instruments

1 Wright, 'Medieval Gittern and Citole', p.10.

2 Details from Page, 'Jerome of Moravia'.

3 Stewart, 'The echoing corridor', pp.348 and 351.

4 For some of the evidence see Chapter 3, n.13.

5 Chailley, *'Tu autem'*, p.29 (including a facsimile of the line of melody,

taken from the Aix-en-Provence manuscript of *Le Jeu de Robin et Marion*). The evidence for associating this melodic fragment with the epic of *Girart de Roussillon* lies in the fact that it sets (and has clearly been designed to set) a decasyllabic line broken 6:4. This break is very rarely used in the surviving Old French epics but is employed throughout *Girart de Roussillon*.

6 Page, 'Jerome of Moravia', pp.90–1. The adjective 'irregular' (*irregularis*) probably implies that the 'unlearned' songs to which Jerome refers did not follow the rules of the modes. Compare the anonymous *Tractatus de cantu mensurali seu figuratio musicae artis* (Gallo, *Tractatus de cantu mensurali*, p.12): 'Irregular music [which] is called rustic or layman's music... in that it observes neither modes nor rules' (*Irregularis autem dicitur cantus rusticanus sive laycalis... eo quod neque modis neque regulis constat*). The point of Jerome's remark would seem to be that tuning 2 is appropriate for music which does not observe modal constraints; this distinguishes it from tuning 1 which, in Jerome's words, 'comprehends all the modes'.

7 See, for instance, Bowles, 'Haut and Bas', p.128.

8 The tuning is usually presented as a uniformly ascending sequence (see, for example, Bachmann, *Origins*, pp.93ff).

9 I am most grateful to Dr Ephraim Segerman for the opportunity to discuss this question at length on many occasions.

10 On Jerome's virtuoso technique see above, pp.69ff.

11 As suggested to me by Dr Ephraim Segerman.

12 Gerbert, *Scriptores*, 3, p.214.

13 See Morrow, 'Ayre on the F♯ string', p.11.

14 *Ibid.* See also Brown, *Sixteenth Century Instrumentation*, p.33.

15 Text in Charland, *Artes Praedicandi*, p.333.

Chapter 11: Conclusions: voices and instruments

1 Marshall, *Razos de Trobar*, p.98.

2 Rastall, 'English Consort-Groupings', p.183.

3   Dimock and Brewer, *Itinerarium Kambriae*, p.48.

4   Quoted in Chailley, 'Chanson de geste', p.11, n.

5   Rohloff, *Grocheio*, p.160.

6   Text in Varnhagen, 'Ayenbite of Inwyt', p.36.

7   See Maillard, 'Coutumes musicales', *passim*.

8   See, for example, Heinrich Eger von Kalkar (Hüschen, *Cantuagium*, p.54), Jacques de Liège (Bragard, *Jacobi Leodiensis Speculum Musicae*, 4, p.21) and Engelbert of Admont (Gerbert, *Scriptores*, 3, p.291).

9   See Page, 'False Voices', for the kind of semantic and terminological difficulties which stand between us and a satisfactory solution of the question.

10 See, for example, Anonymous 4 (Reckow, *Anonymous 4*, 1, pp.66 and 86).

Appendix 1: Terminology of musical instruments

1   Marcuse, *Survey*, p.370.

2   Remnant, 'Rebec, Fiddle and Crowd', p.15.

3   Galpin, *Old English Instruments*, pp.56, 57 (caption) and p.4.

4   For an example from Nicholas Trevet's commentary see Page, 'Early fifteenth century instruments', p.341.

5   See, for example, Bamberg, Staatsbibliothek, MS Bibl. 63, f.351v, and MS Bibl. 64, f.494v, both reflecting attempts to bring the *cithara* into line with Bohemian instruments.

6   Reproduced in Wright, 'Medieval Gittern and Citole', plate 1.

7   *Ibid.*, plate 2.

8   Reproduced in Montagu, *Medieval and Renaissance Instruments* [colour] plate 3.

9   Reproduced after two (slightly differing) nineteenth-century copies in Page, 'Medieval Organistrum and Symphonia', 2, p.80.

10 *Ibid.*, p.81.

11 Reproduced in Galpin, *Old English Instruments*, plate 21:1.

12 For an example see Page, 'Early fifteenth century instruments', p.342.

13 For Old Provençal evidence see Wright, 'Gargilesse', p.67 and n.3, on the illustrations in manuscripts of the *Vidas* which show the troubadour Perdigo said to be skilled with the *viola*. For Old Spanish evidence see Appendix 3:4.

14 The form *rebek* appears in an early twelfth-century table of Arabic and Latin terms (the Arabic has a strong colouring of Romance). For this important table, with details of the manuscript in which it appears (Paris, Bibliothèque Nationale, MS lat. 14754, f.244v), see Lemay, 'Origine arabe', pp.998f.

15 Page, 'Early fifteenth century instruments', p.347.

16 Baines, 'Fifteenth century instruments,' p.23.

17 See above, p.126.

18 *Middle English Dictionary* sv. *giterne.*

19 See, for example, British Library, MS Cotton Tiberius B.V, f.3.

20 For examples see Bachmann, *Origins*, plates 55 and 60, and Panum, *Stringed Instruments*, figures 124 and 125.

21 For an examination of 'harp' terminology in the Dark Ages see Page, *Anglo-Saxon Hearpan.*

22 Panum, *Stringed Instruments*, figures 85–8.

23 See, for example, Steger, *Philologia Musica.*

24 See *Revue Bénédictine*, 29 (1912), p.286.

25 The relationship is discussed in Page, 'Medieval Organistrum and Symphonia', 2, pp.79ff.

26 Ibid.

27 Ibid.

Appendix 3: Literary references relating to the involvement of stringed instruments in French and Occitan monody

1   See further Chapter 3 and the evidence from Jean Renart's romance of *Guillaume de Dole*.

Most readers will no doubt find that items which they would have expected to be included in this list are not in fact present. Choosing the material for inclusion has been a difficult—and no doubt somewhat arbitrary—process. As far as the music-theorists and writers on vernacular poetry are concerned I have aimed at comprehensive coverage. The material from theological treatises towards the end of the appendix, however, is only a minute sampling of a vast quantity of material still waiting to be gathered and assessed. In the case of narrative poems and prose-texts I have not hesitated to include references which, even if they reveal very little by themselves, none the less illustrate some of the formulaic patterns which underlie the presentation of musical life in medieval fiction. I have however omitted references to the performance of *lais* to the harp; most of these are quoted and translated in Chapter 6.

Since the remains of narrative and didactic literature in Old Provençal are so sparse it is worth extending the above remarks to record here the musical references which I encountered in Occitan sources but did not include in the appendix.

Arnaut Guilhem de Marsan *Ensenhamen au Cavayer, 131ff.*

Blandin de Cornualha (ed. Horst), pp.115 and 990ff.

Canso de la Crosada (ed. Martin-Chabot): II, pp.52, 118, 200, 284 and 298; III, pp.182 and 300.

Garin lo Brun *Ensenhamen a la Domna*, 525ff; 539ff.

Guilhem Anelier *Histoire de la Guerre de Navarre*, 271ff.

Jaufre 3073ff; 4485ff and 10786ff.

Matfre Ermengaud *Le Breviari D'Amor* (ed. Azaïs), 2, pp.97ff (also Ricketts, ed., *Le Breviari d'Amor*, 27924ff and 33994ff).

Raimon Vidal *So fo e.l temps*, 1097ff.

La Vida del Glorios Sant Frances (ed. Arthur), p.168

Vie de S.Auzias (ed. Campbell), p.96.

I have also omitted: (1) the celebrated *Supplication* of Guiraut Riquier. Despite its many references to troubadours and instrumentalists I do not find that it reveals anything about accompaniment. (2) The satirical poems against *joglars*. (3) The *Cantigas d'Escarho e de Mal Dizer* in Galician-Portuguese and (4) the writings of the Catalan chroniclers such as Muntaner. These sources all contain many interesting references, but they are either somewhat late (4), peripheral (3), or do not reveal anything about instrumental practice upon closer inspection (2).

2   Arnold, *Brut*, lines 10545–8. Further on the technique of these lists see

Devoto, 'Instrumentos musicales' and Page, 'Music and Chivalric Fiction'.

3 For Vinsauf's recommendations see Gallo, *Poetria Nova,* pp.48–9.

4 Stengel, *Hervis von Metz,* line 569.

5 *Ibid.*

6 Favati, *Voyage de Charlemagne,* lines 413 and 837.

7 I am steering close here to some of the issues raised in recent years by literary scholars in their studies of oral and formulaic poetry. See, for example, Fry, 'Old English Formulaic Themes'.

8 Spitzer, 'Debailadas-bailar'; Devoto, 'Libro de Apolonio', and Artiles, *Libro de Apolonio.*

9 Text from Kortekaas, *Historia Apollonii Regis Tyri,* p.310. I have modified Kortekaas's orthography to the extent of replacing consonantal *u* with *v.*

10 The readings are from Willis, *Libro de Alexandre,* pp.370–1; Criado de Val and Naylor, *Libro de Buen Amor,* p.380.

11 See, for example, Criado de Val and Naylor, *Libro de Buen Amor,* p.378 (all MSS) at 1228b.

12 Rohloff, *Grocheio,* p.136.

13 Kortekaas, *Historia Apollonii Regis Tyri,* p.310.

14 The historical elements in the Vidas have been much discussed. See Egan, 'Vida'; Bec, *Anthologie de la Prose Occitane,* 1, pp.20ff; Wilson, 'Literary commentary', and De Ley, 'Provençal biographical tradition'.

15 For the text of the *Dit des Taboureurs* see Jubinal, *Jongleurs et Trouvères,* pp.164–9.

16 As is assumed, for example, by Riquer (*Història,* 1, pp.63ff).

17 Fay and Grigsby, *Joufroi de Poitiers,* line 1160.

18 Densusianu, *La Prise de Cordres,* lines 2097–8.

19 As in Bachmann, *Origins*, p.127.

20 These manuscripts are: Paris, Bibliothèque Nationale, MS fr.1553 (not 1533 as given in Buffum's edition, p.vii), f.295, and MS fr.1374, f.141v.

21 Buffum, *Roman de la Violette*, p.59, gives this reading in his apparatus.

22 Buffum, *op. cit.*, pp.viiiff gives details of MS C of *Le Roman de la Violette*. According to his account it transmits the romance in the literary language of the beginning of the fifteenth century, while the text it gives is very close to the oldest copy of the work: MS fr.1374 (although MS C is the only witness to the reading that concerns us here).

23 See above, Chapter 6.

24 *Analecta Hymnica*, 3:7.

25 Van der Werf, *Troubadours and Trouvères*, pp.153ff.

26 Grocheio's terms are *dictamen* and *concordantia* (Rohloff, *Grocheio*, p.132).

27 Van der Werf, *Troubadours and Trouvères*, pp.153ff.

28 See, for example (and for details), *Grove 6*, sv *Cantus coronatus*.

29 Text in Coussemaker, *Scriptorum*, 1, p.312.

30 Text in Jubinal, *Nouveau Recueil*, 2, p.244.

31 Text in Oulmont, *Débats du Clerc*, p.168.

32 Rohloff, *Grocheio*, p.130.

33 Carey, *Parfait du Paon*, lines 1409ff.

34 Compare the materials assembled in Faral, *Les Jongleurs*, Appendix 3, items 101 and 106.

35 The part of Peter's text dealing with minstrels is printed at the foot of Chobham's discussion of the issue in Broomfield's edition.

36 f.37v.

Appendix 4: String-materials in the Middle Ages

1   For a review of this issue (with special reference to late medieval England) see Page, 'String Instrument Making'.

2   The best available discussion of medieval string-materials is Bachmann, *Origins*, pp.78ff.

3   On such allegories see Chapter 5, n.6.

4   The evidence is contained in the cywydd (formerly attributed to Dafydd ap Gwilym) *Rho Duw hael rhadau helynt*. The text is printed in Jarman, 'Telyn a Chrwth', pp.174–5. There is an English translation of the poem in Jones, *Welsh Bards*, p.102. There are numerous obscurities and several textual problems in the poem, however; it awaits a full critical edition and study. There has long been a dispute over the authorship of the work; some manuscripts attribute it to Dafydd ap Gwilym and others to Iolo Goch. There is no doubt, however, that it is a genuine fourteenth-century work; see Parry, *Dafydd ap Gwilym*, clxxxiii.

5   By this use of terms I do not mean to imply anything about the composition of the material so-named.

6   Page, 'Early fifteenth century instruments', pp.341 and 346 and *idem*, the Direction of the Beginning', pp.121–2.

7   This tradition of metallic stringing was passed on to the harpsichord. See Page, 'In the Direction of the Beginning', pp.121–2.

8   See Appendix 1.

9   For translation see above, p.96.

10 Sommer, *Vulgate Version*, 2, p.408.

11 Several important string-traditions may have existed which are not revealed in the texts. A case in point is provided by the custom of equipping long lutes (e.g. the Turkish *saz*) with metallic strings, a custom which is observed in many parts of the world and which may have been operative in those (admittedly 'peripheral') areas of Europe where long lutes were used in the Middle Ages—primarily central and southern Spain up to, and including, the thirteenth century. Another tradition of wire-stringing centres upon certain short-lutes which, in Western tradition, have often been characterised by a somewhat 'low-

brow' or at least informal ethos. The line of descent here seems to run from the medieval gittern—an instrument habitually associated with foppish young men and tavern brawlers during the fourteenth century—to take in the Renaissance cittern and, eventually, the mandoline. On the medieval evidence for the ethos of the gittern, see Wright, 'Medieval Gittern and Citole'.

12　On this question see Buckley, *Tiompán*.

Bibliography

Abbreviations

AIM	American Institute of Musicology
AM	Acta Musicologica
AfMW	Archiv für Musikwissenschaft
BBSIA	Bulletin Bibliographique de la Société Internationale Arthurienne
CCM	Cahiers de Civilisation Médiévale
CSM	Corpus Scriptorum de Musica
ELN	English Language Notes
EM	Early Music
FM	Forum Musicologicum
GSJ	Galpin Society Journal
HMT	Handwörterbuch der Musikalischen Terminologie
JAMS	Journal of the American Musicological Society
MD	Musica Disciplina
MGH	Monumenta Germaniae Historica
ML	Music and Letters
MQ	Musical Quarterly
MSD	Musicological Studies and Documents

PL	Patrologia Latina
PRMA	Proceedings of the Royal Musical Association
RBdM	Revue Belge de Musicologie
SATF	Société des Anciens Textes Français
SIMP	Studia Instrumentorum Musicae Popularis
ZfMW	Zeitschrift für Musikwissenschaft

Primary sources: manuscripts

Psalm-commentaries

Most of the unpublished psalm-commentaries listed in Stegmüller's *Repertorium Biblicum Medii Aevi* were examined. The following list comprises only the most important or informative.

Cambridge, Christ's College MS 11
Henry of Cossey

Hereford Cathedral Library MS O.IV.II
Nicholas Trevet (with coloured drawings)

London, British Library MS Royal 19 C.v
Commentary upon the psalter in French

London, Lambeth Palace Library MS 435
Hebrew psalter with Latin glosses

London, St Paul's Cathedral MS 2
Herbert of Bosham

Oxford, Bodleian Library MS Bodley 246
Nicholas de Gorran

 MS Bodley 251
 Nicholas de Lyra

 MS Bodley 318
 Lietbertus of Lille

MS Bodley 727
Johannes Halgrinus de Abbatisvilla

MS Bodley 737
Pseudo-Haymo of Halberstadt

MS Bodley 738
Nicholas Trevet (with coloured drawings)

MS Bodley 860
Anonymous glosses

MS e Mus. 15
Grosseteste (with sketches, f. 43r)

MS Hatton 37
Anonymous glosses

MS Laud misc. 152
Nicholas de Lyra

Oxford, New College MS 36
Michael of Meaux

Karlsruhe, Badische Landesbibliothek MS 184
Arnobius Junior

Vienna, Nationalbibliothek, Cod. Vindob. 927
Honorius Augustodunensis

Douai, Bibliothèque Municipale MS 45 (7 volumes)
Petrus de Palude (with coloured drawings)

Grenoble, Bibliothèque Municipale MS 341
Bruno the Carthusian

Rheims, Bibliothèque Municipale MS 133
Remigius of Auxerre

Troyes, Bibliothèque Municipale MS 144
Petrus de Palude (with coloured drawings)

Sermons

Many sermons by major medieval authors are available in early printed editions. See bibliography, *passim*.

London, British Library MS Arundel 395
Anonymous

Oxford, Jesus College MS E.8
Guido of Evreux

Oxford, Lincoln College MS Lat. 113
Guido of Evreux

Birmingham University Library MS 6/iii/19
Anonymous *Collationes*

Treatises on virtues and vices

London, British Library MS Harley 3823
Anonymous (*De choreis*, ff.372v–78v)

> MS Royal 11 B.iii
> Anonymous

Oxford, Bodleian Library MS Bodley 457
Guillaume Peyraut *Summa de Vitiis et Virtutibus*

> MS Lyell 12
> Guillaume Peyraut *Summa de Vitiis et Virtutibus*

> MS Bodley 251
> Guillaume d'Auvergne *De Viciis et Peccatis*

> MS Bodley 864
> Anonymous *Nota de choreis* (ff.146v–147v)

Paris, Bibliothèque Nationale MS lat.3726
Anonymous, concerning *coreae* (f.42v–43)

Old French fiction

London, British Library Additional MS 12228
Guiron le Courtois

MS Harley 4903
Peliarmenus
Kanor

MSS Royal 15 E.v, 19 E.ii and 19 E.iii
Perceforest

Paris, Bibliothèque Nationale
f.fr 93
Peliarmenus
Kanor

f.fr. 1446
Kanor

f.fr. 22549–50
Peliarmenus
Kanor

f.fr. 1374
Le Roman de la Violette

f.fr. 1553
Le Roman de la Violette

Vienna, Nationalbibliothek MS 2542
Tristan en prose

Miscellaneous

London, British Library MS Royal 8 G.iv
William of Auxerre, *Summa Aurea*

Additional MS 18322
Humbert of Priallaco, commentary upon Peter Lombard, *Sentences*, Book IV

Cambridge, Trinity College MS 0.1.58
Secretum Philosophorum

Oxford, Bodleian Library MS Bodley 196
Honorius Augustodunensis *Gemma Anime*

MS Bodley 749
Bartholomaeus Anglicus *De Proprietatibus Rerum*

Oxford, Balliol College MS 265
Glosses upon Alain de Lille, *Anticlaudianus*

York, Minster Library MS 16.N.3
Pierre of Peckham, *Lumiere as Lais*

Toulouse, Académie des Jeux Floraux MS 500.006 the *Leys d'Amors*

MS 500.007 the *Leys d'Amors*

St Paul in Kärnten, Archiv des Benediktinerstiftes, Cod 264/4
Summa Musice

Books and articles

Adank, T. 'Roger Bacons Auffassung der Musica', *AfMW*, 35 (1978), pp.33–56.

Adkins, C. 'The Technique of the Monochord', *AM*, 39 (1967), pp.34–43.

Albe, E. (ed.) *Les Miracles de Notre-Dame de Roc-Amadour au XIIe siècle* (Paris, 1907).

Altner, E. *Über die Chastïements in den Altfranzösischen Chansons de Geste* (Leipzig, 1885).

Alton, J. (ed.) *Li Romans de Claris et Laris* (Tübingen, 1884).

Anderson, E.A. 'Passing the Harp in Bede's story of Caedmon: a twelfth century analogue', *ELN*, 15 (1977), pp.1–4.

Anderson, G.A. *Notre Dame and Related Conductus: Opera Omnia*. Institute of Medieval Music, Collected Works X (Henryville, 1978), including volume 8, *1pt Conductus—the Latin Rondeau Répertoire*.

—— *Compositions of the Bamberg Manuscript*, CMM 75 (AIM, 1977).

Anglade, J. (ed.) *Las Flors del Gay Saber* (Barcelona, 1926).

—— *Las Leys d'Amors. Manuscrit de l'Académie des Jeux Floraux*. 4 vols in 2 (Toulouse, 1919–20).

Anglès, H. 'La danza sacra y su música en el templo durante el Medioevo', *Medium Aevum Romanicum : Festschrift für Hans Rheinfelder* (Munich, 1963), pp.1–20.

——*La música a Catalunya fins al segle XIII* (Barcelona, 1935).

Arlt, W. 'The "reconstruction" of instrumental music: the interpretation of the earliest practical sources', in Boorman, pp.75–100.

Arlt, W. *et al.*(eds) *Gattungen der Musik in Einzeldarstellungen: Gedenkschrift Leo Schrade.* 1 (Berne and Munich, 1973).

Armandus de Bellovisu, *Sermones plane divini assumptis ex solo Psalterio Davidico thematis* (Lyon, 1525).

Arnobius Junior, *In Psalmos.* PL 53.

Arnold, I. (ed.) *Le Roman de Brut de Wace*, 2 vols, SATF (Paris, 1938 and 1940).

Artiles, J. *El 'Libro de Apolonio', poema español del siglo XIII* (Madrid, 1976).

Bachmann, W. *The Origins of Bowing*, trans. N. Deane (Oxford, 1969).

——'Die Verbreitung des Quintierens im europäischen Volksgesang des späten Mittelalters', in Vetter, W. (ed.) *Festschrift Max Schneider* (Leipzig, 1955), pp.25–9.

Bailey, T. (ed. and trans.) *Commemoratio brevis de tonis et psalmis modulandis* (Ottawa, 1979).

Barassi, E.F. *Strumenti musicali e testimonianze teoriche nel Medio evo* (Cremona, 1979).

Bartholomaeis, V. de (ed.) *Insegnamenti pe' giullari* (Rome, 1905).

Bartsch, K. (ed.) *Altfranzösische Romanzen und Pastourellen* (Leipzig, 1870).

Baum, R. 'Le descort ou l'anti-chanson', in *Mélanges . . . Boutière*, 2 vols (Liège, 1971), 1, pp.75–98.

——'Les troubadours et les lais', *Zeitschrift für Romanische Philologie*, 85 (1969), pp.1–44.

Baumgartner, E. 'Sur les pièces lyriques du Tristan en prose', in *Études de Langue et de Littérature du Moyen Age offertes à Félix Lecoy* (Paris, 1973), pp.19–25.

Bayart, P. (ed.) *Adam de la Bassée. Ludus Super Anticlaudianum* (Tourcoing, 1930).

Bec, P. *Anthologie de la Prose Occitane du Moyen Age*, 1 (Avignon, 1977).

——*La langue Occitane*, 4th ed. (Paris, 1963).

——*La Lyrique Française au Moyen Age* (Paris, 1977).

——'Le problème des genres chez les premiers troubadours', CCM 25 (1982), pp.31–47.

——*Nouvelle anthologie de la Lyrique Occitane du Moyen Age* (Avignon, 1970).

Bechstein, R. and Ganz, P. (eds) *Gottfried von Strassburg Tristan*, 2 vols (Wiesbaden, 1978).

Bedbrook, G.S. 'The problem of instrumental combination in the Middle Ages', *RBdM*, 25 (1971), pp.53–67.

Bédier, J. *Le Roman de Tristan de Thomas*, 2 vols, SATF (Paris, 1902 and 1905).

——'Les plus anciennes danses françaises', *Revue des Deux Mondes*, 31:1 (1906), pp.393–424.

Bender, M.O. (ed.) *Le Torneiment Anticrist* (University, Mississippi, 1976).

Benson, R.L. and Constable, G. (eds) *Renaissance and Renewal in the Twelfth Century* (Oxford, 1982).

Benton, J.F. 'Consciousness of Self and Perceptions of Individuality', in Benson and Constable, pp.263–95.

Bernhard, M. *Wortkonkordanz zu Anicius Manlius Severinus Boethius, De Institutione Musica* (Munich, 1979).

Binkley, T. 'Zur Aufführungspraxis der einstimmigen Musik des Mittelalters—ein Werkstattbericht', *Basler Jahrbuch für historische Musikpraxis* (1977), pp.19–76.

Bliss, A.J. (ed.) *Sir Orfeo*, 2nd ed. (Oxford, 1966).

Bloch, R.H. *Medieval French Literature and Law* (University of California Press, 1977).

Boase, R. *The Origin and Meaning of Courtly Love* (Manchester, 1977).

Boorman, S. (ed.) *Studies in the Performance of Late Mediaeval Music* (Cambridge, 1983).

Borgnet, A. (ed.) *Beati Alberti Magni . . . Opera Omnia*, 38 vols (Paris, 1890–9).

Bossuat, R. (ed.) *Alain de Lille. Anticlaudianus* (Paris, 1955).

Boulton, M.B. McCaan, *Lyric Insertions in French Narrative Fiction in the thirteenth and fourteenth century* (unpublished M.Litt. Thesis, Oxford,1979).

Boutière, J. and Schutz, A.H. (eds) *Biographies des Troubadours*, 2nd ed. (Paris, 1973).

Bowles, E. 'Haut and Bas: the Grouping of Musical Instruments in the Middle Ages', *MD*, 8 (1954), pp.115–40.

Bragard, R. (ed.) *Jacobi Leodiensis Speculum Musicae*, 7 vols, CSM 3 (AIM, 1955–73).

Brewer, J.S. (ed.) *Fr. Rogeri Bacon Opera . . . Inedita*, Rolls Series 15 (London, 1859).

Bridges, J.H. (ed.) *The Opus Majus of Roger Bacon*, 3 vols (Oxford, 1897–1900).

Bröcker, M. *Die Drehleier*, 2nd, revised ed. (Bonn, 1977).

Broomfield, F. (ed.) *Thomae de Chobham Summa Confessorum* (Paris and Louvain, 1968).

Brown, H.M. *Sixteenth Century Instrumentation : The Music for the Florentine Intermedii*, MSD 30 (AIM, 1973).

Bruno of Wurzburg, *In Psalmos*. PL 142.

Buckley, A. 'What was the *tiompán?* A problem in ethnohistorical organology: evidence in the Irish sources', *Jahrbuch für musikalische Volks- und Völkerkunde*, 9 (1978), pp.53–88.

Buffum, D.L. (ed.) *Le Roman de la Violette*, SATF (Paris, 1928).

Bullock-Davies, C. 'The Form of the Breton Lay', *Medium Aevum*, 42 (1973), pp.18–31.

284

—— *Professional Interpreters and the Matter of Britain* (Cardiff, 1966).

Burgess, G.S. *Marie de France: an analytical bibliography* (London, 1977).

Burney, C. *A General History of Music*, 4 vols (London, 1776, 1782 and 1789).

Burnley, J.D. "The 'Roman de Horn" and its Ethos', *French Studies*, 32 (1978), pp.385–97.

Buschinger, D. 'La musique dans le Tristan de Thomas et le Tristan de Gottfried: Quelques jalons', in Buschinger and Crépin, pp.171–85.

Buschinger, D. and Crépin, A. (eds) *Musique, Littérature et Société au Moyen Age* (Paris, 1980).

Carey, R.J. (ed.) *Jean de Le Mote : Le parfait du paon* (Chapel Hill, 1972).

Casagrande, C. and Vecchio, S. 'Clercs et jongleurs dans la société médiévale (XIIe et XIIIe siècles)', *Annales: économies, sociétés, civilisations*, 34 (1979), pp.913–28.

Casas Homs, J.M. (ed.) *Joan de Castellnou Obras en Prosa*, 1, *Compendi de la coneixença dels vicis en els dictats del Gai Saber* (1969).

Casimiri, A. 'Un trattatello per organisti di anonimo del sec. XIV', *Note d'Archivio per la storia musicale*, 19 (1942), pp.99–101.

Cassiodorus, *In Psalmos*. PL 70.

Castets, F. (ed.) *La chanson des quatre fils Aymon* (Montpellier, 1909).

Cesare, G. Battista de (ed.) *Libro de Apolonio* (Milan, 1974).

Chailley, J. 'Autour de la chanson de geste', *AM*, 27 (1955), pp.1–12.

—— 'Du *Tu autem* de Horn à la Musique des Chansons de Geste', in *Mélanges René Louis* (Saint-Père-Sous-Vézelay, 1982), 1, pp.21–32.

—— 'La danse religieuse au Moyen Age', in *Arts Libéraux et philosophie au Moyen Age: Actes du IVe congrès international de philosophie médiévale, Montreal, 1967* (Montreal and Paris, 1969), pp.357–80.

Chapman, R.E. (trans.) *Marin Mersenne. Harmonie Universelle: The Books on Instruments* (The Hague, 1957).

Charland, T.M. *Artes Praedicandi* (Ottawa, 1936).

Chavannes, F. (ed.) *Le Mireour du Monde* (Lausanne, 1845).

Chiarini, G. (ed.) *Juan Ruiz . . . Libro de Buen Amor* (Milan and Naples, 1964).

Cluzel, I. 'La Reine Iseut et le Harpeur d'Irlande', BBSIA, 10 (1958), pp.87–98.

Coldwell, M.V. '*Guillaume de Dole* and medieval romances with musical interpolations', *MD*, 35 (1981), pp.55–86.

Combarieu du Grès, M. de. *L'idéal humain et l'expérience morale chez les héros des chansons de geste des origines à 1250,* 2 vols (Aix-en-Provence, 1979).

Constans, L. (ed.) *Le Roman de Troie par Benoît de Sainte-Maure,* 6 vols, SATF (Paris, 1904–12).

Coussa, Z. 'De quelques emprunts lexicaux faits de l'arabe: les instruments de musique', in Buschinger and Crépin, pp.59–71.

Coussemaker, E. de (ed.) *Scriptorum de Musica Medii Aevi Nova Series,* 4 vols (Paris, 1864–76; R 1963).

Cowper, F.A.G. (ed.) *Ille et Galeron par Gautier d'Arras* (Paris, 1956).

Crane, F. *Extant medieval musical instruments: A provisional catalogue by types* (Iowa, 1972).

—— 'On performing the *Lo estampies*', *EM*, 7 (1979), pp.25–33.

Crocker, R. 'Alphabet notations for early medieval music', in King, M.H. and Stevens, W.M. (eds) *Saints, Scholars and Heroes: Studies in Medieval Culture in Honor of Charles W. Jones,* 2 vols (Minnesota, 1979), 2, pp.79–104.

Crombie, A.C. *Robert Grosseteste and the origins of experimental science, 1100–1700* (Oxford, 1953).

Curtis, R.L. (ed.) *Le Roman de Tristan en Prose,* 2 vols (Munich, 1963 and Leiden, 1976), in progress.

Dahan, G. 'Les interprétations juives dans les commentaires du Pentateuque de Pierre le Chantre', in Walsh and Wood, pp.131–55.

d'Avray, D.L. *The Preaching of the Friars: Sermons Diffused from Paris before 1300*

(Oxford, 1985).

Davy, M.M. *Les sermons universitaires parisiens de 1230–31* (Paris, 1931).

De la Cuesta, I. F. *Las Cançons dels Trobadors* (Toulouse, 1979).

Delbouille, M. 'Apollonius de Tyr et les débuts du roman français', in *Mélanges Rita Lejeune*, 2 vols (Gembloux, 1969), 2, pp.1171–1204.

—— 'Le premier *Roman de Tristan*', *CCM*, 5 (1962), pp.273–86 and 419–35.

—— 'Les chansons de geste et le livre', in *La Technique Littéraire des Chansons de Geste*, Actes du Colloque de Liège, September, 1957 (Paris, 1959), pp.295–407.

—— 'Sur les traces de *Bele Aëlis*', in *Mélanges...Boutière*, 2 vols (Liège, 1971), 1, pp.199–218.

De Ley, M. 'Provençal biographical tradition and the *Razon de Amor*', *Journal of Hispanic Philology*, 1 (1976), pp.1–17.

De Mandach, A. 'Le Berceau des Amours Splendides de Tristan et Iseut', in D. Buschinger (ed.) *La Légende de Tristan au Moyen Age* (Göttingen, 1982), pp.7–33.

Densusianu, O. (ed.) *La Prise de Cordres et de Sebille*, SATF (Paris, 1896).

Devoto, D. 'Dos Notas sobre el Libro de Apolonio', *Bulletin Hispanique*, 74 (1972), pp.295–330.

—— 'La enumeración de instrumentos musicales en la poesía medieval castellana', *Miscelánea en homenaje a Monsenor Higinio Anglés*, 2 vols (Barcelona, 1958–61), 1, pp.211–22.

DeWitt, P.A.M. *A New Perspective on Johannes de Grocheio's Ars Musicae* (unpublished doctoral thesis, University of Michigan, 1973).

Dimock, J.F. and Brewer J.S. (eds) *Giraldi Cambrensis Opera*, Rolls Series 21 (London, 1861–81), including: *Itinerarium Kambriae* (21:6) and *Topographia Hibernica* (21:5).

Dittmer, L. (ed.) *Firenze Biblioteca Mediceo-Laurenziana Pluteo 29,1*. 2 vols, Institute of Medieval Music, Publications of Mediaeval Musical Manuscripts, 10 (Brooklyn, 1966 and 1967).

Dobson, E.J. and Harrison, F.Ll (eds) *Medieval English Songs* (London, 1979).

Donovan, M.J. *The Breton Lay: a Guide to Varieties* (Indiana, 1969).

Doss-Quinby, E. *Les refrains chez les trouvères du XIIe siècle au début du XIVe* (New York, etc., 1984).

Dragonetti, R. *La technique poétique des trouvères dans la chanson courtoise* (Bruges, 1960).

Dronke, P. *Poetic Individuality in the Middle Ages: New Departures in Poetry, 1000–1150* (Oxford, 1970).

Droysen, D. 'Über Darstellung und Benennung von Musikinstrumenten in der mittelalterlichen Buchmalerei', *SIMP*, 4 (1976), pp.51–5.

Dyer, J. 'A thirteenth-century choirmaster: the *Scientia Artis Musicae* of Elias Salomon', *MQ*, 66 (1980), pp.83–111.

Egan, M. 'Commentary, *vita poetae*, and *vida*. Latin and Old Provençal "Lives of Poets" ', *Romance Philology*, 37 (1983), pp.36–48.

Ellinwood, L. 'Ars Musica', *Speculum*, 20 (1945), pp.290–9.

Everist, M.E. *French Thirteenth Century Polyphony: Aspects of Sources and Distribution* (unpublished D. Phil. thesis, Oxford, 1985).

Ewert, A. (ed.) *Marie de France: Lais* (Oxford, 1969).

Falck, R. *The Notre Dame Conductus: A Study of the Repertory*. Institute of Mediaeval Music, Musicological Studies 33 (Henryville, etc., 1981).

Faral, E. *Les Jongleurs en France au Moyen Age*, 2nd ed. (Paris, 1971).

—— *Mimes Français du XIIIe siècle* (Paris, 1910).

Fauchet, C. *Recueil de l'origine et la langue et poésie françoise, ryme et romans* (Paris, 1581).

Favati, G. (ed.) *Il 'Voyage de Charlemagne'* (Bologna, 1965).

Fay, P.B. and Grigsby, J.L. (eds) *Joufroi de Poitiers* (Geneva and Paris, 1972).

Field, W.H.W. (ed.) *Raimon Vidal: Poetry and Prose. 2, Abril Issia* (Chapel Hill, 1971).

Fisher, N.W. and Unguru, S. 'Experimental Science and Mathematics in Roger Bacon's Thought', *Traditio*, 27 (1971), p.353–78.

Flutre, L.-F. *Table des noms propres...figurant dans les romans du moyen âge* (Poitiers, 1962).

Foerster, W. (ed.) *Richars li Biaus* (Vienna, 1874).

Foster, G. *The iconology of musical instruments and musical performance in thirteenth century French manuscript illuminations* (unpublished doctoral thesis, City University of New York, 1977).

Fotitch, T. and Steiner, R. (eds) *Les lais du roman de Tristan en prose d'après le manuscrit de Vienne 2542* (Munich, 1974).

Foulet, L. (ed.) *Jean Renart: Galeran de Bretagne*, CFMA (Paris, 1925).

——'Marie de France et les Lais bretons', *Zeitschrift für Romanische Philologie*, 29 (1905), pp.19–56 and 292–322.

Fowler, M.V. *Musical Interpolations in Thirteenth and Fourteenth Century French Narratives* (unpublished doctoral thesis, Yale University, 1979).

Frank, I., *Répertoire Métrique de la poésie des troubadours*, 2 vols (Paris, 1953).

—— 'Tuit cil qui sunt enamourat', *Romania*, 75 (1954), pp.98–108.

Friedlein, G. (ed.) *Anicii Manlii Torquati Severini Boetii...De Institutione Musica Libri Quinque* (Leipzig, 1867; R 1966).

Fry, D.H. 'Old English Formulaic Themes and Type-Scenes', *Neophilologus*, 52 (1968), pp.48–54.

Fuller, S. 'Discant and the Theory of Fifthing', *AM*, 50 (1978), pp.241–75.

Gallais, P. *Genèse du Roman Occidental: Essais sur Tristan et Iseut et son Modèle Persan* (Paris, 1974).

Gallo, E. *The* Poetria Nova *and its Sources in Early Rhetorical Doctrine* (Paris, 1971).

Gallo, F.A. (ed.) *Johannis Boen Ars Musicae*, CSM 19 (Rome: AIM 1972).

—— *Tractatulus de cantu mensurali seu figuratio Musicae Artis*, CSM 16 (AIM, 1971).

Galpin, F.W. *Old English Instruments of Music: their History and Character*, 4th ed., revised T. Dart (London, 1965).

Gatien-Arnoult, A-F. (ed.) *Las Flors del Gay Saber, estiers dichas Las Leys d'Amors. Monuments de la Littérature Romane*, 1–3 (Toulouse, 1841–3).

Genicot, L. 'Recent research on the medieval nobility', in T. Reuter (ed. and trans.) *The Medieval Nobility* (Amsterdam, etc., 1979), pp.17–35.

Gennrich, F. *Rondeaux, Virelais und Balladen*, 2 vols, Gesellschaft für Romanische Literatur, 43 (Dresden, 1921 and Göttingen, 1927).

—— 'Trouvèrelieder und Motettenrepertoire', *ZfMW*, 9 (1926–7), pp.8–39 and 65–85.

Gerbert, M. (ed.) *Scriptores Ecclesiastici de Musica*, 3 vols (St Blaise, 1784).

Gérold, T. *Les Pères de l'Église et la Musique* (Strasbourg, 1931).

—— *La Musique au Moyen Age* (Paris, 1932).

Gerson-Kiwi, E. 'Drone and "dyaphonia basilica"', *Yearbook of the International Folk Music Council*, 4 (1972), pp.9–22.

Gibson, M. (ed.) *Boethius: His Life, Thought and Influence* (Oxford, 1981).

Glossa Ordinaria. PL 113–14.

Godefroy, F. *Dictionnaire de l'Ancienne Langue Française* (Paris, 1880–1902).

Goldine, N. 'Henri Bate, chanoine et chantre de la cathédrale Saint Lambert à Liège et théoricien de la musique (1246–après 1310)', *RBdM*, 18 (1964), pp.10–27.

Goldschmidt, M. (ed.) *Sone von Nausay* (Tübingen, 1899).

Gonfroy, G. 'Le reflet de la *canso* dans le *De Vulgari Eloquentia* et dans les *Leys d'Amors*', *CCM*, 25 (1982), pp.187–96.

Goolden, P. (ed.) *The Old English Apollonius of Tyre* (Oxford, 1958).

Gorton, T.J. 'Arabic words and refrains in Provençal and Portuguese Poetry', *Medium Aevum*, 45 (1976), pp.257–64.

Gransden, A. 'Realistic Observation in Twelfth Century England', *Speculum*, 47 (1972), pp.29–51.

Grier, S. (ed.) *The Otia Imperialia of Gervase of Tilbury: a critical edition of Book III, with introduction, translation and commentary* (unpublished doctoral thesis, University of York, 1981).

Griscom, A. and Jones, R.E. (eds) *The Historia Regum Britanniae of Geoffrey of Monmouth* (London, etc., 1929).

Guillaume D'Auvergne, *Opera Omnia* (Venice, 1591), including *De Universo*.

Gushee, L. (ed.) *Aureliani Reomensis Musica Disciplina*, CSM 21 (AIM 1975).

—— 'Questions of Genre in Medieval Treatises on Music', in Arlt, *Gattungen . . .*, pp.363–433.

—— 'Two Central Places: Paris and the French Court in the Early Fourteenth Century', in Kühn, H. and Nitsche, P. (eds) *Bericht über den Internationalen Musikwissenschaftlichen Kongress Berlin 1974* (Kassel, etc., 1980), pp. 135–57.

Häring, N.M. 'Commentary and Hermeneutics', in Benson and Constable, pp.173–200.

Handschin, J. 'Aus der alten Musiktheorie, V: Zur Instrumentenkunde', *AM*, 16–17 (1944–5), pp.1–10.

—— 'Über Estampie und Sequenz', *ZfMW*, 12 (1929–30), pp.1–20, and 13 (1930–31), pp.113–32.

Hanning, R.W. *The individual in twelfth century romance* (New Haven and London, 1977).

Hardy, T.D. and Martin, C.T. (eds) *Lestorie des Engleis*, 2 vols, Rolls Series 91 (London, 1888–9). Contains *Gesta Herewardi*.

Harrison, F.Ll. *Time, Place and Music* (Amsterdam, 1973).

Haynes, S. 'Music and genre in the alba', in *Proceedings of the Third British Conference of Medieval Occitan Language and Literature (University of Warwick, 1–3 April, 1985)*. Forthcoming.

Hentsch, A.A. *De la littérature didactique du moyen âge s'adressant spécialement aux femmes* (Cahors, 1903).

Hibberd, L. *'Estampie* and *Stantipes'*, *Speculum*, 19 (1944), pp.222–49.

—— 'Giraldus Cambrensis and English "Organ" Music', *JAMS*, 8 (1955), pp.208–12.

—— *'Musica Ficta* and Instrumental Music, c1250–c1350', *MQ*, 28 (1942), pp.216–26.

—— 'On "Instrumental Style" in Early Melody', *MQ*, 32 (1946), pp.107–30.

Hickmann, E. *Musica Instrumentalis* (Baden-Baden, 1971).

Hilka, A. (ed.) *Li Romanz d'Athis et Prophilias*, 2 vols (Dresden, 1912 and 1916).

Hoffman-Axthelm, D. 'Instrumentensymbolik und Aufführungspraxis. Zum Verhältnis von Symbolik und Realität in der mittelalterlichen Musikanschauung', *FM*, 4 (1980), pp.9–90.

Holden, A.J. (ed.) *Ipomedon* (Paris, 1979).

Holschneider, A. 'Die instrumentalen Tonbuchstaben im Winchester Troper', in *Festschrift Georg van Dadelsen* (Neuhasen-Stuttgart, 1978), pp.155–66.

—— *Die Organa von Winchester* (Hildesheim, 1968).

—— 'Instrumental Titles to the Sequentiae of the Winchester Tropers', in Sternfeld, F.W. *et al.* (eds) *Essays on Opera and English Music in Honour of Sir Jack Westrup* (Oxford, 1975), pp.8–18.

Honorius Augustodunensis, *In Psalmos*. PL 172.

Hubert, M.J., and Porter, M. (eds) *The Romance of Flamenca* (Princeton, 1962).

Hughes, A. 'Viella: Facere non possumus', *International Musicological Society: Report of the Eleventh Congress* (Copenhagen, 1972), 2, pp.453–6.

Huglo, M. 'La chanson d'amour en latin à l'époque des troubadours et des trouvères', *CCM*, 25 (1982), pp.197–203.

—— 'Les instruments de musique chez Hucbald', in Cambier, G. (ed.) *Hommages à André Boutemy* (Brussels, 1976), pp.178–96.

Hugo de Prato Florido *Sermones de Sanctis* (Heidelberg, 1485).

Hume, K. 'Why Chaucer calls the *Franklin's Tale* a "Breton lai"', *Philological Quarterly*, 51 (1972), pp.365–79.

Hunt, R.W. (ed. and revised M. Gibson) *The Schools and the Cloister: The Life and Writings of Alexander Nequam (1157–1217)* (Oxford, 1984).

Hunt, T. 'The Emergence of the Knight in France and England, 1000–1200', in Jackson, pp.1–22.

Hüschen, H. 'Albertus Magnus und seine Musikanshauung', in *Speculum Musicae Artis: Festgabe für Heinrich Hussman* (Munich, 1970), pp.205–18.

—— (ed.) *Das Cantuagium des Heinrich Eger von Kalkar 1328–1408* (Cologne, 1952).

Jackson, W.H. (ed.) *Knighthood in Medieval Literature* (Woodbridge, 1981).

Jaeger, C.S. *The Origins of Courtliness: Civilizing Trends and the Formation of Courtly Ideals 939–1210* (Philadelphia, 1985).

Jammers, E. 'Studien zur Tanzmusik des Mittelalters', *AfMW*, 30 (1973), pp.81–95.

Jarman, A.O.H. 'Telyn a Chrwth', *Llen Cymru*, 6 (1961), pp.154–75.

Jeanroy, A. *La poésie lyrique des troubadours,* 2 vols (Toulouse and Paris, 1934).

Jeanroy, A., Brandin, L. and Aubry, P. (eds) *Lais et Descorts Français du XIIIe siècle* (Paris, 1901).

Jones, E. *Musical and Poetical Relicks of the Welsh Bards,* 4th ed. (London, 1825).

Jonin, P. 'Le refrain dans les chansons de toile', *Romania,* 96 (1975), pp.209–44.

Jubinal, M.L.A. (ed.) *Jongleurs et Trouvères* (Paris, 1835).

—— (ed.) *Nouveau Recueil des Contes, Dits, Fabliaux,* 2 vols (Paris, 1839–42).

Jung, M-R. 'L'empereur Conrad Chanteur de Poésie Lyrique: fiction et vérité dans le *Roman de la Rose* de Jean Renart', *Romania*, 101 (1980), pp.35–50.

Kästner, H. *Harfe und Schwert: Der höfische Spielmann bei Gottfried von Strassburg* (Tübingen, 1981).

Kebede, A. 'The Bowl-Lyre of Northeast Africa. *Krar:* the Devil's instrument', *Ethnomusicology*, 21 (1977), pp.379–95.

Kelly, D. *Medieval Imagination* (Wisconsin, 1978).

Kimmel, A.S. (ed.) *A Critical Edition of the Old Provençal Epic* Daurel et Beton (Chapel Hill, 1971).

Klaeber, F. (ed.) *Beowulf and the Fight at Finnsburg*, 3rd ed. (Lexington, 1950).

Klopsch, P. (ed.) *Pseudo-Ovidius de Vetula* (Leiden and Cologne, 1968).

Knapp, J. 'Musical declamation and poetic rhythm in an early layer of Notre Dame conductus', *JAMS*, 32 (1979), pp.383–407.

Koenig, V.F. (ed.) *Les Miracles de Nostre Dame de Gautier de Coinci*, 4 vols (Geneva and Lille, 1955–70).

Köhler, E. 'Deliberations on a Theory of the Genre of the Old Provençal Descort', in Rimanelli, G. and Atchity, K.J. (eds) *Italian Literature: Roots and Branches* (New Haven and London, 1976), pp.1–13.

Kortekaas, A.G.A. (ed.) *Historia Apollonii Regis Tyri* (Groningen, 1984).

Krüger, W. 'Aufführungspraktische Fragen mittelalterlicher Mehrstimmigkeit', *Die Musikforschung*, 9 (1956), pp.419–27; 10 (1957), pp.279–86, 397–403, 497–505 and 11 (1958), pp.177–89.

—— *Die authentische Klangform des primitiven Organum* (Basel, 1958).

Kupfer, J. 'The Father of Empiricism: Roger not Francis', *Vivarium*, 12 (1974), pp.52–62.

Lacurne de Sainte-Palaye, *Histoire Littéraire des Troubadours*, 3 vols (Paris, 1774).

Ladd, A. 'Attitude toward Lyric in the *Lai d'Aristote* and some later fictional narratives', *Romania*, 96 (1975), pp.194–208.

Langlois, Ch. *Table des noms propres . . . dans les chansons de geste* (Paris, 1904).

Lathuillère, R. *Guiron le Courtois* (Geneva, 1966).

Laube-Przygodda, G. *Das alttestamentliche und neutestamentliche musikalische Gotteslob: in der Rezeption durch die christlichen Autoren des 2. bis 11. Jahrhunderts* (Regensburg, 1980).

Lavaud, R. and Nelli, R. (eds) *Les Troubadours*, 2 vols (Bruges, 1960–6).

Lecoy, F. (ed.) *Jean Renart: Guillaume de Dole* (Paris, 1962).

Le Gentil, P. 'A propos du *Guillaume de Dole*', in *Mélanges . . . Delbouille*, 2 vols (Gembloux, 1964), 2, pp.381–97.

Legge, M. Dominica, *Anglo-Norman Literature and its Background* (Oxford, 1963).

—— 'Pierre of Peckham and his "Lumiere as Lais"', *Modern Language Review*, 24 (1929), pp.37–47, and 153–71.

—— 'La Lumiere as Lais: a postscript', *Modern Language Review*, 46 (1951), pp.191–5.

Le Goff, J. *Pour un autre Moyen Age: Temps, travail et culture en Occident* (Editions Gallimard, 1977).

Lejeune, R. '*Le Roman de Guillaume de Dole* et la principauté de Liège', *CCM*, 17 (1974), pp.1–24.

—— *L'oeuvre de Jean Renart* (Liège and Paris, 1935).

Lemay, R. 'A propos de l'origine arabe de l'art des troubadours', *Annales, Economies, Sociétés, Civilisations,* 140 (September–October, 1966), pp.990–1011.

Leo, F. (ed.) *Venanti Honori Clementiani Fortunati Presbyteri Italici Opera Poetica*, MGH, *Auctorum Antiquissimorum*, 2, Tomi IV Pars Prior (Berlin, 1881).

Le Vot, G. 'Notation, mesure et rythme dans la "canso" troubadouresque', *CCM*, 25 (1982), pp.205–17.

—— 'Sur l'interprétation musicale de la chanson des troubadours: pour une "musicologie appliquée"', in Buschinger and Crépin, pp.99–121.

Levy, J. 'Musikinstrumente beim Gesang im mittelalterlichen Frankreich, auf Grund altfranz. Texte (bis zum 14 Jahr.)', *Zeitschrift für Romanische Philologie*, 35 (1911), pp.492–4.

Lewent, K. 'The *dansa* of Cerveri, called "De Girona"', *Studies in Philology*, 51 (1954), pp.516–38.

Lewis, C.B. 'Die altfranzösischen Prosaversion des Apollonius-Romans', *Romanische Forschungen*, 34 (1913), pp.1–277.

Lindsay, W.M. (ed.) *Isidori Hispalensis Episcopi Etymologiarum sive Originum Libri XX*, 2 vols (Oxford, 1911).

Lindval, W.M. *Jean Renart et Galeran de Bretagne* (Stockholm, 1982).

Linskill, J. (ed.) *The Poems of the Troubadour Raimbaut de Vaqueiras* (The Hague, 1964).

Little, Lester K. *Religious Poverty and the Profit Economy in Medieval Europe* (London, 1978).

Lods, J. 'Les parties lyriques du "Tristan" en prose', *BBSIA*, 7 (1955), pp.73–8.

—— *Les Pièces Lyriques du Roman de Perceforest* (Geneva and Lille, 1953).

Loomis, R.S. *Arthurian Literature in the Middle Ages*, corrected edition (Oxford, 1961).

Lutz, C.E. (ed.) *Remigii Autissiodorensis Commentum in Martianum Capellam*, 2 vols (Leiden, 1962 and 1965).

Maillard, J. 'Coutumes musicales au moyen age d'après le *Tristan* en prose', *CCM*, 2 (1959), pp.341–53.

—— *Evolution et esthétique du lai lyrique* (Paris, 1963).

—— 'Lai, Leich', in Arlt, *Gattungen* . . . , pp.323–45.

—— 'Le lai lyrique et les légendes arthuriennes', *BBSIA*, 9 (1957), pp.124–7.

—— 'Lais avec notation dans le *Tristan* en prose', in *Mélanges Rita Lejeune*, 2 vols (Gembloux, 1969), 2, pp.1347–64.

Manitius, K. (ed.) *Sextus Amarcius Sermones*, MGH, *Quellen zur Geistesge-schichte des Mittelalters*, 6 (Weimar, 1969).

Mansi, G.D., *Sacrorum Couciliorum Nova, et amplissima collectio* . . . (Florence, 1759–67, and Venice, 1769–98).

Marcuse, S. *A Survey of Musical Instruments* (Newton Abbot and London, 1975).

Marshall, J.H. 'The isostrophic *descort* in the Poetry of the Troubadours', *Romance Philology*, 35 (1981), pp.130–57.

—— *Linguistic and Literary Theory in Old Provençal*, 2 vols (unpublished doctoral thesis, University of Oxford, 1962).

—— *The* Razos de Trobar *of Raimon Vidal and associated texts* (London, 1972).

Mayr-Harting, H.M.R.E. *The Venerable Bede, the Rule of St Benedict and Social Class* (Jarrow Lecture, 1976).

McKinnon, J. 'Musical Instruments in Medieval Psalm Commentaries and Psalters', *JAMS*, 21 (1968), pp.3–20.

—— *The Church Fathers and Musical Instruments* (unpublished doctoral thesis, Columbia University, 1965).

—— 'The meaning of the patristic polemic against musical instruments', *Current Musicology*, 1 (1965), pp.69–82.

McPeek, Gwynne S. 'Kalenda Maia: a study in form', in *Medieval Studies in Honor of Robert White Linker* (Editorial Castalia, 1973), pp.141–54.

—— '*Kalenda Maya* by Raimbault Vaqueiras (c1155–1205)', in *Notations and Editions: A Book in Honor of Louise Cuyler* (New York, 1974), pp.1–7.

Michelant, H. *Guillaume de Palerne* (Paris, 1876).

Michels, U. *Die Musiktraktate des Johannes de Muris* (Wiesbaden, 1970).

Miller, S.H. (ed.) and Sweeting, W.D. (trans.) 'De Gestis Herewardi Saxonis', with *Fenland Notes and Queries*, 3 (1895–7).

Misrahi, J. (ed.) *Le Roman des Sept Sages* (Paris, 1933).

Mittellateinisches Wörterbuch (Munich, 1967–).

Mölk, U. *Trobador-Lyrik* (Munich and Zurich, 1982).

Montagu, J. *The World of Medieval and Renaissance Musical Instruments* (Newton Abbot etc., 1976).

Montaiglon, A. de and Raynaud, G. (eds) *Recueil général et complet des Fabliaux des XIIIᵉ et XIVᵉ Siècles*, 6 vols (Paris, 1872–90).

Monteverdi, A. 'La laisse épique', in *La Technique Littéraire des Chansons de Geste: Actes du Colloque de Liège, September, 1957* (Paris, 1959), pp.127–40.

Morris, C. *The Discovery of the Individual 1050–1200* (London, 1972).

Morrow, M. 'Ayre on the F♯ string', *Lute Society Journal*, 2 (1960), pp.9–12.

Morton, A.L. 'The Matter of Britain: The Arthurian Cycle and the Development of Feudal Society', *Zeitschrift für Anglistik und Amerikanistik*, 8 (1960), pp.1–24.

Müller-Heuser, F. *Vox Humana* (Regensburg, 1963).

Mundy, J.H. 'Urban Society and Culture: Toulouse and its Region', in Benson and Constable, pp.229–47.

Murray, A. *Reason and Society in the Middle Ages* (Oxford, 1978).

Musgrave, J.C. 'Tarsiana and Juglaría in the *Libro de Apolonio*', in Deyermond, A.D. (ed.) *Medieval Hispanic Studies presented to R. Hamilton* (London, 1976), pp.129–38.

Mynors, R.A.B. *Catalogue of the Manuscripts of Balliol College, Oxford* (Oxford, 1963).

Nef, K. 'Gesang und Instrumentenspiel bei den Troubadours', in *Festschrift für Guido Adler* (Vienna, 1930), pp.58–63.

Newcombe, T. 'The Refrain in Troubadour Lyric Poetry', *Nottingham Medieval Studies*, 19 (1975), pp.3–15.

Newstead, H. 'The *Enfances* of Tristan and English Tradition', *Studies in Medieval Literature in Honor of A.C. Baugh* (Philadelphia, 1961), pp.169–85.

—— 'The Harp and the Rote: An Episode in the Tristan Legend and its Literary History', *Romance Philology*, 22 (1969), pp.463–70.

Noiriel, G. 'La chevalerie dans la geste des Lorrains', *Annales de l'Est*, 5th Series (1976), 3, pp.167–96.

Noulet, J-B. and Chabaneau, C. *Deux Manuscrits Provençaux du XIVe siècle* (Montpellier and Paris, 1888).

Ollier, M-L. 'Utopie et Roman Arthurien', *CCM*, 27 (1984), pp.223–32.

Opland, J. *Anglo-Saxon Oral Poetry* (New Haven and London, 1980).

Orme, N. *From Childhood to Chivalry* (London, 1984).

Oulmont, C. (ed.) *Les débats du clerc et du chevalier* (Paris, 1911).

Padel, O.J. 'The Cornish Background of the Tristan Stories', *Cambridge Medieval Celtic Studies*, 1 (1981), pp.53–81.

Page, C. 'Angelus ad virginem: a new work by Philippe the Chancellor?', *EM*, 11 (1983), pp.69–70.

—— *Anglo-Saxon Hearpan: their terminology, technique, tuning and repertory of verse 850–1066* (unpublished doctoral thesis, Univ. of York, 1981).

—— *'Bella bis quinis:* a new song from Saxon Canterbury', in Gibson, pp.306–11.

—— 'Biblical instruments in medieval manuscript illustration', *EM*, 5 (1977), pp.299–309.

—— 'Early fifteenth century instruments in Jean de Gerson's "Tractatus de Canticis" ', *EM*, 6 (1978), pp.339–49.

—— 'The fifteenth century lute: new and neglected sources', *EM*, 9 (1981), pp.11–21.

—— 'Fourteenth century instruments and tunings: a treatise by Jean Vaillant?' *GSJ*, 33 (1980), pp.17–35.

—— 'German Musicians and their Instruments: a Fourteenth Century Account by Konrad of Megenberg', *EM*, 10 (1982), pp.192–200.

—— '[The harpsichord]: In the Direction of the Beginning', in Schott, H. (ed.) *The Historical Harpsichord*, 1 (Pendragon Press, 1984), pp.111–25.

—— 'Jerome of Moravia on the *rubeba* and *viella'*, *GSJ*, 32 (1979), pp.77–95.

—— 'The medieval *organistrum* and *symphonia*: 1 A legacy from the East?', *GSJ*, 35 (1982), pp.37–44.

—— 'The medieval *organistrum* and *symphonia*: 2 Terminology', *GSJ*, 36 (1983), pp.71–87.

—— 'The performance of songs in late medieval France: a new source', *EM*, 10 (1982), pp.441–50.

—— 'Music and Chivalric Fiction', *PRMA*, 111 (1984–5), pp.1–27.

—— 'String instrument making in medieval England and some Oxford harpmakers, 1380–1466', *GSJ*, 31 (1978), pp.44–67.

Palisca, C. (ed.) *Hucbald, Guido and John on Music* (Yale, 1978).

Panum, H. (trans. J. Pulver) *The Stringed Instruments of the Middle Ages* (London, 1940).

Parker, I. 'The performance of troubadour and trouvère songs: some facts and conjectures', *EM*, 5 (1977), pp.184–207.

Parry, T. *Gwaith Dafydd ap Gwilym* (Cardiff, 1952).

Pastre, J-M. 'Nature et fonctions de la musique dans les oeuvres narratives allemandes du moyen âge', in Buschinger and Crépin, pp.203–20.

Paterson, L. 'Knights and the Concept of Knighthood in the Twelfth Century Occitan Epic', in Jackson, pp.23–38.

Pattison, W.T. *The Life and Works of the Troubadour Raimbaut d'Orange* (Minneapolis, 1952).

Payen, J.C. (ed.) *Les Tristan en Vers* (Paris, 1974).

Pelaez, M. 'Le Tornoiement as dames de Paris', *Studj Romanzi*, 14 (1917), pp.5–68.

Percy, T. *Reliques of ancient English Poetry*, 3 vols (London, 1765).

Perkuhn, E.R. 'Beispiele Arabisch-Spanischer Glossographie in instrument-kundlicher sicht', *SIMP*, 4 (1976), pp.94–7.

Perrot, J. (trans. N. Deane) *The Organ: from its invention in Hellenistic Times to the end of the thirteenth century* (Oxford, 1970).

Pertz, G.H. (ed.) *Ekkehard: Casus Sancti Galli*, MGH, *Scriptorum*, 2 (Hannover, 1829).

Petersen-Dyggve, H., *Onomastique des Trouvères* (Helsinki, 1934).

Petrus de Abano, *Expositio problematum Aristotelis* (Mantua, 1475).

Piper, P. (ed.) *Die Schriften Notkers und seiner Schule*, 3 vols (Freiburg and Tübingen, 1882–3).

Place, E.B. (ed.) *L'Histoire de Gille de Chyn by Gautier de Tournai* (Evanston and Chicago, 1941).

Plumb, J.H. *The Death of the Past* (London, 1969).

Pope, Mildred (ed.) *The Romance of Horn by Thomas*, 2 vols (Oxford, 1955 and 1964).

Räkel, H-H.S. *Die musikalische Erscheinungsform der Trouvère Poesie* (Bern, 1977).

Ramon Llull, *Obres Essencials*, 2 vols (Barcelona, 1957 and 1960).

Randel, D.M. 'Al-Fārābī and the Role of Arabic Music Theory in the Latin Middle Ages', *JAMS*, 29 (1976), pp.173–88.

Rastall, R. 'Some English Consort-Groupings of the late middle ages', *ML*, 55 (1974), pp.179–202.

Raupach, M. and Raupach, M. *Französierte Trobadorlyrik* (Tübingen, 1979).

Raynaud de Lage, G. (ed.) *Gautier d'Arras: Eracle* (Paris, 1976).

Reaney, G. 'Terminology and Medieval Music', *Festschrift Heinrich Besseler* (Leipzig, 1961), pp.149–53.

—— 'The *Lais* of Guillaume de Machaut and their Background', *PRMA*, 82 (1955–6), pp.15–32.

—— (ed.) *MS Oxford Bodley 842 (Willelmus)* ... CSM 12 (AIM, 1966).

—— 'Voices and instruments in the music of Guillaume de Machaut', *RBdM*, 10 (1956), pp.3–17 and 93–104.

Reaney, G. and Gilles, A. (eds) *Franconis de Colonia Ars Cantis Mensurabilis*,

CSM 18 (AIM 1974).

Reckow, F. (ed.) *Der Musiktraktat des Anonymous 4*, 2 vols (Wiesbaden, 1967).

Reimer, E. (ed.) *Johannes de Garlandia: De mensurabili musica*, 2 vols (Wiesbaden, 1972).

Remigius of Auxerre, *In Psalmos*. PL 131.

Remnant, M. 'Rebec, Fiddle and Crowd in England', *PRMA*, 95 (1968–9), pp.15–28. (See also *PRMA* 96 (1969–70), pp.149–50.)

Remnant, M. and Marks, R. 'A Medieval "Gittern"', in *Music and Civilisation*, The British Museum Yearbook, 4 (London, 1980), pp.83–135.

Rensch, R. *The Harp* (London, 1969).

Rigby, M. 'The Education of Alexander the Great and "Florimont"', *Modern Language Review*, 57 (1962), pp.392–3.

Riquer, M. de (ed.) *Guillem de Berguedà*, 2 vols (Poblet, 1971).

—— *Història de la Literatura Catalana*, 3 vols (Barcelona, 1964).

—— *Los Trovadores*, 3 vols (Barcelona, 1975).

—— *Obras Completas del Trovador Cerverí de Girona* (Barcelona, 1947).

Ritson, J., *Ancient Songs from the time of King Henry the Third to the Revolution* (London, 1790).

Robert-Tissot, M. *Johannes Aegidius de Zamora Ars Musica*, CSM 20 (AIM, 1974).

Robinson, F. (ed.) *The Works of Geoffrey Chaucer*, 2nd ed. (London, 1966).

Rohlfs, G. (ed.) *Sankt Alexius* (Tübingen, 1968).

Rohloff, E. (ed.) *Die Quellenhandschriften zum Musiktraktat des Johannes de Grocheio* (Leipzig, 1972).

Rokesth, Y. 'Danses cléricales du XIIIe siècle', *Publications de la Faculté des Lettres de l'Université de Strasbourg*, 106 (Paris, 1947), pp.93–126.

Roques, M. 'Sur deux particularités métriques de la *Vie de Saint Grégoire* en ancien français', *Romania*, 48 (1922), pp.41–61.

Rosenberg, S.N. and Tischler, H. (eds) *Chanter m'estuet: Songs of the Trouvères* (London, 1981).

Rosenthal, D.H. (trans.) *Tirant lo Blanc* (London, 1984).

Rouse, R.H. and Rouse, M.A. *Preachers, Florilegia and Sermons: Studies on the 'Manipulus Florum' of Thomas of Ireland* (Toronto, 1979).

——— '*Statim invenire:* Schools, Preachers and New Attitudes to the Page', in Benson and Constable, pp.201–25.

Ruini, C. (ed.) *Ameri Practica Artis Musice*, CSM 25 (AIM, 1977).

Sahlin, M. *Étude sur la carole médiévale* (Uppsala, 1940).

Salvat, M. 'Un traité de musique du XIIIe siècle: Le *De Musica* de Barthelemi L'Anglais', in Buschinger and Crépin, pp.345–60.

Secreta Secretorum. Cited from the edition published at Anvers, Mattheus van der Goes, c1488.

Schmid, H. (ed.) *Musica et Scolica Enchiriadis* (Munich, 1981).

Schneider, M. *Geschichte der Mehrstimmigkeit*, 3 vols (Berlin, 1934–5, and 1968).

Schoepperle, G. *Tristan and Isolt: A Study of the Sources of the Romance*, 2 vols (Frankfurt and London, 1913). New ed., 1960.

Schrade, L. *Die handschriftliche Überlieferung der ältesten Instrumentalmusik*, 2nd ed., revised H.H. Marx (Tutzing, 1968).

Schuler, M. 'Die Musik in den Höfen der Karolinger', *AfMW*, 27 (1970), pp.23–40.

Schultz-Gora, O. (ed.) *Folque de Candie* (Dresden, 1909).

Seay, A. (trans.) *Johannes de Grocheo: Concerning Music*, 2nd edition (Colorado College Music Press, 1974).

Seebass, T. *Musikdarstellung und Psalterillustration im frühen Mittelalter*, 2 vols (Berne, 1973).

—— 'The visualisation of music through pictorial imagery and notation in late-medieval France', in Boorman, pp.19–33.

Smalley, B. *The Study of the Bible in the Middle Ages*, 2nd ed. (Oxford, 1952).

Sommer, H.O. (ed.) *The Vulgate Version of the Arthurian Romances*, 8 vols (Washington, 1909–16).

Southern, R.W. *The Making of the Middle Ages* (London, 1953).

Sowa, H. (ed.) *Ein Anonymer Glossierter Mensuraltraktat 1279* (Kassel, 1930).

Spanke, H. 'Das lateinische Rondeau', *Zeitschrift für französischer Sprache und Litteratur*, 53 (1929–30), pp.113–48.

Spitzer, L. 'Debailadas-bailar', *Boletín de la Academia Argentina de letras*, 14 (1945), pp.729–35.

Stäblein, B. (ed.) *Hymnen*, Monumenta Monodica Medii Aevi, 1 (Kassel and Basel, 1956).

Stadler, H. (ed.) *Alberti Magni De Animalibus*. Beiträge zur Geschichte der Philosophie des Mittelalters, 15 and 16 (Münster, 1916 and 1921).

Steger, H. *David Rex et Propheta* (Nuremberg, 1961).

—— *Philologia Musica* (Munich, 1971).

Stegmüller, F. *Repertorium Biblicum Medii Aevi*, 11 vols (Madrid, 1940–80).

Stein, P. 'La musique dans le *Tristan* de Gottfried von Strasburg. Son importance pour l'interprétation du texte', in Buschinger and Crépin, pp.237–49.

Stengel, E. (ed.) *Hervis von Metz* (Dresden, 1903).

—— *Li Romans de Durmart le Galois* (Tübingen, 1873).

Stevens, J. '"La Grande Chanson Courtoise": The Chansons of Adam de la Halle', *PRMA*, 101 (1974–5), pp.11–30.

Stewart, M. 'The echoing corridor', *EM*, 8 (1980), pp.339–57.

Stock, B. *The Implications of Literacy* (Princeton, 1983).

Stone, L.W. and Rothwell, W. (eds) *Anglo-Norman Dictionary* (London, 1977–).

Stubbs, W. *Memorials of Saint Dunstan*, Rolls Series 63 (London, 1874).

Suchier, H. 'Provenzalische Verse aus Nürnberg', *Zeitschrift für Romanische Philologie*, 15 (1891), pp.511–14.

Switten, M.L. *The* Cansos *of Raimon de Miraval: a Study of Poems and Melodies* (Cambridge, Mass., 1985).

Taylor, J.H.M. (ed.) *Le Roman de Perceforest*, 1 (Geneva, 1979), in progress.

Techener, J.J. *Description Raisonnée d'une collection choisie d'Anciens Manuscrits de Documents Historiques et de Chartes, Réunis par les soins de J.J. Techener*, 1 (Paris, 1862).

Thorpe, L. (ed.) *Le Roman de Silence* (Cambridge, 1972).

Tischler, H. (ed.) *The Montpellier Codex* (Madison, 1978).

Tobler-Lommatzsch, *Altfranzösisches Wörterbuch* (Berlin, 1925; Wiesbaden, 1954–).

Ulland, W. *'Jouer d'un instrument' und die altfranzösischen Bezeichnungen des Instrumentenspiels* (Bonn, 1970).

Val, Manuel Criado de and Naylor, E.W. (eds) *Arcipreste de Hita: Libro de Buen Amor* (Madrid, 1965).

Vale, M. *War and Chivalry* (London, 1981).

Vallerie, J.E. (ed.) *Garin le Loheren* (Michigan, 1947).

Van den Boogaard, N., *Rondeaux et refrains du XIIᵉ siècle au début du XIVᵉ* (Paris, 1969).

Van der Veen, J. 'Les aspects musicaux des chansons de geste', *Neophilologus*, 41 (1957), pp.82–100.

Van der Werf, H. *The Chansons of the Troubadours and Trouvères* (Utrecht, 1972).

—— *The Extant Troubadour Melodies* (New York, 1984).

—— 'The Trouvère Chansons as Creations of a Notationless Culture', *Current Musicology*, 1 (1965), pp.61–8.

Varnhagen, H. 'Beiträge zur Erklärung und Textkritik von Dan Michel's Ayenbite of Inwyt, III', *Englische Studien*, 2 (1878–9), pp.27–59.

Vecchi, G. 'Medicina e musica, voci e strumenti nel "Conciliator" (1303) de Petro de Abano', *Quadrivium*, 8 (1967), pp.15–22.

Vernay, P. (ed.) *Maugis d'Aigremont* (Berne, 1980).

Vinaver, E. *The Rise of Romance* (Oxford, 1971).

Vivell, P.C. (ed.) *Commentarius in Micrologum* (Vienna, 1917).

—— (ed.) *Frutolfi Breviarium de Musica et Tonarius* (Vienna, 1919).

Waddell, H. *The Wandering Scholars*, 6th ed. (London, 1932).

Waesberghe, J. Smits van (ed.) *Adalboldi Episcopi Ultraiectensis Epistola cum Tractatu de Musica Instrumentali, Humanaque ac Mundana*, Divitiae Musicae Artis, A.II (Buren, 1981).

—— (ed.) *Bernonis Augiensis de Mensurando Monochordo*, DMA, A.VIa (Buren, 1978).

—— (ed.) *Johannes Affligemensis De Musica cum Tonario*, CSM 1 (AIM, 1950).

—— 'Les origines de la notation alphabétique au moyen age', *Anuario Musical*, 12 (1957), pp.3–16.

—— *Musikerziehung: Lehre und Theorie der Musik im Mittellalter*, Musikgeschichte in Bildern, III:3 (Leipzig, 1969).

—— *Organistrum* in HMT.

Wagenaar-Nolthenius, H. 'Estampie/Stantipes/Stampita', in *L'Ars Nova Italiana del Trecento: 2nd Congress* (Certaldo, 1969), pp.399–409.

Walsh, K. and Wood, D. *The Bible in the Medieval World* (Oxford, 1985).

Ward-Perkins, B. *From Classical Antiquity to the Middle Ages: Urban Public Building in Northern and Central Italy AD 300–850* (Oxford, 1984).

Weakland, R. 'Hucbald as Musician and Theorist', *MQ*, 42 (1956), pp.66–84.

White, J.E. Jr (ed.) *La Conquête de Constantinople* (New York, 1968).

Whitehead, F. (ed.) *La Chanson de Roland* (Oxford, 1970).

Willis, R.S. (ed.) *El Libro de Alexandre* (Princeton and Paris, 1934).

Wilson, E.R. 'Old Provençal *Vidas* as literary commentary', *Romance Philology*, 33 (1980), pp.510–18.

Woledge, B. (ed.) *L'atre perilleux* (Paris, 1936).

Wright, L. 'The Medieval Gittern and Citole: A case of mistaken identity', *GSJ*, 30 (1977), pp.8–42.

—— 'Misconceptions concerning the troubadours, trouvères and minstrels', *ML*, 48 (1967), pp.35–9.

—— 'Sculptures of Medieval Fiddles at Gargilesse', *GSJ*, 32 (1979). pp.66–76.

Wright, R. *Late Latin and Early Romance in Spain and Carolingian France* (Liverpool, 1982).

Zaslaw, N. 'Music in Provence in the 14th century', *Current Musicology*, 25 (1978), pp.99–120.

Zenker, R. 'Der Lai de l'Epine', *Zeitschrift für Romanische Philologie*, 17 (1895), pp.233–55.

Zeydel, E.H. (ed.) *Ruodlieb* (Chapel Hill, 1959).

Zink, M. *La Prédication en Langue Romane avant 1300* (Paris, 1976).

Zumthor, P. *Essai de poétique médiévale* (Paris, 1972).

—— 'La chanson de *Bele Aiglentine*', in *Mélanges Albert Henry* (Strasburg, 1970), pp.325–37.

Index